Stories
from the
Front Porch

JOHN S. CASE

ISBN: 978-1-916954-35-9

For permission requests, contact the Publisher:
Magnolia Bend Press, LLC
P.O. Box 430
Slidell, LA. 70459
www.JohnCaseStoryteller.com

Stories from the Front Porch is a work of fiction. Names, characters, places and events are products of the author's imagination and have no connection to any real person, place or event. Any resemblance is solely coincidental.

Cover graphics by William Blackwell.
Cover photo and design by Kendra Maness.

Photos used by permission of photographers
Kendra Maness, William Blackwell, Wikimedia Commons,
and the Library of Congress. Required attributions can be found in the back of this publication.

Acknowledgements

Writing a book, getting it published, and then getting it sold is a difficult job unless you have had previous major writing success. In my case, my writings are done for my pleasure, in my spare time, and would not exist without the encouragement of so many people.

First, as I have before, I want to recognize my wife, Brenda. Of course, she is prejudiced; but, without her insistence that my stories should be available for all to read, *Stories from the Front Porch* would never have been produced. She is my cheerleader, number one fan, and sometimes, number one critic.

I must mention Kendra Maness. It was for her magazine, *Slidell Magazine*, that I started writing in the first place. Neither this book nor my first two would have existed without her. She has also edited and formatted all my books for publication. Thank you, Kendra.

William Blackwell, a good friend and supporter, has contributed in many ways. He is a magician with a camera and is responsible for much of my success, including enhancing of the cover photo. Thank you, William.

Almost by chance, after fifty years, I was reacquainted with a friend from my college days. She had a very successful career in marketing and public relations. She liked my work, gave me tips, and promoted me in so many ways. She encouraged me to promote myself more aggressively and even set up venues so I could do so. Leslie Westbrook Frigerio is largely responsible for this endeavor. Thank you, Leslie.

Some of my stories are tales of things that happened sometime before I was born. It just so happens that my sister, Sue Case Richardson Stout, was fourteen years my senior. She filled me in on how things were almost a generation prior to my birth. She was a constant source of information and one of my biggest fans.

Unfortunately, while assembling this book, she passed away at age 89. She will never see it in print. Sue, this book is dedicated to you.

Stories From the Front Porch

Dedicated to

Sue Case Richardson Stout

Table of Contents

Acknowledgements iii

Introduction vii

Haint Blue 1

Rigger and Ethiope 7

In Search of Identity 11

Chicken and Dumplings 23

The Heist 29

The Deed 35

Hoodoo Man 41

All American Boy 47

The Clock 57

A Smelly Business 65

The Obsession, Gypsy Woman 69

Three Soldiers 73

Bestseller 85

The Village 91

Fruitcakes 103

Disguised Intentions 107

The Baptism of Tina Jo 119

The Chair 125

Making a Living 139

Eli and Emma 145

Back Home Again 159

The Education of D.J. Gardner 163

Sugar Baby 169

The Serial Killer? 1930 185

Rebellion 193

Interment Delayed 199

The Last Coon Hunt 205

His Legacy 211

Death on the Pearl 217

The Pink Wheel 235

Snake in the Grass 241

Blanche 249

Ring on a Chain 255

It Happened One Christmas 267

The Journal 271

The Sinner's Bench 279

Introduction

The connection of front porches and Southern writing is not by any means a new concept attributable to me. Many writers have referenced the inspiration they have received from the stories they heard sitting on front porchs.

The reason is simple. That is where the stories were told. Before television and air conditioning, on a spring, fall, or summer day, the front porch was an escape from the stifling Southern heat of the indoors and a place for relaxation and conversation.

In early fall, after the crops were laid by or harvested, neighbors would have the time to visit and, to put it plainly, gossip. In my case, not only would neighbors come by, but stranded motorists, hitchhikers, and maybe even a few hobos would find their way up our drive and be comforted by a cool breeze and glass of sweet, iced tea.

Some of the stories evolved from what had happened during the planting season; and larger-than-life characters were created based on the day labor they hired and, of course, the tales they told. Embellishment was a sign of good storytelling. Politics were seldom discussed, as everyone in the community was a Democrat (Southern Democrat, that is), so all were of one accord.

Religion was discussed, as the church was the main social network that existed outside the front porch. Some of these discussions would be heated, as most would try to relate what the Lord had told them.

The stories told and characters described were often about things and people that had existed long ago and only known to them, as they had heard these stories from their parents or grandparents. Again, these people and events became bigger than life and the act of storytelling took root.

It was a wonderful era, and I am thankful that I lived at a time when front porch stories were still being told. Unfortunately, that has changed.

The art of front porch storytelling declined and perhaps disappeared due to several factors. First, better highways and transportation allowed residents more access to places and events outside their rural confinement.

Television came along. The stories they saw there were no better than the ones told on the porch, they were just made visual; a new dimension in storytelling.

Interiors of homes became more comfortable with the availability of affordable air conditioning, making the indoors more desirable than the breeze-swept porch.

Finally, the cost of construction made the porch an expensive amenity that was being used less and less. As a result, they were deleted from many house plans.

The stories I tell are mine. They may be based on an event or character I heard mentioned, but the stories themselves come from the art of listening and trying to duplicate what I heard and put it in written form, with a twist.

The disappearance of the porch, to me, is a sad thing. I understand the reason, but I think their disappearance has prompted a literary decline.

Oxford, Mississippi is considered the Mecca of Literature. Names like Faulkner, Willy Morris, John Grisham, Curtis Wilke, Stark Young, and Joe Brown are all connected to this geography. There is no better example of storytelling than produced by those above, and more.

Just a few miles south of Oxford, near the small village of Taylor, front porches have been reborn. Campbell and Leighton McCool invested their life's savings into the development of a village within a village. More than just a subdivision, this development requires homes to have front porches. Other structures are built to encourage literary art, as well as most other art forms. It is called Plein Air. By the way, Plein Air means outdoors. The McCools understand the need for keeping the practice alive.

At present, I am building a new home. There will be a large front porch.

John S. Case
November 2023

HAINT BLUE

The Gullah people were brought to South Carolina after being captured in West Africa and enslaved. They were a superstitious group and believed in "haints." Haints were what they called ghosts. They believed that the blue color made from local indigo tricked the haints into thinking whatever was coated in it was sky or water, both of which the haints feared.

Rufus built the house around 1910. It was small, with only two rooms plus a kitchen. Both rooms were bedrooms but the larger one belonged to him and Reba. That room also served as the living room. When the house was built, they only had one child.

At that time, Rufus was not what you would call a perfect family man. The sawmill paid their employees on Friday afternoon and Rufus's first stop was Dunnie's Tavern, located next door to the mill. It would be daylight before he would come home on some occasions. Reba didn't seem to mind, as that was not uncommon behavior for most of the sawmill workers she knew. Sawmill work was both hard and dangerous, and she reasoned a man needed some time to unwind.

Rufus was not a big man and may have suffered from a complex due to his size. This often led to fights and, on more than one occasion, he was locked up and did not come home until Reba could raise the bail to get him out. She could tolerate that, too, because she loved him.

As the years passed, the family grew. By 1920, there were five children; still only two rooms, but five children, three boys and two girls. Both he and Reba knew they needed more space, but it was clearly not in the budget.

It isn't known what came first. Did he stop drinking first, or did he get religion first which caused him to stop? It seemed to have happened about the same time. Reba certainly noticed the change and, after twenty years of marriage, had a new respect for her husband.

With his change in habits, Rufus began to excel in his job. Over the next few years, he got several promotions. With more income, he decided to take the beer money he had been spending and buy a piece of lumber from the mill each day. As he walked the mile to his house, he could be seen with some type of timber on his shoulder being transported home.

Over the next couple of years, a room was added to the house. It would be called the girls' room. Then, across the front of the house, a large room was built. It would be a living and dining room. As to the size of the house, it was now adequate for their needs.

Even with added living space, the house still had one basic flaw. It didn't have a front porch. No house in the South was considered more than basic shelter unless it had a front porch. A porch not only added beauty to the structure, it was also a functional addition. There was no air conditioning in those days, nor any electricity for a fan. A porch was the perfect complement to an evening breeze on a hot summer day; and they were used almost daily during all seasons except the coldest winter.

Rufus, with the help of his sons, worked on Saturdays and, in a couple of months, the porch was complete. On one end, he hung a swing and added four rocking chairs purchased from a neighbor. While Reba grocery shopped in town, he went to the hardware store and bought paint for the porch. It never crossed his mind that any color other than white would be considered. The hardware clerk convinced him that the new trend was to paint the floor grey. It held up better and did not show dirt as much as white. The clerk also reached for a gallon of blue paint.

"What's that for?" Rufus questioned.

"The ceiling, of course. Blue paint keeps the bugs away and also the haints. You know, you see it on almost all front porches. The name of the paint is Haint Blue. Like its name says, it is rumored to keep the haints away."

Rufus knew that "haints" referred to "haunts" which implied ghosts.

"Yeah, I've heard about that, but I don't put any stock in it and I don't believe in superstitions either. The Bible says don't seek after wizards to be defiled by them. Read Leviticus, it tells a great deal about that stuff."

For some reason, he took the paint home anyway, but left the ceiling until last to be painted. He was conflicted about using the paint. He liked the color, a light blue-green, but his religious faith had grown. He was concerned about what significance was attached to the paint and its reference as haint blue.

Taft worked at the mill when extra help was needed. Other than that, he sharecropped on the same land his grandfather had worked as a slave. Taft followed the old customs. He planted by the signs of the moon and chanted over the seeds as he carefully placed them in the ground. Whatever he did, it worked. He was a good farmer.

Taft would walk by Rufus's and Reba's house on his way to the mill or to the highway to hitchhike to town. Rufus was on the porch spreading the white paint when Taft came walking by.

"Mr. Rufus, that be a nice porch you done built. Yall's gone enjoy that. But make sho you paint that ceiling Haint Blue."

"Taft, come up here. Tell me what you know about painting the ceiling Haint Blue."

"Well, sir, you got to. If you don't, the haints gone come in yo house."

"What does blue paint have to do with keeping the haints, as you call them, away?"

"Yes sir, it do. You sees, haints are scared of the sky and water. They think that blue ceiling be the sky and they know if they get near it, they will be sucked up from the earth. Also, theys hate water and they think they gone drown. Yes sir, sho do. And it works. You make sho you paint that ceiling Haint Blue.

Reba liked the idea of the blue ceiling. She had waited years for a porch.

To her, it was a symbol of their success. She wanted all the traditional trimmings, including a blue ceiling. Rufus objected based on his religious views. He didn't believe in anything that involved the supernatural. There was a lot of discussion but Reba won the argument; and the ceiling was painted blue, Haint Blue, a mixture of blue and green tints. It stayed that way for years.

Rufus became more involved in his religious practices. After he finished his regular job at the mill, he would tend to the crops and livestock. After all the chores were done, he would study his Bible, often on the front porch. That was his only hobby and pastime. He even became a lay minister and was often called to fill in when a local minister was on a trip or ill. He was respected as a God-fearing Christian.

He was always troubled by the presence of the Haint Blue ceiling. His spiritual side questioned if he was tempting the Lord with this superstitious symbol that existed not ten feet from where he read his Bible.

It was 1941 when, one day, he opened his Bible and again studied Leviticus. He read, *I will set my face against anyone who turns to mediums and spiritists to prostitute themselves by following them, and I will cut them off from their people.*

To him, this was the Word of God. The blue ceiling had to go. He was not sure if having it was in conflict to the Bible, but he believed in being more safe than sorry.

On Saturday, December 6, 1941, he painted the ceiling white. Reba objected; but, even though her religious convictions were not as ingrained as his, it was what he wanted and she would not strongly object.

The next day, after church and lunch, it was a warm day for December, and he took a seat in a chair on the front porch to study his Bible. Only absolutely necessary chores would be done on the Lord's Day.

About 1 o'clock, his youngest son, who was a senior in high school, came into the living room and turned on the radio. The New York Giants were playing the Brooklyn Dodgers in a football game and he liked to follow them because fellow Mississippian, Bruiser Kinard, was a star player for the Dodgers.

Rufus's son heard the radio announcer say that Kinard made a sensational tackle, then the program was immediately interrupted.

"We interrupt this program to inform you that Pearl Harbor has been attacked by the Japanese. Reports are that there is great destruction and loss of life."

It would be the next day when President Roosevelt would make his famous "Day of Infamy" speech and war would be declared.

That was the day, for most, the world stopped turning. War had been declared and it would affect every aspect of American life. The household of Rufus and Reba was not spared. Within six months, all three of their sons would volunteer for the cause.

Reba did not exactly understand the worldwide implications or reasons for the war; all she knew was that her three sons were in danger. She looked for reasons and talked to Rufus about God's will, but this gave her little insight.

A year passed and, after first believing that the war would be short lived, it was common knowledge it would be lengthy. Often, she would not hear from her boys for weeks at a time.

She did not share her thoughts with Rufus, but she more than once wondered if the removal of the blue paint could have contributed to the events and her family's involvement. After all, it happened the day after the paint was removed.

December 7, 1942 came. It had been a year since her world had changed, and she had to do the only thing she knew to do. She, by herself, painted the ceiling Haint Blue. She did not consult Rufus. Eventually, all her sons returned from the war without a scratch.

Rufus and Reba and all the children are now deceased. The house has been neglected and most of it has rotted to the ground. However, if you look where the remnants of the porch existed, you will still see boards painted "Haint Blue."

RIGGER AND ETHIOPE

From the 1800s until 1960, the rural south had an unusual attachment to mules. For example, in 1930 there were 312,366 farms in the state of Mississippi and 370,000 mules. This compares to 102,000 horses and 5,542 tractors.

These animals were used for almost any type of drayage that needed to be done on a farm. Looking at the animal, it is hard to understand that, for most farmers, they were more treasured and loved than horses. Cattle only competed because they supplied milk and beef. We generally love what is beautiful, and mules, compared to horses, just don't compare. Nonetheless, the mule was once held in high esteem.

In 1945, when World War II ended, many farm boys took tractors given by the government rather than using the GI Bill to go to college. They could hire out to other farmers, farm their own land, take part in a government program to limit erosion by terracing hillsides and clear drilling sites for the new, booming oil industry. Partly due to this, by the early 1950s, the mule population was in decline.

Farmers are a superstitious group. They plant by the moon, they align their terrace rows in a certain direction, and they have a specific number of seeds they drop in the earth for each plant, always allowing one for the birds. With all this ritual, some habits are hard to break.

Slowly, the farmers began to "go tractor" to tend the crops that they sold; but they were not willing to do so with the gardens they grew for their family. These gardens were almost a holy site to the family and the care given them was beyond anything done commercially. Most often, there were two sites, one on the hill and one in the lowland. If it was a dry year, the one in the lowland would be the most successful; and, if it was a wet year, the one on the hill would fare better.

Starting as soon as the previous season's crop was turned in, all of the animal waste from the farm was spread as fertilizer. In addition, cotton seeds would be ground into meal and added to the soil. Finally, a large oak fire was built and, when it rendered a large pile of ashes, the ashes were spread to add potassium to the soil.

In March, it was time to break ground. No tractor would touch this soil. Only the sweat of the farmer mixed with that of the mule could put the last touch on this sacred spot. It was a ritual; like being Kosher to a Jewish person.

As early as 1940, my grandfather only kept two mules. Rigger was almost solid white and Ethiope was almost solid black. Both were male, but if you don't believe those two had a friendship bond, I am told, you should have seen them.

My grandfather always worked them together, in a team. Rigger worked the right side, a righty, and Ethiope worked the left, a lefty. At the end of a hard day, when unharnessed, they still stayed side by side, choosing to share the same stall and eating from the same food trough.

It was about a half-mile from the barn to the high garden spot, down a seldom traveled gravel road. Unfortunately, a fruit vendor making his way north from New Orleans approached my grandfather and the two mules from the rear. The old panel truck he was driving had canvas sides and they flapped in the wind. It spooked Ethiope.

Ethiope turned sharply into the path of the truck and was hit, causing serious, painful, and terminal injuries. My grandfather loved his animals and knew Ethiope had to be put down. He removed the harness as if he were removing the crown from a queen's head. He then went to the farm wagon where there was water, removed his shirt, dipped it in the water, and bathed the mule's head while he sent word to call the sheriff.

Again, mules were held in high esteem. You could shoot a horse, shoot a hog, or kill a cow; but the law required the sheriff or his representative to be present to put down a mule.

While the sheriff was en route, my grandfather led Rigger to another field, as if to spare him the sound of the pistol and the grief my grandfather had no doubt he felt.

When it was over, there was no other choice. The tractor had been loaned out that day and Ethiope's body had to be removed from the road. A harness was built, and Rigger was retrieved to escort his lifelong friend's body to a remote corner of the pasture. Rigger would stop and look back after each few steps. It was a procession. The entire farm family, the fruit vendor, and Rigger as the head pall bearer, in solemn order, made their way to Ethiope's final resting place.

Each day, when work was done and Rigger was unharnessed, he would gallop to the spot where Ethiope's body was returning to the soil. It has been told that he would stand perfectly still for several minutes and then walk away. It was as if he were saying, "Ethiope, it was tough without you, but I made it another day."

My grandfather replaced Ethiope with a brown mule. Not only was there no chemistry between the two animals, Rigger held deep resentment. No one could take Ethiope's place, at least not yet. He would kick and bite the new mule and refused to harness with him. That year, Rigger worked alone.

It was Christmas Eve, and I think that was just coincidental, but Jarvis Bowman, a neighboring farmer, came to my grandfather's house leading a black mule.

"Mr. Hezzie, come January, I have decided to go tractor. Maybe old Drummer here can take Ethiope's place. He is a lefty too."

No one in the family had a better Christmas than Rigger. He developed a rapport with Drummer much as he had with Ethiope.

Two years later, my grandfather "went tractor." The two mules could live out their lives in animal luxury. They never again pulled another plow. As close as Drummer and Rigger were, Rigger would never allow Drummer to venture in the area where Ethiope's body lay.

Many of the tools that Rigger and Ethiope pulled remained in the barnyard twenty-five years later. I played on them as a kid. I think my grandfather kept them there to remind him of the special bond between man and beast before "tractor."

⁂

IN SEARCH OF IDENTITY

The phone call was the beginning of one of the most interesting adventures in my life. The call itself was not unusual, as I often have people call and want to stop by to ask me something about the stories I write, the books I have written, and how I get my inspiration. They also want to know, are the stories true?

I welcome them, and I consider it a compliment if someone has enough interest to take the time to know more about what I do. I could tell this call was different from the very beginning. I will paraphrase the first conversation as best I remember it...

◇◇◇◇◇◇◇◇◇

"Mr. Case, my name is Evelyn McNeil and I have read your book *Bogue Chitto Flats*. I would like to visit with you and ask you some questions."

I replied, "Certainly, drop by the office anytime, but call before you come to make sure I'm in. You may not know it, but writing is just a hobby for me. My wife, son, and I own an insurance agency and that requires much of my time. Fortunately, it is the same office where I do most of my writing, so I am usually there."

"Mr. Case, I live in Hot Springs, Arkansas, and I want to make a definite appointment with you. Can we schedule it?"

"Hot Springs? You must have a serious interest to come that distance to discuss the work of an amateur writer. I am flattered."

I could tell by her diction and vocabulary, she was a highly educated person and my heart leapt. Maybe she was an agent and wanted to represent me to a major publisher. In this writing business, you wish for a break. A break that usually never comes.

Two weeks later, she arrived at my office at the exact minute of the set appointment. Her appearance matched the voice I had heard on the phone. She was immaculately and expensively dressed, but conservative, as she appeared to be in her late 70s.

After exchanging a few pleasantries, she got to the point. "Mr. Case, I can afford to pay you what you wish, but I would like to know how much to expect?"

"Ms. McNeil, I don't charge to talk to people about my writing. I am flattered and I guess you could say honored." There was some disappointment, however, as I realized she was not an agent that was going to catapult me to stardom.

"It is more than that, Mr. Case. Hear my story."

Over the next hour and a half, I heard the most amazing story that I have been told in my career of writing and listening. You know, you must listen before you can write. Her story bordered on the paranormal. This is the story she told me...

She said she felt that her birth roots were in Bogue Chitto, Mississippi, as mine were. It was a feeling that she could not explain, as she was raised 300 miles northwest of that small community. She told me that she never believed she was the blood child of the parents that raised her. This was confirmed when, in college, she learned that since both her parents had blue eyes, it was almost impossible for her to have brown eyes. After her mother's death, a DNA comparison proved her suspicion.

This was strange, as most adoptive parents are advised it is best to be open with the child from an early age. Her mother, on the other hand, went to her deathbed without revealing the secret.

She went on to say that, when she was about sixteen, her parents took a trip to New Orleans. In those days, the main route was U.S. Highway 51. When they got to Bogue Chitto, her father drove very slowly, and he and her mother whispered to each other. She remembered that, even though they needed gasoline, they did not stop at the crossroads store on the left side of the road, but pointed to it and continued whispering. She said she was entertained by playing with the words "Bogue Chitto," and intentionally mispronounced them as "Bowl a' Chili." This reinforced the name and location in her mind.

The interest in the small village was intensified when, two years ago, she again took a trip to New Orleans. By then, I-55 was the main route, but she decided to take the Bogue Chitto exit. She pulled into the old store she had remembered from years ago, which was now destroyed by age and storms. Evelyn parked her car. She told me she must have sat for an hour, even dropping into a light sleep or maybe a trance. That is when she had a most unusual experience, and the experience made her need to find out more. In her mind, that crossroad location and that store were familiar; something to do with her childhood.

I thought to myself, what do I or *Bogue Chitto Flats* have to do with this? At this point, I saw no connection.

Then she told me, "I Googled Bogue Chitto and read the history of the village. I also saw your book mentioned. I ordered your book and became interested in the mysteries, such as the one you wrote titled *Bob Smith's Cabin* and the sensitivity you portrayed in *Homemade Ice Cream*. I also saw that you are into genealogy. I found out you made monthly contributions to *Slidell Magazine*, so I wrote to the publisher and got all the magazines with your stories. Being born in Bogue Chitto, if anyone can help me, you can."

I told her I probably couldn't do anything she couldn't do on her own and asked her if she had searched Mississippi's and Arkansas's adoption records. She assured me there was no record of an adoption by her adoptive parents as she knew them.

I told her there was no charge for my help except the expenses I would incur; but she had to promise me that, no matter what we found out, I could write the story. She said she would rather pay me and not be obligated to let me write what she hoped would be her personal story. Eventually, she consented.

How and where do you begin research on an event that is prompted only by a feeling or a hunch? I recalled a friend who had a similar experience, and it was so strong she felt compelled to pull her car to the side of the road. There, she had the premonition of having a Jewish father and the father she knew was not Jewish. It turned out her premonition was correct. Could Evelyn's be also? Well, what the heck, I could write a fictional tale if nothing came from it. I would do it.

About a week later, Evelyn called me to see if I had made any progress. I was embarrassed to tell her I had not even started, but I promised I would go to Bogue Chitto the next week. I asked her to send me pictures of herself, going back to the youngest she had. When the photos arrived, there were four, capturing her image from about four years old to recent. She told me that her first childhood memories, of which she could be certain, were when she was about four. She was with her adoptive parents living in Hot Springs at that time.

I had no first or last name of her potential parents and only access to census records prior to 1940, so this source would be of little help. I concluded that, if she had been acquired by whatever means, it must have been when she was less than four years old. If her present age was correct, she would have been born in 1941 and be in the care of her new parents by 1944 or early 1945.

Since hunches and intuitions were already part of this story, on a hunch, I visited the newspaper archives in nearby Brookhaven. If I had no luck with her story, at the very least, I might find another story to write, as several of the stories I have written have come from newspaper archives.

I suppose a blind hog finds an acorn now and then. The first papers I searched were the year 1944. In a June edition, I found a headline that caught my attention.

Child Missing, Presumed Drowned in Bogue Chitto River

Three-year-old Bonnie Reed was last seen Friday night when her parents put her in bed. The Reed home is deep in the woods, built almost on the bank of the Bogue Chitto River. The recent flooding raised the water level to a depth of about four feet under the house and the current was very strong. The porch has no banister, and it is presumed she fell into the rushing water and was washed away. Her parents did not find her missing until early yesterday morning. A search has started, but since the current is so strong and the river extends far out of its banks, the child could be anywhere. There is little hope of finding young Bonnie alive.

The next day, there was more on the tragedy.

Search Continues for Missing Child

Bonnie Reed, a three-year-old, is missing and presumed drowned. Bonnie was the youngest of seven children and lived with her father Willy and mother Katsy deep in the woods on the Bogue Chitto River. There are six other children, ranging in age from eight to seventeen. The river is presently at flood stage for the second time this spring and the highest it has been in memory.

The family lives in a cabin built on stilts about fifty feet from the river's bed. Mr. Reed is a trapper and hunter. The only access to the home is by a footpath, as they own no automobile. This has, to some degree, hindered the search.

Two days later, there was a third article.

Search Continues for Missing Child

Rescuers have searched the Bogue Chitto River as far downstream as Norfield and found nothing. The search has moved from a rescue to a recovery. Officials have asked those who live in the area to watch for buzzards circling overhead, as they may lead to her remains, but are careful to point out that some livestock have been lost in the flood and this could also attract vultures.

The sheriff was asked if there was any suspicion of foul play and he stated that there was no indication.

No more articles could be found. I was intrigued to know if her body was ever found. Even though I did not think this was connected to Evelyn, I was pleased that it would make a good story for a future magazine edition. Did they ever find Bonnie? I wanted to know. Evelyn's assignment was now secondary. I would now concentrate on a story about Bonnie.

I still had relatives that lived in the area. They directed me to Mr. Wallace. I was told he was in his nineties, but his mind was sharp as a tack. I found him living with his son and daughter-in-law just south of Bogue Chitto. His daughter-in-law made us comfortable on the porch swing and brought us each a glass of sweet tea.

I explained to Mr. Wallace that I was there to find out more about the disappearance of Bonnie Reed, if he remembered the incident. He didn't hesitate. "Yes, I remember it well. I was about sixteen and I went on the search. Later, the teenagers would play a game. We called it 'Looking for Bonnie's Body.' What you call it, a scavenger hunt? Of course, we never found hide nor hair of her."

He continued, "Them folks was strange. They were so poor, they could fart dust. I mean, no car, no electricity, no water except river water. None of the kids ever went to school. I was told, if they were over ten years old, each day they had to catch or kill something, or they wouldn't eat that night. The old man wouldn't share what he had with his wife or kids. We called 'em hermits."

I asked, "Do you remember where they lived?"

"Sure, you know what we called Bauer's Bottom? Just upriver from that."

I had hunted that area as a teenager, so the area was familiar, but I did not remember seeing them or their house when I was there in the early 60s.

"Finally," he continued, "they moved out in the early 50s. The old man went to work as a laborer in the oil field. For that job, they had him digging ditches; the dumber the better and he fit right in. I think they're all dead now, but a daughter lived down in Summit at one time."

On the way back to Brookhaven, I stopped at my friend Tommy's house. Tommy knew those woods like the back of his hand.

He told me he had heard tell of the drowning, but it was about the time he was born. He had seen the house, but it had been gone for years. I wanted to see what was left, but he assured me there was not enough left to justify the walk. Termites, floods and age left only a few posts standing. I was disappointed. I felt if I could just touch something Bonnie had touched, it would help make the story come alive. In writing, being able to visualize is part of the process.

Tommy did save me some time in my investigation. He told me he knew of the daughter. He said he didn't know her personally, but she lived with her son Tucker Purvis, or he lived with her, and she did live in Summit. He knew where they lived, as Tucker repaired four wheelers and motorcycles and had once replaced an engine for him. Tommy told me what street and assured me there would be several disassembled vehicles in the yard. He was sure her name was Ouida.

The next morning, I drove to the place he had described, and it was as he described. There was hardly room for me to get in the drive for discarded engine blocks, wheels, chassis, and the like. A man, who I assumed was Tucker, was working on a motorcycle. I introduced myself but he never looked up. I continued telling him I would like to speak to his mother and told him what it was about. I told him I was a writer.

"She in thar. Not gone talk to you though, but go head on. You ain't the first to come see her bout that."

I made my way through the maze of old Harley and Honda carcasses to the front porch and then to the front door.

The house was more of a shelter than a home. It had no siding, just tar paper over a few boards. The porch leaned from rotted pillars and the back had fallen almost to the ground by the same cause. There was an electric utility meter attached to the home and I saw a pump, so I knew at least they had electricity and water.

It was apparent she had been watching and she met me at the door but did not open the screen, which had more holes than wire. I could see her plainly, though; and, at that moment, I realized there was a connection between Bonnie and Evelyn.

The picture I had of Evelyn was an abstract image of the woman behind the screen. Age the picture image a few years, discount Evelyn's lifetime of facials, hair salons, and Estee Lauder, and facing me was a recognizable facsimile of the same person, just a different model with no chrome.

I told her my reason for coming and, as her son had told me, she had no interest in discussing her sister's drowning. I have some experience in getting stories from unwilling tellers, but she was adamant. I knew it was now or never and I only had one chance.

With the excuse of leaving her a business card, I reached into my leather satchel and felt for the pictures Evelyn had sent. Hoping I chose the adult one, I pulled it out and intentionally dropped it to the porch floor. When I picked it up, by chance, it was the correct picture. I made certain that she saw the photo.

I didn't say a word to her, I just watched her awed expression.

After what seemed like a minute of silence, she said, "I won't talk to you." She then closed the solid door and retreated inside the house.

I had missed an opportunity; but, I had, in my mind, solved Evelyn's question. I just didn't know the details.

I had backed my car from the drive to the street and paused to check my text messages. I took one last glance at the house before driving away. That's when I saw the door of the house open.

Ouida emerged and, like a person with a bad hip, limped her way to my car.

"Is she still alive? Please tell me yes."

"Yes, she is very much alive. She didn't drown and somehow, I think you knew that."

"I did."

"Will you tell me about it?"

She hesitated, then said, "Yes, after all these years, nothing bad can come of telling the truth."

I turned the car back into the drive and she opened the passenger door and got in. At this point, it was the only time her son stood up from his work as if to ask, "What the hell is Momma doing?"

I reached for my recorder, but she refused to let me record the story. In the most botched and almost unrecognizable English, this is what she told me...

◇◇◇◇◇◇◇◇◇◇

"My daddy was a trapper and a hunter. He wasn't lazy. I guess you could say he didn't have a job that paid much money. We also had a cow, some chickens, a pig, and he would make a garden. We had no electricity, or fresh running water. We drank river water and, of course, we had no plumbing or automobile. We walked when we went somewhere, but mostly we stayed in the house by the river. Daddy had a small boat to use if the river flooded and we could paddle to dry land and then walk from there. That is how it started.

"The river was high, and we needed kerosene for the stove. There were seven of us kids and I was about eight years old and next to the youngest. Bonnie was three and the baby in the family.

"I was Daddy's favorite. I don't know why. He would take me to the store most of the time when he went. That day, we paddled the boat to dry land, then walked the mile to the store. He bought a gallon of kerosene and, while paying for it, a car drove up to buy gasoline.

"It was a fancy car; and, in those days, there were no credit cards or automatic pumps, so you went into the store to pay before you pumped your gas. The man was dressed up, a city man. Beside him sat a city woman, too. She had on a hat and gloves.

"Daddy was a loner and seldom spoke to anyone, let alone a stranger, so I was a little surprised to hear him talking to this man, especially when he asked me to start walking home alone. I walked slowly and soon he caught up with me. For the rest of the day, he didn't say one word to me. That night, Bonnie disappeared.

"We were not ever a normal family, but we got along with each other. As poor as we were, we didn't know any other life. After Bonnie disappeared, it was never the same. My two brothers fought with each other and, literally, fought with my daddy. My three sisters didn't get along and it was just a mess.

"The boys were the oldest and left home within a year or two. Soon afterward, two of my sisters left. Don't have any idea where those two went since I haven't seen or heard from them since. Daddy got a job in the oil field and we moved away from the river. He and Momma separated. I don't think they ever divorced. To be honest, I think they just lived common law and were never married.

"My last sister, the one closest to my age, lived out at Fair River and we stayed in touch until she passed away two years ago this past June.

"Well, back to Bonnie. I would see Momma often. She even lived with me, or I lived with her, a few times. She got sick about fifteen years ago. Wouldn't go to the doctor. Said she knew she was dying, and she said she was in terrible pain. That's when she told me.

"Momma told me that Bonnie was an unexpected pregnancy. She was born five years after me. Momma called her an accident. The year Bonnie disappeared was a real bad year. The cow had died, there had been a bad flood just a couple of months before and all the small game had temporarily left to seek high ground. That was what we lived on. Daddy had planted a garden but, with the second flood that year, that's when Bonnie disappeared, it washed the garden out again and it was too late to replant. Nine people couldn't make it under the circumstances. Momma said meeting the man at the store was accidental, but he was the one that approached Daddy wanting to know if there was a child that he might be able to adopt. He and his wife were on their way to an adoption agency in New Orleans; but, if he could skip all the red tape, he would. That is how it started.

"One thing led to another, and a price of $100 was agreed on. Bonnie was selected, as she was still real small and would adapt better. Plus, she was too young to contribute to her upkeep in the woods, the river, or a future garden.

"As it turned out, the man said he didn't need an adoption; he could pull strings and get the proper paperwork done when they got home. Momma made Bonnie drink a lot of Paregoric that night to make her woozy and sleepy. They had to tell us kids something, so they made up the drowning story and, of course, the authorities had to know. I think my oldest brother suspected something. He refused to search for her and wouldn't talk to Momma or Daddy for a long time."

I listened, and I believed what she said was true. I had one other experience with parents selling a baby. When I was young, a neighbor sharecropper sold their child, but they did go through some regulatory process, even though the motive was money. Years later, the young man showed up at my parents' trying to trace his roots; so, I knew something like this was not impossible. But that's another story. I also knew that financial times were bad in Mississippi and the South in the 40s, so many children were adopted from there. I knew about the Orphan Trains.

When she paused, I asked her if she wanted to meet Bonnie. She answered, "Not really, at least not now. I'm glad she's alive."

I left, telling her if she ever changed her mind, let me know and I would arrange a meeting. She thanked me.

I had a moral dilemma. Loosely speaking, you could say Evelyn was my client, but not really. I'm a writer, not a lawyer, I reasoned. Obviously, Ouida, for whatever reason, did not want to meet Evelyn. I owed her some respect too. I knew if I told Evelyn all I knew, she would contact Ouida. I didn't think that was fair to Ouida.

It was a week before I called Evelyn. I told her that she was from Bogue

Chitto, and she has one remaining sister that is living. I even told her she had been sold for $100, but I explained the circumstances of the time. I told her the sister did not want to meet and I would not give her Ouida's name. I feared she would take it on herself to contact her.

Evelyn did not seem surprised that I had made the connection but couldn't understand what Ouida's reservations on meeting were. I tried to explain that, even though they were sisters, the environmental surroundings of their youth had made them two vastly different people, except in appearance. Evelyn did not take my answer well.

A few days later, Evelyn called. "Mr. Case, I've done some thinking. You tell me things aren't good for her, as far as the condition of her home and so forth. I inherited a large sum of money, and I also made a great deal of money in my profession. I would like to buy my sister a comfortable home and give her a reasonable annuity for life. She must be in her mid-eighties. You see, the family sold me. As strange as it seems, I would like to buy my family back. Will you discuss this with her?"

As I drove to Summit that day, I couldn't imagine how Ouida would respond. When I arrived, the utility worker was disconnecting the electric meter. I knew this meant an unpaid bill. I also saw no trace of Tucker.

Ouida came to the porch and, after a few minutes, I told her what Evelyn's intentions were. She was silent for over a minute, and I could see tears seeping from her cataract-filled eyes.

"Mr. Case, if she cares that much about me, I'll see her. In fact, I would love to see her, but I won't take her money. She don't deserve to be used twice. I don't want to hear no more about it."

CHICKEN AND DUMPLINGS

Tennessee Williams' play, *The Glass Menagerie*, had an absentee character named Mr. Wingfield. In the play, he was Amanda's husband and he worked for the telephone company. One of the better lines reads, "He fell in love with long distance." Of course, that meant he deserted the family.

Somehow, that line reminds me of my father. He in no way deserted the family, but you might say he fell in love with a dream. This, in its own way, caused the family problems.

Dad was a smart man with little formal education. He was not averse to hard work, either mental or physical; but Dad always would dream that the grass was greener in another vocation. He would abandon one job before he had an opportunity to see it to fruition just to go on to another "wild goose chase" as my mom often said.

We were considered middle class, well I think we were, but that had to do with Mom's frugality more than Dad's earning power. I knew when the evening meal was tomato gravy and biscuits things were "stretched" according to Mom. Likewise, I knew when there was a ham on the stove, or fried chicken, times were good. I guess you could say that a Dunn and Bradstreet report of my family's finances could have been written based on an analysis of what we ate. I only remember steak, other than round or ground steak, a couple of times.

Dad loved Mom and she loved him. She had to, to stay married to him, but it had to be trying. One time, he spent the utility money to buy me a collie dog. Mother cried, but she filled the lamps with kerosene, and we made do.

Once, he borrowed money from a relative and flew in a private plane to Washington D.C. to patent a self-rocking cradle. That was not successful either. He had a wash board manufacturing business just as washing machines were coming out, and a well bucket company just as wells were having pumps attached. You see, Dad had good ideas, just at the wrong time. He even brainstormed about founding a life insurance company where you only sent in your money if someone in the group died. That idea has recently resurfaced with health insurance but in those days the state curtailed that venture.

On a joyful afternoon, Mom and Dad sat down with my brother and sister as I recorded the story of their marriage and their life. It was their 50th anniversary. They lived in 17 houses and Dad had 28 jobs. That was back in 1980 but, recently, I listened to the tape. It brought back memories and gave me insight into why some things were the way they were.

I now can even better relate as I have raised two children, balanced a job, an amateur writing career, and a family. I have lived the ups and downs. I have felt the emotions that my mom felt, and I am sure my wife has also. I also know where my dad was coming from.

Dad loved to wear a hat. In his younger years, I seldom saw him in a cap, just a hat. His love for hats may have been his vanity, as he had male pattern baldness at age 23. He also loved Stetson hats. Not the western type, but more of the fedora type. In his mind, a Stetson hat was class; and, if he could only afford one classy item, it would be his hat.

Amusingly, the mood Dad was in was reflected in the way he wore his hat. If his hat was sitting square on his head, he was in a serious mood. This is the way he wore it when he went to church. I expect he wore it that way when he went to Washington D.C.

If he were in a carefree mood, he wore it pushed back on his head, revealing his forehead. He also whistled a lively tune when in such a mood.

His emotions ran the gamut from happy to depressed. He called the depressed days his blue days.

Mom, on the other hand, was more even keeled. She was seldom bubbling over with happiness or hampered with being blue. I remember, however, an incident that stands out where both personalities interacted with each other, and I have remembered it for 64 years.

Dad must have shared with Mom that he was having a good week. I have no idea which of the 28 jobs he was doing at the time, but I remember it being a late Friday afternoon and being in the kitchen with Mom. I must have been about eight years old. My sister was married, and my brother was staying in town with my aunt to go to a school function. It was just me and Mom.

Mom had put on a new blue dress. I remember to this day Mom telling her sister that she bought it at Don't Throw Away, a used clothing store, for one dollar. Well, at least it was new to her. I don't remember her dressing real nicely except to go to church and this was not a go-to-church outfit.

I am sure she had pride in cooking a more than average meal and I am sure the dress she wore was to telecast a happy, maybe flirtatious mood to my dad. She set the table with her best china, Blue Willow, and some pale blue depression glass water goblets.

On each plate, she placed a pineapple ring. In the center hole, there was a chopped banana, and it was topped with mayonnaise. The finishing touch was a cherry and grated cheddar cheese. This salad was a favorite of Mom's and, for a few years, it was served often.

For dessert, she had prepared a dish she called a date bar. That was also a standby and served on many Sundays. Of course, only when times were good.

The main dish that day would be chicken and dumplings. It was perhaps the dish she took the most pride in and took a long time in its tedious preparation. She said her secret was she used a hen, not a fryer or a broiler. Even now, I don't know the difference.

We didn't have a car at that time, and I would listen for the Greyhound Bus to stop in front of our house. We lived several hundred yards from the highway, but you could hear the distinct sounds of the bus as it geared down, braked, and stopped. You could also hear the engine as it revved, and the air brakes exhausted as it pulled away.

The arrival of the bus meant Dad was home and would be walking up the driveway in just a minute or so. Then I heard him. He was whistling a happy song. I can still remember, "She'll be coming round the mountain." I rushed to meet him and saw the hat pushed back on his forehead. Even I knew that meant it was a good day.

I intercepted him about halfway up the drive. He seldom brought me any type of surprise. It was not his nature. On that day, he reached into his coat pocket a gave me a bag of potato chips. A bag of potato chips was then much larger than they are today.

I immediately bit into the upper part of the bag where the cellophane is sealed, tearing the bag almost in half. By the time we entered the kitchen, I had consumed most of the bag of chips. Seeing Dad, Mom had a big smile and, as she hugged him, he gave her a chocolate bar. She was beaming.

Then she saw me eating the potato chips. Her mood changed as if you turned off a light switch. From an almost coquettish interaction, she went to a look that projected almost hatred.

Tears came to her eyes and she said, "I've worked in this kitchen all day and now you have gone and spoiled his appetite. I deserve more respect than that. What I do is important too."

She then turned off the stove and went to her bedroom. My memory is dim on what happened the rest of the night. I don't recall eating the chicken and dumplings, the pineapple salad, or the date bar. I know the next morning, the kitchen was clean; and I remember it was years before Mother ever cooked chicken and dumplings again.

You and I would say the incident was no big thing. We would say my mother overreacted, and that would be true. But, over the years, I have thought about what was behind her reaction. It was obviously more than a bag of potato chips. I have considered that she did not feel respected as she was considered just a lowly housewife in those days. I also considered that Dad did not give her credit for what she did as a mother, etc. It could be a hormonal thing; she would have been about forty-four.

Whatever it was, I don't think she ever got totally over it. Within a year, she had enrolled in classes to become a Certified Dental Assistant. This elevated her from the status of a rural housewife, to part of the respected healthcare profession. She was no longer less than equal as a woman or a wife. She was no longer dependent on Dad's good weeks or bad weeks.

The fact that someone's attitude can influence another person exists outside of families. Probably more so than within families simply because we have many more contacts outside the family. I know I have said things to people and, even though they have never said a word, I know their attitude toward me has been forever changed. Likewise, my relationship with others has been changed by what they have said to me. Maybe on another occasion the incident would have been ignored.

I have no conclusion to the problem; but I am cognizant that, if Dad had been more attentive to Mom prior to the incident, it would have been no big thing. Likewise, if we are more attentive to other's thoughts and needs, we can avoid the cold spots forming in our relationships. We must do a better job at being our brother's keeper.

I am often asked where I get the inspiration for my stories. Most, if not all of my stories are based on some real life happening. Most also are enhanced to be more appealing, but some are not. Some are told just as they happened.

I must admit, after 110 stories, subject matter does not come as easily as it once did. After all, one young man can only have so many adventures. I have discussed this with my editor and advised her that I will cease writing on a regular basis if, in my opinion, the quality of my work diminishes past a certain point.

To keep me going, I am doing more study and training on writing than I did in the first five years. I have listened to tape lectures on writing, read Steven King's book on how to write, and paid for writing courses.

I recently attended an excellent workshop sponsored by the City of Slidell. Most, if not all in attendance, were more advanced in their writing career and talent than me.

When you go to a writing seminar, you gain knowledge a drop at a time. You do not attend and leave thinking that you have learned everything you need to know. I compare it to going to church. I do not leave church each Sunday a completely changed person, but I leave a little changed each time. Writing seminars are similar.

We participated in an exercise to help us develop a plot. A dictionary was passed around and each person opened it to a random spot. They then choose a word from the page and we all wrote it down. The dictionary was passed around the table, with each person choosing a word at random. Some of the words chosen were potato, averse, derby, atom bomb and penalty.

We were to write a story of only a few paragraphs that contained at least one of these words. My story was a brief summary of the one you just read.

I used some of my prior knowledge of writing to finish the story. I used a tip that has been the most important I have learned in writing, *write what you know about.* I could not write a story on the "Emotions of a super bowl quarterback" any more than I could the "Apprehensions of a girl's first date."

I had to write what I knew about.

I knew about my family.

THE HEIST

*Police Chief Tom McBride announced there was a burglary at JCPenney®
on Saturday night or early Sunday morning. He did not elaborate on what
was stolen, but indicated it was of little value and the perpetrators may
have been juveniles.*
October 25, 1957

Otis Murphee lived as close to the earth as anyone can. Partly by choice and partly by necessity, he owned almost nothing.

He lived in a two-room shack, deep in the woods, whose only access was a foot path that led a quarter of a mile to the highway. The house was located at the edge of what was referred to as "the Swamp." To some extent, it was a swamp, as the river had changed its course several times over the last thousand years and scarred the terrain with crevasses that, in some cases, and at times, still held water.

These were breeding grounds for mosquitoes, copperheads, and cottonmouths, but they were also oases for wild game hoping to secure food and drink. This made Otis's quest for existence much easier. Within a five-minute walk from his house, he could easily claim the day's food supply for the cost of a few pennies in rifle cartridges. His daily pilgrimage to this natural meat market was necessary, as his home had no electricity or refrigeration.

He planted a few vegetables and there were some fruit and nut trees along the path leading to the highway. Even with this, his diet was mostly protein and not well-balanced. This contributed to his appearance of aging well beyond his years.

For clothing, he would go to the local dump and wear whatever he found. It is believed he did not own a jacket, much less a coat, but his primitive living had made him immune to the elements.

Otis seldom made trips into town or other points of civilization. He did not need to, and he had no money to spend when he went. Those who knew him estimated his annual income, from who knows what source, was less than $100 per year. This he spent on ammunition for his rifle.

By the early 1960's, very few people knew much about him; and, if he had ever had a family, wife, or children, it was not known or expected. No one really cared.

Police Chief McBride was fond of him for some reason. Maybe he just liked the simplicity of his lifestyle or maybe he felt a little sorry for him. When Otis did come to town, the Chief would occasionally drive him home or to the beginning of the path that led to his shack. The Chief also knew that getting him home as soon as possible was the best thing for all concerned on certain occasions.

The locals would tease Otis as you would tease a child. Otis, however, was no one's fool; that is, unless they gave him alcohol to entice him into telling stories. His favorite was about the Indians that lived in the woods near his home. According to him, they would attack almost weekly, and he had killed hundreds over the years. He claimed they had escaped from the reservation and wanted to reclaim their land. It was said that hearing Otis's stories was better than going to a John Wayne movie.

After the alcohol crossed a point however, Otis's mood would change, and he would hallucinate even beyond his imagined battles with the Indians. It was best he be driven home.

Chief McBride was dead now. The new chief, Chief Roberts, was not a native of the county and didn't know the stories of the eccentric who dwelled just south of his town. He didn't know Otis or anything about his proclivity to tell tall tales and sometimes hallucinate; but he would learn.

It was big news in 1960. Laverne Dugan was missing. Laverne was a beautiful thirty-year-old mother and wife. Her husband came home and found their nine-month-old baby in the play pen. It was obvious the child had been there, with no care, for hours. Nothing in the house was disturbed.

Laverne Dugan had keys to the family car, and those keys were at their house. That was not unusual, as she could not have used them anyway. The family only had one car, and her husband, James, had used it to go to work at the local lawnmower plant. What was unusual was that her purse containing her identification, makeup, and $10 also was there. There was no sign of a struggle.

The couple's home was in a small, populated community about three miles south of Otis's, in a jurisdiction serviced by the county Sheriff's office. James called the sheriff.

The sheriff and a deputy arrived, looked around, secured the premises, and called the state police. This was beyond their ability to investigate.

Over the next few days, there were leads, but none panned out. Within a couple of weeks, evidence began to surface that Laverne Dugan was having several affairs. One was with a prominent, older, wealthy gentleman from town. He did not want the infidelity to be made known, and he had the influence to stop the investigation. Soon it was a cold case.

To say the loss of his wife ruined James's life would be an understatement. James was what could be referred to as a "good ole boy." He married way beyond his standing, and Laverne had nothing in common with him. He loved her dearly but had to admit things had not been good at home since the baby came.

There was speculation that he had found out about her cheating and killed her. This caused him to lose his job. Things went from bad to worse. He filed a claim on her $10,000 life insurance policy only to be told that, without a body, she was just a missing person.

With no job and a baby, James was desperate. One night, he went to a small remote cemetery and dug up the grave of a woman of approximately the age and size of his wife. The woman had died five years prior. He took her skull and put it in a ditch not far from his house. When the skull was found a few days later by the county crews cutting the right of way, it was presumed it belonged to Laverne – at first. Then it was noticed that the skull belonged to a person who wore dentures. Laverne had movie star quality teeth.

Eventually, James's conscience got the best of him, and he admitted his actions. He was sentenced to a one-year suspended sentence for desecrating a grave. He did not collect the life insurance money.

The spring and summer of 1963 were among the rainiest on record and much of the land mass around Otis's house flooded. This hampered his ability to acquire food, so he waded to some of the neighbors' houses that he barely knew in search of a handout.

After a couple of weeks, the water receded, and Otis returned to the lagoons that dependably afforded him food. The high water had washed out a portion of the land that, prior to the flood, provided a path to his favored hunting spots. The new route was much longer. The ground was still soft and mushy and, in some places, if he stepped in the wrong spot, he would sink to his knees.

Otis had never been to a doctor of any sort and due to his age, about 60, his eyesight was impaired. Therefore, from where he stood, he was not sure at first what he was seeing. It was too muddy to get any closer, but from fifty yards away, what he thought he had caught a glimpse of forced him to trudge through the mud a few more feet to get a better view. He could not be sure, but it looked like the arm of a person protruding upright from the mud. The hand was somewhat distinguishable, but the arm, if it was an arm, was covered in mud and leaves. Otis continued to the lagoon and claimed his meal of a wild turkey and a gar fish he shot in the shallow water. He then went home.

He reasoned, the next morning the ground would be dryer and he would explore the strange apparition in a little more detail. The next day, he was able to get a little closer. Now, he was positive. It was the arm of a person sticking out of the mud.

Otis was smart enough to know that this could not mean anything good for him. If foul play was involved, he could be a suspect. At best, his hunting area would be disturbed, and the game would be flushed by the excavation of the scene. He was faced with a dilemma. Should he report it or not? Then he remembered the disappearance of Laverne Dugan. He did not know her, but he had seen her a couple of times and, like most men, was enamored with her beauty. The thought of her being in the cold wet earth bothered him. The next day, he walked the eight miles to town.

He met with Chief Roberts and explained what he had seen. Chief Roberts politely thanked him but explained that, due to the alleged location of the body, the investigation would be the sheriff's responsibility. He assured Otis he would notify the sheriff on his behalf. Later that day, Chief Roberts talked with some of the people who knew Otis, found out about the Indian stories, and subsequently dismissed the information he had learned from the man as pure foolishness. He did not tell the sheriff at that time.

It was the practice of the police chief and sheriff to have breakfast once ever few months and share knowledge. This is when Sheriff Case first learned about Otis's visit. He had only been sheriff for a short while and only knew Otis by sight. He reasoned that, at some point, he would stop by and visit with Otis, if for no other reason than to satisfy his curiosity.

It was late August, and a hurricane had blown up from Louisiana. The wind was not significant, but the rain was torrential. This time, Otis's surroundings were flooded to an even greater depth. The water was so deep, he could shoot fish from his front steps. Most were trash fish - buffalo, jack and choupique - but it was better than begging from the neighbors.

When the water receded, Otis was, to say the least, disturbed when he saw the uniformed sheriff making his way up the path to his house. Almost no one had ever visited him, especially law enforcement. Sheriff Case introduced himself, saying his visit was just to see if Otis made it through the storm. In a few minutes, the conversation turned to the subject Otis had shared with Chief Roberts.

"Otis, can you show me what you saw?"

"Well, I can take you thar. I doubt it is still thar with all this flooding. You better git them shiny boots off and go barefooted."

"I have some rubber boots back in the unit. I will be right back."

In a few minutes, he returned wearing the boots and carrying a Polaroid camera. The two proceeded through the mud toward the area where Otis had seen the arm a few weeks prior and before the major flooding.

Sheriff Case, whose eyesight was much better than Otis's, froze in his tracks before Otis even focused on what was visible beyond. Due to the mud, they could not get within 100 yards of the object, but it could clearly be seen. Not only was there one arm visible above the mud, a few feet away, another arm, a leg, and an upper torso were visible. There must have been five or six bodies buried in the mulch.

The sheriff took photos and immediately returned to his patrol car where he radioed the state police. Within an hour, dozens of spectators surrounded what once was the private but primitive home of Otis Murphee. One of the spectators was James, who was sure Laverne had been the victim of a crazed killer.

A young state highway patrolman put on waders and started to the nearest body. He soon sank to above his knees and had to be helped back to high ground. It was impossible to get to the bodies due to the muck.

Within an hour, a lowboy tractor trailer arrived, and a bulldozer was unloaded. The once narrow footpath was cleared to a width that could accommodate vehicles, all of which were destroying the fruit and nut trees that once lined the path and nutritiously sustained Otis Murphee. An oil well supply firm delivered wooden pallets, and a wooden walk was built across the mud.

The same young state patrolman then approached the bodies. He inspected the first one carefully. He shook his head, then began to laugh. He tugged on the arm, and the entire body came out of the mud. It was a mannequin, and still visible was a tag that read, "Property of JCPenney."

That day, Otis Murphee's life was forever changed. No longer could his primitive dwelling be hidden from view and approached only by a foot path. Gone were the trees that provided him nourishment.

But, as it was said, Otis was no fool. He put a gate at the entrance to the widened path to his house. For a while, he charged admission to show people where the twenty-two "bodies" were found. He finished the tour with the story of the Indians. Finally, when this became old news, he became a guide, taking rich city folks hunting. It didn't matter if hunting was in season or not, no one bothered Otis.

Laverne is still missing.

This story has a sequel, "The Deed."

THE DEED

It had been fifty years since Laverne Dugan disappeared. She would have been 80 years old if she was still alive. Some thought she might be, but others felt sure she was dead, a victim of foul play. Years ago, her husband, James, had came home from work and found their nine-month-old son, Steve, in the playpen. Laverne was nowhere to be found, and there had been no sign of a struggle.

The community was basically divided on their opinion of what happened to her. James's relatives felt sure she was the victim of a kidnapper or crazed killer. They felt she would never have left her husband and young son.

It is a well-worn cliché that the husband is the last to know; but, in this case, it was true. Many were certain Laverne was not the person James thought she was. There had been rumors over the years that she had been involved in several relationships. It was well rumored she was involved with Stennis Summerall.

The affair with Stennis caused its fair share of gossip. He was probably forty years older than Laverne and very wealthy. "New rich" they called it. He got into the oil business when the boom hit town. Mostly, he just sat in the lobby of the Inez Hotel and made deals. Oil men from Texas and Louisiana schemed, scammed, and honestly made millions for themselves and a few locals.

Outside the hotel, there was a new Chevrolet that seldom left its parking spot. Stennis had bought it for him and Laverne to use when she could get a babysitter and sneak into town. It would be too obvious for them to be seen in his Lincoln Continental. The Chevrolet was never seen again after her disappearance.

Freddie Baxter was a teller at the bank until he got fired for divulging bank customer's business. He said Stennis had opened an account and put a sizable amount of money in it, and Laverne withdrew it the day before she was last seen.

About fifteen years later, Stennis died. Over the years, Laverne's disappearance faded from the memories of most. At least, the details did.

Steve hadn't given much thought to growing up without a mother. Occasionally, when other kids' moms would come to school, he had wished to have one. But, for the most part, he didn't care. He had never had one. After all, she had disappeared when he was nine months old.

His father, James Dugan, had explained to him that his mother had disappeared and was most likely killed by a crazy person. He was too young to process the horror of such a statement; and, by the time he was old enough to understand the pain and fear of murder at the hands of a stranger, he had heard another theory.

He heard gossip that his classmates had most likely picked up from their parents. They told the story of Laverne deserting the family by running off with another man, adding that she was most likely living in another state. He had also heard that his father may have killed her out of jealousy.

Each of these possibilities had dwelled differently in his mind at various times in his life. The experience had formed in his mind a distrust for women. Now fifty-one years old, Steve had never married and worked as a clerk at the county farmers co-op.

Due to his personality, or lack thereof, Steve's position at the co-op was as high as he would ever achieve. He had not had a raise in five years, but really had not needed one. He lived frugally and had acquired significant assets when his father passed away the year before. A few years after his mother disappeared, his father had inherited his grandfather's eighty-acre farm. Shortly afterward, they drilled a successful oil well on it. Steve's father also had collected $10,000 in Laverne's life insurance proceeds, though at first, the life insurance company refused to pay since there was no body. After seven years, Laverne Dugan was presumed dead.

Steve lived like a recluse and spent no money.

It was a warm day in May when she walked into the co-op. She was looking for cracked corn to feed birds. She appeared to be about Steve's age and, for some reason, for maybe the first time in his life, he felt an attraction to a female.

The smallest package of cracked corn the co-op sold was a 50-pound bag, which was much more than she needed. She said she had rented a room at the Inez Hotel for a month. A genealogy buff, she was using the Inez as a geographical base to explore the records and cemeteries of nearby counties. She wanted to place the seed on the windowsill and photograph the birds as they came to eat. According to her, photography was also an interest.

She asked Steve if a sack ever accidentally got damaged. He told her it occurred occasionally and, if one did happen to break, he would send a small bag of corn to her room at the Inez.

Just before closing, he carefully took his pocketknife and slit a bag of corn. He placed about two pounds in a paper bag, which he decided he would deliver himself. For the first time in his life, Steve felt an emotional sensation he had never experienced.

The two sat in the lobby of the old hotel that still held a bit of its charm. In its day, the Inez had been the town's shining star. Steve learned that her name was Ruby Fulton and she was from Kirby, Texas. Some time, about two grandfathers ago, she had relatives in the surrounding counties. She was retired now and had time to pursue her dream of following her roots all the way to wherever they led.

She then asked him about his family. He told her what he knew, never mentioning Stennis Summerall, wanting to believe that part of the story was not true. She had a probing personality, however, and when he left, he realized he had never spoken to a female that long in his life and had never revealed so much about himself to anyone. She was so easy to talk to.

Within a few days, Steve's new afternoon ritual was to visit Ruby at the hotel. This went on day after day. They talked. This was fun. This was new for him. He bought new clothes and had his car washed and waxed, a treat he usually gave himself only for Christmas.

Would she have dinner at the local café with him? It was in the same building as the hotel. Yes, she would.

From that day on, they were inseparable every day after work until about 9 pm. Nothing more intimate than a greeting hug was shared between the two. Steve never questioned it. Maybe that was the way it was supposed to be. He didn't know. She was the first woman he had more than a casual conversation with.

It was a Saturday, about three weeks into their relationship, when he asked if she wanted to see where he lived. He took her to the home where he grew up, the home where his mother had disappeared. She realized it was decorated just as it must have been fifty years ago. Neither he nor his father had changed a thing.

His mother's picture sat on a table. She was pretty. Ruby asked questions. She wanted to know where the playpen was that he had been left in. He knew where it had been, and he showed her. She did not say a word, just contemplated the disappearance.

He then drove her to the eighty acres that he had inherited. The oil well looked like a giant hammer as it sucked the oil from underneath the soil. It had produced long after it was expected to; but he had been told that when it quit, they could squeeze even more out by injecting CO_2. The oil well had made him financially secure, and that is the only thing about the land he cared about. He dealt daily with too many farmers and realized he was not cut out for that life.

There was a stream on the lower part of the property. It meandered through a sharp turn, creating a nice view in two directions. Audibly, he heard her say, "This is where I want my house."

She then turned to Steve and asked, "Will you marry me?"

"Yes," he said, without hesitating.

For the first time in his life, Steve attempted to kiss someone. She hugged him but turned away.

"No, I have had two romances since my husband died. I think they both did not work out because we became too intimate before we got married. Let's do this right and wait."

That was OK with him. He didn't know any better.

Steve's coworkers advised him to slow things down a bit, but he knew better. Nothing could be better than the new feelings of romance he had.

One afternoon, she told him, "Steve, I would like for you to give me something that I can call my own. I have never owned anything growing up, and I need that security."

"Sure, what would you like? We will go and get you the nicest ring in the store."

"I don't want a ring. I want the land, the eighty acres. I am not interested in the house."

Steve was silent for a moment before answering, "I must think about that."

He wished she had not asked for his property, because he knew he couldn't resist doing anything she desired. That night, he reasoned that she would soon be his wife; so, what did it matter if she owned the property rather than he? What belonged to one belonged to the other. He had no heirs anyway.

Two days later, Ruby delivered paperwork for Steve to sign. He read it and agreed with its contents. They went to a notary, and he signed it.

The next day, he got a call from one of the few friends he had. Tommy Breeland grew up about a quarter of a mile from Steve's home and was the closest thing to a childhood friend Steve had.

"Steve, your lady friend, Ruby, and an elderly lady, Laverne Summerall, were in my office wanting to transfer half the property you gave to Ruby to this Laverne, who she says is her mother. I told them I would have to prepare the papers overnight and have them ready for them in the morning. I thought I should call you. Be careful now, I could lose my license for revealing this information, but you and I go back a long way."

Steve immediately awoke from his deep state of infatuation. "Tommy, I will be right there. Is there anything we can do?"

In less than five minutes, he was in his friend's office. Tommy explained that, although Steve had given her a deed to the property, if she had not recorded it, there was still a chance the sale could be at least flawed. Based on this advice, they hurried to the courthouse. The sale, which was for one dollar, love, and other consideration, had not been recorded.

Time was of the essence. They hurried to the bank. Tommy kept a sizable amount of money in this bank and, from a business standpoint, was well respected. They reasoned the maximum value of the property including the oil well production was $500,000. Based on deposits Tommy had at the bank, a loan was quickly made to Tommy for $600,000, using the land to secure a mortgage. Tommy had explained that, if Ruby had not recorded the sale and they could record the mortgage before she got to the courthouse, the sale would be primed by the mortgage and she would have ownership only subject to the mortgage. In layman's terms, it meant she would have to make the payments. The papers were rushed to the courthouse and recorded. They had made it in time.

The next day, Laverne recorded the deed giving half the property to her mother, not knowing there was a mortgage that encumbered the property for more than its worth. In addition to that, the payments were $5,000 per month.

The next day, Ruby checked out of the Inez at 6 a.m. She went back to Texas, never seeing Steve again. In five months, the foreclosure proceedings were underway. Steve bought his property back at the foreclosure sale.

The truth eventually came out. Like mother, like daughter. Ruby was the child of Stennis Summerall, half-sister to Steve. Laverne had disappeared after finding out she was pregnant with Stennis's child. Stennis supported them well until he passed away. After he died, they had gone through his money rapidly.

Steve now distrusted women more than ever.

HOODOO MAN

The fact that he was born during the Great Depression had no bearing on Dolphus's poverty, disposition, or talent. He was a black sharecropper's son on a poor white farmer's land. As to situations, that was the worst kind of sharecropping. There were some sharecroppers that lived on wealthy plantations where just the trickle down would have been a luxury compared to Dolphus's situation.

On some of those farms, the owner would distribute the unwanted goodies to the class in servitude. Tripe, beef tongue, pigs' feet, and oxtail were all too vile for the sophisticated palate of the landowner, but the caviar of the farm for the struggling underclass.

This type of employment was next to slavery, maybe worse. They were free, free to starve on any farm they wanted, unless they were indebted to the landowner. Then it is said they owed their soul to the big man's store. They could not move. This poor landowner, however, was not a lot better off than Dolphus and his father, and there was no company store. So, in retrospect, Dolphus and his father were lucky.

Maybe he saw the white kids. He may have specifically related to three boys who lived at the top of the hill, sons of the landowner. Why couldn't he do the same things they did? Why couldn't he play ball in that field just next to his house? They played there. It was closer to his house than it was to theirs. He was too young to understand, but then he was told, "That's white man's land."

One of the sons was fat. They called him Chunky. Occasionally, Chunky would play with him. He was the only one though, as he was an outcast too. His size made him too slow to play ball. Dolphus could hit farther and run faster than any of the white boys.

Dolphus was a better athlete than those white kids and he knew it. Why didn't they know it? He reasoned, I can run faster, hit farther, sing better, dance smoother and fish better than any one of them. He knew the spot on the creek where the white perch bit. He knew the time of day and the kind of bait to use.

He also knew that when those boys came, he had to leave; and he may be ordered to catch grasshoppers for their bait. Even the creek appeared to be white-owned.

That was then. Time passed but things had not changed significantly. Chunky was now thinner, but they still played together. Chunky's brothers teased him for having Dolphus as a friend. They said he was slow because he had rather plow a mule than study a book. They said he was weird because he talked about the beauty of the land.

Chunky, both his brothers, and Dolphus grew up. One brother went to the University and became a doctor. The other worked for the railroad. Other than Chunky, the brothers wanted nothing to do with the farm. They agreed to let Chunky have the land in exchange for the mineral rights.

Dolphus still lived with his aged father in the tenant farmer's house and he now worked for Chunky, just as his father had worked for Chunky's father before his passing.

The old black man was still living and would have been at the complete mercy of the son except for one thing. The old man was said to have Indian blood. He proved it and was given some money. It was a meager amount, but $400 was big money during the Depression. Wages were 50¢ per day.

It was early March, planting time. Dolphus knew more about most things farm-related than Chunky. He had learned from his father when to plant crops by looking at the moon. He knew phrases that he would say when each seed was planted that would aid the seed in germinating.

He got the name Hoodoo Man when he was seven years old. His father sent him to the barn to kill a chicken for supper. He wrung the chicken's neck and, to his surprise, the headless chicken continued to live and walk around. People came from miles around to see the headless chicken and Dolphus charged them 50¢ each. The bird lived for five days. It was rumored Dolphus was magic or maybe a witch, thus the name Hoodoo Man was attached. His ability to predict the cycles of the moon only enhanced the meaning of the name.

He became rather popular among most of the black citizens and a surprising number of white ones. The local ministers preached sermons denouncing him and his type as satanic activity. Chucky always defended Dolphus as he knew people get frightened when they don't understand something.

Chunky continued to run the farm much as his father had. His father was not much of a businessman and had struggled to get by. He always had to borrow from the merchants to plant his crop and they charged him extra interest because he was deemed a bad risk. In addition to cash interest, they took ten percent of his crop and held the deed to his land. Chunky continued under the same arrangement.

Dolphus's father passed away; but his father had been frugal and so was Dolphus. They did not have much, but they did not need much. They didn't have, nor need, electricity, a phone, an auto or the like. They never touched the $400, and even added to it out of the proceeds from their share of the crop and the money Dolphus got from his headless chicken.

It was the spring and summer of '57 that broke Chunky. It was a dry spring and then it was a wet summer that flooded his fields and washed much of his plantings away. In '58, the merchants refused him credit. He had been able to pay the merchants, but no one else. It was a small town and word got around. He was a bad risk.

Dolphus asked Chunky about the supplies needed to plant; after all, it was mid-March. Chunky told him they were coming soon. They never came.

Dolphus had enough magic in him, maybe Hoodoo powers or maybe Indian blood, that he could see something was wrong. He confronted Chunky.

"Mr. Chunky, you ain't got no money, do ya? Them folks in town not give you no credit, are they?"

Chunky resented having to share his plight with Dolphus, but he had no choice. He admitted there would be no crop planted that year.

"You can't do that to me. That my livin you foolin with too."

"I've got no choice. I can't get the supplies on credit."

"You don't need no credit. I bez all you need."

"Dolphus, don't let that Hoodoo stuff go to your head. You can't make a crop grow without planting a seed."

"If you listen to me, we have the best crop we ever had. You don't listen, that be why you in the shape you in."

Dolphus had never been this direct when talking to a white man and Chunky had never been talked to like that. For a few moments, the situation was tense, if not frightening.

"Look here, don't get uppity with me. Dolphus, I'm all you got. If you don't show respect, I'll put you off this place. Then I could rent some of it to someone else and get a little income."

"You all I got? That ain't so. I all you got. I can work harder and know more about these crops than you do. Besides, I be the best friend you ever had. You know that too."

"Ok, Hoodoo Man, let me see you wave your magic wand and watch that corn sprout up."

"Don't have to wave no wand. Got to buy seed and fertilize."

"With what, hot air?"

"I makes you a deal. You see, I got money. I make you a better deal than them town men did."

"What you have in mind?"

"Ten percent of the crop and another acre for my own needs."

"That's more than the merchants charge."

"You don't listen. I didn't say anything about interest. Just what I loan you and ten percent of the crop."

"Is that all?"

"No, that ain't all. We gone farm it my way."

"How's that?"

"We gone plant all the land. You gone sell all the cows except a milk cow. Cows has to eat, and in the winter, you have to feed them. We need that land.

"We gone rotate our crops. Last year, where we planted corn, we gone plant cotton. And where we planted cotton, we gone plant beans and so on. It makes better crops."

It was an arrangement Chunky couldn't turn down. After he sold the cows, it was the first time he ever had two cents in the bank.

The two worked side by side that spring and summer. Chunky had renewed energy and, for the first time, Dolphus had a real motivation to work.

In late September, all the crops were harvested and sent to market. Never had that piece of land produced so much income. The ten percent paid to Dolphus padded his account. Late in the afternoon, on an early-October day, the two childhood acquaintances sat side by side and enjoyed a beer. A friendship was recognized and social barriers were dissolved.

The unlikely friendship between the two did not go unnoticed in town. The merchants questioned where Chunky got the proceeds to plant the crop, but neither friend ever told. The next year, the success was even greater.

With the newly recognized friendship, Mr. Chunky was now just Chunky. The success the two farmers were experiencing was beyond what either had ever dreamed of. After the third year, Dolphus told Chunky it was time to expand. He heard that the adjacent land could be purchased. Two hundred acres. The asking price was high, but not too high. Due to it being adjacent to Chunky's land, they could afford to pay a little more than market value. An agreement was reached.

At the property transfer, the attorney called Chunky aside. "Is it your intention for Dolphus to have an interest in the ownership of this property?"

"Yes, that is my intention, and his interest will be 50%."

More land was acquired under the same name and, by 1968, D&C Agriculture was one of the largest producing non-cattle farms in the county. It was also a model of modern techniques and advanced farming systems.

A small branch ran through the center of the property. It was dammed to make a small lake. This was their insurance policy. Pumps and piping ran to a good percentage of the cultivatable land, assuring water when needed.

It was the summer of 1970. It was the driest year on record. Almost all crops failed that year, but not D&C. They made so much money they didn't know what to do with it.

Many of the small farmers who were at the credit mercy of the merchants were going to lose their land. Chunky remembered when he was in that situation and could not borrow a penny. He and Dolphus visited each merchant that provided credit in that manner. They reasoned that repossessing the land would be of no value to them. There was so much to be foreclosed on, there would not be enough labor to farm it and the merchants had no expertise. Dolphus and Chunky proposed giving the merchants a substantial amount of money they had earned to hold off on taking the farmers' land. They also had to agree to provide seed money the next year. It was a gift; D&C expected nothing in return. The merchants accepted the offer.

Dolphus became the first black man to ever sit on the Farmer's League Board. The League published a booklet each year called The Hoodoo Man's Almanac. It gave advice on planting, and most farmers swore by it.

D&C thrived. One day, Dolphus did not show up for work at daylight as usual. Chunky went to check on him and found him unconscious. Chunky knew he had very high blood pressure and always refused any treatment. He was almost angry at Dolphus for not taking care of himself.

Two days later, Dolphus passed away. Chunky's brother, the doctor, had bought several spots in the most prestigious cemetery in the county. He told Chunky he could bury Dolphus there. It was expected that there would be some objection since the cemetery was still segregated. There wasn't.

Five years later, Chunky died.

Today, there are two tombstones, side by side. Each refers to the special relationship the two had as business partners and friends.

To this day, Dolphus is the only black man buried in that cemetery.

FROM THE GREATEST GENERATION
ALL-AMERICAN BOY:
A BIOGRAPHY

On a spring day in 2015, an elderly Marine, accompanied by a younger Marine, visited the Iwo Jima exhibit at the National Museum of the Marine Corps in Quantico, Virginia. When the doors of the exhibit hall opened, the two stepped into a replica of a Higgins boat. A Higgins boat is the New Orleans built vessel that carried so many soldiers to foreign beaches such as Normandy and, for the purposes of this story, to the lava sand beaches of Iwo Jima. Standing in the boat as it was mechanically tossed and rolled, imitating an actual invasion, they watched a video of an authentic Iwo Jima battle that took place in 1945.

Many who boarded those boats, if they returned at all, would return a different person. They came back with pride, and they came back with guilt. They came back with memories so atrocious that, even after seventy years, they still weep. They came back with relationships so firmly established in trust that the friendships would last for the rest of their lives. They were and are Marines.

For this story, the older Marine, approaching ninety, is named Floyd Fogg. The younger Marine had known Uncle Floyd, as he called him, all his life. He could see in Floyd's eyes the exhibit may have been too real. He could see that it brought back memories that Floyd may have suppressed for years. This is Floyd's story.

If the name Floyd Fogg is not familiar, I can understand. However, if you were a sports fan from Hopkinsville, Kentucky; Memphis or Nashville, Tennessee; Slidell or New Orleans, Louisiana, and you were at least ten years old in the late 1940's, then you knew him. You may not have known him as a Marine, but as a Cracker Jack baseball player. You see, the late 1940's and early 1950's were a time when baseball was undisputedly America's favorite pastime. Of course, there was the big league where Stan Musial, Ted Williams and other legends applied their skills. But, additionally, many small towns had their own teams.

These teams were staffed with starry-eyed young men who, since childhood, had dreamed of being on the field at Yankee Stadium or Wrigley Field. Floyd was one of those, but he was a far cry from being average; he had the whole package.

Floyd was born in the town of Lacombe, Louisiana, as the sixth of seven children in 1926. When he was four years old, his father took advantage of a job at the local creosote plant and moved to larger Slidell. They lived near the plant in one of the company-owned houses. Across the street from the house was a baseball field.

Parents with the last names of Ezell, Gomez, Broom, and McQueen provided enough young boys for at least two ball teams. And play baseball they did, every available minute, year-round. The baseballs were castaways from more affluent sportsmen. They were held together with black friction tape. The bats were in similar condition, only coming into their possession after they had been broken and repaired with nails.

Here, with this primitive equipment, Floyd would learn the skills that would take him to the next level. In grammar school and especially in high school, he would compete with such Slidell names as Decker, Cochran, and others, who proved worthy teammates, as he etched his way into local stardom and beyond.

It seems that Floyd was destined for success in everything he attempted. I am sure Floyd would tell you it was the Will of the Lord. You see, Floyd is a very religious man. You will see that his faith was forever carved in stone in a pledge he made to the Lord on a beach in the Pacific Ocean.

Floyd lettered in baseball, basketball, and football. Baseball was always his favorite sport. However, after a successful high school career during which he became Slidell's first All-State basketball player, and just after graduating high school, he became the varsity basketball coach at Slidell High. The reason: all eligible coaches were at war.

This could have proved difficult as some of the players were older than him, but he had the skills; and Mr. McGinty, the principal, would apply the discipline to make a good thing out of a bad situation.

The season started with a loss. The loss could be attributed to the fact that he had to bench a player prior to the game for disciplinary reasons. He did not lose any more, racking up fifteen straight wins and winning his conference title. He was one of the first to put in a press defense. This could be an inkling of things to come for Floyd and his athletic endeavors.

At seventeen years old, he joined the Marines. The day he finished coaching the high school team, he was called to active duty. Goodbye Slidell. Hello Uncle Sam.

After basic training, he was sent to Maui, Hawaii. There they trained some more. Then he was sent to a place that, a year prior, he had never heard of, Iwo Jima. Geographically, it was a world away from Slidell and a universe away from baseball.

I feel history is best told through the writings and publications at the time the event happened. The following article appeared in The Times Picayune on March 23, 1945 by sportswriter Wm. McG. Keefe and it sets the stage for what would come:

It was just a year ago that the Slidell team came into the office for a group picture. Leading its team as its coach and former star, was a handsome 17-year-old youth named Floyd Fogg, a Slidell boy. The school had been unable to get a coach and Fogg, waiting to go into the Marine Corps to which he had volunteered, coached the team to a championship.

One year later, Mr. and Mrs. Edward Fogg of Slidell received word from the Office of War Information that their son, Private Floyd Fogg, had been wounded in action on Iwo Jima. No soft touch - Iwo Jima.

So this fine lad, whose dash and courage on the court were echoed in his quick enlistment in a branch of the service that gives quick action, carried this courage to a distant land, where in less than a year from when he changed

Floyd finally saw combat on February 19, 1945. That is when he stepped on the landing net and descended to the Higgins boat. Like most 18-year-olds, Floyd had never been shot at before. I am sure it crossed his mind, just as it did for thousands of others over the next few days, that this may be his last boat ride. A long way from Bayou Liberty, Bayou Bonfouca, and Lake Pontchartrain, the familiar waters of his childhood. When his foot hit the beach, he stopped and prayed. He asked God for protection and promised he would spend the rest of his life assisting others.

I could write a book on Floyd's war experience, another book on his sports adventures, and then finally conclude with a volume based on his service to God and community. I have not the space; therefore, I must be brief.

It was the assignment of the 23rd Marines, 4th Division, to secure a Japanese-held airport. After this was successfully accomplished, a stand of woods had to be crossed. This provided a great place for enemy snipers, and they were there. His unit had to temporarily pull back a few hundred yards. In relative safety, Floyd noticed that a buddy of his, Dick Freeby, was not accounted for. He had to find him. He disobeyed his superior officers and, under fire, went back to the hot zone for the rescue. He found Dick, who was seriously injured. He was bleeding profusely and Floyd knew his chances of survival were slim. Floyd fashioned a tourniquet to slow the bleeding. He twisted it tight with a pencil and told Dick not to let go of the pencil. It was Floyd and this pencil that saved Dick's life.

In all branches of the service, you are taught to never leave your weapon behind. Floyd could not manage the weight of the seriously wounded Marine and his friend's weapon, a heavy Browning Automatic Rifle (BAR). Floyd had to threaten his friend with leaving him behind if he did not drop the BAR. Finally, Floyd convinced him that, if they were to have a chance, he had to leave it. Again, under heavy fire, Floyd made his way back, running zig zag, to relative safety. The corpsmen took over the medical treatment of Dick, evacuating him to the hospital ship. Floyd had no idea whether his friend lived or died.

During the early part of the invasion, Floyd was wounded with shrapnel. He was evacuated to the hospital ship and ordered to the hospital in Hawaii. He did not want to leave his unit and his Marine buddies. He convinced the commanding officer to let him return to battle.

Floyd had a fond attachment to the hospital ship that he, Dick, and another Marine you'll read about later were sent to. The ship's name was the U.S.S. Solace. It was, and is, a symbol to Floyd of hope and a chance to live on. Iwo Jima taught Floyd and others the meaning of life.

On March 8, 1945, for the fifth time, Floyd and his fellow Marines had taken Hill 514. Basking in their victory, they peered below into what could best be described as a crevasse. In the side of the adjacent hill, there was a bunker that was occupied by the Japanese.

At first, it was believed it could be eradicated by machine gun fire. Unfortunately, the machine gunner was shot and killed. Next, it was decided that a large TNT bundle, called a 17-pound satchel charge, if hurled appropriately, may also work. There is a difference between a baseball and a 17-pound satchel but, with Floyd's baseball skills, he was the best choice.

Just prior to being chosen for the task of throwing the satchel, Floyd teamed up with a fellow Marine named Felix Aucoin. They had something in common - Felix was from Algiers, Louisiana, some 30 miles from Slidell. Felix was to dig the foxhole for both, while Floyd threw the satchel.

As it turned out, Floyd pitched a strike, and the bunker was silenced. He then returned to assist in digging the foxhole which would serve as their shelter for the night. Before it could be completed, a mortar shell struck nearby. Floyd was rendered unconscious by the concussion but awoke to someone reaching for his dog tags. Collecting one of your two dog tags was done as a record of your death in combat. Floyd regained consciousness, and vehemently denied he was dead. The corpsman reaching for his tag was none other than fellow Slidellian Joe Koll, who later became a well-known jeweler in Slidell.

He then noticed Felix, his foxhole buddy. He had not fared so well. Floyd could see that his leg, for all practical purposes, was missing. Felix was taken away and, again, Floyd would not know if he lived or died.

Floyd, himself, was also injured. He had two dislocated shoulders and two ruptured eardrums. Blood was pouring from his ears. This would be Floyd's last military battle. He would be sent to the hospital, first in Hawaii and then to Oceanside, California. Six months later, Japan would surrender, and Floyd would come home.

I have learned from experience that I should write on subjects that I know. You may think it strange, but I know more about the military than I do about baseball. Therefore, I will not be able to tell the baseball part of Floyd's life as effectively.

If you ask Floyd about his military life, he will tell you, but only in a matter-of-fact way. It was an obligation, a patriotic duty, one he would have never avoided. But now, he wanted to move on.

Today, if you ask him about baseball, his face lights up. He is twenty-four years old again, playing third base for one of the farm teams of the Chicago Cubs.

To this very day, Floyd can name many of his teammates, give you the season record, give you scores of important games, and quote his RBI, home runs and batting average. If you want to enjoy being with Floyd, ask him about baseball.

While in high school, he was approached by a man named Bruce Hayes. Bruce was a scout for the Nashville Vols, a farm team of the Chicago Cubs. He, coincidentally, was a relative of the local Abney family.

"Son, I've been watching you play baseball, and you are good. How would you like to play this game and get paid for it? You have what it takes." Floyd could hardly believe his ears.

Unfortunately, this dream would have to wait as his military obligation occurred at just the wrong time. Eventually, the war did end, and Floyd came home.

Enjoying Slidell and Mama's cooking was short lived. Prior to the war, Bruce told Floyd that when the war was over, he would be calling him. He did, the very day Floyd came home. The next day, Floyd was off to another chapter in his life, ten years of baseball. Ten years that would see him with half a dozen teams and a temporary resident of as many cities. Ten years that would see his wedding to Shirley McDaniel and the birth of his first son, Larry.

Floyd played in all divisions of baseball as he worked his way toward the majors. If batting averages of 327 and RBIs of 144 impress you, then you would want Floyd's baseball card. Floyd modestly tells the story of a young reporter in 1948 coming into the locker room and informing the team that Floyd had 144 RBIs. This was more than the great Smokey Burgess had the prior year. Years later, when statistics were published, they may not back up that story. Floyd is quick to point out that he was sorry he had been under the wrong impression. But I see no reason for Floyd to apologize. Who knows? Maybe Smokey's numbers were incorrect also. The official record for Floyd is 127 RBIs.

Players were traded frequently among other teams in the league. Occasionally, cash would be exchanged along with the trade. In 1951, New Orleans sold Floyd to the White Sox. As a token of the respect the team owner had for him, Floyd was given $5,000. That was a tidy sum in those days. Also, about this time, the citizens of Slidell, primarily four prominent citizens, took up a collection and bought Floyd a new 1950 Oldsmobile. A nice gesture for a favorite son.

It looked like 1953 would be his year. He was to report to the Chicago White Sox training camp. Shortly after arriving, Floyd broke his finger. He was sent home to rehabilitate and join the team later; but, when later came, the offer was not as good as expected. He would spend one more season in the minors, then he was forced to make a decision.

His baseball career was over, but it would never be out of his system. This would partly lead to the next phase of Floyd's life. After baseball, Floyd returned to the town who appreciated what he had done. They appreciated his war effort, and they appreciated his putting their small town on the map. He was, and would remain, a favorite son of Slidell, Louisiana.

Floyd had known that someday his baseball career would end. Wisely, he had taken steps, along with his wife and brother-in-law, to establish an insurance agency. After all, his name was a household word.

Being self-employed gave him other opportunities. It gave him the time and freedom to return something back to his community, the community that had loved and supported him. You remember the pledge he made to God and himself on the beach in 1945? Part of that pledge was to help other people. Floyd was not the type to not honor a pledge, especially one that he had made to God.

Far from the final chapter of his life (in fact, in the prime of his life), Floyd became a leading voice to make his community better. You see, Slidell did not have a hospital. People had died waiting for the drawbridge to close so they could get to New Orleans and the medical facilities it offered. Remember, there were no interstates then, and New Orleans was the better part of an hour's drive.

As a leading member of the Kiwanis Club, Floyd and his fellow club members approached the parish about funding a hospital. Floyd was the main thrust in the movement. They were told that, if they could get land donated, the parish would attempt to sell bonds to construct a hospital.

It was not easy, but Floyd was successful in persuading Mrs. Brugier and Mr. Jahraus into donating several acres. Slidell would have a hospital, thanks to Floyd and his club members. If Floyd did nothing else, I cannot help but think about how many lives this one good deed has saved.

If you thought Floyd would never give up baseball, he didn't. He coached youth teams for most of his life. Even today, at 90 years old, he teaches batting at his home in Pearl River, LA. He has a batting cage and a pitching machine and offers his services free to those who cannot afford it.

Like most people, life has not always been a bed of roses. A hometown hero is not immune from tragedy. First, his only daughter, Cheryl, passed away from a sudden illness when she was thirteen years old. Later, his wife Shirley, a victim of cancer, would pass. Reflecting on Floyd's deep religious faith, I can recall at Shirley's funeral, Floyd telling me, "John, she is finally with her daughter. I know she is happy."

Floyd learned a lot from baseball. He learned early on if you lose a game, you don't give up. After each tragedy, he rebounded. Later, he would marry a wonderful lady, Maribeth, who is such a complement to him still today.

Occasionally, Floyd will go to a minor-league New Orleans Zephyrs game. He is self-conscious when people point to his picture by the elevator, denoting him as a Louisiana Hall of Famer. Then they play the "Star-Spangled Banner." The memories flood his mind.

For just a few minutes, his mind takes him back to the 1950's, when his fellow townsmen drove hundreds of miles to see him play. He remembers a certain game or certain player. He can smell the game and the boys of summer.

Yes, he likes to go to the Zephyrs games. It is total enjoyment for him, until the fireworks start. That is when the noise, the explosions, take him back to the beach. He puts his head in his hands as if to say, "Let's go. Get me off the beach and back to Maribeth."

Epilogue:

Old-timers still talk about watching Floyd play ball. Some say they drove to Memphis to see him; others say they saw him in Chattanooga. His stats are all over the internet.

One day, a stranger knocked on his door. There stood a man that looked familiar but, if Floyd knew him, it was from years past. The stranger reached down and tapped an artificial leg.

"Hello, Froggy, it's me."

It was Felix Aucoin. Froggy was Floyd's Marine nickname.

At some point, Floyd and Dick Freeby, the Marine with the BAR that he rescued, also made contact. They have visited each other, and there remains that Marine bond between them.

Of all the true stories I have written, I have enjoyed this one the most. I had made a rule. I would never write about living people. I think you can understand why. But, you know, rules are made to be broken. If ever Slidell had a hometown hero, it was Floyd Fogg. I could not resist this story. We both cried, and we laughed together. Neither Floyd nor I are ashamed to admit this.

Floyd is a very modest man. He will tell you the real heroes are the ones whose bodies still lie beneath foreign soil or who came home in boxes, not to parades of laughter. He will tell you that, in the scheme of life, baseball is just a game.

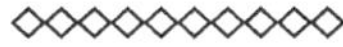

Floyd Fogg passed away on April 23, 2018, peacefully. The world lost another of the Greatest Generation.

55

THE CLOCK

The call was not unexpected. She had lived longer than any of us imagined. After my grandfather passed away two years prior, she never faced reality. She talked to him as if he were alive almost constantly; and, I suppose, in her lucid moments when she realized he was gone, she decided to just give up. Those two really loved each other for 65 years.

I was in college, and I came home for the funeral but went back to school the very next day. There was nothing that I was needed for anyway. I was just a grandchild.

The rural homestead had remained intact and in her possession after my grandfather's passing; but, with her passing, it would be sold and the assets of the real property dispersed between their eight children. The personal property would also be divided, but the grandchildren were told they could have their pick of the leftovers.

My grandparents had provided a stable homeplace for countless family members, brothers, sisters-in-laws, nieces and nephews. They were also a revolving motel of sorts for itinerant ministers that were passing through. My grandfather, being a rural mail carrier, at least had an income during the

Depression. Their home was an oasis for comings and goings, with some guests staying for a day or two and others for months at a time.

Whatever the length of the stay, the house guest would invariably leave some of their personal property behind. I remember a trunk with Great Aunt Tera's clothes in it. She died in 1932. There was Uncle Oscar's gas mask that he left after his return from WWI. Then, World War II came along. Four sons saw active duty. Four sons brought home souvenirs to become part of the collection. There were literally dozens of automobile parts placed neatly on a hillside behind their house. It looked like a growing crop of transmissions and motor blocks.

I remember there was a box that I was forbidden to open. It was a small box about the size of a cigarette pack. I was told it held an ear that had been cut from a Japanese soldier on Okinawa. One day, I got the nerve to open it. There was nothing in the box. I have always tried to figure out which cousin beat me to opening that box and took the ear.

Another non-relative contributor to this junk was Peach Tree Davis. Peach Tree was a traveling arborist, using the term very loosely. He was much like a Johnny Appleseed. He traveled in a covered wagon, two mules, his wife, and most (if not all) of their possessions. He was a transient, but he carried with him hundreds of small peach trees. It is believed he got some type of state grant to distribute these trees to farmers, encouraging them to plant fruit orchards.

Like most people, he trusted my grandfather; and my grandfather allowed him to use an old barn for his campsite while in the area. Peach Tree had used my grandparents' property as his base of operations many times over several years and his visits were not only welcomed, they were joyfully anticipated.

A visit to that storage shed was like a modern segment of the TV show, "American Pickers." Unfortunately, even though I had given myself the self-appointed title of being the favorite grandson, I was not a party to the distribution of this junk.

There were three reasons for this: One, I was a grandchild and the direct children rightfully had first choice. Next, I was away at school and not present to make any picks. Finally, I had no place to keep anything of any size as I was a student with no real home of my own.

A month after everything was cleaned out and taken, I visited the homeplace one more time. It was a very sad time for me, as I had been extremely close to my grandparents. Living nearby, I had spent many happy hours at their house. The few items that remained had a history. There was a slide rule. I knew my uncle had used that when he studied engineering at Mississippi State. There was a bucket with hundreds of holes in the bottom. I knew it had once been a homemade shower designed by another uncle. I saw an old muzzle-loading rifle and a very old pistol in a burn pile. The stocks were missing and they were severely damaged. I took the old guns and laid them aside. I might choose to keep them.

Under the wringer part of an old, disassembled washing machine, I saw a piece of finished wood. I lifted the wringer and found a clock. I recognized it. I had seen it in that shed for years and I seemed to recall when it sat on the mantle in the main room of the house.

It was a Seth Thomas clock. I knew that it had been replaced by another Seth Thomas that my grandfather wound daily. The clock was an ornate rectangular shape, taller than wide.

The last time I saw the old homeplace while in my family's ownership was that day in 1967 when I walked away with the pistol, the rifle, and the clock. I had not been the victor, but I got the spoils anyway. I was pleased to have something with which to remember that part of my childhood. Tokens, pieces of a piece of life that had been so simple but would never return.

That night, at my parent's house, I set the clock on a table by my bed. The key was missing but I assumed it would not run anyway, as it had been replaced and relegated to the shed. So, there I sat with a broken clock. I realized that there was something special about this clock, or at least it was to me.

I thought, *You know, that clock has a face. So do I.*

I had seen many things in my limited 20 years. What more had that clock's face seen from its position on the mantle of a home that was much like Grand Central Station for various people? It had witnessed deep discussions about the value of life and God's place in one's life. My grandfather, who was also a lay minister, used the room where the clock was placed as his spiritual office. I am sure it had witnessed disagreements between family members that were not pleasant. I expect it had witnessed childbirth, as the master bedroom was also a main room of the house. Maybe it had witnessed proposals of marriage. I knew that it had witnessed funerals, as in those days, they were held at the home. I imagined it had watched as my grandmother hugged each of her sons goodbye as they went to serve their country. I bet, if it could talk, it would tell of the joyous reunion when they came home.

The clock took on a personality. I found myself talking to the clock, and then I found myself answering on its behalf. Those are the best kinds of conversations.

College years and military training saw a great deal of transition in my life. Many things I owned were misplaced, lost, or maybe even stolen. Not the clock.

Some ten years after I acquired the clock, my uncle, the one who had left the slide rule in the shed, visited our house. By that time, I was married. He noticed the clock which, not in operating condition, sat on a table with other what-nots.

"Dang, ole Peach Tree's clock," he said.

I had heard the stories of the traveling arborist. Those stories were well established in family lore, but I had no idea that the clock had belonged to him.

"Yes, I was always told it was his. He left it with Papa the last time he ever stayed at our place. He told Papa that he was going down to Louisiana. Tangipahoa Parish, I think I was told. He didn't like to go down there because twice he had been robbed. He left most of his non-essential property that had value with Papa to keep until he returned. The clock was a nice clock, and it ran then. Neither he or his wife ever returned to reclaim it."

"What happened to him?" I asked.

"We never knew. Lots of rumors. Never heard from his wife, either. Some say he got murdered. Others say his wife left him and he just drifted off someplace."

"When did all this happen?" I asked.

"Before I was born. About 1922, I would think. Papa talked about him a great deal. You know those peach trees that were behind the garage at the old home place? They came from him."

Some years later, Mother called me. A long distant call is one financial splurge Mother would make as she had to keep in touch with her children. In the conversation, she said she had a strange visitor. He was the grandson of Peach Tree Davis. His name was Charles and he was writing a book about his family history and wanted to gather all the information he could find on his traveling grandfather.

Mother remembered Peach Tree and his wife well, and I am sure she gave him a great deal of insight into who he was. Mother did learn from his grandson that he had been shot in a robbery attempt and died a few days later, only briefly regaining consciousness. His wife returned home but died a very short time later of T.B. Mother learned that they actually had a home up in Smith County.

Mother continued, "I told him that you had the clock. He didn't ask about it; but, after I told him, he seemed to lose interest in anything else that I was telling him. He did ask your name and address. I hope you don't mind me giving it to him."

I no longer talked to the clock as I had when I was trying to conjure fond memories. It was just a non-working knick-knack that sat on a shelf with other items that had no value to anyone except me. I decided to see if it could be repaired. Now living in Louisiana, I took it to the clock shop in the Pere Marquette Building. The repairman told me it may take a few weeks before he could get to it.

While the clock was being repaired, we traveled out of town for the weekend, arriving back home after dark. I noticed that none of the motion-activated lights turned on as we pulled into the garage. I thought that was strange, as I had replaced the bulbs only a month or two prior. I reasoned it was a faulty motion sensor and continued to park the car.

If it is your home, it has a spirit of its own. You can tell if its premises have been violated without visually seeing anything. You can feel the presence of evil. Occasionally, this proves to be a false sensation; but, other times, it is alarmingly real. The experience that followed was somewhere in between.

Our house was small. The den was the main living area and that is where most of our possessions were kept. I first noticed the books on the bookshelf were leaning and not meticulously spaced as my wife was known to do.

I noticed cabinet drawers ajar. Entering the bedroom, I noticed a window had been broken. After days of checking our belongings, we could not find a single thing missing. Coins were in the jewelry box, guns were in the closet, and all the electronics were undisturbed.

I remember feeling the insult when the investigating officer asked if we kept drugs, either prescription or illegal, in the house. I assured him that we may only have some pain killers as a result of dental work, but checking found that they were in the medicine cabinet. In time, the incident was forgotten.

Several years passed and I received a call from the grandson, Charles Davis, that had visited my mother years before. He asked if he could visit and see the clock. According to him, after careful family research, it was the only item that he could pinpoint having belonged to his grandfather. I welcomed him since I am a genealogist-type also.

Charles arrived early on a Saturday morning. He was several years older than I had expected. He appeared to be a pleasant and courteous type.

After a few minutes, I took him to the den and lifted the clock from its resting place. He nervously turned the clock in different directions to examine it. I asked him to be careful, as I had spent considerable money having it repaired.

"You had it repaired?"

"Yes, about ten years ago. It took extensive reworking of the mechanics, but it works fine now."

"So, it has been totally disassembled?"

"Yes," I answered.

He seemed disappointed to hear it was working. Then, his attitude changed.

"Well, since this appears to be the end of my search, I will tell you the truth. You see, the story goes like this, and I am sure it is true: Grandpa had been robbed in Louisiana on more than one occasion, but he needed the income so he continued to go to that area. He did not believe in banks, so he was always in danger of being robbed."

Charles then paused and took a deep breath.

"Well, if I'm going to tell it, I might as well tell the truth. Grandpa had a good bit of money. His peach tree sales and getting paid by the state is true; but, under those trees were gallons of moonshine whiskey. That is where he made his money. He made big money. However, the same people who bought the whiskey knew he was an easy target to rob."

Charles' story continued, "Twice a week, while in Louisiana, he would leave my grandmother at this place he stayed. Much like when he stayed with your grandparents. Late in the afternoon, he would leave and travel to a secret spot and drop the money in a steel barrel he had buried somewhere near the Louisiana-Mississippi line. He only put coins in there, but it is believed there were lots of them. Before he died, he regained consciousness for a few hours. He told my grandmother the map to the barrel was in the clock back at the Stringer place. Unfortunately, she died before the family could find out which Stringers or where they lived. Over the years, we have inquired with many Stringer families, mostly in Marion County, to no avail. Finally, by coincidence, I ran into your mother.

"Like most families, we have those who are not so honorable. I will confess that my cousin broke into your house years ago in search of the clock. I apologize for that."

After listening to the story, I told him he was welcome to examine the clock, but anything that may have been inside would have been removed by the repairman. I also told him I had opened the clock prior to taking it to the clock shop and found nothing inside.

He told me that his grandfather had another stash near their home that had been found. It had over $5,000 in silver coins in it.

I commented, "Wow, some business for the 1920s."

As he left, I could tell he was disappointed almost to the point of dejection. Charles was a well-dressed fellow and had arrived in a late-model luxury automobile. I don't think the monetary value of this cache had anything to do with his quest. I think he just got obsessed with the hunt, like hunting for buried treasure. I felt sorry for him.

A few days later, I picked up the clock. I noticed something that I had not seen before. The working mechanism of the clock, including its face and hands, were placed on a decorative base. There was some distance from where the two were attached to four externally mounted legs. This gave the appearance of a drawer, but there was not one.

I examined how the clock and base were attached. They were attached by a series of tiny brass screws, but some of the screws were missing. In their place were tiny rusty nails. I had an eyeglass repair kit and carefully unscrewed each tiny brass screw. I then took a needle-nose pliers and removed the small nails. The bottom dropped off.

Taped to the bottom of the base was an age yellowed page. I opened it. I somehow thought I should contact Charles and let him be involved in the exciting discovery. On the other hand, I had too much curiosity.

It was written in pencil. It was not a map at all, but it was rather detailed directions to what he termed "My Bank Account."

It read:

Go to the old Jewish Cemetery near Chatawa. On the northeast corner of the cleared field, there is an oak tree. You must go at 10 a.m. on May 1st. The sun will cast a shadow. Follow the shadow 150 feet from the tree. You will be standing over a buried steel barrel that has my deposits in it.

I know nothing about astronomy, but had my son contact his friend who is a world class ocean sailor. He gave me the corrective measurements as I did know the sun slightly changes directions over time. He told us the direction change over the timespan from 1922 until 2016 was insignificant. I learned this in January, and I knew the sun would change directions between then and May 1st. I had to wait.

I immediately attempted to find the Jewish Cemetery on FindAGrave. (That is not the real name of the cemetery or the location. I have intentionally not given that information, as I do not want to encourage vandalism.) Now, all I had to do was wait until May 1st. I counted the days. I must admit, I thought about calling Charles, but the excitement of finding it alone overruled that. I don't think that I thought I would come home with riches. Honestly, I don't know what I thought the outcome would be.

At 7 a.m. that May morning, the sky was overcast. Would there be a sun today? No sun, no shadow. About quarter to ten, the sky cleared, and the sun shone brightly. The shadow formed. As it lengthened, I measured.

Even before the tape measure was stretched, I knew the treasure would not be found. Over the exact spot left on the note, there was a substantial building where cemetery lawn equipment was kept. I looked in the window. The building was erected atop a concrete slab.

I saw no use in telling Charles that I had solved the mystery. Sometimes it is best not to know.

A SMELLY BUSINESS

I am proud to say that, in my entire career, I have never been fired.

That does not mean that there hasn't been a bump in the road.

In the 1960's, there were few summer jobs for teenagers. Mr. Bitsy Hart had a crew of teenagers that cut rights-of-way for the utility company. I was not strong enough for that, or maybe I was too lazy. It was hot weather and it was hard work.

There were no McDonalds or Burger Kings, so there was little opportunity; and, when there was opportunity, the pay was low. If I recall, when I was sixteen years old, the wage was about $1 per hour. But, one summer I planted corn for $4 per day, sun-up to sunset.

I had saved some money and had been given some birthday money, so I bought an old pickup truck for my sixteenth birthday. It had a rusted body but the engine was good. I paid $300 for it. It was transportation in its most basic form. Little did I know, buying that old Chevrolet truck would lead to losing my first good paying venture into the business world.

My dad had a cousin who owned a commercial chicken farm. The building housed thousands of chickens and, explained simply, a conveyor belt ran under the cages to catch the droppings. The belt transported the chicken manure outside and dumped it in a pile.

Once a week, a truck would come from Baton Rouge and pick up the waste. I suppose they converted it to fertilizer, but I'm not sure. It was July and the weather was hot and dry. The waste company went on strike, resulting in no manure pickup. The pile was growing in size and stench daily.

Finally, the odor got so bad it began to affect the egg-laying cycle of the thousands of chickens housed in the adjacent building. Even a few of the neighboring farmers had similar problems and complained.

Cousin Smith called me and asked if I would use my truck to haul off the waste. I had to load and unload it, but he would pay me $7 per truck load. He arranged for me to spread it in a farmer's field that was nearby.

I calculated that I could do three loads per day and gross $21. Those were not bad wages for even adult laborers at the time.

I also found out that some of the ladies in town wanted to use the loads as fertilizer in their flower beds. They would give me $10 a load. Now I was making $51 a day! I hired a helper, which allowed me to deliver five loads per day rather than three. I was now grossing $85 per day. I paid the helper $10, so I was netting $75. Not bad for a sixteen-year-old kid in 1963.

I had little expenses as I was illegally burning untaxed farm gas in the truck. It only cost 10¢ per gallon. I got it from my uncle and I probably did not pay him even that much. I was doing good.

By the end of July, it had not rained in about thirty days. The dry weather allowed my business to grow rapidly. Word got around. A very wealthy, prominent lady called and asked for a load of chicken manure. We delivered it and spread it around her azaleas. It just so happened that the Garden Club was meeting at her house the next day. They saw how nicely we had spread the fertilizer and all of them wanted a load. My business went viral, and this was five decades before social media.

My parent's phone would ring eight or ten times a night with customers calling for "John's Secret Nitrogen Supplement" as I had named it. Chicken manure did not sound sophisticated. Even the newspaper took notice. They published a picture of me rolling a wheelbarrow with a load of this "high nitrogen" material. The title of the article was "A Smelly Business."

That night, a call came to my parents' house and my dad answered. He knew the lady calling and knew she had a difficult disposition. She had once cut her neighbor's hedge and two of her live oaks, all without the neighbor's permission, just because she didn't like them. It was the gossip of the town and a lawsuit followed.

She had a large yard and a long, winding driveway. On each side of the drive were azaleas. She told Dad that she wanted to buy enough fertilizer to cover all her plants. She was not concerned with how much it took or what it would cost.

It took three loads to accomplish this. That night she called and wanted me to put an additional load on her plants. The next day we did. A few nights later, she called my dad and wanted a third load. At this point, Dad informed her this fertilize was fresh and had not composted. It was strong and would burn her plants. She insisted anyway. She wanted a third load. We complied.

We had delivered nine loads and she owed me $153. Most people would give me and my helper a tip and I was counting on this. Dad told me that she was too tight to tip, and to just be content with getting paid. She was to pay me the next afternoon.

That night, there came a huge summer rain. It rained most of the night. When I pulled up in her long driveway, I knew I had a business problem. The stems of the azaleas were burned so badly they were almost clear. The limbs and stems were all drooping.

I hesitated when going to her door. As it turned out, I did not have to. She and a man I knew came out. She was crying and yelling at me, accusing me of poisoning her flowers. I was speechless. I was sixteen years old; she was a well-known, prominent lady. Those flowers, well, they did look terrible.

The man with her was a local attorney. I had done yard work for him the year before. He asked her to go inside so he could talk to me privately.

He explained to me that she wanted to sue me for destroying her landscaping. He knew I had no money and no insurance. He also knew my dad had no money or insurance; so he would try to make a deal with her. If I would agree not to charge her the $153, he believed she would drop her complaint. I was naïve, intimidated, and frightened. I agreed.

As I said, she was well-known, and the story of our problem spread through town. It basically destroyed my reputation as a horticulturist expert. About that time, the strike ended at the Baton Rouge plant and I would have been out of business anyway.

A few weeks passed and her plants did not survive. She attempted to hire someone the dig them up but, due to her personality, no one would work for her more than a couple of hours.

I was surprised when the phone rang and it was her. She wanted to know if I would remove the manure, dig up the dead plants, and replant new ones.

Before I could answer, she said, "I know how I treated you and I know I hurt your business. If you will be fair with me, and I know you will, I will pay you whatever you charge."

She concluded by adding, "But you be reasonable now."

I charged her $17 per load to remove the manure, $3 per hour for me and $2 per hour for my helper to remove and replant. I then sneaked in the $153 she owned me in the first place. She never questioned the bill.

For the next couple of years, she used me for odd jobs. Then I went to college and she gave me work when I was home for the holidays.

Years later, when I married, for a present, she sent us an entire place setting of Strasbourg Silver.

Cousin Smith is now deceased, the chicken house is empty, but the building is still standing. The lady with the bad disposition has also passed away. Her yard has been subdivided into two sites. I never pass either place without thinking of my Stinking Business of High Nitrogen Supplement.

Wow, life was simple then.

❧ ◆ ❧

THE OBSESSION, GYPSY WOMAN

One of my earliest memories is of a collection of cars - old, large, black cars that were parked on a vacant piece of land on the east side of Highway 51, just north of Bogue Chitto, Mississippi.

The cars themselves have become as elusive as the subject of this story, as they are rare. They were Packards, Hudsons, and Desotos. There must have been thirty or so such cars, and almost all had a type of camping trailer either attached to it or at least parked nearby.

I remember when we would pass them, my dad would say, "Well, it must be February, the Gypsies are here."

Dad would go on to explain that, years earlier, they would arrive in January. They were not using automobiles then. They traveled in elaborately decorated wagons drawn by two horses. He told me they always led a third horse, so they could periodically rest one of the others. Dad admired the way they cared for their animals.

I now know they were most likely in route to Meridian, Mississippi. There, the American Gypsy Queen was buried. Once a year, they came from all over the country to visit her grave.

Who were these gypsies and what about the Gypsy Queen? Gypsies are a worldwide culture of nomadic people. They are believed to have originated in India. Their culture is deeply engrained in their roots. They tend, or at least then they tended, to preserve their practices and seek only to be left alone.

Emil Mitchell became King of the Gypsies in 1909. This made his wife, Kelly, the Queen. They were camped in Alabama, just over the state line from Meridian, when she died in childbirth, delivering their 14th child on January 31, 1915. She was 47 years old.

The entire gypsy nation wanted to pay tribute to their queen, but it would take days for them to arrive by horse-drawn wagons. Meridian was the nearest town that had an icehouse, so they took her body to Meridian and kept her on ice until the crowd arrived. Over 20,000 attended the funeral.

As a young boy, I was fascinated by the gypsies' mysterious lifestyle. A few times, they had camped at a place nearer my house when they were probably not on their way to Meridian. At night, I could hear their music. It pervaded the still, hot summer air. Even to this day, when I hear night crickets and the buzz of summer mosquitoes, I remember their haunting music, its melody, and the beat from the late 1950s and '60s.

We were told they stole chickens and children. It is possible some chickens came up missing, but there was no proof that a child had ever been stolen. Not literally, but you might say it happened to Johnny Allgood.

You have all known at least one person like Johnny, and maybe several; a person who acts just a little differently from the norm. Some people would call him peculiar. Not peculiar to the point that he was an outcast, but peculiar to the point that he was never described by anyone as their best friend.

He dressed differently than most of his peers. Long after flat-top haircuts were passé, he still wore that fashion, held up by Butch hair wax. He still cuffed his blue jeans rather than leaving them straight; and, while others were wearing penny loafers, he wore high-top Keds tennis shoes.

Conversations with him were broken, as if he could not concentrate for any great length of time on any one subject. He was intelligent and, in his brief interludes into side subjects, he was often astoundingly interesting.

Johnny lived not far from me. We were not close friends, as he was a couple of years younger than me. Due to our close proximity, I would see him from time to time. Before we were able to drive, we walked almost everywhere and I would see him as he walked a path that crossed the back of our property, near the barn.

One day, he diverted from the path and approached me.

"Hey, the gypsies are there. You want to go see 'em?"

Being fascinated by their music and lifestyle, something about the proposal interested me. I knew that we would have to hide in the woods some distance away and avoid them seeing us. I think I was intrigued by the assumption of danger. We really didn't know if they were friendly or not. We also didn't completely dismiss the kidnapping of children either, though we didn't consider ourselves children.

"Yea, I'll go with you."

It was about a 30-minute walk, and it was dusk when we heard the music start. Soon, we could see the glow of the campfire and a great bit of activity around it. By the time we found a hiding place that offered us a good viewpoint, it was dark.

That is when she first appeared. Little did I know that this was the birth of an obsession for Johnny. I think we both were instantly attracted to her; not for what we saw, but for what we thought we saw. She stood behind the fire and in front of an old, silver Airstream trailer. Her silhouette projected on the trailer. It was like watching a movie on an actual silver screen.

None of her specific features could be seen, just a shapely female body as she moved to the music. We both imagined she was beautiful, even though it was only our imagination due to the distance and the lack of lighting.

That is when I felt it. Cinched against my throat was the curved handle of a walking cane being held tightly by a man in blousy pants that made him look much larger than he was. I saw Johnny's eyes get as big as saucers.

The man grabbed the back of each of our shirts and ordered us to come with him. We approached the fire. The music stopped. The girl disappeared, as did all the women except one. She was an elderly woman, and she began to scream orders to the men. I think she was speaking English, but the dialect and the rapid cadence made her less than comprehensible.

We were forced to sit on the ground. The woman came within inches of our faces, as several men stood by her side and on each side and behind us.

"What you do?" she asked. "Steal what little we have? Wait for us to go to sleep and pilfer our goods? Damage our cars? That is what you do? We do you no harm, why do you bother us?"

Johnny was almost in tears, and I was close as well. "No, we came to hear the music," I answered.

"What else did you do?" she demanded.

I could not believe what happened next. Johnny, who by this time had regained some composure, said, "We watched the girl."

I didn't think this was a good idea, so I immediately said, "No, we didn't see her. We came to hear the music."

My statement made no sense, as the girl had been plainly in sight, and it certainly hit a nerve with the gypsies. The man who had caught us rushed over to Johnny and put the cane rather harshly on his shoulder.

"The girl is my daughter, you not look at her. You are not our people. You bring shame. Leave and don't come back."

We left.

I never went back, but Johnny did. He had literally become infatuated with a shadow. The very next day, he walked beside the highway where the gypsies were parked. He kept his distance but scanned the encampment for the object of his obsession. Finally, he saw her. He told me that she saw him and waved.

The few times I saw Johnny that year, all he would talk about was her. About two years later, Johnny came to my house with his guitar. He played a song he had heard on the radio and memorized. The song was about a gypsy woman.

He told me that if she came back in February, and he felt sure she would, he was going to go to their campsite and ask them to let him play and sing the song that night. I told him they may resent such a proposition, as they tend to be very private. My advice did not faze him. That is exactly what he did.

Somehow, he began to build a rapport with the caravan. Soon, he was allowed to see the girl, but only in her father's presence. He told me she was even more beautiful than we had imagined. Each year, he spent more time with the gypsies.

Johnny dropped out of school around Christmas of his senior year. He worked construction for a few weeks but, when February came, he made sure to be near the gypsy camp. I was later told it was the biggest caravan that had ever parked there. The music lasted all night, and those that lived nearby said it was a very festive celebration.

The caravan left two days later and has never returned.

Neither has Johnny.

❧ ◆ ☙

THREE SOLDIERS

Brandon Beck was a twenty-year-old town favorite. His dad was a favorite before him and, most likely, his grandfather before him. The family boasted of doctors, judges, mayors, and star athletes. They also were proud of their patriotism, as his dad was a veteran of WWII, his grandfather a veteran of WWI, and his great-grandfather served with the Confederacy in the Civil War. They were true town blue bloods, and just the mention of the Beck name demanded respect.

No one in the community was surprised when it was announced that Brandon had dropped out of the University to join the military and fight for his country as the war in Vietnam escalated. It was 1965.

He was the first white citizen from the community to enter the military at the beginning of the Vietnam Conflict. The community reacted by treating him as a hero. There was a parade the day before he left. Speeches were made, the high school band played patriotic songs, and hundreds of people were on hand when he departed for basic training. His parents drove him to Fort Polk, escorted to the Louisiana line with police cars and flashing lights. The community knew he would make them proud.

A hundred miles away, another young man was entering military service. He was a high school dropout and subject to the draft when he turned eighteen. Probably only a few in the small community knew him, and those who did just called him Sammy. His family had not been mayors or judges. His father had practically deserted the family when he was small, but would drop in occasionally; and what little money he brought with him was welcomed. Then he was gone again. His mother worked as a domestic. At the time of his induction, she was ill, but no one knew the severity.

When Sammy left on the bus for basic training, there were no bands, no parades, and he went to the bus station alone. To his knowledge, Vietnam could have been in the next state or in the next universe. He had heard little of it.

◇◇◇◇◇◇◇◇◇◇

It was eight miles from Jace's house to the bus station. Jace Magee rode shotgun, his dad drove, and his mother sat in the middle. It was a quiet ride. All that could be said had already been spoken.

Mr. Paul Simmons, the chairman of the local draft board, tried to explain it to Jace, but Jace didn't understand. His dad didn't understand either. It was not like 1942, when he enlisted. The country had been attacked. In 1942, his father feared the Germans or Japanese would invade America, even their rural hometown, raping, killing, and burning. That was reason enough to fight, and he gladly served. But Vietnam? He didn't fear an invasion and neither did Jace.

Mr. Paul, as Mr. Simmons was called, served as a volunteer on the draft board and owned a service station at the corner of Fourth Street and Azalea. That was where the Magee family bought their gasoline. Jace knew Mr. Paul had a lot of influence with who went to service and who didn't, and Jace didn't miss a chance of letting him know he didn't want to go to Vietnam. These conversations ceased when Mr. Paul told him that every man had a duty to serve his country when he was called, and no explanation had to be given. Jace didn't share that feeling but realized he had not found an ally with Mr. Paul.

Just a little over a year ago, he knew this day would be a possibility. He had graduated from high school and wasn't going to college. Without that deferment, he would be eligible for active military service. He tried to honorably avoid it.

He first applied to the National Guard. Years earlier, it had been filled with poor young men who needed the Drill money to make ends meet. Recently, there was a waiting list, but those on the list weren't poor anymore. They were the wealthy, those with connections. If a position came open, one of those would get it. Little did they know that, even by getting into the National Guard, they may be called to duty. Many were and, even though they may have wanted to avoid Vietnam, they served admirably. Jace was not one of those whose family could get him in.

Jace got a job offshore working on an oil rig. He had been told that working in the energy industry was an occupation contributing to national security and would get him a deferment. It didn't.

He then tried to plead that he was the only child in his family. Maybe this would keep him out of combat, at least. That remained to be seen.

As a last resort, he considered Canada. His parents left the decision to him, but they all knew that he would never be able to come home again if he chose to do so. Going to Canada to avoid the draft was a safe haven, but one that was considered just next to treason. He couldn't do that. His family may be low-income farmers, but they had pride. As much as pride, never being able to come home was the main deterrent to this alternative.

Halfway to the bus station, he was already feeling homesick. He had never been more than one hundred-fifty miles from home. Except when working offshore, he had only spent the night away from his parents five times; and, until four years ago, had hardly heard of Vietnam. Four years ago was when Brandon Beck left to go. That was a big deal in 1965, and that brought Vietnam home to the county.

It occurred to him that the old truck in which he was riding was bought the same year he was born. It was also nineteen years old. It was the only vehicle his family had owned in his entire life. He couldn't help but compare it to himself. By all accounts, he was in his prime; but the old truck probably would not make it the two years until he returned.

The thought of some stranger cutting his hair as he had seen of the new recruits on the newsreels disgusted him. He was determined that wouldn't happen. The day before he was to depart, he had gone to the barber shop. The barber, aged beyond his years from decades of standing for work, and the only one that had ever cut Jace's hair, cut it as gently and as short as he could. That wasn't close enough. Jace asked him to shave it. He then offered the barber a dollar, the usual charge.

"This one's on me, son. When you come home, you have another free one coming. Just remember, always find a tree you can get behind. I spent most of WWII looking for a tree. I made it, and you will too."

The scene at the bus station was somber, as a dozen draftees and their families were there. One very pregnant and very young woman hung on to her husband, burying her head on his shoulder, sobbing uncontrollably. Other mothers, along with some girlfriends, cried. Some of the fathers just looked lost and bewildered.

There were only two buses in the docking area. On the front of one, the destination was posted "Memphis." On the other was posted "New Orleans." Obviously, one bus was going north, one south. Finally, his bus arrived. Its destination was labeled "Fort Polk." It would be traveling west.

Jace let the others board first. Maybe he was thinking he would get a last-minute reprieve; but finally, it was his turn. He hugged his mother, then shook hands with his father. He tried to be upbeat, if for no other reason than to comfort his mom. He reminded her it was only basic training and he may be assigned a non-combat position. Maybe in some exciting place like Japan.

"Son, keep your head down," were his father's departing words.

"Dad, its only basic training. Maybe I'll be a cook."

He would come home for the first time after finishing basic training. Just before departing Fort Polk, his company was called to formation. Each trainee was given his orders for AIT, Advanced Individual Training. He

76

scanned his orders, looking for anything other than what he saw. His was labeled 11B. "11 Bravo" meant he would be going to infantry training. Even this classification did not necessarily mean combat, but it was a step closer.

He tucked his orders in the pocket of his dress greens, which was the required uniform for traveling off base, and pondered what he would tell his parents. That question churned in his mind the entire 13 days he was home. On his last day at home, he told them of his assignment, but still held hope of a non-combat station.

When it was time to leave for AIT, it was a different scene at the bus station. He was the only passenger in military uniform, and his parents were pleased to know that he would be going back to Fort Polk, at least for ninety days. It was close enough to visit if they wished.

Suddenly, Jace's parents took an interest in international affairs, especially anything to do with the war in Vietnam. They subscribed to a newspaper for the first time in their lives and watched all the TV networks. They had hope. American opinion was turning against the war. They read that in 1965, 55% of Americans supported the war. Now, in 1969, 52% opposed the war. Also, President Nixon wanted to have a peaceful end. It was the first time his family had ever supported a Republican, with the hope that the war was coming to an end.

Twelve weeks after he returned to Fort Polk, he graduated AIT. Another company formation was called. Orders were issued again. He scanned the paper more nervously than he had three months prior. His assignment was not what he hoped for.

Again, he would return home for two weeks before reporting for duty. He didn't tell them that he would be sent to a combat area. For the first time in his life, he told his parents a lie about something important. He justified it by reasoning that it would keep them from worrying.

He had a friend that had been ordered to Japan. He would send his letters to him and let him mail them. His parents would never know.

Three months into his thirteen-month tour of duty in Vietnam, on a hot summer day, Jace's father watched as a strange car kicked up dust coming down the lane to their house. Not recognizing the car, he turned the tractor toward the house, arriving shortly after two men dressed in military uniforms got out of the sedan.

"Mr. Magee, I am Captain Edward Smith, and this is Sgt. Ed Weaver. We have some news that is not what you want to hear, but it could be worse."

"What news, what happened to Jace? What could happen to Jace in Japan?

"Sir, I know nothing about Japan, but your son has received a serious, I must say, life threatening injury. So serious we are required to advise you."

"What happened, a car wreck?"

"No sir, we have been given little detail, but it appears he stepped on a booby-trapped explosive."

"Lord, have the Vietnamese invaded Japan?"

"No sir, he was not in Japan. He was in Vietnam."

"How and when did he get there?"

"Sir, the records show that he was injured on his 92nd day of being in country."

"What country?"

"Vietnam, sir."

About this time, Mrs. Magee had walked toward the car.

"What's this all about?" she asked.

"Jace has been seriously wounded in Vietnam."

"Vietnam! Oh my God," and she began to weep.

"How bad is my boy hurt?"

"Mrs. Magee, I regret to tell you, he has lost both legs."

"Where is he now?" she asked.

"I have not been informed of where he is, but rest assured he is in a fine hospital and, when able, he will be coming home."

"What's left of him," she mumbled.

"Hush, Mama, he's alive. He will come home alive, not like Brandon Beck, who came home in a box."

"When will he get here?" Mr. Magee asked.

The captain answered, "That depends on him. He will go through

78

psychological counseling and physical therapy, and then the fitting of prostheses."

"Can we go see him?" Mrs. Magee asked.

"At this time, I don't know where he is, but you will soon be notified. If he is sent to Walter Reed, he will have the same doctors that the President of the United States would have. They do have family quarters, but it has been my experience that soldiers with these types of injuries at first don't want to see anyone."

The officer handed Mr. Magee his card, extended his sympathy, and offered any assistance he could in the future. The couple watched as the military car left in the same ascending dust as it had arrived.

It would be three days before Jace's name was mentioned again by his parents.

◇◇◇◇◇◇◇◇◇◇

It would be a year before Jace came home. He arrived by plane from a rehab hospital in St. Louis. Out of respect to him, the other passengers allowed him to deplane first. A rowdy applause could be heard outside the fuselage from the seated passengers. This would be the extent of his homecoming welcome. Not like Brandon Beck. When he came home, the town closed for the afternoon and lined the streets as his body was driven from the funeral home to the cemetery.

His parents waited for him to come down the airstair and walk toward the gate. With artificial legs and two crutches, his gait was slow and unstable. He greeted his parents with embarrassed distance, barely hugging his mother and briefly shaking hands with his father.

In the car, his first words were, "I don't want to talk about it. Don't ask me." Not another word was spoken on the drive home.

He resented that the old truck, which he had predicted would be useless by now, had more life in it than he had in himself. It was just another thing to hate.

Each passing day, he warmed a little to his family, but it was obvious he held no patriotism for his sacrifice. His emotions were immature. Why had he not had a reception like Brandon Beck? In his opinion, being dead was less of a sacrifice than being legless. The local paper had not even asked for an interview. It is doubtful he would have granted one anyway.

It was a year before Jace even went into town. His spirits were better, but he was still bitter. He wondered often... *if I had just gone to Canada.*

On one trip into town, his father dropped him off on the corner near the bakery and the town's only funeral home. He stared at the funeral home. He asked himself, "Do you have to go through that funeral home to be respected in this town?" He stood and stared.

As Jace stood there, Mr. Danton, the owner of the funeral home who was returning from lunch, approached him.

"Hello, son. I believe you must be the Magee boy, is that correct?"

"Kind of obvious, sir, since I am the only guy in town with no legs."

"Not unusual to me. During the Korean War, I buried several with no legs or no arms. Some with no legs and no arms. War is terrible thing."

"At least you buried them. They didn't walk the streets like some freak, as I am."

"Son, what happened to you is a terrible thing. I respect you, but I don't feel sorry for you. If I felt sorry for you, I wouldn't do what I'm about to do."

"What's that, sir?"

"Offer you a job."

"A job? Can you see me digging graves on my crutches?"

"No, I can't, but I can start you as a mortuary assistant. Then, you can get your license. Besides, I need some help. Your duties will be limited, of course, but we can adapt and accommodate. By the way, speaking of adapting, we don't dig graves with a shovel anymore, either. We use a backhoe."

"I bet you do need help with all these war deaths."

"No, that's not it. In fact, Brandon Beck is the only one I have buried."

"Why do you need help?"

"Population getting older. Economy is better. People want nicer funerals."

An occupational future was not something Jace had thought much about. His veteran's disability provided some income and he lived with his parents.

"Come by tomorrow and talk to me."

For some reason, the offer interested him. He was there the next morning when the funeral home opened.

Mr. Danton showed him around. Their last stop was the morgue. There, Mr. Danton opened the door, rolling out the corpse of a young man killed in an auto wreck the night before. He rapidly threw back the sheet, revealing an unpleasant sight. Mr. Danton watched Jace's reactions carefully. Jace didn't flinch.

"Jace, you have the aptitude for it. The job is yours."

Salary was negotiated, which was more than Jace had expected. In addition, there was a small apartment adjacent to the facility. He could live there free.

The employment was a good fit. Jace excelled. His spirits brightened and life returned to some degree of normalcy. At Mr. Danton's encouragement, Jace joined a support group for disabled veterans. Some were not even as lucky as he. Slowly, he accepted his state, and even seemed to take pride in the fact that he had survived and had come home. His life no longer centered on his disability.

He and Mr. Danton became close. Jace confided in how he at first resented not dying and getting the hero's homecoming that Brandon Beck had gotten. He alluded to it several times over the years, but Mr. Danton never responded.

One day, the funeral home was empty, no funerals were scheduled, and no one was in the morgue. It was just Jace and Mr. Danton. Jace made the statement again but admitted it was not of major importance to him anymore. Mr. Danton interpreted this to mean that Jace was healed of this emotional millstone. Mr. Danton went to a safe, opened it, and took out an envelope. He handed it to Jace, motioning for him to open it.

Carefully, Jace removed the contents. It was a military dog tag. It read:

Sam Brown Jr.
Type A+ RA 438694226
Protestant

Jace studied it. "Whose is that?" he asked.

"The fellow most likely buried in Brandon Beck's grave."

"How do you know that?"

"I always open military caskets. Several mistakes were made in Korea, so it's just something I do.

"In this case, I had additional suspicions, as the Beck family did not ask me to retrieve the body from the airport. They didn't use the military, either. It came to this facility by private transportation.

"For some reason, these dog tags were in there. They shouldn't have been. They are seldom sent home with the body."

Jace pondered, "It was probably just an accident… they accidentally fell in."

"Maybe, but it wasn't Brandon in the casket."

"How do you know?"

"Everyone in this town knew that kid, including me. The body in that casket was a negro."

"Shit. What do you make of it?"

"Just a mistake, I suppose; but they had already planned the parade and the town was closed for the funeral. There is a chance that the real body was lost in battle, so why put the family through the grief? I went on with the funeral."

Jace thought... *Well, Brandon did not come home in a box, as I have thought all these years. His body was not the one that circled the town on its way to the cemetery. What honor was given, was not given to Brandon.*

For a year, Jace mulled over what he had learned. Who was in Brandon's grave, and where was Brandon's body?

In October 1978, Jace's 10th high school homecoming reunion was held. Jace was now much more confident than he had been, and a well-respected citizen of the town. He would attend. To his surprise, one of his classmates came dressed in his U.S. Army dress greens. He was a Captain and wore a Vietnam service ribbon. He sought Jace out.

"Thank you for your service, Jace. I and all of us understand your sacrifice."

Jace learned that his classmate was in a position to have access to almost any personnel records. He shared the story of the black man in Brandon's grave. The Captain listened carefully and promised to research the matter. Jace had looked at the dog tag so many times, he knew all the information on it by heart, including Sam's service number, which was also his social security number. He gave it to the Captain. It crossed Jace's mind that this was the only time he had trusted the military. He, for the first time, felt real pride for his service and wanted to explore what he could about the body in Beck's grave.

About three weeks later, the Captain called. "Sam Brown Jr. was killed in April of 1966. He was from Forest, Mississippi. Records indicate his insurance was to be paid to his mother, but she was dead. It was paid to his father, Sam Brown Sr. The body was claimed at the Jackson Airport by unnamed transportation and delivered to Danton's Funeral home.

"Wait, Jace. There is more. Brandon went AWOL about that time. They traced him somehow to Japan and lost him. The military believed he was in Canada."

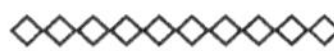

By this time, Jace had an automobile that could be operated with hand controls. It took some time, but he located Sam Brown Sr. still in Forest. He drove to Forest and was not surprised that Sam Sr. was still the drunk he had been in 1966.

The first question asked was by Sam. "Can you buy me a bottle of gin?"

Jace perceived this to be a good idea, as it would lubricate his willingness to tell everything he knew. He was correct. Within five minutes, he learned that a man named Beck had given Sam Sr. $2,000 to let him bury his son somewhere. He didn't remember where. That was all Jace needed.

Where was Brandon Beck? He felt sure he was not dead, or at least was not dead in 1966. How could he find out?

The resentment Jace held for the glory Brandon had received and the lack of it given to him had disappeared. He was torn. He did not need to get even. He was over that, but a wrong had been done. He drove to Brandon's parents' house.

They welcomed him in, and immediately commented on the sacrifice he had made for his country, but quickly added, "At least you could come home. Our son couldn't."

"Couldn't or didn't?" Jace asked.

Jace wasted no time in dropping the dog tag on the table. There was silence. A lie that the Beck family had perpetrated for 13 years was exposed with the drop of a small piece of metal.

"Mr. Beck, I suspect your son is in Canada. Am I correct?"

There was almost a silent answer. "Yes."

Jace broke the silence. "President Carter gave amnesty to those who went to Canada, as well as most deserters. Why did you not bring him home?"

"Honor. The Beck name is a family of honor. Please, Mr. Magee, this is terribly embarrassing. Promise you won't tell."

"You mean you want him to stay in Canada?"

"I must, for the family's namesake. You see, we sent him to the University.

He stayed there two years. Unfortunately, he enjoyed fraternity life, but only enrolled in school one semester. He did, however, enlist; he lost his deferment and was set to be drafted. Mr. Paul Simmons cooperated in not letting the other draft board members know. He let him enlist."

"Mr. Beck, you talk about family honor. What is honorable in duping a community into believing your son is a hero? What is honorable about a young man named Sam Brown lying beneath the soil, with not one letter of indication that he even existed? Who made the real sacrifice, Mr. Beck? Your son or Sam Brown? You think about that. Maybe there is honor to be claimed yet, but that is up to you."

Jace left without receiving an answer.

That night, Jace flipped the dog tag like a coin while lying in his bed. He couldn't sleep. He thought about the years he wasted, feeling that death was the only honorable end for a soldier and that disability was just a curse. He remembered things that he had attempted to forget. He remembered, on two specific occasions, saving the lives of fellow soldiers. He had contributed. He had done something good. He thought about how he almost gave up on life and himself.

He then thought about Sam. What was his military story? How was he killed? There was no homecoming celebration. His family didn't want him. In that, Sam and the Becks had something in common.

Lastly, he thought about Brandon, a person who, at one time, he held undeserved contempt for. His parents didn't want him either, or at least as he was. What was Brandon doing now? He had a Vietnam wound too, just not a wound in the flesh. What was worth more, being dead or never being able to come home? How had Brandon processed that? Was he still in Canada? Was he happy?

He concluded that the real losers were Brandon and Sam. The real winner was he, himself.

In the early morning hours, he got up, went to the safe, and placed the dog tag inside. It has remained there for years.

BESTSELLER

It's inevitable. There comes a time in everyone's career when they stop, look, and listen. It usually occurs at about the age of forty and it doesn't happen overnight; it gradually sneaks up on them. One day, they come to the full reality that they have not accomplished what they had wished at that point in their life.

By this time, they most likely have invested fifteen or more years into their profession and changing careers is a frightful thought. If they should change careers, what will they do? How will they pay their bills if they must take a cut in salary? Will they have to relocate? All these questions are frightening, and most accept their present fate and keep plugging on in their present profession.

There are a few that have the courage to make the change. Experts suggest that the success of the decision is about fifty-fifty. If they fail, they usually return to their old profession and plod through their life in mediocrity. On the other hand, those who succeed usually have unprecedented success.

Daniel was at that point in his life. He sat at his desk in a corner office near the rear of the bank. It was nicely furnished, and the name plate indicated he was a vice-president. He realized that he was on target as far as his position and income for his age, but his chances of making big money were very limited. Money was actually the minor issue; he wanted job satisfaction. He calculated that he was almost halfway to retirement, and then he most likely would retire as a regional vice-president. Banking, a very respected and honorable profession, has many layers of bureaucracy.

The more he thought about it, the more he dreamed. What disappointed him in his career the most was that, when he retired, someone else would just take his place. In a couple of years, he would not be remembered as having ever existed. Someone else could do his job just as well as he had.

The thoughts of his career, or lack of satisfaction in it, began to occupy more and more of his time. However, his career was not the only lackluster part of his life. Not wanting to admit it, he had to doubt the success of his marriage. It was unrewarding, too.

It had not always been that way. He remembered their wedding day. It was joyous. Even more than most newlyweds, they were truly devoted to each other. Helen was beautiful, and it was said they were the most handsome couple that had stood at the altar in years.

They had dreams. He would be successful, in what they didn't know; but, in their immaturity, the world was theirs for the taking. Their dreams included a nice home, maybe a second home in the North Carolina mountains, and children. She, a registered nurse, would then become a stay-at-home mom.

A banking job seemed a good place to start. He would make contacts, have community respect, and the benefits were good, even though the salary was less than he had hoped for. He reasoned he would excel so the income would take care of itself, or other doors would open. Other doors did not open, or hadn't to this point.

Two years after they were married, they received the most disappointing news. Due to medical issues, she could not conceive. It was a change of direction for both, but mostly her. She would delve into her career, becoming the most at nursing; and this she did. She went back to school and received her designation as a Certified Registered Nurse Anesthetist (CRNA). Soon, her income exceeded his. But, with success, there is always pressure. Pressure can manifest itself in marital problems, among other things.

Your fortieth birthday is a milestone in life. It is the beginning of middle age, and he realized he was halfway through his career's life. If he was going to change things, it was now or never. What would he do?

He thought about becoming a financial planner. He had the contacts that he had made at the bank, and he was trusted. If successful, he could make the money he dreamed of and be his own boss. He still questioned, what mark would he leave on society when he was gone?

This mental debate went on for months. One day, he knew what he wanted to do. He wanted to be a writer. He had written several articles for the banking industry that were well received, and he wrote an article for the local newspaper covering his 20th high school homecoming reunion. It, too, was well accepted.

He dreamed of being more than that. He dreamed of being featured in a national magazine, writing novels and even screenplays. For once in his life, he was enthusiastic about what he wanted to do.

He made some inquiries. A regional magazine agreed to purchase his stories for five hundred dollars per month. He would be a stringer for the local paper, maybe another five hundred a month. He could count on another magazine purchase occasionally to add to his income, and he had some savings he could draw from. Helen also had her income.

He would do it, leave his job and security to pursue his dream. He wasn't expecting his first negative. It was Helen. No longer did she trust that he could give her the emotional things she wanted, and no longer did she give him the encouragement and support he needed. She was successful in her career and their relationship had drifted as two ships passing in different directions. The thrill was gone, and it takes the thrill to see a marriage through difficult times.

She would not follow him in his dream. He would have to go it alone, middle-aged and single. The day he moved his belongings, there were tears from both of them; so some hint of devotion remained, but not enough for a reconciliation.

Five years passed. Now he had the same doubts about his writing career as he had felt in his banking profession. The only difference is that he still wanted to be a writer; he still had the desire. Not a part-time writer, but a professional writer. He still had dreams of a bestselling novel with royalties from movie rights. This hadn't happened. There was some success. Several short stories had been purchased and published, the newspaper and magazine he had arranged in the beginning had worked out, and he got a few paid speaking engagements. It made a living, but barely.

As for Helen, she had not found inner satisfaction either; but she realized life was about as good, or bad, as it would be for her in the future. There was something missing, something even her financial success could not provide.

◇◇◇◇◇◇◇◇◇◇

He had attended all the writing conferences, taken creative writing courses, and followed all the instructions as best he could.

Daniel kept a list of the things all writers should do. The first was to write something every day. This he did religiously. Sometimes, he would write the end of a story with no idea of the beginning. At other times, he would write the first few paragraphs with no idea of the ending. It pleased him that, after months, an idea would bloom, and he could add a pertinent beginning or end to these story fragments.

Most of the time, he had to suppress what his mind wanted to dwell on. He missed her. There was still an emptiness in his life. He promised himself, he would not write about that emptiness. After all, she was not willing to follow his dream. Thoughts of her would be disruptive. He was also disturbed to find out that she had not been well. Headaches, maybe from job stress. For the headaches, she self-medicated with the drugs of her trade that were readily at hand. She was addicted, but still functioning.

His career was, to say the least, at a point where he did not want it to be. With all the drive and desire he possessed, so far, profound words had never emanated from his keyboard.

On this day, his mind was blank. More barren than usual. No golden words or exciting literary ideas or plots came forth.

He looked back at the list of things writers should do. One should have a comfortable place to work. He moved his desk away from the window.

Maybe the outdoors distracted him. She had always loved being outside. He remembered their dream, the mountain home; but he quickly dismissed the thought.

Next on the list was to think about a real person and, when you write, fictionalize about some aspect of their life or personality, like mentally drawing a caricature. He left his desk and moved to the front porch. Maybe he did need fresh air and nature. There, he made a list of all the people that had influenced his life. Hers was the first on the list.

He returned to his desk, and then he remembered. He remembered the first day of the first writer's conference he had ever attended. The speaker said, "Above all things, write what you know about." He knew about her, or at least at one time he had. Again, he tried to dismiss her from his mind, as the last time he had seen her, she seemed unsteady on her feet. The chemical abuse had taken its toll. No longer was she the beauty she had been. But then his thoughts reflected, and he realized what he was seeing; someone as troubled as he had been and was now. He realized she had that right just as much as he did.

He hurried to his computer. He made several attempts to start and then, he wrote the first line. "I saw her today, not as a photo in color but as a black and white negative. The positive, accented by the light spots on the film, and the less flattering, darkened by the dark tones. She just needs a touch up. That will be my job."

She, too, was seeking help from her inner self. Smart enough to realize her demise, she too tried to pinpoint the real cause. Was it job stress or something more important in her life that was missing?

When he called her, she was very receptive and appreciative. Could they start over? They made no promises to each other but looked forward to dinner at an old familiar place.

After that night, they visited often as he continued the book. Yes, a book, not a short story. The book would be about them. She, slowly and without outside help, recovered from her dependency. This was part of the story.

One night when she was visiting, an old movie, *The Days of Wine and Roses,* was on television. The plot stirred emotions in both of them: a couple fighting their way through alcohol addiction, which eventually causes their relationship's demise. Neither said a word through the entire movie.

The book he wrote could have been a sequel to that movie, but with a happy ending. It was bought by a reputable publisher and, even though it was not a bestseller, Daniel got an advance for the second book. He remembered the first thing he learned in his first writing course. He wrote what he knew about.

Now, several bestsellers later, they enjoy the view from their North Carolina home. She thrives in the beauty of the outdoors, and he thrives in the support and inspiration from her that made his dreams become reality.

❧ ◆ ❧

THE VILLAGE

When I was young, I heard old timers talk about the accident. They always started the story with, "Well, about sixty years ago, when I was a kid..." Somehow that made the story seem less real; because, as a twelve-year-old, that far back was beyond my imagination. As a boy, years rolled by slowly; and thinking about something or someone from 60 years past made the people and times almost unimaginable.

Through the years, I had recalled bits and pieces of what I heard then, but I realized I may have had several stories mixed up. Some of the descriptions of the horrible incident remained in my mind; but, as I began to write stories (some factual, some fictional), putting this story on paper just would not evolve.

Some years ago, I wrote a book of short stories titled *Bogue Chitto Flats, Stories from a Southern Town*. Most of the stories were inspired by tales I had heard from older relatives and their friends. This story did not appear in the book. As I have stated, I just couldn't get it to come together.

Somehow, my book fell into the hands of a man named Charles Percy in Connecticut. He wrote me a letter and asked if I knew anything about the sawmill explosion in a community they called The Village. He thought it was a story that I would like to tell and should tell.

I answered the letter and informed him that I was aware of there being a serious accident before the turn of the 20th century, but I had not researched it, and certainly had never written about it. He wrote again asking me why I did not feel it was a worthy story. I explained to him that the only records I could most likely obtain were newspaper articles from that time. Writing a story based on that information would just be a journalistic repost. Previously, when I had written similar stories, they had not been well received. For the story to attract attention, it needed something of human interest other than recanting about an explosion that killed thirteen people. I responded that I would be interested in writing the story if I could find something about the social changes that the incident inspired; but, in those days, that would not have been newsworthy and not recorded.

A few days later, Charles Percy called me. He said he knew exactly what I meant, but he felt sure he had some information that would change my mind. Talking to him stirred my interest. I realized that, based on the information he held, and the manner by which he had obtained it, I could write about much more than the fact that it was a tragic accident.

He told me his grandfather, Tom Percy Sr., was killed in the accident. At the time, Charles' father, Tom Jr., was only ten years old. Tom Jr. had been obsessed with the accident that killed his father his entire life.

A few days later, I received a large envelope in the mail. Inside were copies of letters, notes, and graphs. It was evident from what I saw, Tom Jr. had made an almost lifelong study of the accident, its cause, the people affected, and even its influence on The Village itself. His notes and letters spanned over fifty years.

Based on the information I received, this is the story as best I can tell it. To assist me, I have consulted news articles from that time, Find-a-Grave.com, Ancestry.com, Newspapers.com, Genealogybank.com and the Library of Congress. I also conducted several interviews, but only one proved helpful. Very sparingly, I have made assumptions to fill in gaps where no information existed, but I think these assumptions are logical.

The Story...

It was a February morning and Jordan Magee dreaded getting from his bed and embracing the coldest morning he could remember in his 35 years of life. He cursed as the breath from his mouth created a rush of fog as it encountered the unheated room in his primitive mill provided house.

He dressed slowly, seeking the warmest clothes he could find. After tossing aside a few wool shirts that were threadbare, he went to the woodshed to split extra wood. As frugal as he was, the extra wood would be needed to kindle a small fire in the wood burning stove that would warm his house the entire day.

Jordan was known to have a sour temperament, and the cold weather did not improve his mood. He would later recall that his movements seemed to be slowed, as if he had a feeling of impending doom. He milked the cow, gathered some eggs, ate some fried sausage and sourdough biscuits left over from the night before, and started for the door of his house. Beside the door was a rack, and from the rack he lifted a belt, and on the belt was a holstered pistol. He never left home without it.

Jordan was, in some respects, the village bully. He had killed three people over the years, but all were deemed killed in self-defense. Mill towns attract a rough clientele. Nevertheless, most people left him alone and tried not to agitate him. His mood could change at the drop of a hat.

He was late for work. He briskly walked the half-mile to the mill.

Henry Evans was the antithesis of Jordan Magee. He was a small, mild-mannered man who, on Sunday, served as a preacher at a small church. His main job was that of a filer. Keeping the blades sharp was his responsibility and it was important. A dull saw not only slowed production, it was dangerous. It could sling splinters. Before he was hired, a dull blade cast a splinter that entered Felix Smith's head through his eye and exited in the back of his neck. Miraculously, Felix survived, with his only disability being the loss of his eye. Felix attended Henry's church and Henry would often point to him in the church pew and call him "God's Miracle."

Henry's routine was to arrive at work early to make a check of all the equipment. That morning, he realized something was wrong. There was not as much activity of men moving about the mill yard as there should have been.

Duke Chastain owned the Village Mill. The mill was one of the largest in the state and, at times, would employ up to 150 men. Sawyers, loaders, trimmers, and even locomotive engineers were necessary to operate the small gauge railroad that transported logs.

The Village had a population of about 600 people and those included men, women, and children. Most of the male citizens worked at the mill. A few others ran supporting businesses such as a dry goods store, blacksmith shop, and there was a small bank.

Duke had been a wealthy man, but he had overextended his debt with the purchase of a new locomotive. It was ordered a year prior, before the recent recession had been realized and the demand for lumber reduced. The locomotive had been delivered last month, and payment was due in full.

Despite owning one of the toughest industries in existence, Duke had a soft heart, and laying off employees hurt him. He had commented that it was the worst part of owning a business. In making his decision on who to let go, he first looked at the roster and rated those who performed the poorest. He even kept some that had less than pristine reviews. He kept them because they had large families. He then dismissed the single men and the ones who had children that were old enough to help support the family. He did not layoff the three fireman that maintained the boilers. Not that they were good employees - in fact, they were not - but because it was the hottest, nastiest job at the mill and no one else wanted it. When he finished, he passed out 75 dismissal notices. Those who lost their jobs did not realize it, but it may have saved their lives. It was, however, the beginning of the end for The Village.

Tom Percy was the superintendent of the mill and was Duke's right-hand man. He was the grandfather of Charles Percy who had contacted me. Tom was hard-working, honest, and dependable. The men respected him for his fairness, and he was respected in the community. He was on the school board and a deacon at the Baptist Church. He was the most educated of the employees, having completed the 8th grade, and the highest paid.

Other than Tom Jr., he had a wife, Rita, and a younger daughter, Emma.

He had depleted most of his earnings sending Emma to New Orleans for the treatment of a yet undiagnosed disease. She and Rita were to return from New Orleans on the train the day of the accident.

It was the responsibility of the three firemen to keep the boilers in working order and make sure the "steam was kept up." The boilers were never extinguished completely, as that would take too long to get power to the machinery when the mill opened at 6 a.m.

The mill was powered by three boilers housed in a building called the boiler room. In the past few weeks, the use of one boiler had been discontinued due to the recession. When the firemen arrived that morning, both the other boilers were reportedly cold. The firemen knew that Duke would not be pleased, as only a few men had jobs that could be done without power.

Adding a little coal to the lumber cutoffs, they attempted to raise steam as fast as possible. In the meantime, the idle workers gathered around the warming boilers. The white men got the privilege of standing closest to the heat. The black workers formed a row outside of this, but still close enough to receive some comfort. This would ultimately save many of their lives.

Conley Ford was a twelve-year-old boy that came to the mill with his father that morning before going to school. He had climbed into the rafters over the boilers to keep warm, but not get in the way of the firemen or the other workers. This turned out to be another story that one day Henry would point to as "God's Miracle."

It happened at exactly 6:41 a.m. This is known because the concussion of the explosion stopped the clock on the bank three-quarters of a mile away. Reports say that the noise could be heard five miles away. Parts of the boilers were located a half-mile from the site. An engineer on the mainline railroad was backing into the spur belonging to the Village Mill and saw the disaster from a distance. He said he saw the body of a small man, or boy, go through the roof and into the air as high as 200 feet.

In the few moments after the explosion, it seemed as if the world was dead. Nothing could be heard; as if the noise was so intense, it had frightened the sound waves and driven them in the opposite direction. Jordan was almost at the mill when he heard the screams and moans of men dying and scalding. As tough as he was, at first, he chose not to view the carnage; but then, he knew he had to do what he could.

Approaching the boiler room, he stepped over the bodies of men he knew and had worked with. In some cases, he could not recognize them due to the damage. Men lay stacked on each other like broken broom straws. Some hung from trees, or at least their body parts did, and many were alive, writhing in pain.

Then he saw what would change his life forever. Tom Percy was trapped under an extremely heavy piece of metal, with steel and wood timbers further pinning his leg to the floor. He was on his back and the boiling water was about three inches deep, boiling him alive. He was screaming in agony.

Due to the scalding water and the weight of the debris, freeing him was virtually impossible. Jordan looked around for Henry. He had never before had any use for a preacher; but, if one was ever needed, it was now. Soon, Henry was kneeling as close to Tom as the hot water would allow. While Henry prayed, Tom begged for death.

Suddenly, Henry stopped his prayer, paused and looked at Jordan. Then, clearly and distinctly, he said, "Shoot him, Jordan."

A square timber was brought so that Jordan could use it as a bridge to get closer to Tom without stepping in the hot water. This was not a time for a bad shot. He unholstered his pistol and pulled back the hammer. The wailing of pain from all but Tom seemed to cease, as if giving Tom the last bit of respect. Jordan balanced himself on the timber bridging the hot water and placed the pistol on Tom's forehead. His hand began to shake.

Tom said, "Do it Jordan, please do it, the pain is unbearable. I need to die."

To those watching, it seemed like an eternity. Then, Jordan lifted the pistol and tossed it into the boiling water that now was beginning to recede.

With the hot water receding, maybe there could be a rescue; so plans were made. Timbers and jacks were brought in to lift the debris and free Tom's body. No one noticed that the building, which had at first not burned, most likely due to being soaked in water, was now beginning to burn rapidly.

Henry sent for a bucksaw. Henry prayed as Felix Smith and Jordan placed the saw just above Tom's knee. There seemed to be a mental battle as to which of the two men would draw the saw first, making the entry into Tom's scalded flesh. Henry would later say that God's mercy was rapid. After the first pass with the saw, Tom passed away.

Rita knew that morning that it was one of the worst days of her life. She just didn't know that it would only get worse. As she boarded the train to come home, she held back tears. The doctor had told her the evening before that 8-year-old Emma would not survive till summer.

The train headed north and new passengers boarded at each stop. At Hammond, Louisiana, she heard the boarding passengers talk about an accident at a sawmill. Bits and pieces of the conversation let her know that it was an explosion, and many lives were lost. Then she heard the words she did not want to hear, "The Village Mill."

Maybe he is ok, she thought; but, even reasoning in the most positive way, she knew that the dead would consist of friends and neighbors.

As the train pulled into The Village station, she saw a group of her best friends. As she and Emma stepped onto the platform, her minister approached. She fainted.

The Percys did not live in a mill provided house. They had a large home that was one of the nicer in town. It was about a mile from the mill and Tom Jr. had heard the explosion. Most likely due to his youth, he did not immediately associate the noise with a serious happening. Then, the neighbor knocked on the door. She lived next door, and her husband owned the dry goods store. She told him to come with her.

Tom Jr.'s notes dwell on the lady that informed him of the accident in more than just a passing manner. He reflects on that specific incident several times. As I studied the notes, I could tell by his early writing that he held contempt for the way she broke the news, or the lack of breaking the news, to him.

All she told him was that there had been an accident and she needed to

take him to the mill. He had no idea what he was going to see. What he saw
was his deceased father lying in a pool of bloody hot water. The imprint of
pain was frozen on his face.

Later in Tom Jr.'s writings, he reasoned that she herself did not know
what they would see. I noticed, in several instances, Tom Jr. seemed to
mellow through the years.

The final count was 13 dead, including three black men. Of course, in
addition to Tom Sr., the three firemen were killed. Miraculously, the young
man that was seen going through the roof lived. Eventually, he overcame
his injuries and just the scars remained. He was another example of Henry's
"God's Miracle" characters.

The mill was insured by Great American Indemnity Company. Soon,
lawsuits were being filed on behalf of the families of the deceased and, in
some cases, those that were injured. The final settlement awarded Tom's
family was $3,000. It was reasoned that he should be compensated for pain
and suffering as well as a death award to his family. That was a major sum
then, as it would be about $96,000 in today's money.

All the others that were killed got $200, except the black workers' families,
who got $100. Most of the scalded and injured got less than $75.

The mill never reopened. The equipment was sold to a new mill in Louisiana
and a few of the employees moved there. Tom Jr. had corresponded with
them or their children in several letters. These letters were dated in the 1930's.

For employment, or maybe adventure, twenty young men joined the
Army and went to the war in Cuba. Tom Jr. does not mention any specific
names, but he does report that seven died from disease or injuries.

Only one of the black workers was identified by name according to Tom
Jr.'s notes. His name was Luther Adams. He left a wife and one son, Frank,
who was 15 years old at the time. I think Tom Jr. enjoyed keeping in touch
with him, and I was able to find out more while writing this story. It is a
story of success:

Frank and his mother bought 10 acres of land on Big Creek. It was on a
hillside that sloped toward the creek. It was cheap because all the timber had

been cut and the lower part flooded occasionally. This could be a problem for farming, but it could also be a blessing since the flooding deposited rich, fertile silt.

He and his mother planted the entire parcel in watermelons and, even in the years when there were floods, there was enough produced from the hillside to provide a meager living. In drier years, they did well.

After about the fourth year of planting, Frank got permission to demolish the old mill cabins. With a mule, he dragged the virgin heart pine 12 x 12 floor joist timbers and built a substantial cottage. His farming skills improved also. He learned that if he placed metal filings from the old blacksmith shop around his plants, it produced a sweeter melon. His melons became highly sought after.

I was able, through Ancestry.com, to locate his grandson. He tells an interesting story about his grandfather Frank. There was an old, dilapidated house on the property, probably built in the 1840s. When new, it was a substantial dwelling but had long ago become uninhabitable. Frank decided to demolish it. As he tore it down, he found an old flour sack hidden in the wall attached to a window weight. Rats had eaten the sack; but, in the sack, he found one silver dollar. As he continued the demolition, he found over 500 similar coins that had dropped to the floor.

The grandson still owned the property, even though he lived in another state. He told me that after Hurricane Katrina, he demolished the old cabin that Frank had built from the mill cabins. The heart pine floor joist and beams he sold to a lumber company to make heart pine floors. There were 12 of them and he got $500 apiece. Coincidently, he told me that they ended up in a home being rebuilt after the storm in Louisiana.

Jordan Magee never lifted a gun in anger again and never carried one on his body. He loved guns and moved to a nearby larger town and became a skilled gunsmith. When WWI happened, he volunteered as a civilian to work in a weapons factory assembling arms for the cause.

Tom Jr. notes that he must have had remorse knowing the ultimate use of what he was making. Jordan moved back and bought a piece of property where he built a cotton gin. The gin, he notes, was powered by the one boiler that was salvaged from the explosion. Tom also notes that he had perfect attendance at the Henry Evans' church until the day he died and is buried in that cemetery.

Henry Evans was dead, apparently, before Tom started doing his research. He did find, correspond and apparently visit with Henry's son, Alexander Campbell Evans. Alex, as he was called, became a very well-known minister. Alex had the notes from his father's most outstanding sermons and had used parts of them in his own services. The notes were in the packet I received.

Henry tells about the explosion and the carnage he saw on that day, but only briefly. Then he tells about praying to save Tom Percy. Then he says:

It was just like Abraham and Isaac. You know God commanded Abraham to offer his only son Isaac as a burnt offering. As I prayed beside Tom that day, asking God to save him, I felt the Lord tell me he had to be a sacrifice. God was testing me to see if I had the faith of Abraham. I knew God was speaking to me, and I know He told me to relieve Tom of his earthly suffering. I know God told me and gave me the strength to order Jordan Magee to shoot him.

Then, just as He did to Abraham, when I trusted my faith, He did provide. He provided a way for me to not have Tom's blood on my hands. He did it through the weakness of another man. This man was not really weak, just acting through the Angel of God. That man sits in this audience today, and he and I know the Angel of the Lord said to him, "Step aside Jordan, this is my doing."

Yes, the Lord took Tom that day, but He did it His way. Brothers and Sisters, we must live life His way.

Tom Jr. and his mother lived in The Village on the money that was given to them from the accident for another year. Then Emma died. They then rented their house to others after dividing it into three apartments. This provided a little income, which allowed them to move to a larger town. Rita got a job as a seamstress and, with the insurance money, they survived rather comfortably.

Tom Jr. became fascinated with the accident and boilers in particular. He got a job repairing boilers with the railroad, and then started his own boiler repair business. He had the reputation of being the best in the business.

At age 30, he was asked to go to work for Hartford Steam Boiler Insurance Company inspecting boilers and making safety recommendations. The company took note of his talents and eventually he moved to Hartford, Connecticut and retired as an officer in the company.

There was not a happy ending for The Village, at least not for a long time. First, the bank closed. Then, the dry goods store closed and, slowly, the people began to leave the area. I visited the town while researching this story and found that, in the 1980's and 90's, there was a rebirth.

Better highways made the commute to more populous areas of employment convenient, and a smaller community with affordable real estate became desirable again. Houses began to be restored. The school was rebuilt. Interestingly, not a person I talked to knew about the accident. I could not even be certain where the mill had once stood.

Duke Chastain lived another 30 years. His obituary tells of what a fine man he was and his business successes - president of the bank, elder in the Methodist Church, and so on. Funny, it never mentions that he once owned one of the biggest sawmills in the state.

Henry Evans never worked in a sawmill again. He got a job as a rural mail carrier, farmed forty acres, and continued to preach the Gospel. He is buried near Jordan Magee and Felix Smith in the church cemetery. His epitaph reads, "Miracles Occur But You Must Have Faith."

FRUITCAKES

My grandmother was a very talented actress. Very few knew she was skilled in that manner, and revealing it to you may come as a surprise to those who knew her. Even her youngest son did not know the secret she kept until many years after her death.

You see, my grandmother, MaMa, could not read. She would sit on the front porch and hold the newspaper as if she were reading it. She would laugh at times and grunt with disapproval as she moved her head from side to side. If illiterate means you can't read, she was illiterate. I think she did enjoy and, to some degree, understand the comics.

Now if illiterate means lack of intelligence, she was certainly not illiterate. There are so many examples of why, and some of them came as a blessing to her grandchildren.

Since we did not find out about her lack of reading ability until after her death, we wondered why there was not an abundance of recipes that we would inherit. She could not write or read; therefore, no recipes. Fantastic cooks just don't use recipes, but they had to learn some way. Someone taught them, and they remembered. A sign of intelligence.

She loved her grandchildren but we never experienced her taking us on her knee and reading to us. She told stories, very simple ones; and, sometimes, she would leave out a part that would make it understandable to a child, but we had heard them before and knew the part she left out.

In place of holding us in her lap and reading to us, on summer days, she would put our head on her apron as she sat in the swing. There, we were drugged by the bouquet of the good things from her kitchen that clung to her apron. This was especially true in the holiday season.

MaMa, as a rule, only had two spices in her pantry, salt and pepper. There was no cinnamon, ginger, or nutmeg and she never heard of thyme, rosemary, or coriander. Her complexity of flavors came from the sourdough she used in her breads, cakes, and pie crust. It came from real butter and yes, her favorite condiment of all, bacon grease.

She took some short cuts. She reconstituted dried apples for her apple pie. Come to think of it, maybe she did not take short cuts. Maybe she was making apple pie before they had access to fresh apples; after all, she goes back some years.

There are always exceptions to things. That exception would be fruitcake season. It was an operation extraordinaire and began with summoning her three daughters back to the house, even though they actually had family responsibilities of their own.

It was then that she broke the rules. She bought cinnamon, ginger, brown sugar, white sugar, molasses, cloves, mace, and all types of candied oranges, glazed cherries, lemon rind, candied citron, dried figs, and candied pineapple. Then there were the nuts, both pecans and walnuts. Each had to be hand-shelled, being careful to save some unbroken ones for decoration.

There were two dining rooms in her home; a formal one, which was almost never used, and an informal one that was used for everyday purposes and to feed the white field hands. The coloreds ate on the steps of the adjoining porch.

This informal room was where the cakes were assembled. This may take a period of four or five days. Piles of each of the good things I described were placed directly on the wood table. The stacks looked like pyramids of goodies. I learned at an early age this was the best place to enjoy the fruit cake. My opinion, but strongly mine, was that the cakes were better raw than cooked. The nuts and fruit I would sneak without her knowing, but the bowl of flavored dough I was freely allowed to scrape and eat. She called it sopping the pan. More on this later.

The process was detailed; and, years later, my aunts tried to recreate all the ingredients and steps, but they could only remember fifty-two. Surely many were left out. The ordeal would culminate with the cake mixture being placed in a pan and cooked in a pressure cooker, one at a time. In my time, she had shortened her list of recipients to twenty-five, but I understand that she had cooked as many as forty.

Recipients would be diverse. I remember two ministers that lived in Texas each got one. She met them in 1926, or there about, when they came through to hold a tent revival.

The rural mail carrier got one. I think this was out of respect to the fact that her husband had held that job prior to retirement.

Her doctor and his nurse got one. I'm not sure why.

Several of her nieces and nephews who lived in the area got one, as did her eight children.

Let me not forget that in my early years she sent one to President Eisenhower, as she had to every president since 1910. There was a four-year pause. During WWII, she had someone write President Roosevelt and tell him that he wouldn't get another cake until he brought her four sons home from the war. Poor fellow died before he got another one of MaMa's cakes. I don't think that contributed to his demise, however.

Finally, the product was finished, and she picked the worst looking cake to make her test cake. Maybe it had stuck to the pan or something. She would be awarded the first bite. On more than one occasion, this almost turned fatal as MaMa was diabetic. On at least two occasions, she had a diabetic reaction to the sugar and had to take her insulin shot. The shot was too much, and she had to reverse that by drinking a Coke. By this time, we were at the emergency room where she promised all the medical personnel that they would be getting a cake.

I, too, had to visit the emergency room once, as the dough I had eaten apparently swelled in my stomach. They thought I had appendicitis until I told them the amount of dough I had consumed. I will not tell you the remedy.

She passed away in August, and that Christmas no cakes were made. Yes, we got a letter from the son of one of the Texas preachers inquiring as to where his cake was, as if he had a right to it. Others questioned the absence of the tradition, but we did not hear from President Johnson. This was most likely because she had not sent President Kennedy or him a cake. She didn't like them either.

The next Christmas, an attempt was made by her daughters to recreate the unwritten recipe. The mixture, they said in retrospect, was too thin and bubbled up, clogging the relief valve on the pressure cooker. It exploded, thus ending the tradition.

MaMa couldn't read, but she could remember that recipe by heart. She was intelligent. With her passing, the tradition ended, as it does when we lose any of our kin. The moral of this story is to listen and learn from your elders. Then, write down what you learned.

DISGUISED INTENTIONS

Going back to your hometown after a long absence is always an experience. It is not that Ron had not been back. He returned often when his parents were living, but they passed on in the 90s. After their deaths, his trips from Virginia to Mississippi were less frequent. His last visit was almost five years ago; and, each time he had come back, there seemed to be less of the town he had known years before.

The interstate highway changed things. He remembered, in the 60s, the business district consisted of about a five-block square area. Then there were the neighborhoods. The more affluent lived on the south and west side of town. As the density of housing diminished, it eventually vanished into rural logging and farming communities.

Then, the interstate, built a mile and a half west of town, replaced the U.S. highway that once was the artery that pumped economic blood into the area. The town moved to the interstate.

He was pleased that he found an exquisite boutique hotel in the center of the old downtown. The Inn on Whitworth had been a mercantile store then; but now, it was surprisingly upscale, capturing the lure of antiquity with modern features and contemporary art. He could tell he would be comfortable there. It would be his home for awhile, maybe a couple of days, maybe a week or more. He had a curiosity to satisfy. He didn't realize it, but he also had a long-time, slow-burning, romantic fire he needed to control.

Ron Ferguson wasted no time starting his investigation. After checking into the hotel, he drove a few miles out of town and found the driveway. Even though it was overgrown with weeds and debris, it appeared passable. The drive was more like a short road, or at least that is the way he had remembered it. Of course, the last time he had been there was a half century ago.

After negotiating a couple of turns, he could see the house and was relieved to know it was still standing. He was puzzled that it was not located a greater distance from the main road. In his memory, it had been deeper in the woods. He knew that, in your mind, things you remember from your youth always remain larger, bigger, and better than they likely were. By now, the drive was impassable. Small saplings were standing and fallen trees blocked passage. He would walk the remaining two hundred yards.

He had not walked through the door of that house in more than fifty years and had not even passed the drive in over twenty-five. Just inside the door, he was amazed that it was much like he had remembered. After all that time, the smell was the same. Musty, moldy, sweet, and sour - a real plethora of aromas that were collectively unique to this one place.

He stood for a moment where the front door had been. The door itself was gone now; but, from his vantage point, not much else had changed. He remembered the first time he came there. It was with Mr. Graves, the Industrial Arts teacher. Mr. Graves had taken the class to show them the type of construction and the quality.

He remembered his teacher's words as if he had written them down. "They don't build 'em like this anymore. Not a nail in it, just wood pegs and perfect joiner work. She'll still be standing when you and I are dead and gone."

He was correct. Structurally, the house was much as it had been then. He remembered Mr. Graves pointing out that it was made entirely of virgin heart pine and cypress. It was old when the class toured it, very old by Southern standards.

Rumors abounded that it was a haunted house. Most old, abandoned houses had that reputation, but this one was different. No one knew who owned it, or even who originally owned it. At least, that was the story then. Located out of town, some distance and hidden in the woods, no one really cared. Its unknown ownership had proven to be a mystery, almost an unbelievable mystery in this day and time. He was not sure if all he had remembered was correct, but it was told that no one had title to it. The surprising thing was that, with land values rising, no one seemed to care. Had it been forgotten, or was its haunted reputation a market deterrent?

The sensation of fright is a strange emotion to describe. It is said that it does one good to cry occasionally. Nowhere does it say that one should be frightened; but, from time to time, we seem to take pleasure in it. It's obvious this fetish exists by the popularity of frightening movies and scary books. Alfred Hitchcock, Stephen King, and Dean Koontz are the masters of the craft. This old house had been a perfect setting for such activity, a perfect set for a horror movie.

It was not a place you would go to on your first date; but, after a little familiarity, it could be an interesting venue. Teenage girls were easily frightened and seemed to enjoy it; and teenage boys loved playing the macho protector.

Still standing in the doorway, he smiled remembering one such experience. Out of the clear blue, Julie Williams, his girlfriend, had broken up with him. They had been dating steadily for over a year. She gave him no reason. She simply wanted to date others and, in short, he was not in the picture. A put-down like that hurts a young man's pride. With his friends, they planned revenge.

Julie soon developed a more-than-casual relationship with the brother of a friend who was a freshman in college. Losing your girlfriend to an older guy is a special affront. She was only a junior. Being older, the new boyfriend was not in the click with Ron and his friends, but some knew him well enough. A plan of revenge was put in motion. They planned it for weeks.

Julie's new boyfriend was named Larry Wade. He was told there would be a Halloween party at the old house, and he should come with Julie. There would be soft drinks, a fire for hotdogs and, of course, spooky house décor. The extent of the decorations was not revealed. The house had a spooky reputation already.

The father of one of the guys in the group owned a funeral home. They were able to secure a damaged casket and a makeup technician. The casket was placed in the house with nothing but a flickering kerosene lantern for light.

When Julie and Larry arrived, they did not enter at first, but other couples did. There was ample screaming that could be heard from those inside. Finally, Julie and Larry entered.

After going through all the usual Halloween gore - spaghetti for brains, grapes for eyes, and red Kool-Aid for blood - they worked their way to the back room. Lying in the coffin, looking more dead than a real corpse, was Ron.

Julie almost fainted. She peed her pants. Embarrassed, she ran to the car. The fair maiden was not won back, but a bit of revenge was exacted. She got a new name, WeeWee Williams.

Ron explored each room of the house and was disappointed that younger generations had painted most of the walls with graffiti, but pleased to see that most of the windowpanes were still intact. The glass was not clear, but wavy and imperfect; and, to some degree, made the trees in the distance obscure. This lured him outside.

He carefully walked around the perimeter of the old house. He had never explored the land surrounding the house. The lure was the old house itself, but now he was interested in the house and the land. He began to circle the house in wider and wider circles, kicking at old bottles and discarded debris.

About fifty yards in the rear of the house was a clump of what, at one time, may have been a hedge. It was thick and made the small area it covered almost impassable. It was obvious that no one had gone to the trouble to explore there in many years. The area interested him.

Pushing one bush back at a time, he made his way to the center of the cluster. There, he found three depressions in the ground. One was longer than the other two. Could these be graves? If so, who would be buried there? He had seen sunken graves before and these depressions in the ground looked just like those. He knew that bodies interred without caskets or those with wooden caskets will cave in over time due to rot and decomposition.

With the toe of his boot, he scraped back the decaying leaves surrounding each of the small ones. He found nothing. Then, he scraped the leaves from the larger grave. On the west end of the depression, he uncovered a cross made of the same wood the house appeared to be made of. Fastened with a rusty nail, not a peg, it still appeared old.

By now, it was getting late. He was satisfied that the effort he had made to research this old place had real interest. Who is buried there? Is anyone buried there? Could it be fake graves just to take a Halloween party to the next level? He didn't know; but, he now knew he would be in town for awhile. Tomorrow he would visit the land office.

Back in his hotel room, he reflected on what a difference a half-century had made in his life. He was now retired, divorced, and bored with having nothing to do and few to do anything with. Maybe the mystery of the old house was just an excuse to come home and reminisce. Maybe there was a reason he himself did not understand. Maybe there was some clue as to the history of the house he could solve. Investigations had been his life; since, after completing college, he had joined the FBI. His hobby had been genealogy and, since leaving the FBI, he had spent many hours searching wills, marriage records, and censuses. He wondered if the ownership of the house was still unknown; or, for that matter, had it always been known? Was unknown ownership just part of the myth? At least the research would relieve his boredom.

His soul searching went from the old house to something more personal. His marriage had failed, but that was long ago. While working, there was little time to kindle a new relationship; and he was smart enough to know that the reason his first marriage failed would still be an obstacle. Maybe now, he had time; but dating sites were not his interest and trolling bar rooms held even less interest for him.

He found the hotel accommodations better than expected and awoke fresh, with his energy spurred by the excitement of his intended research. At nine o'clock, the land office at the courthouse opened. So far, he had not seen one person that he recognized; but his desire to reignite an old flame led him to believe that would soon change, and that may be a big reason for his returning. When he saw her, for a split second, it was that dagger-in-the-heart feeling.

People change over decades; but, the moment he saw her, he knew who she was. Her beauty was still there. The blonde hair looked natural, not like that of older women that try to remain blonde into their seventies and eighties but can't pull it off.

She still had the petite, cheerleader figure. What little makeup she wore was applied exquisitely. He got pleasure in knowing someone his and her age could still look so good. Green had always been her color, and that was what she was wearing. He knew who she was; but, at this point, she had not seen him.

When she turned, she glanced in his direction. And then, glanced again. A double take, to make sure she saw who she thought she saw. Her thoughts were not as flattering of him... a little overweight, grey hair thinning, but a reasonable preservation of what he had been.

He spoke first. "Julie Williams, you're the last person I expected to see here," he lied. "It is great to see you," he said, trying to make the meeting seem totally coincidental.

"Ron, just call me WeeWee. Everyone still calls me that. Even my grandchildren. It is great to see you, too. What brings you here?"

"I came to solve a mystery. I want to attempt to find out who really owns the old haunted house."

He lied again. Or, at least, didn't tell the whole truth.

"You're in luck. The county owns it. About three years ago, they hired Geoff. Remember him? He is the best title attorney in the county, to research it. When he finished, the county acquired it for unpaid taxes and some other legal reasons that are above my pay grade. Geoff also filed some detailed notes with the title as to his findings. So, with that being done for you, what are you going to do next?"

"Find out who lived there and why it was abandoned for so long."

Ron made copies of all of Geoff's notes. That night, he studied them carefully, charting a timeline of the property transfers. He learned the original owner was George Dawes Sr.

He made detailed notes to add to what Geoff had provided as an expert genealogist would do. He realized this would mean nothing to one not familiar with genealogy, so he simplified his findings in a spreadsheet.

1865--- George's son, George Jr, was living about 30 miles away from his father's place. Married with no children. ~Source, Post Civil War Census (PCWC).

1865--- Surrounding George Jr's property, the families were Smiths, Dickersons and, of special interest, widow Stella Windsor and three children. Note: All three were born pre-1864, the youngest born in 1863. ~Source, PCWC.

George Dawes Sr. had acquired his land by federal grant in 1820. It consisted of one entire section. That would be 640 acres, or one mile square. George had one son, George Jr, mentioned above, whose property was about 20 miles north of his father's.

Ron would learn George Jr was born in 1840. George Sr died in 1867 and his will left everything to George Jr. ~Source, Geoff's notes.

1870--- George Jr is now residing on the land his father owned, which he inherited. ~Source, will of Georges Dawes, Sr and 1870 Census.

1870--- Widow Windsor is now living again on part of the property George Jr inherited. Her marital status is not shown, but no male head of household is listed, and she now has an additional 2 children, for a total of five children. ~Source, 1870 Census.

Possible Conclusion: She had followed George Jr to the new location. At least two children born after being a widow.

1855--- Marriage record found: Josiah Windsor married Stella Tanny. ~Source, Lawrence County Marriage Records.

1862--- Josiah Windsor died, Oxford, Mississippi, after being wounded at the Battle of Corinth. Mustering pay does not reference wife, only an attorney representing his father. ~Source, Confederate Civil War Records.

Possible Conclusion: At least one of her first three children was born after Josiah's death. Josiah could have known this; therefore, no pay was left for her.

1882--- George Jr had sold most of the land he inherited, retaining 140 acres and a home located on the northern part of the property and the old house located on the southern part where Stella lived. ~Source, Geoff's notes.

Ron had read about the South during Reconstruction enough to know that poverty was rampant. It was especially harsh on widowed mothers with small children. Hardly anyone had money and, if so, not enough to share. It was not unheard of for a mother to compromise her morals to feed her children. In those days, it was certainly not accepted; but many knew it was a mother's ultimate sacrifice, prostituting herself to assure her children would survive. Could this be what had happened to Stella? Did she follow her clandestine lover? Or maybe she lived on the land Dawes had inherited as her means of feeding her children? What happened to her? What happened to Dawes? Why was her home abandoned and never sold or occupied?

The next morning, Ron returned to the Land Office. WeeWee seemed to beam as he came through the door.

"Hey there, Kojak. Still working on mysteries without any clues?"

"I still have mysteries, but I do have some clues, WeeWee. I guess I shouldn't call you that?"

She interrupted, "Call me WeeWee. It's ok. After all, you had a great deal to do with that."

"Ok then, WeeWee. Are there any Windsors living in the area today?"

"Sure, Heady Windsor Smith. She is the head librarian."

"Do you know her well?"

"Yeah, really well. Our kids grew up together. We thought at one time her son would marry my daughter. But I think you have personal experience with young love. Kinda fickle, wouldn't you say? I wish those two had married. My daughter couldn't have picked a bigger loser than the guy she chose. Followed in my footsteps, I suppose. Oh... I'm sorry, Ron. Yes, I know her well."

Ron tried to explain the scenario of who the father of Stella's children could have been. She got lost in his explanation, so he showed her his spreadsheet.

Then he asked her if she thought he could discuss that with Heady.

"Ron, you were always bold. There's nothing like a man who walks in and meets a strange lady and says, 'Guess what? Your grandpa was a bastard, a real bastard.' I suggest you break the ice first. But I'll call her and tell her that you are a good guy and you need some information. Ok?”

“That would be great. By the way, it does not appear you are having sweet dreams about that ex of yours. Has there been, or is there now, another? And, if not, let me get to the point - how about dinner tonight?”

“I have no sweet dreams about my ex. Yes, there have been others. And no, there is not now another. And finally, I would be honored to have dinner with you tonight. But, let’s get out of town. Being alone, I eat at all the local places too often. Since tonight I have an escort, let’s go somewhere. Dixie Springs, the Mallards, is open again. You remember that place?”

“You bet. Six-thirty? Oh, what’s your address?”

“Three doors away from where you are staying. I have a condo above the men’s store where you worked in high school.”

The dinner conversation was typical of two that had not talked in years. She asked about his wife, or ex-wife; and he had the same questions for her. He acted surprised, but she eventually married the Larry guy who took her to the haunted house the night she earned her nickname. Of course, he already knew that. He had spent his life investigating much more complex things than that.

“It lasted twenty years. He was married to his job and there was no time for me. Computers. He was on the cutting edge. We moved to Silicon Valley where he helped found a software company. It owned him. I didn’t. We have one daughter. In the settlement, I got 15% of the stock. Good move on my part. You can’t turn the computer on without seeing his company’s icon. I don’t have to work, to say the least.”

He was not as open with her but did divulge the basic truth. “Being married to a cop, any kind of cop, is tough.” She hated secrets. He could not divulge much of what he was doing. “The day after my son’s seventh birthday, I came home, and she was gone. I had been at work and missed his birthday. I think I missed them all. She took everything. Even the saltshakers that used to be on my mother’s table. You remember them, the ones that looked like windmills.

“She was good about me seeing our son, though. She asked for child support but no alimony, so I was not surprised when she married two months after the divorce. My son and I are close, and he says she is happy.”

"We need to get back," she said. I got you an eight o'clock meeting with Heady. So you would not have to be so blunt, I greased the wheel for you."

If ever anyone looked like a librarian, Heady was the model. Not at all unattractive, but just the librarian look. Hair swept back into a bun, glasses on a chain, thin, wearing a long skirt and flat shoes. She welcomed him into her office, shutting the door.

"Mrs. Smith, thank you for seeing me and I hope you can help me solve a mystery."

She interrupted, "No, thank you for pushing me toward what I have suspected for a long time. WeeWee told me what you suspect.

"I think you are on the right track. My dad's aunt all but told me as much. She said their dad, my grandfather, was not a Windsor. I even got curious as to the Windsor in the puzzle and found he died in 1862. My grandfather was born in 1877.

"I don't think the human gestation period is 15 years. My great-aunt also told me that his real father had the same first name as a famous president. I hear you think his name was George Dawes. Like George Washington?"

"It could be."

"How do we find out?" she asked.

"A little science and a little trickery. I want you to fill out three generations of your family tree. Use Ancestry.com. There is a place to put your suspected relative's name. Here you will put Dawes. Then send it in for your DNA analysis. Some Dawes relative is most likely looking for answers too. If it is a relative, they will match you. You will then know the grandfather was a Dawes, and the Dawes connection may take you to George. I think it will. It will take a few weeks."

Two nights later, Ron had not told WeeWee about the graves. There had been too much excitement about just making a possible family connection. After a light lunch at Betty's, they returned to the Inn on Whitworth. One of their favorite pastimes was sitting behind the plate glass window guessing if a passerby was related to a classmate, or maybe even the classmate them self. At this point, he told her about the graves.

"Have you told anyone else, Ron?"

"No."

"Who could they be?"

"I have some theories."

"What are they?"

"Well, assuming we are correct that she was being kept by Dawes and had children by him, I have this idea. Dawes got into financial trouble in the mid- to late-1880s. It is evident by delinquent tax notices and the fact he sold some of the land below market value.

"Probably by the mid-1880s, Stella's older children had grown up and left. Some of them would have been true Windsors and some Dawes.

"There is no record of when these deaths occurred or even if they are real graves or not. But I have a theory."

"Go on," she prodded.

"When times got financially bad, let's just assume that Stella and her two youngest were still living there. Dawes was no longer able to sustain them. I read many folks in those days died of pellagra. It was a horrible disease that affected both your body and mind. It was caused by the consumption of too much cornbread and little else. Death was imminent.

"I believe they died of this, or something similar, all in a short period of time and he buried them on the property. The small graves are the children, and the larger one is her. I believe that, to hide the shame, this second family lived reclusively. He never sold the property or allowed it to be occupied because he wanted the graves to never be found. He planted hedges and probably kept them filled with dirt until his death. He hoped no one would ever know he had another family."

Ron went home to Virginia with the intention of returning in a few weeks. It was obvious a romance had rekindled between he and WeeWee. Sooner than he had expected, there was a phone call. It was WeeWee.

"Ron, she got a hit! Heady got a hit! A Dawes lady is a third cousin, and she goes back to George Dawes."

"Wow. But somehow, I knew it. I will be down in a couple of days."

She didn't want to admit that she had missed him and looked forward to his return. She didn't know if the feeling was mutual, but strongly suspected it was. The first day he was back was a Wednesday. That was her afternoon off. As the sun set, they went to the old house. They entered and wandered their way to the room where, many years before, the casket had sat. Nothing was said. In a moment, he could see her tears glistening from the little light that still prevailed.

"Ron, what's your real interest in this old house?"

"I have an interest – some."

"It's more than that, Ron. And you know it.

"The night I saw you lying in that casket, I knew I had made a mistake. But then you caused everyone to start calling me WeeWee. I couldn't give you the satisfaction. I just wonder how life could have been for us."

He didn't answer, and they started toward the door of the room. She was slightly ahead of him, and he reached and took her arm. They turned toward each other. There was an awkward pause that seemed to last for a full minute. Then, he said, "My real interest, and reason for coming, was you. The land office, the mystery of the unknown ownership, and your employment there, all fit into a perfect puzzle to come back. To come back for you."

He took her face in his hands, lifted her chin, and they kissed. The kiss was even more passionate than the high school kisses of their youth.

When they reached the porch, there was little light. "You know, WeeWee, I don't think there is any reason in telling about these graves. Just let 'em be."

The two of them took pieces of lumber and leaves and covered the sunken holes. They hoped the bulldozer that was coming to wreck the house would permanently cover them over.

Julie "Weewee" Williams Wade
and Ron Ferguson
invite you to celebrate their marriage.
They will be receiving friends
at the Inn on Whitworth
from 7-10 pm
Saturday, October 12, 2019

THE BAPTISM OF TINA JO

It took me a few minutes, but the photo posted on social media looked familiar. Then I read the caption, *Old Swim Hole on Highway 51 South.* Like aging people, the years can change nature's terrain also; but, like seeing an acquaintance from the past, with a closer look, you wonder why you didn't recognize it to begin with.

How familiar I was with that place, and for so many reasons. Not the least was its connection to Tina Jo Brewer. Not that she was the first, because she was just one of many. I myself would be baptized in that creek, but that would be four or five years later.

The picture reminded me of my dad's comment, "This is a nice rocky bottom place to swim and baptize, but if they keep cutting timber near the banks, by the time you're my age, it won't be deep enough to piss in."

I considered that strong language for my dad to use and felt a little sacrilege that he was referring to our baptizing creek. Lots of sins had been forgiven by that water; it wasn't fair to say anything about pissing in it.

My daddy wasn't a preacher but, at that time, he was tall and strong. A lot of people asked him to baptize them. I think part of the reason was that my grandpa, who was the preacher, was too old and feeble to do the job. I am sure they feared that if he dipped them in the water, they may not come out. So, Daddy was a good choice.

Creek baptizings were a spectacle, a ritual you might say. Larger, more modern churches had indoor, heated baptisteries; but Jesus was baptized in a river, so some people wanted to follow his example.

If it was to be a creek baptizing, people tended to get motivated to be saved in the spring or summer. Obviously, the creek water was cold in the winter. To be truthful, it was cold in the summer, too, as it was fed by numerous springs from upstream. The warm spring weather brought people out. Some would bring picnic baskets to the occasion. There also would be gospel singing, which was a source of entertainment at the time.

I thought the whole process was somewhat archaic. Why did you have to embarrass yourself by getting drenched in a creek to be saved? The Methodists, Presbyterians, and even the Catholics didn't do that. Maybe when it came my time, I would join one of those churches.

The ceremony would start with a prayer and most likely a couple of gospel songs. Almost always one song would be "Shall We Gather at the River." After this, the repentant was led into the water holding on to my daddy's arm. Then, another prayer would be said leading to the submersion.

Back to Tina Jo. There was a larger than normal crowd there that day and I noticed the crowd consisted of more men than usual. I thought I knew the reason. The reason was Tina Jo. You could say, anytime she was around, she was the main attraction.

Tina Jo's appearance was somewhere between beautiful and sleazy. With a change of dress and more properly applied makeup, she could have been a model somewhere. Maybe, as she was that day, she could have been the bartender at the local country and western tavern. It needs no explanation that, if she leaned over the bar, she would have gotten big tips.

It had not rained in some time and the level of the water in the creek was low. The water, if it flowed at all, flowed slowly. The yellow or gold pollen had settled over the creek, as if to paint it gold. It was the only time I saw the phenomenon and I equated it with nature offering a special decoration for Tina's special day. I thought maybe Tina was going to be baptized in golden water. Is there a special meaning to that? I still don't know, but I remember it.

In conservative communities, women did not wear pants, especially for religious events; but for baptizing they most often did. This provided more modesty. After the event, they would go into Mr. Cleves's house that was located adjacent to the creek, change clothes, and reappear as the new Christian women they were. Usually, there would be applause, and some would become emotional to the point of tears.

Just before Tina Jo and my dad went into the water, it was my job to go into the creek and splash around to make sure there were no snakes. I would be on standby in the water with a stick, just in case one appeared.

Tina Jo did not disappoint. She wore a rather close-fitting white linen skirt with a like blouse. As she walked into the water, her clothing became transparent. I noticed the panic on the church ladies' faces, but the men were mesmerized. It got worse.

Dad went through the normal protocol. He asked her if she believed that Jesus Christ was the Son of God and died for the forgiveness of her sins.

She said yes.

Dad then leaned her backwards into the water, raised his left hand, and said, "I baptize you in the name of the Father and the Son."

As her upper torso came out of the water, it was obvious she was not wearing a bra. The cold water emphasized this.

Dad recognized this and, for reasons still unknown, he pushed her back under the water. He then said, "I baptize you in the name of the Father, the Son, and the Holy Ghost."

Maybe Dad thought the Holy Ghost would intervene and block the view of her upper torso. It didn't. It was as visible as if she had nothing on.

Believe it or not, something even worse was about to happen. I was following close behind as she and Dad waded from the creek. I saw it about the same time as all those watching did. It was obvious she didn't have panties on either.

There was more. As if she had not placed the highest indignity on the sanctimonious group already, there was a tattoo plainly visible on her rear. Debate would go on for weeks, arguing if it was a T for Tina or a cross for Christ.

I saw things differently. The gold pollen had seeped into the fabric of her clothing, and I saw what I thought was a religious miracle - a beautiful woman clothed in fine linen and gold. Others didn't see it that way.

There was commotion among the women. One, who had spread her lunch on a tablecloth, ripped the cloth from the ground, spilling the food. She rushed to make Tina Jo a respectable woman. It was as if all the women descended on her at the same time and, when she was deemed modest, they retreated to a gathering within my hearing distance.

"What kind of woman would be caught dead without underwear?" I heard one ask.

"What would the doctor say if she had to go to the hospital?" another said.

Another said she did it on purpose, just to get attention. There were few kind remarks.

This happened on a Sunday afternoon. It was the gossip on front porches and telephone party lines throughout the entire community for the next week and even for months to come.

I am sure Tina Jo was made aware of the dissension she had caused. Knowing a little about her, she may not have minded it. Maybe she did have a sleazy side, but she did come to church the next Sunday. She had been shunned by the pious, so she inconspicuously eased into the building and took a seat at the rear right side of the church.

As the church filled, not one woman sat on that side of the church. It was awkward; but what was to come would bring even more attention to the conflict.

Ministers do their best to prepare an appropriate sermon, but sometimes it is not received in that light. My grandfather started the sermon with several readings. The first:

Revelation 19:8

She was given clothing of fine linen, bright and pure. For the fine linen she wears is the righteous acts of the saint.

He then read Revelation 3:5

Like them, he who overcomes will be dressed in white. And I will never blot out his name from the Book of Life, but I will confess his name before My Father and His angels.

He didn't stop there, he quoted a few more scriptures mentioning white linen and gold. I don't think the ladies in the crowd heard any of them. They were hiding behind the hand fans given to the church by the local funeral home.

Unfortunately, the sermon did little to rectify Tina Jo's transgression. That was the last time she ever attended that church.

Tina Jo must have moved away; or, at least, I never saw her in person again. I am sure her absence was appreciated by most of the female congregation members.

Mrs. Fanny Flowers worked for a company called Luziers. They manufactured ladies' bras and I think they are still in business today. At that time, Mrs. Flowers would visit your home and, in its privacy, properly fit you. My mother used her services. I have no idea how long a bra lasts, but I think Mrs. Fanny came every year or so and Mother would order a couple, maybe three. The measurements were kept on file and, when the bras were delivered by mail, there would be a catalog showing other colors and designs that you could order based on your history the company had on file.

It was a few years after the baptizing. I was probably 18 by then, and Mother's order arrived in the mail. Inside was a magazine of other possible designs. It was in color, which was unusual for the time, and it featured real models. I guess you could say it was the nearest thing to a Playboy Magazine I had been exposed to, so I took it to my retreat and studied it carefully. On page two, there she was. Tina Jo, in living color. She had become a model, of sorts.

I would learn through an acquaintance of hers that she had made her way to Dallas and attempted to become a fashion model. She learned she was not the type needed at that time. The prototype was now the flat-chested, anorexically thin type, as portrayed by Twiggy. The Marilyn Monroe types were passeé.

As to her religious endeavors after she never attended our church again, I just don't know. However, I expect, knowing her, she continued to dress in white linen and delighted in being the main attraction.

THE CHAIR

Karon never knew her father. She was the only child of an only child and, when small, lived with her mother and grandparents. They lived in a comfortable environment and she received ample attention and more than just the necessities of life. Despite being fatherless, she not only survived, she thrived.

Mary, her mother, worked four hours a day at a small manufacturing plant and attended afternoon and night school at a nearby community college. She hoped someday to become a registered nurse. She was determined to be successful both as a mother and as a medical professional. Looking back, it could be her way of atoning for a mistake.

In the summer before Karon entered grade school, her mother had received her designation as an RN and moved the two of them to New Orleans. She had graduated top of her class. Ochsner Hospital was expanding and hiring the top personnel from both medical and nursing schools. Mary could make almost twice as much money there as she could back in her hometown. The two moved with the blessing and assistance of her parents.

It was in the first grade that it occurred to Karon that her household was different from some, or maybe most. That was when she first realized there was no father in her life.

She remembers the first time she questioned her mother. "Mom, why can't my daddy take me to school like Jennifer's does?"

It did not come as a surprise, as Mary knew it would be a question someday asked. Even knowing that, she was not completely prepared.

"Sweetie, your dad can't be with us, but that means I don't have to share my attention with anyone, and I can give it all to you." And that is what she did.

From time to time, Karon would make an inquiry into her paternal heritage and each time she would get an evasive answer. It is a women's nature, more than a man's, to keep inner secrets; and, at a young age, Karon realized this. She knew there was something her mom just didn't want to tell. After becoming a teenager, she never asked the question again. Mary advanced rapidly at Ochsner and Karon grew up a model child, succeeding in all her endeavors. After high school graduation, she attended LSU. She majored in accounting, married another accountant and, at some point in time, moved to Jackson, Mississippi, not far from where both she and her mother had been born.

Her mother never married, and Karon and Mary had an extremely close mother-daughter relationship. Often one or the other would catch the train from Jackson to New Orleans and visit. Both would make sure to press their faces closely against the window as the train passed through their old hometown. Mary especially loved it when the train would stop for passengers. It would give her an opportunity to scan the crowd on the street, as if she was searching for someone; and maybe she was.

The old man shuffled down the street. He had returned home after spending 55 years in a nearby city. If you asked him why he returned, he couldn't or wouldn't tell you. He had no reason to come back. The last days he had lived there in his youth were painful. She, the only one he had ever loved, had left him, and WWII had started. He had to join the service or be drafted. He reasoned it was more comfortable to sleep in a bunk than a foxhole, so he chose the Navy. His commitment at the time seemed like it would be an eternity. As his orders read, for the duration of the war plus six months.

As months, then years, passed by, the war continued. His homesickness dissipated, but his love for her still burned. Where did she go and why did she go? She could have at least said goodbye and given some explanation.

When the war was over, he was discharged in Chicago. He rode the Illinois Central train home. His parents' home was only a few blocks away from the depot and he had not told them he was coming. He would walk home when the train arrived. Maybe there was another reason he wished to walk. Her house was only one block out of the way, so he would make a detour. He had not been back in over four years. During that time, and the two months before he left, he had not heard one word from her.

Soon her house was in sight. The war had changed things. Did her family still live there? He recognized that her family had the same car they had before the war, so he knew at least they lived there. Then he saw the child's tricycle in the driveway. It was like he was stabbed in the heart with a blade of ice. He quickly made some mental calculations. A child lives in that house. She must have a child he reasoned. That is something he never considered. He was confused and crushed.

He arrived home from the military in December. He weighed his options. One was the GI bill. He could go to college and there was time for him to enroll for the second semester. He enrolled at Mississippi State and pursued a civil engineering degree. Later, he would graduate and be employed by the Mississippi State Highway Department. He would live most of his working life in Natchez. He never married. It would be years before he would ever come back to his hometown. He only had been back twice. Once, for his father's funeral, and two months later, for his mother's.

Now retired, he had decided to come back home. He was 75 years old. At least he had some siblings there and a few cousins. There would be someone he could keep an eye on and they on him. The town was no longer the same as it had been in his youth. When he left, all the shopping he needed to do was contained in about a four-block downtown area. Now there was an interstate highway; which, coincidentally, he helped build. Its construction came at a price. The town had moved toward it. Shopping for someone his age was no longer within walking distance and convenient. The Piggly Wiggly and the Sunflower Grocery no longer existed.

He rented a room in an old hotel that was in poor repair, but 55 years ago it had been the crown jewel of the community. He was a conservative spender, so he liked it being inexpensive.

Each day, on foot, he would extend the distance he explored from his room. One day, he had ventured a few blocks farther than usual; and there it was, in a consignment shop window.

He was sure. But, to make sure, he hurried back to his room. His chair was identical, just a little larger. He tilted it back. He remembered the day he took a wood burning set and lettered "His" on the bottom. He had lettered "Hers" on the smaller chair.

He hurried back to the consignment store and asked the shop owner if he could see the chair. She agreed. Then, he turned it upside down. Yes, it was there. "Hers."

"Where did this come from?" he asked.

"A client dropped it by a few weeks ago."

"Who was it?"

"I can't tell you sir, that information is confidential."

"Can you tell me how old she was?"

"Well, you are correct, it was a female. I shouldn't tell you, but she was about 55."

"Are you sure she was not older?"

"Yes sir, I am pretty sure."

The shop owner could tell he did not like her answer.

"I'll tell you what sir. I will contact her and give her your name and number. If she is interested, she can call you. Do you have a phone?"

"Yes, I have a phone. How much is the chair?"

"She wants $300 but she may take less."

"Do you deliver?"

"Yes sir, but that will be an extra $25 if it is here in town."

"Yes, just over at the Inez Hotel. So the total is $325?"

"No sir, there will be sales tax, so it will be $346."

"Do you take a credit card?"

"Yes sir, but we have to charge you an extra 5 percent."

He angrily replied, "Ok, how much now? I don't care how much it costs. I want that chair."

"That will be $363.30."

As he handed her his Visa, he remembered the day he and Mary had bought them. She paid ten dollars for his and he paid the same for hers. She and her mother had put new upholstery on both. It was one of the happiest days of his life. However, on this day, realizing she was probably no longer living, this was one of the saddest.

Later that afternoon, the shop owner's teenage son delivered the chair. The young man surveyed the old man's belongings. There were two chairs, the one he was bringing made three. There was an aluminum lawn chair with a TV tray beside it. This appeared to be the old man's favorite place. On the tray was a package of chewing tobacco and the TV remote. On one side of the room was a chest with four drawers; and on the other side, a large screen TV with a VCR attached.

The other chair looked identical to the one he was delivering, except it was larger. Both had the same upholstery, and both looked like they had seldom been used.

Three days later, his phone rang. "Mr. Higgins? I am Karon Moore. I understand you bought my chair and asked to contact me. May I ask why you are so interested in me and my chair?"

Again, the words "my chair" rang deeply in his mental interpretation. Why was it her chair? How did she get it? Why is it not Mary's chair?

Chocking back his resentment, he said, "I have a chair just like it only larger. I had a friend, Mary, that had one also."

Karon's demeanor and tone changed from lack of interest to one of a more intent, quizzical mode. "Did that Mary happen to be Mary Martin?"

"Yes, that's her."

"Mr. Higgins, I would like to talk to you. Can I come and see you Saturday? Will you meet with me? I am her daughter."

"Yes, let's meet on the bench in front of the bakery. Say 10 a.m?"

"Yes, I will be there."

It was Thursday. There was some reluctance and dread beginning to set in. For 57 years, he had nursed the emotional pain but had learned to manage it. It was still there but not all consuming. In his saddest moments, he could imagine that someday she would appear and come back to him. That was not her make up however, and he knew that. She is the one that left; walked away from a five-year relationship without so much as a goodbye. He, too, was a stoic type. Since that day in May of 1942, he had never inquired as to where she was; nor, as far as he knew, had she tried to contact him. Did he really want to awaken the painful giant inside him, the emotional tragedy that had followed him daily for 57 years? He had doubts. Now, with her being deceased, was this meeting with her daughter a blessing or a curse?

The small grey BMW convertible maneuvered into the vertical parking spot between the corner men's store and the bakery. It was a cool, comfortable day; and, in the south, there are only a few days that it's cool enough to let the top down on a convertible. It was down that day.

Before she even opened the door, he could see her well. Yes, she was Mary's daughter. He would have recognized her if he had passed her on the street. He was the only person on the bench that morning so recognizing him was obvious. He stood and waited for her to extend her hand. Southern ladies always extend their hand first. Her mother would have done that.

After a few cordial pleasantries, she said, "Mr. Higgins, I am curious as to your interest in the chair. You see, when my mother decided to downsize, we sold a lot of her things. She had a rather large shotgun style home in New Orleans, but in her new apartment things wouldn't fit. The chair that you purchased was the last thing she parted with. My husband carried it to his pickup to bring it to the store, but she stopped him. She asked him to place the chair on the ground beside the truck and then she sat in it.

"She seemed to drift into a dream world, then asked that we leave and let her be alone for a few minutes. She said she needed some private time. About a half hour later, she came inside. We could see that she had been crying. She said, 'Take the chair.'

"It was obvious the chair was important to her, but it was never mentioned again. Apparently, there is a story. Can you shed some light on it?"

It seemed to him the few years they spent together back then was an eternity. That was from the 7th grade until just after graduation in the 12th grade. Many things were very private. He did not know what he should tell her daughter that he had just met. He certainly would not tell her about the first and only time during their long courtship that they were intimate. That was only a few weeks before she left. He always wondered if their sin had caused her to leave. Was God punishing him? But why would he punish her? At church, he had heard God punished people for that. But why would God punish you for loving someone? He had loved her and, at the time, he was certain she loved him.

"Your mom and I dated from the seventh grade until graduation. Everyone knew, and we had our parents' blessings, that we would marry in the summer after graduation. Starting three years prior, on each gift giving occasion, we would give each other something that would contribute to us establishing our household. We knew things would be tough and finances would be limited. One year, I gave her a plate, knife, fork and spoon. She gave me the same. I still have that. On one occasion, she gave me a coffee pot and I gave her a toaster.

You see, we had it all planned out. I would go to college, she would work. She would go to nursing school while I worked. She would work until I got my masters or maybe my PhD. Then we would have children. We would have been almost 30, but it didn't happen that way."

"What happened, Mr. Higgins?"

"I don't know. Did she ever mention me?"

"My mother was a very private person. I don't even know my father's name. I know he was killed at Midway in 42. We both used her maiden name. Mother had secrets she never shared."

"Yes, I am sure she did."

After a few minutes of conversation, he had enough courage to ask the hard question.

"Tell me about her and when did she pass away?"

"Oh, Mr. Higgins, Mom hasn't passed away. She is very much alive."

If you had observed his demeanor when he heard those words you would have realized his life had changed forever. He bounded from the bench as if he were in his thirties and did not hesitate to ask, "Where is she?"

"She is in New Orleans. But she will be moving here in about a month. They are remodeling her apartment. She just wants to come back to her roots. There is a culture shock between New Orleans and this community. She always missed it, but never had the courage to come back. Once she told me something I didn't understand about this town. She said there are memories that are too tender to be brought to the surface on a regular basis. 'It's best I stay away,' she said. Somehow, last year she changed her mind."

"Where is her apartment?"

"Oh, she is combining four rooms at the Inez. The carpenters are making it a beautiful place. Just not big enough for the parlor grande, the buffet or the chair."

He was speechless. Then, almost inaudibly, he said, "I live in the Inez." They talked another half hour and Karon left.

For the first time in years, he went to the men's store on the corner and bought clothes other than khakis. He let the young proprietor advise him on what he should purchase. In his mind, what the young man picked out did not really appeal to him but, after all, he was buying for what would appeal to her.

He then went across the street to the barber shop. He had seen the ad. Grecian formula. Did they have Grecian Formula? Would it really remove the grey?

He knew where she would live. It was the only apartment with construction activity. He visited it several times each day. His anticipation and excitement grew as it neared completion. Had Karon told her about him? Surely, she had.

The apartment was complete. She would arrive at any hour, he assumed. He took the elevator to her floor at least a dozen times a day. Days passed, and she did not arrive. Then, one day, a moving van came and began to unload furniture into her unit. Surely, she would be there soon; but the van was unloaded, the furniture just stacked in the apartment and left with no Mary in sight.

Two days later, Karon's BMW parked in front of the hotel. There was still no sign of Mary. In the entry he stood, and she smiled as she saw the transformation that had occurred in him over the last month.

"Look at you Mr. Higgins. You got some snazzy duds on there. Lookin good, sir."

Almost rudely, he dismissed her compliment and answered with a question, "Where is Mary?"

"I just got a cell call from her. She will be here in thirty minutes. Can you help me take this to her apartment?"

"Surely," he said, as she handed him two bags of previously refrigerated groceries.

Karon was surprised to find the door unlocked, but more surprised at the large bouquet of flowers on a table with the other furniture in disarray.

"Where did those come from?" she asked.

"I bought them. It was a few days back and they are not as fresh as I had wished. I thought she may expect something since it has been so long."

"Mr. Higgins, she wouldn't expect anything. I haven't told her about you. I thought the surprise would be better. She will love the flowers. You remembered her favorite, chrysanthemums."

For years, he had suffered from a nervous stomach and the excitement of the day had intensified the symptoms. He would run back to his apartment and take some Pepto Bismol. Then, he would come back and wait.

Before he returned, Mary arrived and made her way to the apartment. Giving Karon a hug, her eyes locked onto the flowers.

"Who..." before she could continue, Karon interrupted.

"Stop right there, Mom. Turn around."

He stood in the doorway.

It was the most awkward moment of either of their lives. He walked toward her but paused just in front, waiting for her to extend her hand. She didn't. Another awkward pause and then she threw her arms around him, and they both sobbed uncontrollably.

As she regained her composure, she said, "Tim, my precious Tim. How many times have I dreamed of this moment."

Karon left the room, but in a few minutes she returned.

The three spent the afternoon arranging furniture. By late afternoon, most of Mary's pared down belongings were in place. It was obvious Karon kept moving some furniture to make space for something.

"Mr. Higgins, it's time."

He returned to his apartment and, in a few minutes, returned with the "Her" chair. There were more tears.

"Well folks, it's getting late, and I must get to Jackson. I have an audit in the morning. We got a lot accomplished and Mr. Higgins, you were a Godsend. I will leave the rest of the day up to y'all. Be good now."

That night, they went to dinner. The conversation was just as it had been when they were in high school. Both realized there were places they couldn't go. He never asked about Karon's father. He never asked about why she left. After all, it was not important. She was back.

For the next few years, they spent almost every waking minute with each other. Soon, he moved his chair into her apartment, and they would sit facing each other. She taught him the secret of making Sazaracs, a drink she had developed a taste for in New Orleans. In May, he made her Mint Julips to remind her the South consisted of more than just New Orleans.

They made a trip or two to the Big Easy, listened to music on Frenchmen Street, played tourist riding the street cars and the river boat President. They spent some fall days at Lake Lincoln and even went to a few hometown football games. The games were still in the same stadium where she led cheers as he sparingly played football. The stadium, the crowd, even the game had changed; but they accepted change because they had changed, too.

He spent most nights at her apartment. For breakfast, she would serve him in the dishes they had bought long ago. They were happy. All was forgiven. Karon would visit and became very fond of her mother's new old friend. He was no longer Mister Higgins, he was Mr. Tim.

They were older now and, on the occasions when they were under the weather, each would stay at their own place. His stomach disorder had continued to progress and was passed off by the physicians as IBS. On this day, it had been especially bad. He would spend the night at his place.

The next morning, she set the table for two and waited for him to arrive before she started the bacon and eggs. They were both early risers and, when he did not come down by 8 a.m., she called his cell. No answer. She went to his apartment, inserted the key, and felt resistance as she opened the door. She pushed hard and then she saw a foot lying near the opening. She called maintenance.

It appeared he had passed several hours prior. The key to her apartment was clutched in his hand.

In his will, he left most everything to Mary. At some point in time, while young, they had given each other a Sterling Silver hairbrush set. After his passing, she kept it, both his and hers, on her dresser. She also kept both chairs.

Karon noticed that her mother's health began to decline. She was not as jovial when they visited. It was as if, after Tim's passing, she had failed to thrive. After all, her life had come full circle. She no longer enjoyed traveling to Jackson or New Orleans and, as time passed, she seldom left her room. Karon visited often.

One afternoon, as Karon started to leave, her mother asked her to stay for a while longer. She asked her to sit in "His" chair and she sat in "Hers." They faced each other.

"Sweetheart, I thank you for accepting me as your mother and the decisions I made not to tell you the full story of my past or of your father. It is a sad story and one that I am ashamed of. You are my blessing and, of course, I am not ashamed of you.

"You see, Tim and I dated through high school. It was a foregone conclusion that we would marry, and I had all the intentions of doing so.

"Things were different then. Honestly, I am not sure that we were any more moral than now. We were just self-righteous, or pretended we were. Pre-marital sex was rampant, but you denied it. It is kind of hard to talk to you about this, but about two months before we were to get married and just after graduation, we had our very first and only totally intimate encounter, if you know what I mean.

"We had waited so long, but we still regretted it. But it was done.

"About a week after that, Mother asked me if I would go to Hattiesburg and help care for her sister who was extremely ill. I loved Aunt Jane and just spending Friday and Saturday night with her was not a problem. I knew I would miss Tim though.

"The very day I arrived in Hattiesburg, a car pulled into the next driveway. The most handsome man I've ever seen, dressed in a Marine officers uniform, stepped from the back car door only feet away from where I was unloading my things.

"Karon, I had a feeling like I had never had before or since. My heart sank and I got chill bumps just looking at him. Then he dropped his duffel bag and ran to assist me. His hand just barely touched mine. It gave me chills. Looking back, you would call it infatuation, but now I know it was a mistake.

"Within minutes, he asked me to go have a soda later that evening. I meant to say no, but the words were uncontrollable. My mouth said yes.

"The next night, we went to a movie. Sunday evening, I went home feeling so guilty, but I could not tell Tim what had happened, although I know I should have.

"The next weekend, back in Hattiesburg, that Friday night he asked me to go to a drive-in movie. I will never forget, we saw *Casablanca*. That is when he kissed me. It was a thrill like none other I have ever had. The only person I had ever kissed was Tim.

"The next night, we went for a ride in the country. He took me to his grandparents' home, a beautiful place on Black Creek. They were deceased, but the family kept the place as a weekend retreat.

"We sat in the swing on the front porch as the sun set and then it began to lightly rain. He told me about his military obligation. He was a Marine Lieutenant, a fighter pilot. He said he would be flying a Grumman Wildcat. This sounded so exciting to me. Then he told me that he was being shipped to the Pacific in two days.

"He was a big, tough Marine, but he was sad. He said he had a premonition he wouldn't return. Then he kissed me, more passionately this time than ever before. He kept emphasizing that he wouldn't come back alive and that God had sent me to him as a present for giving his life for his country. I made a mistake, a bad mistake. You are the product of that mistake, but remember, you are my blessing. As it turned out, I would learn later, he was shot down on June 7, 1942, on his very first mission.

"I had no idea I was pregnant, but I couldn't face Tim. I felt so guilty. I chose to run away. I ran away from Tim, the Marine that was dead, and

I never even gave Tim a reason why I left. It was very unfair. But then, I realized something was wrong. Soon I realized I was pregnant. Then I was glad I had not told either of them.

"I found out that Tim was leaving for the Navy in a few days. Knowing his personality, I knew he wouldn't chase me. He respected and loved me too much. Oh, how miserable I was. Before Tim died, he told me that it had never crossed his mind that there was another man, until he saw the tricycle.

"That's enough for one night, but you know most of the story. You really know more than I had planned to tell you. Maybe next week we will talk more."

The conversation haunted Karon. There were so many questions. Her mother had not, or would not, reveal her father's name. Tim loved her so much, certainly he would have forgiven her; he may have even thought that he was Karon's father, and they could have all been a normal family. But, no, she reasoned, because her mother loved him so much, she had rather leave than tell him or deceive him.

When the phone rings at two in the morning, it is never a good thing. Karen's phone rang and the ID said King Daughter's Hospital. She was told she should come as soon as possible. Her mother had suffered a stroke and the outcome didn't look good. She left immediately.

When she arrived, she was directed to the chapel. She needed no explanation.

After the funeral and over the next several weeks, Karon closed out her mother's apartment. She sold many items, gave some away, kept a few, such as the chairs, and packed some of her mother's personal items. One item was the silver brush set. First, she put her mother's set in a box. Then she picked up Tim's. She says now that she knew something was special about his brush. It is as if it generated heat in her hand. She saw his silver hair, pre- and post-Grecian formula, in the bristles. Well, it was worth keeping. He was the nearest thing to a father she had ever had.

One night, she awoke from the most realistic dream she had ever had, one of those detailed dreams. At sunup, she examined his brush carefully.

With a comb, she removed all the hair from the bristles. It cost $1,000 but she had to know. She sent it off along with the hair from her own brush.

Six months later, the letter came. She nervously tore into it. She carefully scanned the disclaimers before getting to the results. Her eyes focused.

Based on our extensive examination, with the DNA technology present today, the genetic makeup shows that this is a father and daughter match. The odds are so positive that the unlikely probability is not calculated.

Now she knew. Her dad's name was Tim Higgins.

Two days later, she traveled to the mortuary. She had a marble tag made to be attached to his gravestone. It read, MY DAD.

MAKING A LIVING

Moonshining means making illegal whiskey. The stills were usually deep in the woods so the revenuers (federal agents) could not find them. Bootlegging was the illegal sale of alcohol, whether the alcohol was illegally made or not. Both were a way of life in the South and were economic forces. We learned this early in our childhood, about the time we learned the Ten Commandments.

Robert and William Eades were brothers. Being brothers is basically where their similarities ended. Robert was an achiever. William would become what you would call a "ne'er-do-well."

They grew up poor, but Robert seemed to always be at the right place, at the right time, with the right work ethic. William, on the other hand, was not as fortunate, and ethics were not in his personality.

At nineteen years of age, Robert got a job at a local funeral home. Within ten years, he owned it. William worked odd jobs, but he was mostly interested in automobiles. If he had a talent, it was body and fender work. If he had the frame of an auto, he could almost completely rebuild the body. Sometimes, however, this talent was misdirected.

At some point in time, Robert decided to buy a new hearse for his mortuary business. William wanted the old one, and Robert practically gave it to him. There is not a lot of value in a used hearse.

Before long, a new, modern paint job made the vehicle even more beautiful than it had been when it was new. William contemplated selling it to a family-owned funeral home in a smaller town as a backup. Then, he had an idea.

William had no interest in moonshining. It was too much work. Bootlegging was much easier, and he had a plan. Alcohol, except for beer, was illegal in Mississippi. Moonshining was big business but selling bonded whiskey (whiskey that was not homemade) was also profitable. Bonded whiskey meant the federal taxes had been paid, which satisfied the federal agents. They were not interested in getting into the state's business of enforcing the law against those who sold alcohol that was federally legal.

Rather than sell moonshine, an entrepreneur may go to Louisiana and buy bonded legal alcohol, transport it back to Mississippi, and resell it. The federal taxes had been paid, so the only law he was breaking was state or county law.

Enforcing temperance morality was left up to the local sheriffs. Most of them could be coaxed into turning their head for a monthly stipend, up to the point that the moral majority (churches) put pressure on them. Then they would have to make an arrest.

As a rule, bootleggers did not mind an arrest by the sheriff. It was a fine they could easily afford, and they got free newspaper advertising, letting everyone know they were in business. William did not feel that way. He did not plan to get caught in the first place.

The shiny hearse was used to go to the Louisiana state line, load the whiskey, and transport it back to one of several counties. The whiskey would be in pint or half-pint bottles, placed in a false floor that William had welded to the bottom of the hearse.

Eventually, there was a rumor of what was going on, so additional security measures had to be taken. That is when William hired his nephew Bob, Robert's son.

Bob was more like William than he was like his father. He did not work much; but, when he did, he worked at the funeral home for his father. William made him the perfect offer. All Bob had to do was ride on the passenger side of the hearse and look sad. He would play the part of a grieving relative.

If someone came near, especially law enforcement, he would start crying. He was even known to wail so loudly that people in passing cars could hear him. He had a jar of sliced onions to produce tears if needed, and a box of Kleenex. William and Bob would borrow a coffin from the funeral home and put it in the back, often filling it with booze. This allowed them to transport more contraband and made their trips more profitable

They were stopped a couple of times but, when the officer saw the tears in Bob's eyes, and the coffin, no questions were asked. This went on for some time. They were making big money.

Eventually, a new sheriff was elected. He was a candidate of what would be called the "religious right" and vowed to close all alcohol sales, gambling, and dancehalls. There was nothing illegal about dancing, but religious constituents considered it sinful, so he would close them down based on the loud music disturbing the peace. The election of the new sheriff was a religious victory. The largest church in the county boasted on live radio that it was the turning point of ridding sin from the community. The minister reminded the listeners that first comes alcohol, then comes dancing, then comes fornication, then comes divorce, and then we have fatherless, hungry children.

William realized he had to be vigilant and proactive in hiding his activities. About three months after the election, he was tipped off that he would be stopped and searched by deputies. He gave the tipster $20 and thanked him.

His biggest delivery to date was scheduled for Thursday. He and Bob had a plan.

Miss Minnie Stanton had died about two weeks earlier. She was an old maid, and her only living relative was a niece that lived in Maine. The niece contacted the funeral home to make arrangements. She told Robert that it was unlikely she and her family could make the interment, but please give her two weeks, until that Friday, to attempt to make the trip. If she did not make it before Friday, the funeral home should go ahead and bury her. The niece would send the money.

It was Thursday, and no one from Maine had arrived. Bob took a cheap coffin from the coffin room and attached a false bottom in it. In the floor of the hearse and in the bottom of the coffin, he placed pints of Ancient Age, Jack Daniel's, Maker's Mark, Beefeater Gin, and Johnny Walker Scotch. It was all good stuff, basically legal as far as the Feds were concerned, but would be a feather in the cap of the new sheriff if seized.

After the whiskey was packed, Miss Stanton's body was placed in the coffin. William had added additional springs to the hearse, as to not tip off anyone by the vehicle looking overweight. They left at 9 a.m. By 9:30, they were almost to the Lawrence County line. That's when the flashing red light appeared in the rear-view mirror.

Basically, William detested all law enforcement; but when he saw Deputy Billy Joe step out of his car, he seethed with anger. Billy Joe had been married to William's sister and put a mortgage on property their father had given to her for a home. Billy Joe then divorced the sister. She could not pay the mortgage, so Billy Joe bought it at a Sheriff's sale for pennies on the dollar. They had not spoken since.

"William, your goose is finally cooked. We know what you've been doing with this ole hearse. You can't fool us," Billy Joe sneered.

William didn't answer.

"Open up the rear end of this whiskey wagon and let me inspect it."

William did as he was asked.

"How do I open the lid on this coffin?"

William handed him a key.

"Be careful, we been waiting two weeks on her family to bury her and she's a little ripe."

"Yeah, smells like 90 proof I bet."

By this time, Billy Joe had wedged himself into the hearse in a tight spot between the side of the vehicle and the coffin. He weighed about 275 pounds and had to lay on his side to fit.

He inserted the key, turned it, raised himself up on his arm, but still could not see inside the coffin. He reached inside the coffin, expecting to feel bottles of whiskey. Instead, he felt the dead flesh of a 97-year-old woman.

He screamed and worked himself out of the hearse as if he were a gymnast, wiping his hand on his uniform.

"Get the hell out of here, William! And you better not tell anyone I put my hand on a dead person."

William had the idea that this brush with the law was a little closer than he wished, so he decided not to continue the delivery, but to return to the funeral home and unload the whiskey and the body.

Robert was on a trip and management of the facility was left to his assistant, Troy, and to a lesser degree, Bob. On arrival, William and Bob noticed the staff was in a buzz.

"Bob, we got problems," Troy said. "Miss Stanton's niece and her family just arrived from Maine, and they want to view the body. We can't find it."

"No problem. You know the weather is supposed to be stormy tomorrow. The weather is always bad when we bury an old person. I put her in the hearse, the old one, because I thought it was more in keeping with her age and era. Since she had no family present, I wanted to give her a proper sendoff. I had given up on the family coming, and if they were not here by late afternoon, I was going to bury her."

Miss Stanton's niece heard this. She thanked Bob for being so thoughtful and said there would be no reason to open the casket or remove it from the vehicle. The family would just accompany it to the grave site.

In addition to the niece and her family, William, Bob and two funeral home employees would attend the burial. There was no need for the normal entourage of pall bearers. Miss Stanton didn't weigh 80 pounds anyway.

The grave was some distance from a suitable parking spot for the hearse. Bob and William supported one side of the coffin and the two attendants the other. As soon as they attempted to lift the casket, the attendants knew something was wrong. It was like laying to rest a four-hundred-pound body. They struggled, but finally made it to the mechanical device that was already in place.

This appeared to be the end of William's whiskey trade, but it wasn't to be.

Two months later, the sheriff arranged a private meeting with William. They agreed on a business arrangement.

Soon, some of the best liquor was being sold at some of the best dance halls with some of the best bands in the state.

Every other January, the sheriff's wife got a nice, shiny, new car.

ELI AND EMMA

If you're looking for a bedtime read that will give you sweet dreams, this story isn't for you. If you close your eyes to the bad things that happen in life, you will not like this story. If you embrace your prejudices to the point of pretending things didn't happen, maybe you should read another story.

I feel, however, that many of our social problems emanate from our unwillingness to face the reality of our past; more so, the reality of the dark side of our past. Something can be gained from coming to grips with the bad and ugly as well as the pleasant and the good.

I have heard a lot of axioms in my life and some of them I believe to be startlingly true. For every happening, there is a cause; or, more scientifically, for every action there is a reaction. Certainly, the events of October 1907 were the culmination of previous actions and would be typical of happenings that would have future repercussions. As you will see, I specifically point to the breakdown of the family unit.

There are a few other characters in this story, but the main characters are Eli and Emma. They are the exact opposite of each other. Eli is black, Emma is white. Eli is 53 years old, Emma is 17. Until that event, Emma had a loving, caring family. Eli doesn't remember having a family.

I think I'll tell you about Eli first. I have no specific reason for doing so, because both are equally important. There is no story without both Eli and Emma, and what happened on that October morning. For some reason, I feel that Eli is the more complicated personality. I feel that studying Eli's history is key to understanding so many social problems of the 19th and 20th century.

Eli was eleven years old when the Civil War ended. His ancestors had lived for 80 years on the Williams' plantation. The owner then, Mr. Zeb Williams, was known to be a kind master. He demanded respect and obedience but never used the whip. Unfortunately, in 1858, he died with the fever, and the management of the plantation fell into the hands of his twenty-five-year-old son, Zacharias Williams. Of course, he was called Zack or "Masser Zack" as the slaves would say.

Zack Williams was not the businessman his father was, nor was he the manager of personnel that his father had been. Whether you are in a 21st century corporate office or a slave on a 19th century plantation, you are aware of management dysfunction. The slaves knew there was trouble in the air long before the first shot was fired at Fort Sumter. They could feel the resentment and disdain Zack felt for them. It seemed to increase each time he went to a community meeting.

Those were the meetings where the possibility of war and secession from the United States were discussed. More importantly, those meetings shared the news of the slave uprisings. It was told that, in some cases, entire white families were butchered with pitchforks – men, women, and children. Zack began to plan.

He reasoned, for his slaves to plan a successful uprising against his family, it would have to be due to their trust and familiarity with each other. In order to limit the possibility, he would sell some of his slaves and purchase others to take their place. It would be the technique of divide and conquer. This would break up families and the familiarity and trust the slaves had with each other. Before Eli's mother gave birth to Eli, Eli's father was sold to the Parker plantation in St. Francisville. This was the first time a family on the Williams' place had been sold apart. I believe that this practice, and similar ones, would greatly contribute to the happenings that were to come.

Eli

When Eli was six years old, the war started. His mother was sold to a farmer down river. Eli was not allowed to go with her and was given to another slave household on the plantation for them to raise. He never saw his mother again.

The ending of the war meant little to him. He had been too young to do much work, and the concept of slavery or freedom was beyond his comprehension. More importantly, he was adrift in a sea of suffering humanity, harnessed with poverty, as he had never learned the art or skills of farming, or any other trade for that matter. He was not invited to stay and sharecrop as many were. At eleven years of age, he was a vagabond in the countryside; a drifter without means, without direction, and helpless, if not hopeless.

He lived off the land and begged for handouts as he drifted. Eli was almost a feral child. He slept in abandoned sheds, in the open, in the woods, or in crude shelters he made from fallen trees.

When he was fifteen, a stolen hog was found butchered near his campsite. The assumption was that he had done it. He was stripped, spread between two trees, and whipped by a group of local men. They left him tied and bleeding; he was not discovered for three days. The ants had covered his body and were thriving on the dying flesh and sweetness of his blood.

Some of the women in the community heard about his plight and, accompanied by their sons, tended to his wounds. They provided him with clothing and food until he was well enough to travel. Then, he was ordered to move on. Now Eli was not only a homeless drifter, but he had also become filled with resentment and hatred for anyone white. He became labeled as a troublemaker and a thief.

Psychologists will tell you that behavior is learned, not inherited; but I think some tendencies toward behavior are passed on. If that is the case, then there is reason enough to understand the personality that Eli developed. For the next few years, he had numerous brushes with the authorities; some were most likely his fault, but some were just attributed to him because of who he was and his reputation.

Oluda

In the 1740's, Eli's great-grandmother, Oluda, was captured and sold to the slave traders at Badagry, Nigeria. The description lists her as "a fit female, about twenty years old," healthy, with good teeth and apparently good breeding stock. An examination tended to indicate she had previously given birth, but no child is mentioned as being present with her when she was taken.

Oluda is further described as tall and thin with more than average size breasts, a symbol at the time of being a good breeder. Her description says her skin "has a healthy sheen" and her teeth are perfect and white. The traders knew she would bring a high price at auction in New Orleans.

A woman's beauty can lead to bad fate or good luck. She was holed in the bowels of the ship like all the rest of the dozens of slaves that were being transported to New Orleans. There, they would just subsist, chained, with minimal food and water. They would lie in their own waste until the stench got such that they were brought topside, and their quarters were rinsed with fresh seawater. They, themselves, were drenched in the brine and returned to the hole.

About two weeks into the voyage, during the second cleaning of the hole, she was kept back and not allowed to return. She was washed again and then confined to the deck. There, she was assaulted by as many as ten seamen almost every night until they reached New Orleans.

When she was put on the auction block, she was dressed in nothing but a waist cloth. No one, except possibly she, knew she was pregnant. She was purchased by the owner of a small plantation upriver from New Orleans. He was not pleased when, after the purchase, he found out she was pregnant. He wanted her for breeding purposes and already had plans for who he would mate with her. He was hoping for a strong male, as he intended to expand his land holdings.

He was even more disappointed when he saw the baby was of white ancestry. This is not at all what he wanted. It was believed that slaves who mixed with whites produced children that were inferior in strength. Their lighter color also made them less obedient, as even at a young age, they knew they were different and should be privileged. From these roots came the elements of rebellion and anarchy.

All this is known because Mr. Duplessis, her first owner, kept good records on the lineage of his slaves, just as he did the lineage of his livestock. He wanted to guard against too much close inbreeding. This mixed-race child, a girl, was sold to the Williams family when she was fifteen. These ancestral records were sent with her, which provided little that could not be seen by her skin color. The Williams family kept similar records. This child would become the grandmother of Eli.

Annag MacGruen

About 1780, Annag MacGruen and his wife, Cairistiana, arrived in America. It is not known if these were given names or ones they adopted due to their religious beliefs. Annag was a well-educated, Scottish Presbyterian minister. The name Annag means merciful, and the name Cairistiana means a Christian woman.

The young couple migrated to the Philadelphia, Pennsylvania area where Annag set about advancing the Presbyterian doctrine and belief. One of his first sermons was titled, "The Meaning of Presbyterianism." Little is known about this sermon, but it put forth that John Calvin's belief was that the greatest threat to Christianity was greed and the desire to acquire wealth, fame, and pleasure over their desire to serve God. It was as if he was foretelling the future of his descendants.

Annag's offspring followed in his footsteps and stayed learned and faithful ministers of the Presbyterian Church. Their names became more American, and their last name was shortened from MacGruen to Green. His great-grandson, William, moved to the South and established a prosperous Presbyterian congregation among the plantation owners in the Driftwood region.

One of the unwritten tenants of Presbyterianism is patriotism. Their prayers, their sermons, and (even today) their music exude a patriotic ambiance that is almost spiritual. This basic belief would change the course of history for William Green.

As the talk of secession increased, his sermons were more and more based upon the importance of loyalty to the Union. In his mind and in his heart, just as his father's and grandfather's before him, he had not been able to justify slavery with his religious convictions.

As the probability of secession neared, his congregation justified their actions as patriotism to their state, the South, and their cause.

The elders approached him with the outline of what his sermon was to be. It was to be based on Galatians 3:18, *There is neither Jew nor Gentile, neither slave nor free, nor is there male or female. For you are all one in Christ Jesus.*

The next Sunday, all the slaves from the surrounding area were brought to church and baptized in the nearby creek. They were then told they were no longer slaves, but free in Christ Jesus. Nothing else in their lives changed, however.

Being a pastor would never have the same meaning for William after that day. His feelings for his profession changed when the same elders asked him to base his sermon on a list they provided him:

~ Abraham was a slave holder.

~ Abraham was ordered not to free his slaves, but to circumcise them.

~ The Laws of Moses did not abolish slavery, but regulated it.

~ Christ received slaveholders as believers.

~ Paul told slaves to be content in their lot.

William knew he could not preach that way, but he would continue his duty. If war came, he would be needed; if for no other reason than to console the mothers and widows of those who might be killed. This he did.

After the war, he was never comfortable in the pulpit. He would not compromise what he believed to satisfy the wishes of his congregation. He would make a career change. The South was rebuilding. With the carpetbagger rule, there were few to be trusted. He could be trusted. He formed a farmers' co-op with himself as the manager. It prospered.

In 1875, he purchased (at a very fair price to the farmers) the assets of the co-op. Green Hardware and Farm Supply was established. His oldest child and only son, Benjamin, seemed to have the same business keenness as his father. However, he did not have the patience and humility that his father had. There was nothing ministerial about him. It was as if the words of his grandfather, Anaag, were written for him. He was filled with greed, pride, and ambition.

Benjamin wanted desperately to advance in politics. He used every avenue to speak before people to his advantage. It was evident his speeches did not carry the sincerity and humility that his father's had. He was not always truthful; nonetheless, in those conflicting times, he said things the public wanted to hear.

Most annoying to Benjamin was the unfairness the carpetbaggers placed on the white citizenry. They put slaves he had known as a child in government to rule over him. This he resented. He began to form a deep prejudice against the freed slaves.

It cannot be denied that he and his father would not only be successful, the business was successful beyond expectations. Soon, a gin and grain storage were added, along with a railroad spur connecting this agrarian community to the rest of the world to export crops.

By the turn of the century, the timber industry was in full swing, and large mills were building small railroads (dummy lines) deep into the forest. You could buy a locomotive at Green's Hardware and Farm Supply.

Emma

Emma was William and Sue Beth's only other child. She was eight years younger than her brother, Benjamin. Given all the attention and all the benefits of affluence, she developed into a beautiful, talented young lady. She was described as a sweet girl and, since her mother's death the year before, had assumed some of the duties her mother had held in the community. She planned to go to college the next year and fulfill her dream of becoming a teacher. Those plans would change.

On an October Saturday morning in 1907, she left on her prize horse, Vicksburg, to ride to her grandmother's home some two miles away. It is something she did almost every Saturday. At some point in the day, Vicksburg returned riderless to his barn.

It was just assumed that she had not tied him well at her grandmother's house, something had spooked him, and he had found his way back home. There was no cause for concern, until it began to get dark. When it was learned that she had never arrived at her grandmother's, panic went through the community.

Search parties were formed and tracking dogs were brought from the county penal farm. It was almost midnight when she was found. She was about 100 yards off the road near a ravine. Her clothes were mostly torn away, there was a bad gash on her head, and she was unconscious.

It was obvious that she had been sexually assaulted. She was carried home and a logging train was dispatched to bring the nearest doctor. The doctor did not leave her side for forty-eight hours. Late the second day, she regained consciousness.

She told the authorities she remembers Vicksburg raring up, but she remembers nothing else. She did not see her attacker, nor did she have knowledge of the assault. That did not keep the neighbors from searching the area for the possible perpetrator.

Three years prior, Eli had settled about two miles from where the assault took place. The rumors had always been that he was untrustworthy, but there had been no incidents since his arrival. He supported himself by weaving baskets that he made from white oak strips.

Near where Emma was found were freshly cut stumps and limbs from several small white oak trees. They could not have been cut more than two days prior.

Benjamin called a community meeting of men only. At first, the crowd was peaceful. But, within a few minutes, the crowd was stirred into an angry mob. Benjamin had tried and convicted Eli of the assault on his sister. The crowd started to Eli's house.

Word got back to William of the justice, or lack thereof, that was in process. He ran as fast as he could toward Eli's shack. By the time he arrived, Eli was being beaten by Ben and two of his friends. William yelled, "Stop, let the law run its due course!"

Those were his last words. William grabbed his chest and immediately slumped to the ground. Temporarily, the lynching was halted. Seeing that reviving William was hopeless, Benjamin turned toward Eli with even more vengeance.

A rope was produced and placed around Eli's neck. The other end of the rope was thrown over a limb. Eli was hoisted into the air. As he hung there in pain, Benjamin built a fire beneath him. As the flames climbed, the rope was pulled, lifting Eli higher so he could get the full effects of the flames for a longer period.

Thankfully, someone had mercy. A shot was fired, striking Eli solidly in the head, instantly killing him. Maybe the shooter was the only honorable person in the mob.

The mob ambled away, leaving Eli hanging. A buggy was brought, and William's body was carried home for the preparation of burial. It would be two days before Eli's body was retrieved. His neighbors, who prior had been too frightened to come out of their homes, took Eli and buried him.

Emma healed rapidly for a while. Then she began to regress. Mornings were extremely difficult, and the smell of breakfast cooking made her nauseous. It was determined that she would travel to the doctor on the train the next day.

It had never crossed her mind and, when the doctor gave her the news, he had to explain the situation to her... She was pregnant.

The only family member with whom she could share the news was her brother Benjamin, who was now head of the house and running the family business. Again, she was naïve. She had no idea how he would react, and certainly was not prepared for his actions.

She would be forced from the house. No sister of his would have a baby fathered by a slave. He gave her two hundred dollars and a mule that was 15 years old. He told her to never be seen in those parts again.

It was December 1, 1907 when she walked out of the comfortable, luxurious home that had been hers all her life. She was traveling to a place, but where, she did not know; how she would survive, she had no idea. She had taken several ham stuffed biscuits and a jar of molasses.

She headed south. The day was cold, and January would be colder. She heard that it was warmer farther south. If she could just get to New Orleans. She had heard that it never snowed in New Orleans.

The first night, she found an abandoned shed not far from the road. The next morning, she awoke to find the mule had died. She was now on foot. New Orleans was a long distance away.

After the third day, she had no more food. She kept walking and, finally, in an almost-dream state, she saw the smoke from a chimney in the distance. With her last bit of strength, she stepped on the porch. That is the last thing she remembered.

Bessie

A day later, Emma awoke. She was in a warm bed and a large woman was standing over her. She felt strange garments on her. They were scratchy, not soft as the ones she was accustomed to. The woman held a bowl that had a steaming substance in it.

"You's almos dead when you comes to my poach, chil'. Who be you anyhow, and where you come from?"

"I am Emma Green and I am from Darby. I mean, I was from Darby. I have no home now."

"Where you headed, honey chil'?"

"I don't know," and she began to cry.

"You hush up that cryin. You can tell me later, but nows you gots to eat. You's at Bessie's house."

Emma had forgotten how good boiled chicken and broth could be. The cornbread was good too. She wondered about her future. What would be the future of her child?

It was the next day before she told Bessie the whole story. Bessie listened without saying a word.

Finally, when Emma finished, Bessie shook her head. "Colored man, you say? This ain't good. You say his name be Eli. Eli Williams? I heard of him, kind of a bad one, I hear. I ain't got no sympathy for him the way he did you, honey chil'. If you askin me, he gots what he deserved.

"Now, us gots to take care of you and dat baby. You's welcome to anything I gots. Dat baby be comin' about June or July. I gots enough canned stuff to gets us by. I gots a cow, and I gots plenty chickens. If I plant an early garden and if the weather be warm, we's have fresh vegetables to keep you going till you birth dat baby. Don't you worry, honey chil'."

As the months passed, Bessie and Emma became the best of friends. Bessie told Emma that she and her husband had done good and made that little homestead until he died of the flu back in 1900. She did okay, though; never been hungry or cold.

The Baby

It was June and Bessie had been in the garden all day, hoeing the vegetables and packing water. Emma was way too far along to be of any help. When she stepped on the porch, Bessie could hear her. The sound progressed from sobs to screams. At first, Bessie didn't even go inside. She went to the well and drew plenty of water and then to the woodpile to get some firewood. It was time.

If Emma had any luck at all, it was that the birth was relatively easy. Bessie made a big pot of sassafras and made Emma drink it. She said it would make her sleepy and ease the pain. Before she dozed off, Bessie said, "Well, it's a boy, but it be a surprise."

In a few minutes, the word surprise registered with Emma. "A surprise? What do you mean, Bessie? Is my baby okay?"

"Yo baby fine, and guess what? It's a white baby, too. Ain't a bit of dark in this chil'."

"How can that be, Bessie?"

"Honey chil', it mean that Eli was not the one who did this to you. Some white man did it. Low down, lower dan a slave. I hope somebody cuts his man off."

Emma was confused. This opened a whole different avenue of opportunities for her. When she got stronger, she would go back home and surely her brother would accept her and her child. Surely.

It had been a month since the baby came. He was healthy and she was too. It was July now. She would head back home next week. Bessie had arranged for a friend with a buggy to take her.

The Saturday before Emma left, there was a knock on Bessie's door. Opening the door, there stood Benjamin and his best friend, Nathan. Emma could not wait to show Benjamin that her baby, his nephew, was white.

As soon as she saw him, she knew he was not there to apologize. "I will not have a baby in my family with black blood. Give me the little bastard," he said.

"Look Brother! He is white. He has red hair."

Benjamin's attitude softened. "How can that be? We know it was done by Eli."

"Brother, it couldn't have been. I never knew who did it. I was unconscious."

He asked Nathan to leave, allowing him to speak with his sister alone. "Emma, if this gets back to Darby, they will know we lynched an innocent man. That can't happen. I could get arrested. We have to get rid of the baby."

"What do you mean 'get rid of the baby'?"

"I will take the baby to New Orleans and give it away. I have told everyone you have been in Europe to recuperate. No one knows you were pregnant. Get him ready to travel. Don't leave any sign that he has been here."

"No! He's my baby."

"The longer he stays here, the more you will get attached."

Bessie, who had been in her garden, was now listening from the back door. She came in, armed with a fire poker.

"You's ain't takin that young'un nowheres. You gits, and don't you come back."

Surprisingly, Benjamin and Nathan left.

"Miss Emma, them's kind will be coming back, but I's got a plan. Archie will gets his wagon and take you into Brookhaven tomorrow. You goes to the sheriff. We's hear he be a good man. Show him da baby. Then, if anything happens to dis baby, ever body done knowed who done it. We leaves at first dark and be there by daylight."

Archie's mule ambled his way along the dirt road pulling a wagon with Bessie, Archie, Emma and the baby. At daylight, they arrived at the sheriff's office. It was closed so they sat in the wagon until 6:30 a.m. when Sheriff Applewhite came in.

Sheriff Applewhite knew Emma because he had known her father and brother as being prominent wealthy citizens from nearby Darby.

"Well, Miss Emma! When did you get back? Your brother tells me you have been on a vacation to Europe to recuperate." He nodded at the child in Emma's arms. "Obviously, that's not the whole truth, is it Miss Emma?"

"No sir. This is my baby. You see, it's white."

"Miss Emma, this just proves there is no place for lynching. Sometimes you get them right, but sometimes this happens. One day, they're going to lynch an innocent white person and there'll be hell to pay."

"My brother wants to take the baby away. He says nobody can see it is white or they will arrest him for killing Eli."

"Miss Emma, I won't let that happen. You come inside so no one sees you and let me go home and talk to my wife."

In about an hour, he returned.

"Miss Emma, I want you to spend the night with me and my wife. I don't want anyone to know you're here. You folks are Presbyterian. Your daddy built that church over there and it has two hundred members now. Tomorrow is Sunday. My wife will get you and the baby some Sunday clothes. I think it's time this baby is baptized in front of God and the whole congregation. You will hide in the preacher's office. Then, when the preacher signals, you come out. I will get the preacher to call your brother up to be the Godfather. He can't refuse, and then he will have committed to take care of this baby as if it were his."

The expression on Benjamin's face when Emma brought the baby from the back room caught the attention of the entire congregation. When he was called forward to be the Godfather, he could barely stand. It was as if the whole congregation knew the whole story.

With reservation, Benjamin took his sister and the baby back to the family home. It was a strange and cold relationship.

In a few days, Emma took the baby to visit Sheriff Applewhite. "Sheriff, there is something I need you to help me do."

"What's that, Miss Emma?"

"I want to do something for Eli. This community needs to ask for forgiveness. I want to visit his grave."

Emma, Sheriff Applewhite, and the baby trudged their way to the corner of a cotton field. There were a dozen or so graves. Most were not marked, but a couple had wooden crosses on them.

The sheriff reasoned that the one with the freshest dirt was Eli's. Emma approached, carrying the child.

"See, Eli? You didn't do this." She waited as if expecting an answer.

"Sheriff, do you think the community will regret what they did to Eli?"

"Someday, maybe, Miss Emma. But not now."

Epilogue

There were no legal proceedings brought against Benjamin for the lynching of Eli. However, society did get justice in a minor way. After he campaigned for U.S. Senator, he was soundly defeated. Also, Green's Hardware and Farm Supply began to fall on hard times.

Benjamin moved from the community, leaving the family home and business to Emma. She made it profitable again.

One day, Sheriff Applewhite stopped in to visit. He complimented Emma on how she had turned the business around.

Emma replied, "A farmer must have credit. Even with credit, it's an iffy endeavor. I give credit to every responsible person, regardless of color. My brother never did that."

The sheriff was silent for a moment.

"Miss Emma, you never know how an event will change things. Everything that happened in the past was terrible; for you, for Eli, and for our community. But it seems as though some good may have come out of it. Maybe you have opened the door for peace and understanding and, perhaps, change."

"Sheriff, can I ask you something?" Emma asked.

"Yes, Ms. Emma, I don't know that I can answer it."

"Do you have any idea who is the father of my child?"

"Ms. Emma, as sheriff, what happened was a serious crime. I am talking about what happened to you. I have worked on that case since the day you brought the baby to my office."

"Well, have you any idea?"

"I have a hunch, but it is not well founded, and we can't ruin another life on speculation.

"Please tell me who you suspect."

"No Emma, not now."

BACK HOME AGAIN

I am fascinated with one's desire to stay associated with the place of their childhood; you might say, a connection to their roots. I once thought this was more prevalent with people from the South, and accomplished scribes such as William Faulkner, Willie Morris and others have penned numerous references to this tendency. I still think we Southerners tend to be more attached to the real estate of our youth than those from other geographical locations, but we do not have a monopoly on this.

I personally have written more than one article or story based on my visits back to my roots in Lincoln County, Mississippi. Age and passing of those who lived there have made my trips less frequent. When I do go however, I get a sense of refreshment or renewal. Even though this was a dual-purpose trip, it was one of those journeys.

My purpose in going was to attend a graveside service and a celebration of life for my first cousin, Janis. This story is about that, but it is about much more. It is about a change in viewpoint, life experiences, and observation.

In recent years, since I have no direct family to stay with, I book a room in a nice boutique hotel in the heart of Old Brookhaven. It is a wonderful place to stay. Created out of an old mercantile building, it has only a few rooms, but they are nice. It has a lobby with appropriate art and comfortable seating. Having been an old store front, there is a glass window which gives a view of what was once the commercial area of the town.

Don't let the word "commercial" allow your mind to wander and envision fast traffic, noisy industry, or anything of the sort. The view is of the old buildings that have been urban renewed and Railroad Park. Outside on the sidewalk are benches and tables, some for two and some for more. Almost next door is Janie's Bakery, an establishment where, as a youngster, sixty-five years ago, I bought donuts, some of the best, for a nickel each. I would usually order a chocolate milk to finish the not-so-healthy snack.

Little has changed and plenty has changed. I arrived after a two-hour drive about 8 a.m. My room was not available so early and I did not expect it to be, so I took a seat at a table for two on the sidewalk. I ordered a donut and a cup of coffee. Yes, the donut is no longer a nickel.

I watched as people came by walking their dog or strolling with their child. Not one failed to speak. I thought that some of them may be the children or grandchildren of my contemporaries, those I knew when I lived there 55 years prior. They could have been, I'll never know. They wouldn't look the same, but neither would I.

After being seated a few minutes, a black man came and sat down by me, at my table, uninvited. I was pleased, as I thought I could get some community reaction from a different point of view. I also thought that, 55 years ago, his uninvited seating would have been a social taboo. Yes, things had changed.

In a few minutes, I realized the man had some mental challenges and had a fixation on radios. He asked me several times if I had a radio which, I suppose, he wanted me to give him. I had no radio to give. We sat mostly in silence as his interest was only in radios.

Finally, the time of the graveside services approached. Janis was born and raised in Brookhaven but had lived for many years in the San Diego area. That is where she raised her three sons. I had only seen her a few times in those years as the trips she made home were minimal.

I was amazed at the entourage of those who came for her last homecoming. Her three sons and their spouses, of course, from different parts of the western U.S., her grandchildren, her brother and his three sons. There was a smattering of cousins from both sides of the families, making a congregation of, I would guess, thirty people. Lots of effort went into traveling that far to say their final goodbyes, but they were her close family, and it would be expected.

It was a hot morning, and the eulogy was presided over by her oldest son. I had never met him before, but something told me he must be a minister. He had that aura and ease of presentation. All her children had an air of class and sophistication. Could it be that a little of the South ran in their blood? But then I pinched my prejudiced self and just enjoyed the event. I don't like the word "enjoy" as it relates to a funeral, but they assured me and all that attended, that is what Janis would have wanted.

Then I was taken back to the early 1960s and shockingly awakened. Her brother's son, her nephew, began to sing an a cappella version of the Lord's Prayer. I had not heard my grandfather's rich a cappella voice since the early 60s . He passed in 1965, but there it was, as if a recording of him belched from the mouth of his great grandson. What you hear about genes is true.

There is more about Janis's send off but let me continue with my day of reminiscence. I had recently purchased a drone, a radio-controlled small aircraft with a camera. I drove to the home of my childhood friend Tommy. As kids, our favorite pastime was to go to the river. That would be the Bogue Chitto River for sure, and it was about a mile walk from our houses. We fished there, we camped there, we swam there, and hunted there.

Over the years, the underbrush has grown to the point that access to our favorite spot is hard to negotiate. I have concluded that I may never make that trek again. I decided that we would visit it together one more time by drone. It was not the same, but a high-tech way to wind down the day.

I returned to the hotel and took my seat outside on the sidewalk and again was visited by Radio. We talked some but mostly he sat quietly. An air and heat repairman came to do a repair at the hotel. He spoke to me and to Radio, calling him by that name, Radio. He then called me aside and told me that the community looks after him, as if to insinuate I was to be kind to one of the town's adopted.

I sat on the bench, watched the trains come by, and thought about days gone by until 10 p.m. Then I retired. Sunday morning, I took my coffee to the bench on the sidewalk. Chris Kristofferson's *Sunday Morning Coming Down* kept ringing in my mind. The sidewalks and streets were empty except near the houses of worship; and it seemed that, somewhere in the distance, a lonely bell was ringing reminiscent of the song mentioned.

I then reflected on the closing part of Janis's eulogy. I had learned it was in her will to be buried back home, adjacent to her mother. In closing, her son placed a flower on her grave as we all would eventually do, and said, "Mother, I will probably never be in this spot again but Rest in Peace."

My first thought was that was such a callous statement. You won't be visiting your mother's grave? That is blasphemous. No Southern boy would do such a thing. Then I remembered, he has roots too, a place he is attached to and that is California. I then equated this with his deep religious convictions that she is not there, she has departed, and he will see her in the by and by. I wanted to think that his deep faith was a Southern thing, but then I stopped and just thanked God for it being the common denominator.

Janis was back home again, and it was time for me to go, back Home. You see, like Janis, I have lived away three times as long as I lived in Brookhaven. "Away" is home now, but Back Home will always be a sweet respite and a refreshment for my mind.

In departing the hotel, as I loaded my overnight case in my truck, Radio walked by. Rest assured, if there is a U.S. mail service, he will have a new radio.

Epilogue: He did.

THE EDUCATION OF D.J. GARDNER

There comes a time in any writer's life when they feel their mind has created its last story. Then, out of nowhere, comes a mental flicker. I do believe you have to train your mind to be receptive to these bits of inspiration.

Such was the case when I met with some old high school classmates for lunch back in my hometown. There were less than a dozen there; most have moved away, many are deceased. They meet monthly, but I can only manage to drive the two hours about once a year.

Naturally, we reminisced about old classmates, those we haven't seen since graduation, and those that are deceased. A name came up that had crossed my mind many times over the years. His name was D.J. Gardner.

I have learned through experience that you never know when a happening will take place that you'll remember for the rest of your life. Such was the case on the second day of class in my fourth grade. Only recently, after almost sixty-six years, did I take the time to discover some of the answers.

It started when he walked into the classroom. Even for a school in a semi-rural environment, he was a spectacle. Most of us had been in school with each other since the first grade. We had never seen him before, or anyone dressed like him.

He was taller than most of us, skinny to the point of appearing undernourished. He wore farmer's overalls, the type with the bib up to the neck and held on by straps over the shoulders. Maybe twenty years prior, this would not have been so unusual, but not in 1957. We had moved on to blue jeans and t-shirts, especially on hot September days in a classroom with no air conditioning.

His hair was cut short around the sides. A few boys had similar haircuts given by their parents by placing a bowl over their head and cutting around it; so that wasn't so unusual. His was different, though. The hair on top of his head was long and greased down with something heavier than hair oil. Someone would later say it must have been sausage grease. He wore high-top brogans, which none of us wore. Black lace-up Keds tennis shoes were now in vogue for us.

His clothes, though unusual, were clean; and he was clean, something you could not say about all the students in our school. I mostly remember his shyness, but he posed with an almost continuous smile. Where did he come from? We had never seen him before. Did he move here from some other place?

He didn't say but one word all day, and that was to answer "Present" when the roll was called. At recess, he stood under a tree on the playground as the rest of us played kickball or something similar. Recess also doubled as our physical education class in those days.

At the end of the day, I wanted to see where he went, but he quickly exited the building and disappeared. He would return the next day, but not for long.

The next morning, he was present, dressed in the same manner. Around 9:30, a man appeared at the classroom door. No one had to ask who he was. It was as if this man had cloned our classmate, who, by now, we knew as D.J. Gardner.

The man was dressed just like his son, but his clothes were dirty, as if he had already put in a hard day's work. He stood at least six feet tall, very erect, except for his head that was attached to a long neck and bobbled forward.

He walked up to the teacher's desk and said something we couldn't hear. The teacher asked him to step into the hall.

The door was open and we could see him and the teacher plainly. He

164

placed his thumbs into the straps that held his overalls, as if to position himself in a pose of authority. We could hear the conversation.

"Mrs. Davis," that was the teacher's name, "I have come to get my boy out of this here school."

"Mr. Gardner, we have been through this already. We have truancy law in this state. Your son must be in school until he reaches the ninth grade."

Mr. Gardner responded, "He ain't never been in school before and when y'all tested him, you put him in the fourth grade. He's gittin learnin, and he's gittin all he needs."

There was some of the conversation we didn't hear, or at least didn't understand, but then Mrs. Davis asked Mr. Gardner what he had against education.

In a roundabout way, this is how he answered.

"My family has owned 160 acres since before the war. My grandfather only had one son, that was my daddy. And he only had one son, that was me. And I only got one son, that's D.J. My grandfather worked hard to keep that property away from the carpetbaggers and scalawags. My father and I have continued to make a livin there and none of us had as much education as that boy already has.

"If he gets educated, he may think he's smart and do things different from us. He may even borrow money on the land and invest in some brainstorm or wild idea he has. He could lose our farm. I know best for mine and he ain't going to school."

With that, Mr. Gardner took his son and left.

That's the last we saw of D.J., but I often thought about him. Recently, in search of a story, I tried to locate him. Unfortunately, I found him on Find A Grave as he had passed in 2016 and was buried at New Zion Church, a small Baptist church at the edge of the county. I drove to the church and found his grave:

D.J. Gardner
1946-2016
Husband

Next to him on the same stone was:

Annie Ruth Smith
Wife of D.J Gardner
1936-2015

It immediately occurred to me that she was ten years older than him.

I didn't notice a car as it entered the church parking lot, but soon a man began to approach me. He identified himself as Brother Alan Wells, pastor of the church. After a few introductory comments, I told him of my interest in the grave of D.J. Gardner. He listened carefully and invited me to his office.

He was familiar with the story of D.J. and Annie Ruth. They had been church members for many years.

"Mr. Case, before we start, let me show you something."

We walked out the rear door of the church. Immediately adjacent, there was a large, modern building. On the building were the words, *D.J. and Annie Ruth Gardner Family Life Center.*

Brother Wells looked at me and said, "Not bad for an uneducated farmer. Let's go inside and I'll tell you the story."

"You see Mr. Case, D.J. was an only child. So was Annie Ruth. Her family owned 160 acres adjacent to the Gardner family. You noticed she was ten years older than he. Even though she was older, he was the nearest neighbor, and she had a fondness for D.J. Her parents were the opposite of D.J.'s and insisted on her getting an education. She always wanted to be a teacher. She took D.J. under her wing and taught him everything she had learned. That is why he was placed in fourth grade, even though he had never attended a real school.

"She graduated from college and got a job teaching just down the road. When she was 26 and D.J. was 16, they married. Even with the age difference, it was a good marriage. He worked offshore 14 days and was home seven. She taught school. When her parents died, D.J's were already dead, they joined the land and turned it into a first class farm, cattle and cash crops.

"On his seven days off, he did the heavy work and, while he was away, she kept things going. They had no children and accumulated some money. A few years ago, they leased the mineral rights to some oil company and got a lot of money.

"When they died, they willed everything they had, including the land, to this church, with the stipulation that we could never sell it. It is now leased to a cattle farmer and provides considerable income to the church."

As I left the minister's office, I couldn't help but think of the Biblical passage that says something to the effect... He who has most, will have least, and he has least will have most.

During my drive back home, it occurred to me that maybe I have one more story left in me. I began to think and lay it out in my head. You see, you must see a story before you can write it, so pictures of those two days with D.J., years ago, began to become perfectly clear. By the time I arrived home, the story was written in my head. All I had to do was put the images on paper.

SUGAR BABY

Big Trout, Louisiana is not a town. It's not even a village, and to call it a community would be a stretch. It doesn't have a stop sign or a red light, a post office or a movie theatre. A crossroads is a better description, but it is actually just a boat dock. There is an icehouse from which fisherman pack, sell and transport their catch.

There is a school, a very small one, with 48 students in grades one through twelve. Some students arrive by boat, but most are transported by Mr. Dyson's school bus. Mr. Dyson is not a native of the area; no, not by a long shot. From Nebraska, he came to Big Trout as an engineer for an oil company, retired, and just stayed in the area. The small stipend he got from the school didn't nearly cover the cost of his bus and its operation. He just saw a need and liked the kids.

Corrine Bourgeois was one of the students. It would be hard to say what her ancestry was. Certainly, there was French, probably Acadian French. Almost as certainly there was Spanish, as her great-grandfather was a Rodriguez. Maybe a little African American somewhere back there but they became Creoles as they descended. Corrine was a genetic melting pot, but the proportions of each ethnic group combined to create an almost breath-takingly beautiful young woman.

Her skin was just a little lighter than a good summertime tan and it stayed that way even in the winter. Her hair was dark. She wore it long and it was naturally wavy. Green eyes and the figure of a centerfold, she was beautiful and had been since she was a baby.

The genes also produced the smartest girl that had ever attended Big Trout Community School. She would achieve a 34 on her ACT, a very high score. She was popular and liked by her fellow students, as well as the entire little community.

Corrine wasn't from a poor family, but they were by no means rich. Her father, William, as his dad and granddad before him, was a fisherman. Her Uncle Ted, a bachelor, worked offshore as a tool pusher and made good money. The two brothers built the docks and the icehouse, so I guess you could say they owned the town. Ted had no other nieces or nephews and was extremely fond of Corrine.

Yes, there was a boyfriend, Raymond Boutee. He had all the genetic blessings that Corrine had, just in male form. A very handsome and athletic young man, he and Corrine started dating early their sophomore year.

Even though Corrine's family were as well to do as any in the immediate area, she lived a rather sheltered life. Corrine had never been to Baton Rouge, the state capital, and only once to New Orleans. Her parents had taken her there when she contracted a virus and became very ill. Back then, they said they thought it came from a mosquito but could not be certain.

In her cloistered world, she had no ambition other than repeating the life patterns of her parents, grandparents, and their parents before them. She would marry Raymond; he would fish like her father or work on the rigs like her uncle, and she would work in the icehouse and have babies. As a junior in high school with a boyfriend she loved, she had no desire for any other lifestyle.

Only 125 miles away from Big Trout, Jimmy Sinclair's life was much different. It had drastically changed, especially in the last year. He and his wife Mary had plans to travel; travel all over the world. They could afford it easily. They had paid their dues and had been fortunate.

Jimmy came from a middle-class family and was afforded a good education, culminating with a college degree in Business. He worked for a bank for three years but found it too confining. Only bank presidents make the money that would satisfy his dreams. Mary was a nurse and the job paid well. She could support the two of them while he explored other opportunities.

She continued to work and he began diverse entrepreneurial ventures. He bought his first fixer-upper house. He sold it and made a nice profit. He realized the profit on that one house was almost as much as he would have made in an entire year at the bank. Mary soon quit her job. In their career, he and Mary would flip over seventy-five houses. On some, they made as much as $100,000. Only on one did they lose money. You might say they had the Midas touch.

He then invested twenty-thousand dollars in a startup stock. The year was 1997 and it was called Amazon. The price was eighteen dollars per share. The stock was now worth $3,000,000 and that was just a fraction of his assets. They sold their home in Metairie, an affluent New Orleans suburb, bought a condo in the French Quarter and built a home across the lake in Madisonville.

He planned to enjoy the fruits of his labor. He no longer labored over stock market reports and would never have to flip another house. They would travel. It isn't as if they had never made trips before, but their new plan was to be gone most of the year. They had no children, no pets, and no business that needed to be tended.

Hong Kong and Taiwan seemed to be of interest, so they took a one-month trip to Asia. It was great; that is, until the third week. Mary became ill, nauseated, with fever and weakness. They assumed it was the unusual diet of the area and, in a few days, it passed.

When they returned home, Mary was alarmed that she had lost twelve pounds. Maybe she picked up a parasite on the trip? She made an appointment with her doctor.

He ran some tests, referred her to a couple of specialists, and finally gave her the news. She had pancreatic cancer. Her prognosis was not good. He estimated she only had ten to fourteen months. She passed away three months later.

Mr. Dyson felt sorry for the kids from Big Trout. In one way, he appreciated their remote, simple lifestyle; but, on the other hand, he felt they needed to see more. They should see more of the world, not just the fishermen, the boats, and the dock. After they saw it, they could make their choice to stay in Big Trout or leave; but at least they would be exposed to other options.

The summer after Corrine's junior year, Mr. Dyson, at his own expense, planned a trip for the entire high school - all sixteen students. His school bus would take them to places some, if not most, had never been. For those who could not pay, he provided food, hotel rooms and some spending money.

Their first stop was Baton Rouge. They went to the State Capitol and had their picture taken by the bullet in the wall that was fired at Huey Long's killer, or maybe at Huey himself. They stood on the deck, hundreds of feet above the ground, seeing the largest city they had ever seen and the Mississippi River.

Next, they toured the LSU campus. Mr. Dyson had arranged for a guide. They first saw Tiger Stadium and were allowed to walk on the field. It was the first time some had ever seen a real football field. Then, the Maravich Pavilion and finally, a tour of the campus, then lunch.

At lunch, the guide told them that, if you were a Louisiana resident and graduated from a Louisiana high school, you could attend LSU tuition free. It was called the TOPS program. You would have other expenses, but there were grants, loans, and work study programs. He told them if they wanted to go to LSU, nothing stood in their way.

Then Mr. Dyson's bus headed down I-10 to New Orleans. The next day, he treated them to lunch at Acme Oyster House, then a tour of the Superdome. Later that afternoon, they took a tour of the St. Louis Cemetery with a visit to the grave of Marie Laveau.

The next morning, they went to Tulane University. There was no football field at that time as the Tulane team played in the Superdome. That didn't matter, though; Corrine was drawn immediately. She loved the beauty of the campus and its approach on St. Charles Avenue. She loved the streetcars. Never had she seen such homes, such activity, such hustle and bustle.

As at LSU, the guide had told them of the reputation of Tulane University, its history, and the fine medical school associated with it. Corrine was the first to ask a question.

"Sir, is the TOPS program available for tuition?"

Mr. Dyson smiled as he realized that, for at least one person, the efforts and expense he had incurred had paid off. Corrine had seen something besides Big Trout.

The guide told her that TOPS would only pay the average of the Louisiana public university cost. Tulane was a private school and rather expensive.

That would have been disappointing for most, but not for Corrine. When the guide continued, her spirits lifted.

"Tulane has large endowments. Scholarships, loans, and grants are available to deserving students."

That day, Corrine knew whatever it took, she would graduate from Tulane and its medical school.

Never in Jimmy's imagination had he dreamed that he would be a widower at 62 years of age. He tried to take a trip or two alone but realized the loneliest place in the world is a place without someone you care about. His money and wealth had little meaning. Four years would pass and all he had saved was of little value without Mary.

He had dinner with a few ladies, but if they were divorced, he could see problems. He probably judged them unfairly, but he reasoned the divorce must have been at least partly their fault. He didn't understand that. He and Mary had almost never quarreled.

The few times they had, he remembered how miserable he was until they made up. That was usually in a few hours. They never once slept in separate beds.

Remarriage was out of the question. He had seen what happened to his friends. Only about one in four had found happiness. He'd rather be lonely than miserable.

Corrine returned home and prepared for her senior year. She would make the best grades she could, and almost overnight she lost interest in Raymond. She felt guilty that her desires now did not include him. She also regretted the intimacy they had shared when she thought that one day, she would marry him. But her drive to be different, to get away, canceled out the guilt. She felt sorry for Raymond, as he just didn't understand. That reinforced the fact that he would continue the Big Trout lifestyle. There was nothing wrong with that, but it was not what she wanted.

At first, she didn't mention to her parents what she intended to do, not until she had all the facts. Then she put it in presentation form. Tuition cost, room cost, meals, books, etc. She then subtracted the TOPS grant and a scholarship that she felt she could count on. The total was ominous. She was $20,000 per year short.

She did not expect any objection to her going to college from her parents. They were pleased. No one in the family, and maybe even no one in Big Trout, had ever gone to college except Mr. Dyson. The money was a different matter. $20,000 was out of the question. Maybe $10,000, but not $20,000.

Her parents said they needed to think about it overnight and see if there was any way to make it work. The next morning, her dad was home when she got up. This was unusual. He had usually been fishing for hours by now.

"Sweetheart, let's go see your Uncle Ted. He has always considered you his own. Maybe he can help. Bring all the facts and figures. You know he's a detail person. Your mom and I can afford $10,000."

Uncle Ted listened carefully and looked at her financial projections. He used his calculator to check her figures.

"You can't do it, honey."

Corrine almost cried, but realized her uncle owed her nothing. Then he said, "Nope, you can't eat in New Orleans for what you have projected. That's an expensive town. I'll give you $12,000."

Corrine did cry.

She graduated high school with the highest GPA in the history of the school.

Three years passed. Jimmy was 66 years old now. He had a few friends and played golf almost every week with some of them. Most were older than him, as he was able to retire early.

Corrine had finished her junior year at Tulane. Her grades were good enough for med school, but not the perfect scores she had wished for.

After golf, locker room talk can get rather open. What he heard that day would change the rest of his life and Corrine's.

One of his golfer friends, David Willoby, was the loudmouth of the group. He was also a gossiper.

"You guys hear about Ralph Wilson?"

Ralph was a sometime golf partner but had not been around in a couple of months.

"Yep, the old dude has him a Sugar Baby. Twenty-one years old, I hear."

Jimmy responded, "What is a sugar baby?"

David continued, "Well, he tells me there's a website that hooks older men up with young women that need money for tuition."

"You mean, it's an escort service? Prostitutes?" Jimmy questioned.

"Not the way he tells it. They just have dinner together and maybe she goes on a trip with him, things like that. He said when you interview, you cannot discuss sex. Probably doesn't matter, he couldn't do it anyway, too old."

Some of the group laughed, Jimmy didn't. This idea may have merit. He was lonely. A college student could be intelligent and maybe a good dinner partner. He could see merit in that.

A couple of days after the discussion with the golfers, Jimmy was home with the TV on in the background to break the solitude. The headline news story told of a boat exploding at the Big Trout Docks and Icehouse. The icehouse was destroyed and five people killed. Four others were injured. The owners of the icehouse and dock, William and his wife, and his brother Ted, were among the dead. William's daughter, a Tulane student home on break, was only slightly injured while trying to rescue her family.

The names had no meaning to Jimmy at that time, but they would.

A couple of days later, Jimmy scanned the internet searching for a Sugar Baby site. There were a couple, but only one appeared to be a source of college students. He wanted intelligence in companionship, not just a female body. To be truthful, he didn't know what he was looking for.

The site charged a substantial fee to be listed as a Sugar Daddy, and no fee to list as a Sugar Baby. You had to submit your real name, and you would be vetted for criminal activity, and to verify other information you had submitted. You would then be given an alias.

Sugar Babies were handled much the same way, with no fee. Corrine knew about the site. She had seen a news feature on TV. It said thousands of students were using this means to help with tuition expenses. With the loss of financial support from her parents and uncle, she needed assistance. She had three years invested at Tulane; she had to finish, no matter what she had to do.

Both their profiles came up the same day. His alias was World Traveler and hers Doc to Be. He flagged her name for the administrators at the website and, the next morning, there was a friendship acceptance. The fee was now $1,000 to be able to correspond with her directly. He was warned that, if there was any mention of a sexual liaison, he would be terminated. This was a companion site, not anything else.

His first correspondence was something to the effect that he was financially secure, 66 years old, with average looks for his age, not overweight, liked to dine out at the best restaurants and maybe travel if possible.

She responded with more detail. She told about the death of her parents and uncle. They were her money source. She had one more year of undergraduate school and had too much invested not to finish. Maybe she could have applied for financial help, but it was too late. She was quite forward. "Can we meet for dinner?"

At this point, the administrators of the program interrupted and reminded them that the first three contacts had to be approved by them. They had to know where and when they were going. Regardless of how compatible or incompatible they were, he would be responsible for sending the website $300, plus giving Doc to Be $300 with transportation paid to and from her residence.

Jimmy knew her story was true, as he remembered hearing about the accident on TV. He suggested Restaurant August, not as noisy as Galatoire's, and one of New Orleans' best. She agreed, the administrators of the site agreed, and the site charged $300 to his credit card.

It would be two nights before their dinner date. He went to Rubenstein's on Canal Street and was honest about the occasion. He had developed a close relationship with one of the salesmen over the years. The salesman chose trousers, a shirt, and sports coat that did not try to subdue his age. It did, however, have some brightness that enhanced the assets of a 66-year-old man.

Jimmy arrived thirty minutes early and took a seat near the maître d' just in front of the bar. He was a stickler for promptness. If she was politely late, that would not impress him. He hoped she would not be a game player. She wasn't. She arrived five minutes early by Uber.

He was swept away by her beauty. She was much more beautiful in person than in her photograph. He complimented her as to that. She replied that she wanted to be desired by who she was, not how she looked. Jimmy realized she was a deep, complicated, and truthful person.

"Corrine, would you like a drink? I am going to have a gin martini, but you may have anything you want."

"Just ice water, I don't drink."

"Are you opposed to drinking?"

"No, not at all. I just don't spend money that I don't have on things that I don't need."

When the menu arrived, he watched as she examined it. "Jimmy, I have never eaten in a restaurant like this. I don't know what to order. I see salad of duck confit. My daddy cooked duck and I liked it."

"Corrine, this duck is not going to be anything like your dad's. His may have been better." They both laughed.

"I see Snapper Pontchartrain. My dad caught a lot of snapper, but I never knew they were in Lake Pontchartrain."

Jimmy laughed, "They're not. They are named that because the recipe came from the way they were prepared at the Pontchartrain Hotel."

"Oh. It must be good?"

"It is."

"Then I will have it."

The night went rather smoothly, Jimmy realizing there was a larger age difference and cultural difference than he had expected. She had spent three years at Tulane but a lifetime at Big Trout.

Finally, he asked her if she would like to continue the relationship. She didn't hesitate and answered affirmatively.

He said, "This is new to me. How do we begin?"

"Jimmy, this is new to me also but there are certain things I have to have financially."

"Go on."

"$2300 per month and it must be for a year. I can get loans for med school, and I will make enough money to pay them back, but I am in a real bind now."

"$2300?"

"Yes, and that is for three weekends a month, Friday and Saturday, but I want one weekend free. If you expect more, like going out of town with you, that will be $3,000 per month. I must be back by Sunday noon; I must keep my grades up.

Jimmy didn't answer for several seconds. "Do you want dessert?"

"Yes, blueberry shortcake and coffee."

"Demitasse or espresso?"

"I'm not sure I know what those are, you choose."

Since Jimmy had not committed to the arrangement, Corrine later would say that she was almost in tears. She thought Jimmy was a nice fellow, but she did not have time to play games, and she needed the money.

He walked her to the Uber. "Here is the $300 and an extra $100 for the transportation. And, by the way, I think I'll take the $3,000 program."

She beamed, quickly kissed him on the cheek and disappeared into the Uber.

Their next two dates, both monitored by the website, were the next weekend. This satisfied the website's requirement that they monitor three meetings. She made her first exception to what she had told him at Restaurant August. Since school had not started, she agreed to Sunday lunch at Commander's Palace.

After lunch and dessert, he asked her when she would need her money and how much. She had it written down and handed the paper to him as if she were presenting him with a bill.

"Jimmy, I have to pay tuition and make some deposits. I need $12,000. That will be four months in advance."

Jimmy had expected something like this and quickly wrote her a check for the requested amount. He then handed her a check book, and some papers to sign.

"I have opened a special account. Sign those papers and you can write checks on it as you need. I deposited $36,000 in the account. You'll never have to ask me for money again. I think you'll feel better if it is that way, and I will too."

Corrine reached across the table and grabbed his hand. "Thank you. You can trust me. I promise."

Jimmy did trust her. He did not regret the arrangement at all. If it didn't work out, it would not be the first time he had made a not so good investment.

The relationship continued in much the same pattern as it began. Lunches and dinners in New Orleans at its finest restaurants. At a mid-November evening meal at Bayona, another of his favorite places to eat, the subject of Thanksgiving came up.

"Jimmy, I haven't thought about it. Thanksgiving was a big thing for my family in Big Trout. This is my first Thanksgiving without them. I don't know what I'll do."

"Corrine, come spend Thanksgiving with me in Madisonville. I will have dinner catered and you can relax from your studies. If the weather is warm, we will take a boat trip on the lake."

Corrine had dreaded when this day would come. He had never asked anything of her but companionship. Was this a forward step? She then realized the thought of where this may lead was not as bad as she had feared. After all, he had lived up to his agreement and even more.

"I would love that, Jimmy."

There were no classes the week of Thanksgiving. She reasoned that she did not want to stay with him a whole week, so she told him she needed to catch up on studies and would come to his house on Wednesday.

Tuesday night, she carefully chose the clothes she would take. She had never dressed casually around him, as the restaurants they frequented were upscale. Lots of thoughts ran through her mind on what she should and shouldn't take. The weather was warm, so there may be a boat trip. Thankfully, she thought, it is too cool for a bathing suit. Shorts and a long sleeve blouse will suffice.

Then she was forced to think about what she would wear for bedtime. She had hoped she would not have to consider that, and she knew she didn't. It was not in the agreement. On the other hand, he had been so kind and considerate, she didn't want to hurt his feelings. She packed a very modest pair of flannel pajamas.

Her Uber arrived in Madisonville just before noon. His home was not as large as the ones on St. Charles Avenue, but larger than any in Big Trout, and beautiful. Her thought was, "I've never spent the night in a home this beautiful."

They greeted each other with hugs, and he helped carry her luggage in, just two small bags. "Let me show you around, Corrine. This, of course, is the living and dining room and back there is the kitchen. Down that small hall is a bath and down this other way is my bedroom with the guest room next to it.

When he opened the door to the guest room, she did not get the idea it was for her. Magazines and financial papers were scattered on the bed. He then opened the door to his bedroom. There was a king size bed and the largest TV she had ever seen except in the bars around school. The room was immaculate, the sheets were turned down and freshly pressed.

"Now, let's go upstairs."

The door at the top of the stairs opened to almost another house. There was a parlor room and then a bedroom. It was also pristine. The sheets were turned back and also freshly pressed. There was a vase with a dozen roses in it.

"This is your room. No one has ever slept in it. Let me get your things."

She was relieved; but in a strange way, it occurred to her that she did not appeal to him. No girl wants to feel that. By this time, they were back in the kitchen.

"Let me cook Thanksgiving dinner for us. I'm a good cook, especially if you like seafood," she said. How about some vegetables and a shrimp dressing, or maybe oyster? I really want to."

He replied, "Suit yourself, but you don't have to. I will take us out to dinner."

"Nope, drive me to the supermarket, one that has good seafood."

"I'll tell you what. You take my wife's car. It hasn't been driven one hundred miles since she passed. Just enough to keep the battery charged."

He gave her directions, some cash and the keys. The car was not a new model, but she could tell it was a fine car, an Infinity. Her family had only a Ram pickup. She purchased the items she needed and returned to Jimmy's.

That evening, they sat on the porch overlooking the Tchefuncte River. They watched the boats pass by, on which sat what she imagined were trophy girls, prominently being displayed by the elderly owners of the boat. She thought, *I guess I am a trophy girl to some extent, but he is kind enough not to put me on display.*

She respected him even more.

The Thanksgiving dinner she prepared was traditional for Louisiana - turkey and oyster dressing. She was a good cook. She told him most people from Big Trout are.

Saturday night, she surprised him. "Tonight, we have Snapper Tchefuncte. Jimmy, there are no snapper in this river, but I named it that because this is where I created the recipe." They both laughed.

Before she realized, it was Sunday noon. It had been a fabulous, carefree holiday. When the Uber came, he lifted her bags into the trunk, and she hugged him. He felt that the affection was genuine. He was thankful she was in his life.

For the Christmas holidays, she repeated the Thanksgiving routine; but for New Year's, he had a surprise. He took her to the Grand Hotel in Point Clear, Alabama. When he entered the room, he was more surprised than she. There was only one bed. He began to apologize and, before she could say anything, he had gone to see if another room with two beds could be arranged. It couldn't. When he returned, she had already unpacked her bags.

This would be one of the most nervous nights of his life. After spending time in the Bird Cage lounge, they went back to their room. It was late and even she had a drink that night, a cosmopolitan.

"Why don't I go back to the Bird Cage and give you a few minutes of privacy. I won't be long."

"You don't need to, but if you wish."

She showered, dried and dressed in the flannel pajamas she had worn Thanksgiving. When he returned, she was already in the king size bed. He showered and changed and slipped into the other side of the bed, hoping she was asleep. She wasn't.

"Jimmy, I know that this is not part of the agreement, but if you want to kiss me, it's ok."

"No, Corrine. You're somewhere between a daughter I never had and my best friend."

"Just hold me then. I miss having someone hold me."

Jimmy flipped the light off and put his arms around her. For the next three nights this was their routine. She had the time of her life.

The year passed quickly, and June came. His contract with Corrine was expiring. They decided to have their last dinner where it all began, Restaurant August.

Again, she arrived by Uber early. They sat at the same table, but this time there was no unfamiliarity. They laughed and spread the occasion over four hours.

"Corrine, do you want to continue this arrangement through medical school?"

"No, I already have loans for that. I could not have made it without you. You saved my career, and I will always love you for that. I can make it from here." She laid her hand over his on the table.

"There is one thing, Jimmy. I can make it financially, but I can't make it without you in my life. I'd like our friendship to continue just as it is, but with no financial strings attached."

When it was time to leave, Jimmy signaled the maître d'. When they walked to what she expected to be an Uber, a shiny white Infinity drove up.

"You know, it was my wife's car. It's seven years old, but only has six thousand miles, and it's not doing me any good in my garage. Here is the bill of sale, insurance for a year, and a $400 gas card. It's yours."

Medical school was more difficult than she had expected. She struggled but survived. Four years of the toughest academic curriculum she had ever encountered, but she made it. Then the internship and residency. She was selected to the school of Ophthalmology. Her total commitment had been eight years and, throughout it all, had visited Jimmy as often as she could. He was there for her. Kind of like a father, but in some ways more.

They celebrated his 78th birthday. Yes, he had aged. She knew that he now primarily lived for the joy she brought him. A few days after his birthday, she got a call.

"Doctor Bourgeois, I am Nurse Paxton at Lakeview Hospital in Mandeville. We have a patient here, a Mr. James Sinclair. Your information was in his wallet as an emergency contact."

"Yes, I am. What has happened?"

"Mr. Sinclair has suffered a massive stroke. It would probably be best for you to come as soon as possible."

"Yes, I'm on my way."

"Hurry, Doctor."

Corrine canceled her patients for the next two days and left for Mandeville immediately. Upon arriving, she was escorted to his room. Gone was the healthy color that he had possessed when they met twelve years prior. Gone was his ability to give her that reassuring hug. He was alive, but barely.

She took a chair by his bedside and took his hand. She imagined she could feel him squeeze it, but maybe she just wanted to believe that. Hours passed. She never let go of his hand.

Sometime about two in the morning, she heard the sound of the monitoring equipment change. If he was gripping her hand, it was limp now.

Nurses rushed into the room, asking her to step outside.

"No, I am a doctor. Let him be. That is the way he would have wanted it."

Only a few of his golfing friends came to the memorial service. Of course she was there. She was the only one that cried.

Three weeks later, she received a letter from an attorney in Covington informing her that she was named in Jimmy's will. She was asked to contact the law office for an appointment regarding the succession.

The appointment was made, and she traveled across the lake. "Doctor

Bourgeois, Jimmy Sinclair was a wealthy man. He had only one living relative, a nephew. In his will, he left the nephew a million dollars. For you, he left his Amazon stock. Today's value puts it at a little over $3,800,000. He also left you his home on the river. In addition, $25,000,000 remains to be put into a foundation. This foundation is to provide tuition for young women who wish to attend any Louisiana college. He named you the chairman of that foundation, if you accept. The condo in the French Quarter was left to the foundation for emergency housing."

"Dr. Bourgeois, what was your relationship with Mr. Sinclair, if you don't mind me asking?"

She replied, "Somewhere between the daughter he never had and his best friend."

The attorney responded, "He sure thought a lot of you."

Shedding uncontrollable tears, she said, "And I of him."

THE SERIAL KILLER? 1930

Other than a few businesses in town, only 28 people had telephones in the entire county. All, including the business phones, were managed by Estelle Harper from a switchboard located in her home. She shared the duties with her two grown daughters, Mabel and Eula May. Eula May had a learning disability. Back then, it was thought that she was just a little slow, but today it would probably be diagnosed and treatable as dyslexia. If you tried to call Rupert Jones at number 21, she would invariably ring Ms. Tiny Jean Smith at number 12. This could be problematic sometimes because Rupert was the undertaker.

Just as telephones were few in the county, so were the number of law enforcement officers. There were four to be exact, the sheriff and three deputies. Each deputy worked an eight-hour shift and shared one car. The size of the force was adequate as there was almost no crime, and the crime that existed was overlooked. Crimes such as moonshining, gambling, and cock fighting were just considered honest ways of making a living at the time.

There was no radio communication with law enforcement, so a unique method of transmitting emergency messages was devised. Each home that had a telephone had a blue light bulb installed on the front of the house. If there was an emergency, Estelle or one of her daughters would notify all the county telephone subscribers to turn on the blue light. When one of the deputies passed and saw the light, he would know to stop and use the phone to call Estelle, and she would give him the information that was needed.

It was mid-afternoon when Western Union received the telegram. It was addressed to all law enforcement agencies. It was a lengthy message, and it was what you would call a BOLO (be on the lookout) for Thad Jorgensen.

The message stated that it was believed Thad had killed his wife, two children, and his in-law in St. Paul, Minnesota. He then broke into a home in Iowa, killing an elderly couple and stealing their auto. The auto was found abandoned in Arkansas and a doctor had been car jacked and his car taken. It was a grey 1930 Chevrolet Coupe, license plate number 2356.

The fugitive was to be considered armed and extremely dangerous and should only be approached by trained personnel. It was believed he was headed to Mississippi or Louisiana.

The local Western Union office called Estelle and she called all the telephone subscribers with blue lights. Due to it being mid-afternoon, the deputy on duty did not see the light that was turned on. It would not be noticed until the sun had gone down when Deputy Green passed Felix Danton's house and saw the blue glow.

After receiving the message, Deputy Green drove to the sheriff's house where they laughed at the likelihood that such a notorious criminal would be in such a rural county. If he were in Mississippi, he would probably head to a large town like Meridian or the Gulf Coast, but most likely he had gone to New Orleans. New Orleans was a big town, and he could just blend in with the crowd.

The next day, a grey Chevrolet Coupe turned the corner in front of Deputy Green. The car was unfamiliar, as he knew and could recognize almost every car in the county. He read the license plate, 2356. He turned on his siren. The car pulled over and the driver exited the automobile and started walking toward the deputy. The deputy pulled his pistol and the man stopped immediately and raised his hands.

"Get on the ground," Deputy Green ordered.

"What's wrong, officer?" as he complied with the deputy's orders. "If I was speeding, I'm sorry, there is no need for this action. After all, I ain't no killer or nothing."

The deputy laughed, "You ain't no killer no more. I done apprehended you and, after I get you booked, departments from Minnesota, Illinois and Arkansas will be on their way to talk to you. That is, if I can keep the locals from hanging you. You about the most famous guy we've had here since Tom Austin. Even you ain't as bad as him."

"Bad? I ain't done nothing."

"What's your name, mister? I know before you tell me it's Thad Jorgensen. I've always wanted to catch me a guy like you. Spottin' that car tag was just good detective work on my part."

"Wait a minute officer! I'm not Thad Jorgensen. I am Delous Walker."

"Yea, and I'm Abraham Lincoln. Put your hands behind your back."

Shortly, the word was out, and the Western Union operator sent notice that Thad Jorgensen had been caught.

Two hours ago, hardly a citizen in town had ever heard of Thad Jorgensen. The word was getting around, and it was not all true. The exaggerated story being told was that he had kidnapped three children, held them captive for days before throwing them alive in the Mississippi River. Then some of the true story was mixed in.

Sheriff Cox arrived at the police station and jail in his own car. The county could not afford a car for him, and he was more of an administrator now. He had spent 10 years in the military and 10 years with the state police. Being sheriff was more of a civic duty to him than being a law enforcement officer, but he was the most qualified crime investigator of the four.

When he arrived, he did not like what he saw. Several men were gathering near the jail and were loud and agitated. The sheriff entered and met the prisoner. Somehow, he knew something was not right about this case. The man he saw was dressed in almost rags. He had cardboard in the bottom of his shoes, as the soles had long ago worn through. Someone that had carjacked and murdered as often as this guy supposedly had done, would have at least stolen a pair of decent shoes.

"Undo the handcuffs, Green. If he looks outside, he won't be going anywhere. Some of those guys have ropes."

The prisoner immediately looked panicked.

"You got to believe me. I ain't done much wrong, if anything. Who do you think I am, anyway?"

The sheriff told him he was suspected of being Thad Jorgensen and explained the allegations against him.

"I ain't him. I am Delous Walker and I ain't hurt nobody."

The sheriff questioned, "Whose car is that outside?"

"I don't know," the prisoner answered.

"How did you come by it?"

"That is what I was coming to tell you when I got stopped. You see, I was walking down the road. I walked thirty miles in the last two days. Nobody would pick me up. I went down a logging road to relieve myself and I see this car. There is a dead man lying in the woods close by. I come to tell you."

"How far away?"

"'Bout six miles, just south of that next little town north of here."

"Well, Mr. Walker, can you take me to the spot?"

"Sho can."

The crowd outside had grown to more than a hundred men and their attitudes were angry.

"Green, tell the crowd we are coming out and if anyone steps even accidentally in my way, I will kill him."

Green replied, "Sheriff, them's our people out there. You can't shoot one of them to save this murderer."

"We don't know that he is a murderer. There will be no lynching on my watch as long as there is breath in my body. Do you understand that, Green?"

"Yes, sir, but don't count on me to shoot one of our own."

Agitated, the sheriff was very direct. "I need you too much to fire you right now, but I should."

Green did as the sheriff directed. The men stepped back and allowed the sheriff and his prisoner to make their way to the car.

The prisoner directed the sheriff to a dirt trail off the main highway. Just as he had said, there was a dead man lying in the dirt. He looked much more like a criminal than the prisoner and, after examining the body, the sheriff left with his prisoner to find a house with a blue light. He then placed a call to number 21, Rupert, the undertaker.

Tiny Jean was confused when she answered and the sheriff abruptly said, "We got a cold one here. Come get him."

The body was picked up and examined at the funeral home. It was then photographed, and distinguishing features were sent to all law enforcement interested in the apprehension of Thad Jorgensen.

The town settled down since the murderous lunatic was presumed dead. There were no grounds to hold Walker as he had not stolen the car, just used it to report a dead body. He was released on foot just before dark on Saturday evening. Who killed Thad would be another mystery.

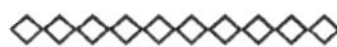

The next morning, the news was startling. The body described was not Jorgensen. Nowhere was it mentioned that he had terrific scars on his body due to a boiler explosion when he was young. Who was this man?

It was not until Sunday afternoon that it was learned that a salesman with Swift Packing Company had failed to check in as planned. He typically would either stay at the local hotel or, if he felt like it, drive on and check into the Jung Hotel in New Orleans. His family was concerned.

Never, in this town, had local law enforcement been so busy. A suspected killer had been arrested and released. A suspected killer's body had been found but proved not to be him. A salesman had not arrived at his destination, causing concern to his family. An unidentified "John Doe" was lying in the local funeral home waiting identification. This was a lot of action for a four-man sheriff's department.

The sheriff now turned his attention to the missing salesman with a strong premonition that it had something to do with the dead John Doe. If John Doe was the missing salesman, his name was Dennis Overby from Memphis, Tennessee.

The sheriff then posted the particulars of the description of the deceased man as related by Rupert Jones. He included the fact that there was a scar on the right side of his body. Possibly a sign of an appendectomy. There was also a missing left small toe.

Within hours, Dennis Overby was the name of the corpse, and his body was being prepared for shipment to Memphis when the Panama Limited train came through town that evening. After a long two days, the sheriff went home.

Monday morning, a county highway worker saw something suspicious at the edge of the right of way. On closer examination, it was the body of a local woman. It appeared she had been dead only a very short time. She was identified as Nellie Hinton, a well-respected lady that was a nurse at the local hospital. At the time of her death, she was on her way to work for her seven o'clock shift. Something went badly wrong. Where was her car? Where was Dennis Overby's car?

The sheriff reasoned that Thad Jorgensen had hijacked Overby, killed him and taken his car, abandoning the doctor's car which had been found by Walker. If the murder of Nellie Hinton was connected, then Jorgensen, at some point in time, while in possession of Overby's car, could have killed Mrs. Hinton in order to switch cars.

Another telegram arrived. Relatives of the murder victims in St. Paul offered a reward for the apprehension of Jorgensen and likewise did the relatives of the Iowa couple. The reward was sizable for the day, $800. A BOLO was posted for Mrs. Hinton's car which was a 1924 Ford and the automobile of Dennis Overby which was a 1927 Dodge.

Just two miles from the Mississippi-Louisiana border, Overby's car was spotted. The driver was taken to the Magnolia, Mississippi jail awaiting the arrival of Sheriff Cox. The sheriff was shocked to see who was being held for the murder of Overby. Delous Walker.

With the prisoner secure in the rear of his car, Sheriff Cox was aggravated that he had been wrong in his assessment of Walker's innocence. So aggravated, he did not say a word to his prisoner.

"I'm sho glad you come and get me, Sheriff. You a good man."

The sheriff did not answer.

"I should have known something was wrong. I usually don't get that lucky."

Glancing in the rear-view mirror, the sheriff said, "What do you mean, lucky?"

"Getting a ride all the way to New Orleans and, better yet, being given a car to drive."

"Ok, Walker, tell me another lie. Tell me what happened."

"I slept in an abandoned barn until just about daylight this morning. I was walking down the road. I see two cars on the side of the road and a man standing by this Dodge. He said he was on his way to New Orleans and had a friend following him in the Ford. They got in an argument and the friend thumbed a ride and left him there with two cars. He said he had a sale for the Ford in New Orleans and, if I would follow him in the Dodge, he would give me $25. Sheriff, you know how long it's been since I had $25 in my pocket? A long time."

Sheriff Cox felt he was being lied to again but felt the story was worth probing.

"Where is the man in the Ford?"

"When they pulled me over, he just kept going."

"You did not tell that to the officer that stopped you?"

"He didn't ask."

By now Jorgensen would be in New Orleans and had probably abandoned the Ford. The sheriff sent a telegram describing the car and the man as Walker had described them to him.

It was Officer Arceneaux's first day on the job. He spotted the Ford at Morrison's Restaurant on Gentilly Boulevard. He didn't know if the driver had abandoned the car or was inside the restaurant. The officer drove on past, not wanting the driver to spot him if he was nearby. He parked and watched the car.

In a few minutes, another New Orleans policeman passed by. Officer Arceneaux signaled him to stop. They both approached the car. It was not occupied. They then entered the restaurant. There Jorgensen sat, and he made no effort to avoid the arrest.

Two days later, Delous Walker received wired money by Western Union. It was the reward money, $800. He had never been so wealthy. The sheriff suggested he buy a pair of shoes, but he said he saw no use in wasting good money. He then cut a thick piece of cardboard and placed it in his shoe.

REBELLION

If writers catch the essence of reality, they have well demonstrated the attachment Southerners have for the place they call home.

With "home" I mean home place, town, community, crossroads, or even state. It is as if that one geographical location will guide their thinking, their ambitions, and their outlook on life. It is a common thread that binds them together and it seems to make life easier, as a crutch helps someone to walk.

There are contradictions, however. Raymond Thompson had other ideas about life. Rebel, malcontent, non-conformist, and a target for bad luck, all that he was. Yes, but somehow, he drew us to him like a magnet.

Nothing about him was normal. Some things you are better off not knowing; but, whatever, he was strange and powerful. Even powerful at a young age. Uncanny, almost as if possessed by some alluring magic, we watched him and followed him, if only at a distance; sometimes wishing to follow him and sometimes knowing to avoid him.

Maybe it was because he did not have a geographical center hold, the one Southerners rely on so much. After all, he had been raised all over the county; and, everywhere he went, he left his mark. Not always a good one and not always a bad one; but, from the time he was nine years old, he never left a place that he was not remembered.

Too much happened in his presence for it to be coincidental. I first met him when we were both nine years old. His family rented a house on Louis Maxwell's place. Not far from the house they rented was Louis's barn where he kept his hay and other farm equipment. On that day, he had about a dozen calves in stalls for some reason.

Ray, as he was called, sneaked out to the barn to smoke. Somehow, a fire started. He was the second kid I knew that caused a fire from smoking. Instead of running away, he turned all the calves loose, then ran for help. None of the livestock were injured, but the barn burned to the ground.

Ray was an unpredictable kid. Most nine-year-olds would have made up some lie, but not Ray. He told the authorities exactly what happened, and he was immediately arrested.

Old Judge Hemphill was the only judge we had. He presided over all the trials, whether it be first-degree murder or a misdemeanor juvenile case. This legal proceeding was not going to be a murder trial, but it certainly was being treated as more than a misdemeanor juvenile case.

I think it was handled that way because, even at nine years old, Ray cast the persona of an adult. He was confident, he had no fear of authority, and I think adults were troubled about his attitude. That attitude can best be described as, no matter what you do to me, you can't hurt me.

I don't remember the circumstances, but somehow my dad knew Ray's dad and heard about the hearing. It probably wasn't a full-blown trial, just some type of juvenile hearing. Dad decided to go, and he let me go with him.

My daddy was not a lawyer. No, far from it. But he was well respected, and Judge Hemphill let him speak. I think that was the proudest I ever was of my daddy. He saved Ray that day.

Ray's dad had hired some lawyer and, even at my young age of nine, I could tell he was worthless. I guess you get what you pay for. He was trying to impress the judge with all these juvenile precedents, but you could tell the judge was not impressed.

My dad asked to speak. The judge said he could.

"Your Honor, what you have here is a kid that is trying to act just like me and you."

My dad was smoking a cigarette as he talked. The judge had one burning in the ashtray on his desk.

The judge replied, "L.W., get to the point."

"The kid was just smoking. Imitating you and imitating me. Now, we know he's too young to smoke. But if you punished every nine-year-old who has smoked a cigarette now and then, you would empty the grammar school."

At this, the district attorney spoke up. "L.W., the boy burned down a barn full of hay, a bush hog, and over a thousand dollars' worth of miscellaneous tools."

Dad responded, "No, you are wrong. These were destroyed by an accident. If the boy had been burning the trash that his family puts in their 55-gallon drum every week, and the wind caused it to set the grass on fire and it spread to the barn, we would not be having this trial. It would have been an accident."

The district attorney spoke up again. "Your Honor, he was not burning trash. He was smoking a cigarette, and he is nine years old."

To this, Dad replied, "I think he is too young to be smoking, but he is not the only person who has accidentally set a fire from a cigarette. Pinckney Smith set my woods on fire five years ago and burned my pulp wood. You didn't have him in here."

The judge replied, "Is that all, L.W.?"

"Almost, your Honor..." and then Dad gave, what I would call today, his closing argument.

"This kid is guilty of smoking a cigarette. He happened to be smoking it near Louis Maxwell's barn and, for whatever reason, the barn ignited. I feel sorry for Louis. The neighbors have already pitched in and raised him a new barn, better than the old.

"So, if you punish this kid in a harsh way, you are treating him differently than you would if it were me or Pinckney Smith, and I don't think that's fair. Give the kid a little community service or let him work for Louis or something; but don't send him to reform school. You have never reformed anyone by doing that. Look at that Lucus kid, came back and robbed the bank, first week."

"Thank you, L.W. Please take your seat."

The district attorney stood to address the judge.

The judge said, "Sit down, I have heard enough." He motioned to Ray, "Stand up, son. Young man, I am going to do you a favor. I am going to give you ten years of probation. I don't know if the state will let me do it or not, but I am going to do it anyway. The only thing you cannot do is smoke. If I catch you or hear about it, you will go to the reform school. In ten years, you will be nineteen and, if you want to kill yourself with those cigarettes, go for it. But, in the meantime, be healthy."

Things did not go so well between the Maxwells and the Thompsons and, within a few weeks, the family moved to another house.

Ray's family was not poor. In fact, they were middle-class. It was unusual, but they were one of the very few middle-class families I knew that never owned a home. They would just move from place to place. I am not sure if they moved because of the way Ray was, or Ray was the way he was because they moved. I know wherever they went, something happened.

A couple of years after the barn burned, the family was living in a nice brick home that had belonged to Otis Calcoat's parents. They were both deceased now. Otis wanted someone to live there, more or less to watch after the house and a few cows that were on the two-hundred acres. Mr. Thompson didn't mind that, especially as a partial trade for rent.

There was one problem, however. There was a small lake or large pond on the property that was filled by a spring fed creek. It had a hard clay bottom, and the water was almost perfectly clear. Try as he might, Mr. Thompson could not keep the trespassers out of the pond during the summer. It was a favorite swimming lake.

He did not have much concern for them drowning, most kids could swim back then; but they would leave the gate open and let the cows out. Also, they would leave trash on the banks where they picnicked. Someone once cut the fence and drove their car to the water's edge to listen to the radio.

Ray was a good swimmer but did not have the luxury to spend too much time at the pond. On this day, he was cutting grass along the backside of the dam. Several kids that he recognized as high school football players and their girlfriends had come to swim.

Red Danvers was a big, strong kid that played running back. He was popular and talented. He was in the group. There must have been twelve or fourteen teenagers there. They had brought a picnic lunch, watermelons, and most likely some beer; but from the tractor Ray was driving, he could not tell.

Some people are just lucky. On that day, Red was. Ray had let the tractor run out of gas. If he had not done so, he would have never heard the screams. He ran to the other side of the dam where the kids had been swimming. All of them were panicking, pointing into the water, but none of them were making any effort to do anything.

Ray realized someone was underwater. He did not know who, but he instinctively dove in. Maybe he saw a bubble rise or maybe it was just luck; but he dove as deep as he could beside the spillway valve. At about fifteen feet, he saw a form. Finally, he reached an arm and began to fight his way to the surface, pulling a body that was almost twice his size.

As soon as he surfaced, the others in the party swam to meet them. They pulled Red to the bank and immediately began artificial respiration, as CPR was called then. Red quickly responded and began to vomit a stream of water and bubbles. After a moment, he took a breath.

The group did not wait for an ambulance. Ambulance service was poor at best and, of course, there were no cell phones. He was put in a car and rushed to the hospital. It would be a few days, but he would recover.

No one knows exactly what made Red almost drown. Some say he got a cramp because he ate watermelon; others said he had too much beer and tried to dive to the bottom of the spillway valve. It was the deepest part of the lake. But, as a result, word spread that a two-hundred pound football star had been saved by a one-hundred pound eleven-year-old former barn burner. Instantly, Ray was a community hero.

His heroism didn't last long. Due to saving Red's life, word got around about his heroic act. About two weeks after the incident, the newspaper came to his house to interview him. After the interview, Ray thought the reporter had gone, but he had not. The reporter had gone to his car to retrieve his camera for a photo. When he returned, he found Ray on the back steps, smoking a cigarette. That was the photo he published.

It would be a year before we heard from Ray again. Reform school had changed him; but, as my dad had predicted, not for the good. He resented authority and rebelled in any way he could. Nothing serious, just riding his bicycle on the sidewalk downtown, intentionally throwing trash on the streets, and most memorably, stopping his bike on the railroad tracks, making the train apply emergency breaking procedures. Of course, Ray rode off before there was any real danger.

It seemed the community could not wait for him to grow up and, hopefully, leave. Most left the community, at least temporarily, at about eighteen. But, if anything can change the course of a man's life, it is the entrance of that special female.

I don't mean to say she was out of his league. He was a good-looking kid and smart. After reform school, he rejoined his class as if he had never left. I am not sure why she was attracted to him; except that she may have wanted to rebel just as he had. When she rebelled, the town noticed. After all, she was the Baptist minister's daughter. She was also one of the most popular and prettiest girls in town. Somehow, their compass points pointed to each other, and their contemporaries knew they were an item.

Up until this point, she had played the preacher's daughter role perfectly. She would later say, "You should never raise a child in a fishbowl. Everyone in town watched me. I had had enough."

They were both nineteen. He could now smoke, and she followed him in anything he wanted to do. They drank beer too; and it stands to reason, other things not approved of by her raising.

One night, they drove to the edge of town and parked. It was a spur of the moment decision, but Ray's impulses were always spur of the moment. I can picture them on a high ridge, overlooking the lights of town, saying their goodbyes to the community and their past. But there were no high ridges near that town.

It could have been her idea, not his. But, on impulse, they decided to run away. No prior planning, no intention of eloping as to marry. Just put the town behind them. They didn't even carry a change of clothes.

He had fifteen dollars in his pocket, she had five. He had a tank of gas. That was enough fuel for about 250 miles. They headed west. By daylight, they were in Texas. They saw the oil rigs and the refineries and, by luck, saw a billboard advertising work in a refinery. They both applied and were both hired.

They lived out of their car until payday, and then had enough money to get a cheap hotel and buy a change of clothes.

Yes, their parents tried to find them, especially hers. But it would be almost a month before they were tracked to Texas. They had broken no laws, both were nineteen; and neither one, for whatever reason, wanted to return.

Their relationship was good. They never considered marriage. Why should they? That would just be conforming. Vows would not make them any more or any less faithful to each other.

Their first trip home came six years later. There was a visit to her parents first, then his. In a short time, they realized that, for whatever reason they had left to begin with, the reason had not changed. In seven hours, they were on their way back home, Texas.

INTERMENT DELAYED

The Boys ---

It was a Saturday morning in 1954. As had been their routine for the last year, Ralph and Richard, friends that lived in the same rural area, met to look for adventure, as they called it. For some time, they had been fans of the Hardy Boys Mystery series of books and pictured themselves as crime solvers, like the fictional Frank and Joe Hardy.

The boys had read all the books in the series, often arriving at the library early on a Saturday and not leaving until they had read an entire book. They were disappointed that there were no real mysteries to solve, but that did not dampen their imagination. On this Saturday, like most Saturdays, they were in search of a mystery, armed only with a writing pad, pencil, camera, and their bicycles. This would not be an ordinary Saturday.

The Old Couple ---

A short pine limb was nailed to the door. It served as a latch, not a lock. There was no lock and no need for one. There was virtually nothing in this house to steal, and the house was not at all inviting.

If you passed the house at night, you could see the glow of a kerosene lantern through the rough sawn board siding that did not seal the cracks.

There was no electricity, no running water and no indoor plumbing. A wood stove served as heat for the two room, less-than-basic lodging.

No one remembers if the house was at any time a decent place to live. Now, it leaned north on its rotted foundation, with the outdoor toilet located behind the house leaning in the opposite direction. You might imagine that some tornado had lifted the entire place and dropped it askew. It was fitting for the inhabitants.

Very few folks, if any, were alive that remembered either of them in their younger days. It seems that they were always old and looked older than old. He was bent, bald and boney, but long. He looked like Ichabod Crane with a head, but kept it bowed as to keep it from being taken. It is not remembered what he did for a living; but, in addition to this shelter and outhouse, he had acquired 30 acres of surrounding land. The land was as worn as he, and all 30 acres did not have enough cultivatable land to raise a family garden. It never had; but it certainly didn't now.

Forty years ago, he sold the gravel rights to the county to maintain the gravel roads that crisscrossed the area. With their draglines and bulldozers, they had scooped and scarred the land to a frightening depth. The only high spot was the site where the dwelling stood, and it teetered on the edge of the man made ravine. The high land, on which his house was placed, extended only about 15 feet beyond the outer walls of the house. The house site was much like an island in a waterless ocean. If you walked farther than 15 feet from either door, you would fall a distance of at least 40 feet to the bottom of the gravel mine. The excavators had left a six-foot-wide piece of earth that served as walking access to the public road, which itself was gravel and seldom traveled. The other 29-plus acres resembled a small Grand Canyon.

The money from the gravel is the only known source of income he ever had, but that ceased 20 years ago. The gravel no longer met specification, so the contract was canceled.

In retrospect, it is hard to know what he offered that would attract a wife. It is said that, if people live together long enough, they will begin to look like each other. As it applied to them, there was no better example. Some thought they were brother and sister. She was not bald; however, maybe she would not have been so unsightly if she had been.

Walking was their only method of transportation. Passersby knew them and maybe pitied them, but giving them a ride was a mistake to be made only once. In all weather except the hottest days of summer, they wore matching long, black, thick, wool coats. When not in use, they must have been stored with mothballs, as this odor only amplified the body fragrance that exists without basic hygiene. In addition, he chewed tobacco and she dipped snuff. Each would roll the window down to spit, having the wind return most of the spittle to the car's interior and onto their black coats.

The community knew they were there and may have felt pity, but not enough to show any great concern. They were just allowed to exist, and no one noticed them anymore than they would have noticed two stray dogs on the side of the road.

The minutes of the County Supervisors' meetings mentioned the payment for the gravel. Other than that, his name is mentioned only one other time. In 1929, the county paid for the burial of his only two sons. They were killed when a school bus on which they were riding got hit by the Chicago-bound City of New Orleans train at Thayer Crossing. The county buried them in the pauper's cemetery located at the county's penal farm.

Neither he nor his wife had been seen in months, but no one missed them and, most likely, no one cared. In fact, the grocer had asked him to not come back the last time he had been in. He was alone and the smell of his clothing made it unbearable for other customers. The grocer agreed to deliver his needs to the roadside and reduced the price for his cooperation. This was fine with him. He had no pride.

The Discovery ---

On that hot August Saturday morning, Ralph and Richard, in search of adventure, were riding their bikes and decided to go down the road where the old man and his wife lived. They had seen the house and the couple and knew what their parents had said about them. Bums, not civilized. The boys were curious.

From the gravel road, it was obvious that no one lived there any longer, as the foundation had dropped on one side to the ground and the roof had caved in. But the boys were curious.

They turned the pine limb latch and pushed the door open. They had heard how bad these folks smelled, but they were not prepared for the odor that came from the house. The missing tin from the roof allowed for plenty of light and it did not take but a few steps in the small house to realize this would be an adventure they would someday tell their children.

A chair sat at the end of the table. On the table was an open can of putrefied Vienna Sausage. The chair was empty, but scattered around the chair on the floor were bones. A great deal of dried flesh still clung to some of them. The only clothing seen was a pair of men's undershorts.

Then they entered the bedroom. There was nothing unusual to see except on the floor, at the edge of the bed and neatly placed in rows, were dried or dead flowers and small limbs with dried leaves. They photographed the scene carefully, as the Hardy Boys would have done.

Sixty years later, each one of the boys tells a similar story. They both admit that, for some strange reason, probably based on the Hardy Boys Mysteries, they wanted to take possession of the scene. It belonged to them. They would be the ones who found the dead body and they would get whatever glory they imagined went with it. They began to take more photographs and make notes.

Looking back, they admit they did not know what to do next. What would the Hardy Boys do?

Although they hated to give up control of the situation, they decided to notify the sheriff. There was a payphone at the crossroads and, after the two-mile bicycle ride, they reluctantly dialed "0" and asked the operator to connect them to the sheriff. Disappointed that the deputy answering the call did not believe them, they were determined to only share their find with someone of real authority. At the crossroads, they knew a state trooper or other official would pass by eventually. So, they waited. After about a three-hour wait, they could see the officer's car from a distance. The siren was mounted on the top center which made it distinguishable, even from far away.

As the car approached, they moved their bicycles to the center of the road, forcing the officer to stop. The boys explained why they had stopped him and, unlike the sheriff's deputy who had talked to them on the phone, the state trooper could see the sincerity in their eyes.

They hid their bikes in the woods and got in the back seat of the patrol car. This was rapidly becoming the most exciting day of their lives.

Arriving at the shack, the officer did not even enter the door. Having experience with the smell of human decomposition before, he radioed for backup.

Soon, the property (what little of it there was) was covered with law enforcement and curious neighbors.

With the excitement, and little being known about the strange couple, no one questioned the wife's whereabouts at first. Finally, the coroner, who was also the funeral parlor owner, arrived. He opened the door to the other room of the two-room house. There was a different, but similar, smell; not as strong as the one at the kitchen table.

He pulled back the covers on the bed. Nothing was there. Then he looked under the bed. They swept away the dead flowers and limbs to remove another body. She had died fully clothed except for one missing shoe. Her clothes contained dried mud with red clay, gravel and sand. It was obvious she had been dead significantly longer than her husband. The coroner estimated he had been dead about six months, and she longer, but he was uncertain about how much longer.

Back at the makeshift morgue in his funeral home, he carefully examined the bodies, or what remained of the bodies. There was nothing unusual about his, but hers concerned him. He called the doctor to come over and give him an opinion. The doctor confirmed that she had two broken legs, a broken arm, and a severe back injury. The body would be sent to the state crime lab for additional testing.

In a few days, the examiner called the county coroner with a question. What about the bits of sand and gravel that were found on her clothing? Did the coroner have any idea where this would come from? Should this be of concern?

The answer was easy. They lived in a gravel pit.

The cause of death could not be totally determined, but one clue led to the conclusion. At the edge of the drop off to the pit from where the house stood, the missing shoe was found. It is believed she fell to her death. She could have been going to the outhouse or she possibly could have been a sleepwalker.

Solving the Mystery ---

The time of her death could not be established and is a question authorities wanted answered. Ralph and Richard had their opportunity. They examined the photos they had taken on that day carefully. Their attention was centered on the skillfully placed flowers and leaves that had been disturbed while removing her body from under the bed. There were four hundred and twenty of them.

The first one was a Japanese magnolia. They went to the library and found that it only blooms in late February. They surmised that these flowers were tributes he left for her and that she must have died in February or early March. As a token of his devotion, he had placed a flower or, in winter, a dried leaf or stick, for 420 days or until his death. If he had been dead about six months, this would mean she died about 600 days previously.

They took their findings to the coroner, and he concurred. Their detective work earned them a front page write up in the local paper. It also catapulted both their careers, as they would each retire from a career in law enforcement.

After the death and circumstances were made public, the attitude of those who had known them changed. From being an odd, poorly dressed team of filthy misfits, the emphasis was now on how devoted they were to each other; or, especially, he to her. So devoted that he could not bear her to leave their home, even in death; and he would honor her daily with his meager floral tokens. To add to the mystery, where did he get the flowers? His property was so barren it could not nurture a thorn bush. He must have had to make daily long-distance walks, regardless of weather.

The county would have one more involvement in their lives. The couple would have to be buried. Public opinion pressured the authorities to not bury them in the paupers' plots. Someone donated a plot in the city cemetery. Their meager remains were buried together, just a few hundred feet from the most respected mayors, newspaper editors, and educators.

When the story is told today, little is said about their oddness; only his devotion to her is remembered.

THE LAST COON HUNT

The raccoon is a very smart animal. They are fast, sometimes almost vicious if cornered, and appear to have the power to reason. They can learn to unlock latches and other accomplishments and retain this knowledge for up to three years. They can be a nuisance, as they can destroy crops and scatter trash. They have been observed with one raccoon holding the garbage can open while the other plunders its contents. Catching a raccoon, locally called a coon, takes some skill, patience and physical endurance for both the dog used to track them and the dog owner.

During the poverty of the Great Depression, coons were hunted for meat. Many families made it through the tough times eating coon and baked sweet potatoes. This was prevalent in rural, more impoverished areas well into the 1950's. Out of the necessity, to harvest the food source, hunters became adept at training dogs that could pick up a coon's scent, trail it and chase it into a tree where it could be captured.

By the early 1960's, very few people ate raccoon, but a sport had evolved; a sport whose success depended on the skill of the dog, and the skill of its owner. Daryl and Sonny, when they were both seniors in high school, were the best coon hunters for miles around.

It is said that, when you look back on your life, you can count your true friends on one hand. Nothing could be truer than the friendship between Daryl Hart and Sonny Smith. It had been thirty years since they had seen each other; but, on the weekend of their 50th class reunion, the bond was as if it had never been broken.

The friendship could have ended just prior to high school graduation if the facts had been known, but circumstances were never revealed that would threaten their close relationship. These two friends loved to coon hunt. Even the old timers would tell you, as teenagers, they were the best at the sport. There was not a better dog than Daryl's black and tan dog named Dan, unless it was Sonny's blue tick hound named Rowdy. It's hard to say which was the better dog, or who was the better owner; but no one questioned the fact that one of these two was the best.

Coon hunting was usually done on cold winter nights. This was most likely because the coon's habitat was deep in the swamp that, in warm weather, would be infested with both mosquitoes and snakes. The cold weather also added to the ambiance of the occasion that was just as much a part of the sport as the hunt. Good friends, maybe a half dozen, would gather to tell tall tales of past hunts and listen to the dogs run. On cold nights, they would build a fire, adding to the allure of the occasion. They would gather around the fire and wait until the dog or dogs had "struck." Struck meant picked up a scent. There was no question when this happened, as each dog has a specific bark. The dog's bark has a certain sound when it strikes, and another when it "trees." Trees is the term used when the dog has trailed the coon to a specific tree.

Each dog has his own unique voice, but some are chippers - they make a sharp sound as they trail the coon - and others are howlers. Dan was a chipper and Rowdy was a howler.

In Utopian thought, this was before young adults experimented with more mind-expanding drugs, and even before the use of any considerable amount of alcohol. It was not, however, unusual to see someone light up a cigar. The favorites were Honey Rum Crooks. They were cheap and you could buy them at Pistol Sasser's store on the way to the hunt.

Bogue Chitto was a small community, a village you might say, and everyone knew each other. Most of the teenagers had been in school together from the first grade. Most attended the First Baptist Church and their dependence on each other had formed a very close-knit circle. Even the adults knew most of the kids in the area.

Coon hunting was their favorite recreation; that is, other than basketball. If there was not a game on a weekend night, they would be coon hunting. They had done it without parental supervision since they were twelve years old.

There were lots of good coon hunters in the area and surrounding counties, but the fame of Daryl, his dog Dan, and Sonny, with his dog Rowdy, had become legendary. It was March, and warm weather would be coming. There was only time for a few more hunts.

The community must have known that the era of coon hunting was coming to an end, or that these two boys would be moving on. Not many stayed in the small town after graduation. Before it was too late, everyone wanted to know who had the best dog - Daryl or Sonny.

Word of the "Great Hunt" to crown the "Bogue Chitto Coon Dog King" had spread throughout the area. Both boys wanted their dog to win and, regardless of friendship, it was heated competition. Wagers were placed at Dude Morgan's Pool Hall.

Rules were drawn up. The winner was the dog that had the first verifiable "tree." In other words, the coon had to be seen in the tree the dog had indicated. The dog owner would rule when his dog had treed, and then the hunting party would go to verify.

Due to the popularity of the contest, there was concern that there would be a crowd, and this would distract the dogs. It was decided that only four people would accompany each hunter and his dog.

Even with these rules, dozens of people, maybe as many as a hundred, wanted to witness the event. They were allowed to come; but they were required to park and stay in Busby's field, about a quarter of a mile away.

Daryl would release his dog Dan by the old sycamore tree at the section marker, and Sonny would release his dog Rowdy about two hundred yards away by the squirrel tree, an old hickory that was famous for having eight squirrels shot from it in one day.

As they say, a lot of water had run under the bridge in the fifty years since the two old friends had hunted together. Neither lived in Bogue Chitto anymore. Daryl lived in North Carolina and Sonny in Louisiana. They had seen each other once at the funeral of a friend, but that was thirty years ago.

Coincidentally, they had both booked rooms in the same hotel in Brookhaven, the nearest town of any size. Once they realized they were in the same hotel, the importance of the class reunion was secondary. They had a lifetime of catching up to do. The reunion festivities lasted until almost midnight Friday night and, when they returned to the hotel, the conversation was brief before retiring. Saturday night, they both decided to skip the reunion and just visit with each other.

They talked about winning the State Basketball Championship their junior year, still questioning how they won when both had fouled out with eight minutes remaining in the game. They tried to recall the Freshman's name who came off the bench and scored twelve points in those closing eight minutes. They couldn't recall.

They talked about the class trip that lasted twenty-five days their junior year; how they rode a school bus and camped all the way to Hoover Dam and back. The trip influenced their lives. If not for the trip, they may have never left Bogue Chitto. Each agreed that not leaving Bogue Chitto may not have been a bad thing.

Eventually, they began to reflect on the coon hunts. Neither had coon hunted again since that night. Both tried to explain why, and both agreed the reasons were numerous: Coon was no longer a part of the Southern diet, the loss of land available for hunting, transition to deer hunting... but, mostly, there was no opportunity for them to do it together. And there would never be two dogs like Dan and Rowdy.

They talked about Dan and Rowdy and the contest. Each could sense that the other was holding back on details of the hunt in depth. There was something that neither wanted to tell.

After a few awkward pauses in the conversation, Daryl brought the discussion to a point, "I was never happier than when we found Rowdy alive."

Sonny responded, "I remember, you crazy fool, you were so excited you jumped in the river, and it was thirty degrees. What made you do that?"

Daryl didn't answer.

Sonny continued, "Well, I was glad you won. You and Dan deserved it. I guess, after all these years, I can tell you what I tried to do.

"You see, I had read they have a coon dog graveyard in Alabama where the best coon dogs in the world are buried. I wanted Rowdy to be in that graveyard someday. I had to win."

Sonny continued, "If you remember, I had a pet coon we kept in a cage. We called him Bandit. About three hours before the hunt, I took Bandit down to where I knew you would release Dan. I walked him about a half mile in the woods and then circled back to where your truck would be parked. I could just imagine how the crowd would be laughing when Dan returned to the release point fifteen minutes later.

"It didn't happen that way, though. Dan was smart. He struck on a fresher scent and went for it.

"I never told you and, since you won, I guess I should have. But it bothered me all these years that I would do such a thing to my best friend and his dog."

Sonny watched Daryl's expression. He just smiled and exhaled deeply.

Daryl spoke up, "Well, since this is true confession night, I have a story to tell you...

"I didn't know anything about a dog graveyard, but Delos Howard had offered me a two-hundred-dollar stud fee if Dan won. That was a lot of money in those days. I had to win. So, I had an idea how to do it.

"I put some red cayenne pepper in a paper bag. You know, those bags your mama used to put your sandwiches in to take to school? My intent was to scatter it all around the hickory tree before you got there, so I went about an hour early. I knew if Rowdy got a nose full of pepper, he would be useless. When I arrived, there was a crowd already gathering and I didn't have an opportunity to scatter the pepper. I put the bag in my front jeans pocket.

"When Dan struck, I could hear Rowdy already on a fast trail going toward the railroad. I knew you heard it, too. You remember, we always tried to keep the dogs away from the railroad. I knew and you knew it was about time for the Number 3 freight train to come through. Then I heard the train coming.

"When the train passed, I didn't hear Rowdy again. I remembered, just the year before, Clem Britt's dog was killed running under a train trailing a coon. I also knew Rowdy wouldn't pull off the trail either.

"Dan was still trailing, but I pulled off the chase to go look for Rowdy. I beat you to the track as I hoped I would. I knew how you loved that dog. I walked up and down the track. If he had been killed, I didn't want you to find him. I saw no blood, but I didn't see Rowdy either. That's when you got there and that's when it happened."

"What happened, Daryl?" Sonny questioned.

"Just as I told you, I saw no blood. I realized the bag in my blue jean pocket with the pepper had broken. I had a hole in my jean pocket and, let me tell you, that pepper has no respect for tender parts.

"As you recall, we looked for Rowdy about thirty minutes; then we heard him. He struck. You called him off because Dan had treed, and we both knew my dog's voice and he was not lying to us. There was a coon in that tree. I was burning so bad I couldn't think straight.

"Finally, just by the river, Rowdy comes up unharmed. I didn't jump in the river to celebrate, I did it for relief! Never had pain like that, not even when I had kidney stones.

"You conceded that I was the winner, and I took the two hundred dollars and went to Junior College. Dan died while I was gone, but I came home and buried him. To tell you the truth, I buried him in the family cemetery. I didn't tell any of the relatives. They wouldn't have approved."

Sonny smiled, "You SOB, you were as devious as I was! But I have a follow up to the story. Delos Howard told me he had some puppies by Dan. I bought one of the puppies and later bred her to Rowdy. Some folks didn't like the fact that I mixed a blue tick with a black and tan, and I guess they were right. Maybe coon hunting is just in the blood. I didn't coon hunt anymore, but I wanted to train that dog to deer hunt. Never could break it from chasing coons. It could be on the trail of the biggest buck in the woods, but if it crossed a coon trail, off it went."

After both had revealed their transgressions, they reflected on other hunts. One they remembered was the night they got lost. It was a Sunday night and they missed school the next day. Because they missed school, Coach Calhoun suspended them from the Wednesday night basketball game. They lost.

They also talked about the guys who hunted with them. Some were deceased but some very much alive. They talked about Tommy. He was the designated tree climber. They tried to guess how many coons he shook out that had been treed by Dan and Rowdy. They agreed to meet soon and deer hunt. They did. Somehow, without Dan and Rowdy, the hunt was disappointing.

HIS LEGACY

Wilfred, the old man was as predictable as the Number 2 freight train. Each day at precisely three in the afternoon, he would put on his hat and take the keys to his old Pontiac off the nail on the back porch. Backing the old car out of the garage carefully and slowly, he unknowingly raced the engine because he could not hear well anymore. Not only could he not hear, but his neck was fused and his only aid to backing was a rear view mirror. He did not see well, either.

Making a slow, but methodical, journey out of the driveway and onto the gravel road, he drove the half-mile to inspect his investment. It was a forty-acre plot of land. Years ago, he had owned 140 acres; but, over the years, he had sold much of it. Some he sold to his son-in-law, but most he sold to Purvis Nations.

He had sold the land because he needed the money; and besides, he could not farm that much anymore. Two vegetable gardens, a pasture for a milk cow, some chickens and a couple of hogs had become an ambitious achievement for someone his age. Yet, he had to keep going. His pension from the U.S. Postal Service was $20 per week. His diabetic wife's doctor's bills were almost that much.

He got comfort in knowing that his investment was about to mature. Just as the money from the last land sale played out, he would have something to fall back on. He had planned it that way.

Twenty years ago, in 1940, he was forced to retire from being a rural mail carrier. Heart trouble, or so he was told. It was just before the war, and things were inexpensive. Then the war, the victory, and the inflation. In 1945, he had his financial plan. Selling the land was not part of it, but it became a necessity with the rising cost of living. He didn't want to sell the land in the first place. He wanted to leave it to his children. That would be his legacy. He didn't mind the sale to his son-in-law. It was still in the family. He regretted selling to Purvis. Purvis was not one of them. A nice guy, but he had other means of income and he wasn't dependent on the land or its produce to live comfortably. You could say he was just a hobby farmer, and the land was just a tax write-off.

In 1945, Wilfred planted the 40 acres in Loblolly pine. Pulpwood was the new industry. It was less labor intensive than cotton or corn, but it needed about 20 years to mature to its full potential. He had thinned it in 1955 and given the little profit to his grandson to buy a band instrument.

Each day he walked the land, looking for infestation of pine beetles or other diseases. He had never had a problem. He knew that the main threats to his future income would most likely be from two sources: fire and low pulpwood prices. Some years ago, he had control-burned his trees to rid the underbrush. Underbrush, if left to thicken, becomes kindling if a fire starts. The wind changed that day and the fire almost got out of control. He decided he would take his chances and never control-burn again. That was eight years ago.

These days, he didn't walk the entire land as often. He was 85 and suffered from arthritis. He still liked to view it from the comfort of his unairconditioned automobile and through eyes that were almost milk-white with overripe cataracts.

What he couldn't see, he imagined. The faded vision mentally displayed a rose-colored portrait of his security. In his mind, he saw much more timber than was there. He heard pulpwood prices were rising. In a few weeks, he would sell and then be financially secure. After all, how much longer would he live? He was a realist. If the timber did not bring a good price, he would most likely have to sell the land to Purvis. Again, he didn't want to do this. That land was for his children.

Purvis Nations owned five hundred acres adjacent to Wilfred's property on the south side. The land wrapped around the rear of Wilfred's property and extended to the river. Purvis had dabbled in all types of farming: corn, cotton, peanuts and soybeans. He had recently decided to experiment with cattle. In the early spring, he planted a hundred acres in Byhalia grass. In July, he placed thirty head of imported French Charolais cows and a bull on the property. It was a sizable investment. By late August, there had been no rain. The grass dried and died and there was no grass for the cattle.

Purvis began to supplement the grass they were not getting with crushed corn he purchased at the county co-op. That was expensive. Surely it would rain next week. It didn't. By September, the grass in the cattle pasture was as dry as a powder keg.

Wilfred's daughter, Ellen, had built a home on two acres he had given her on the north side of the pine farm. She and her husband had cleared the land, but the yard grass was as dry as Purvis's pasture. She would tell later that she remembered the phone call as if it were yesterday. A fire observation tower located eight miles south called her and told her they were seeing smoke somewhere near her home. Did she know anything about it? She had not been outside all day. She remembers it was about 3 p.m.

She went outside and immediately smelled smoke. Then she saw it. She could even see some flames as they belched over the trees in the distance. She recalled that it reminded her of what she imagined hell fire would look like.

By this time, neighbors were arriving and attempting to contain the blaze. Soon, the forestry department arrived with a jeep that had a plow behind it. They would attempt to cut a fire lane, but the trees were planted too close together to allow navigation. Then a large bulldozer arrived.

The local high school was called, and all junior and senior boys were allowed to leave school to help fight the fire if they wanted to. Not a one refused.

Wilfred's daughter then realized the fire was coming toward her house. She was home alone and was at a loss as to what to do. Desperate, she decided to seek help from the neighbor across the highway. Maybe they could load and move some of the keepsake items that she could not replace. That is when the sheriff pulled into the driveway.

With the excitement, Ellen did not notice the somber expression on the sheriff's face. Then he asked her to sit down. Her immediate reaction was that this was not a time for sitting; but the sheriff almost pushed her into a chair.

"Miss Ellen, I have bad news. Your father arrived and attempted to fight the fire. He has had what I believe to be a heart attack or a heat stroke. I don't think he will make it."

Ellen then heard the siren as the ambulance passed. In a matter of minutes, she heard it going back the opposite direction.

"Miss Ellen, I know you want to be with your father. I will do all I can to save your house."

Ellen didn't bother changing clothes. This was not a time that she cared about looking presentable. In five minutes, she was on her way to the hospital. How could a day that had been good, go so wrong?

The fire now had reached Purvis's field where the cows were. A low flame was racing across the dry grass as if it were gasoline, and the cows were retreating. There was a fence between the pasture and the river. The cows were trapped.

Tommy, a young neighbor who left school to fight the fire, took his motorbike, grabbed a pair of pliers, and raced through the shortest part of the flames. Reaching the fence, he began to cut the wire. If he could just get the cows to go through, they could find the river. It was wide but shallow. The fire wouldn't cross it.

One cow was obstinate and began to run the opposite direction from the cut fence opening. Tommy chased the cow on the bike and finally succeeded in driving it through the downed fence. He then parked his bike and proceeded to drive the cattle through the thick woods to the river.

Now he was trapped. His only hope was to get in the river with the cows. He did.

The old man was a survivor. He began to regain consciousness and, in two hours, he was deemed stable. He would have to remain in the hospital for a few days, at least; but his will to live was strong.

Ellen hurried back to her home. To her surprise, there were twelve pickup trucks in her driveway and all her furniture, even the trash can, was loaded on the trucks and safe. To the south end of her property, she saw the bulldozer as it cut a double path between her property and the fire. Her home was saved.

Wilfred lost his entire pine farm that afternoon. They didn't tell him about it. Not then, anyway. Purvis lost nothing except a fence. Tommy lost his motorbike.

Before Wilfred was released from the hospital, he had a visitor dressed in a coat and tie. No, it was not a doctor. It was a land-man from an oil company. They wanted to lease his land for mineral rights. The lease brought more money than he would have gotten from his timber.

In four more years, he would pass away; the next year, his wife would follow. As he had hoped, the land was left intact for his children, his legacy, and he still had $366 in the bank.

Purvis Nations bought Tommy a new motorbike.

In 1985, the family harvested a new stand of pulpwood from the property. Each child got a few thousand dollars, which some needed. They then sold all the property to Purvis Nation's son.

So the legacy ends.

DEATH ON THE PEARL

Deep friendships usually don't develop overnight; but, for some relationships, there is a defining moment when an occurrence solidifies a bond that may have been growing for a long time. Such was the case with Freddie Brumfield and Johnny Mays.

During the mid-1930s in rural communities, a high school graduating class could be very small. This was due to the area being sparsely populated; and the fact that, by high school, many had dropped out. Education may not have been deemed important. Freddie and Johnny were two of only 18 students in the class of 1942.

With so few to choose from, you were friends with almost everyone; but, in their case, they developed a special bond. It was due to an incident that happened on a cold, late-October night in 1938.

The friends enjoyed fishing on the nearby Pearl River and hunting in the adjacent Honey Island Swamp that lay just on the opposite side of the river. On that day, their plan was to squirrel hunt. Using a small skiff and outboard, they traveled two miles downstream from the boat launch and lashed the boat to a cypress tree on the opposite side of the river.

That afternoon, the weather worsened and it began to rain. The boys realized they needed to get back to their boat and return to the dock. Both boys pulled the starter rope until they were exhausted, but the outboard wouldn't start. They realized they were stranded until help came, which could be the next morning.

Neither felt any life-threatening danger; but they realized, to have any comfort from the cold and rain, they would have to improvise. They gathered firewood and drained gasoline from the outboard. To further ignite the wet wood, they carved kindling from a fat pine stump. As dark set in, the straight-line wind gusted to 60 miles per hour. Without the fire, they would have been in danger of hypothermia. It was, to say the least, a very uncomfortable experience and they were pleased to be rescued the next morning. Neither knew what a mystery that night would produce in the years to come.

There is something almost universal that kids and even teenagers enjoy doing. That is to build their own cozy, small place. Young children may place blankets over chairs to create dark rooms beneath. Older kids will build a fort. Others built tar paper shacks. Based on their experience of being stranded on the river, Johnny and Freddie had a much grander idea. They would build a houseboat. It would be their get-away and maybe a place that some other stranded fisherman or hunter could shelter if needed.

They scavenged material. The boat would float on pontoons built of 55-gallon drums, welded together and coated with tar to retard rust. There would be ten drums on each side. It would be twenty-five feet long, eight feet wide and include a front porch.

They built four bunks inside and heated it with a small potbellied stove. A kerosene stove was used for cooking and kerosene lamps for lighting. It was quite impressive when complete and they moored it to the same cypress tree to which they had tied their skiff when they were stranded.

They used it often. Over the next few years, the two became maybe closer than brothers.

For a high school graduate in the waning years of the Great Depression, there were few opportunities for young men, and even less for young women. Freddie knew he wanted to be in law enforcement. Due to his love for the river and the swamp, he thought of being a game warden.

Johnny was less outgoing than Freddie, and maybe less ambitious. He had not given much thought to his career. One thing he did know was that, two days after graduation, he would marry Mary Ellen. The two had been an item since seventh grade and never dated anyone else. Mary Ellen spent her senior year planning her wedding, but she had a more pressing obsession. She wanted a baby as soon after marriage as possible and spent even more time planning for that.

On December 7, 1941, their lives, as well as the rest of the world's, would change. President Roosevelt said it was the "Day of Infamy." Pearl Harbor was bombed; and shortly afterward, both Johnny and Freddie knew their future would be redirected.

In April of 1942, they knew it would be their duty to enter the military. Johnny tried to explain to Mary Ellen that it was the thing to do; when, in fact, he had no choice. If he did not join, he would be drafted. She insisted on marriage before he enlisted and maybe she could have a baby while he was gone. Johnny knew this was not a good idea. There were already local boys that were being killed in combat. He didn't want to leave a widow; or worse, a widow with a child. Mary Ellen resented him for that but promised she would wait.

Freddie chose to join the Marines. Johnny, on the insistence of his mother, joined the Navy. She said if he had to die, she wanted him to die clean, not in some muddy trench like the photos she had seen of WWI.

No one knew at the time it would be over three years before they would return home. Each time the mail came, Johnny would search for a letter from Mary Ellen first. He expected a "Dear John." After all, she resented the postponement of their wedding and being a mother was most important to her. When he received a letter, he quickly read the first paragraph and the last. Somehow, he felt he could get the gist of the letter quickly. The "Dear John" letter never came.

Both Freddie and Johnny were involved in combat. Most notably, Freddie at Iwo Jima among other places; and Johnny would be at the invasion of Okinawa. Freddie would be wounded, not life-threatening, but he would be awarded a Purple Heart.

Johnny would later tell his story, or at least part of it. He remembered the dawn of Easter Sunday. As the sun rose, the invasion fleet was in place.

It seemed as if he could see ships anchored for miles. He said, at first, it was the most beautiful morning he had ever seen. But then the kamikazes came. That is all he would talk about, but that does not begin to tell the story.

His ship got hit by a downed kamikaze. Luckily, the entire explosive package did not activate; but there was damage, and he was struck by shrapnel. There were several wounds, mostly to his lower abdomen.

As soon as possible, he was evacuated to a hospital ship, the USS Mercy. In a few days, a doctor gave him the news. No one knew how it would change his life.

Bedside manner was not the long suit of military doctors during wartime. There was too much to do; and if a wounded soldier was not critical, they were given little attention. On that day, the doctor briskly approached his bed.

"Sailor, you're going to be fine. You are lucky, but there is one small problem."

"What's that, doc?"

"As a man, you will be fine. You can do anything you did before, except you can't have children. Other than that, everything down there is good. Go home and shoot blanks. You're lucky."

With that, the doctor departed.

It would be a year before Johnny was discharged and, each day, his mind dwelled on what he would tell Mary Ellen. She wanted children more than anything. Her letters were filled with the hope of him returning, their marriage and children, lots of children. What would he tell her?

He chose to tell her nothing, and he would regret that for the rest of his life. On November 27, 1946, they were married. They rented a small two-bedroom cottage and immediately Mary Ellen decorated the spare bedroom as a baby's nursery.

Freddie came home about the same time and got a job as a deputy with the sheriff's department. Both were considered local heroes for their military service, and Freddie's outgoing personality made him a favorite in the community.

Johnny got a job at the shipyard, dismantling small craft that had been used in the war effort. An unreasonable amount of his take-home pay was spent by Mary Ellen, buying things that would be used when the baby came. Of course, Johnny knew this was a waste of money, a baby was not coming.

He felt guilty. Even though the two were happier than he had ever imagined, he feared she wanted a baby more than anything else.

A couple of years passed. Mary Ellen made an appointment with a doctor in New Orleans to see if he could determine her inability to conceive. He found nothing and suggested she have her husband tested.

When she revealed what the doctor had told her, it led to the most severe disagreement they had experienced in their marriage. He refused, reminding her that she had never complained about the frequency or the quality of their intimacy. She tried to reason that, medically, it went beyond that; but he could not let his secret be known and refused her request.

Soon, their marriage seemed to cool. Nothing serious, but she no longer discussed the subject with him, and he felt a distance coming between them.

It was now 1951. The parish sheriff had decided to retire. Freddie would run for the position. With an outgoing personality, being a war hero, and the backing of the retiring sheriff, Freddie won 69% of the vote. His first week on the job, he asked his best friend Johnny if he wanted a job as a deputy. Johnny liked the idea, but Mary Ellen thought it too dangerous for a father-to-be. Johnny turned the job down.

It would be unfair to say Johnny and Mary Ellen's marriage deteriorated. He worshiped her and she him, but she felt incomplete with the lack of being able to become pregnant. She realized it was a problem she had to deal with and attempted to turn her interest to other projects. She thought about opening a daycare; at least she could be around children. There was not a daycare in fifty miles, but she did not have the space in their small home or the money to get started.

She volunteered to help any way she could at the school, aiding in the teaching and caring for elementary children. She became a Red Cross volunteer and a member of the PTA, even though she was not a parent. All this involvement took time away from Johnny. He sensed a lull in their relationship, but nothing that really concerned him. After all, they had been married six years. Her time away from him was missed, but not resented.

It was late June of 1953. Johnny came home from work and Mary Ellen was beaming with excitement.

"Johnny, I have a surprise. I want to blindfold you so I can surprise you."

She carefully secured a bandana snugly around his eyes, tying it in a tight knot at the back of his head. She then led him through the small house to the spare bedroom. Then she slowly unfastened the blindfold.

Johnny didn't understand what he saw. The bedroom had been transformed back into a nursery with all the items Mary Ellen had collected over the years but had been in storage for the last two.

She watched carefully to capture his surprise and excitement.

There was some, as he asked Mary Ellen, "So you have decided we will adopt?"

"No, no, no Johnny. I'm pregnant."

What excitement Johnny had displayed ceased immediately and he turned and walked out of the room and into the back yard.

He was caught off guard. Never in his wildest dreams had he expected Mary Ellen to be unfaithful. He wondered who it was. He had no knowledge of any male friends, only the ladies in her volunteer groups. Why would she do this? Except for her being childless, he felt they had a perfect marriage. How could she do such a thing? How could he raise a child that he knew was not his?

Out on the lawn, alternating through fits of rage and grief, he contemplated what he would do. He had to get away. As far as he knew, at this time, it would be final. She had breached the ultimate trust.

Mary Ellen was completely shocked by his actions. She reasoned he must be having some type of breakdown. Why would you not be excited about your wife's pregnancy?

In about an hour, Johnny came in. He didn't speak, just went to a closet and pulled out his Navy duffel bag. In it, he placed the barest of necessities, including a few clothes, shaving equipment, and his work boots.

He said nothing to Mary Ellen as he attached the small boat and trailer to his truck and left for the houseboat. The next day, he didn't go to work, nor did he go the next day. This wasn't like him. He was a hard, dependable worker. His employer came to his house and asked Mary Ellen about his absence. She could not, or would not, tell him what had happened. She didn't know herself.

In a small community, news travels fast, and the rumor was gossiped that she and Johnny had separated. No one in the community could believe it or had any idea why.

One afternoon, Freddie was waiting at the shipyard gate when Johnny got off from work. It was about a week after he left home.

"Johnny, do you want to talk about what's happening? I've done some checking and I know you are living on the houseboat. I know things are not good between you and Mary Ellen. Do you mind sharing? I'm very concerned about both of you."

The friendship between the two was still close and Johnny needed to confide in someone.

"Freddie, Mary Ellen is having an affair. I don't know who with, but there is no question she is having an affair."

"Johnny, how do you know?"

"Freddie, I just know." He did not mention the pregnancy, nor had he ever confided in Freddie about his war injury.

"Johnny, I will do some checking and see if I can turn up whoever it might be."

"That's not necessary, it's over. I'm not going back."

Three weeks passed. Johnny began to think more clearly. He missed Mary Ellen and knew he still loved her. He reasoned, maybe it was only fair that she got pregnant by someone else. She wanted a baby so bad; she could not have one with him. Maybe it was just physical, with no emotional attachment, for the purpose of conceiving. If so, maybe he could live with that.

Each day, he drifted more and more toward reconciliation. He decided that on Saturday he would go home and have a talk with Mary Ellen. It was Thursday.

Friday morning was a beautiful morning. He felt good going to work that morning and had basically determined he would reconcile with Mary Ellen. He had some concern that she had not attempted to contact him, but reasoned he deserved it. It was now early July.

July weather can change quickly, and afternoon storms were not uncommon. The rain came about 1 p.m. and lasted until after 3 p.m. Luckily, it was over when he arrived at the boat dock from work to take his skiff to the houseboat.

Before Johnny moved onto the boat after leaving Mary Ellen, the houseboat had been used occasionally, but less frequently than years before. Maintenance was bare minimum; and the right pontoon, the first 55-gallon drum, had a gradual leak and a gaping hole in the upper portion of its end. This caused the starboard side of the boat to ride lower in the water. This had one advantage. It made the step onto the porch easier, as it was not as high out of the water.

Johnny skillfully maneuvered the skiff for a docking with the houseboat. He steered it a few yards downstream and then turned against the current to have more control. Before he even reached the boat, some twenty feet away, he knew something was wrong. He could see a red tint in the rainwater that had blown onto the porch.

After tying the skiff to the boat, but before stepping out of it, he knew something was seriously not right. He had shot enough animals to know what he saw looked like diluted blood.

The door was partially open. What he saw was something he would think about for the rest of his life. Lying on the floor, in a massive amount of blood, was Mary Ellen. The blood had begun to coagulate inside the houseboat, but Mary Ellen was warm to the touch. It may have been only due to the July heat. Due to the amount of blood, he knew she was dead.

Her head was lying on its right side; and on the left exposed side was a cut. It extended in a circular pattern from her ear, toward her chin and circled across her neck to her shoulder. Most of the blood had come from the neck area.

For a few minutes, he just sat on the floor by her body and wept, some of the blood seeping into his pants. *Who could have done this?* he wondered. *Maybe the father of the baby?*

He had to do something. The nearest phone would be about a mile from the dock. There was a payphone there and he would call Freddie.

Johnny tried to relay the happenings to Freddie but, through sobs, it was hard to tell the story. Finally, Freddie told him to wait for him. Don't talk to anyone. He was on his way.

The two friends made their way by skiff back to the boat. After examining Mary Ellen's body, Freddie asked the inevitable question.

"Johnny, we're friends. I don't believe you did this, but if you did, don't tell me. It is important for your sake that I do not know."

"Freddie, you know I didn't do this, and I don't have any idea who did."

"Johnny, we'll talk about that later. We've got to get her body to the funeral home. The coroner will come by tomorrow and examine her."

The two friends loaded the body of Mary Ellen in the skiff and returned to the dock. They had wrapped her in a blanket from the boat and, luckily, no one was at the landing. She was placed in Freddie's patrol car. It was the saddest moment in Johnny's life.

"Johnny, don't talk to anyone. Don't say one word. I'll see you in the morning. You go to your house and spend the night. Don't go back to the boat. We will have to search it for any evidence we can find. Do you hear me?"

"Yes. I hear you."

That night, there was no sleep for Johnny. He lay down on the bed he and Mary Ellen had slept on for years. Somehow, this felt like an invasion of privacy, so he moved to a large rocking chair. It was one Mary Ellen had bought to rock the baby, but that was years ago. Still no sleep.

Investigation Day 1

The sheriff had asked a physician to perform an autopsy. The coroner was just an elected position and the present one had no medical training. The best he could do with any authority was to pronounce her dead, which he did and then departed.

Meanwhile, Johnny, Freddie and his chief deputy, Paul Stone, went to the houseboat. The hot July day and the abundance of blood had attracted flies. The smell was not pleasant.

The sheriff noted:

No sign of a struggle.

No obvious footprints in the blood except what most likely are Johnny's and mine from the day before.

Most disturbingly, there is no indication of how she got here. Since there was no skiff attached, she had to be brought here by someone.

What was the motive?

Investigation Day 2

The doctor reports that she died of a cut from the ear through the neck, cutting the jugular vein. She bled out quickly.

She was pregnant.

Sizable bits of rust were found in the wound. Who would take a rusty knife with them to murder someone?

The weapon used to cut her neck and into part of the crew neck shirt she was wearing appeared to be dull, as if to tear more than cut.

Freddie surmised, based on the weapon, or lack of a good one, the murder was not premeditated.

By the third day, the incident was the main subject of gossip. The public found out the couple were separated, she was pregnant, she was found on the houseboat, and she had been transported there by someone.

On the fourth day after the discovery, the following letter to the editor appeared in the local newspaper:

It is obvious who killed Mary Ellen. It could have been no other than her husband. It is well known that our sheriff and the killer have been friends for many years. For the sake of decency, he should recuse himself from the investigation. It should be turned over to the District Attorney to investigate and the husband should be arrested. He not only killed his wife but his unborn child.

Maybe it is time to elect a new sheriff for this parish.

Anonymous

Investigation Day 5

Sheriff Freddie arrived at his office early that morning. He avoided breakfast at the local cafe because he didn't want to hear the criticism of the dozen or so that met there for breakfast. He understood that the evidence against Johnny was great, but years of friendship give you insight into someone that defies all evidence. In his mind, he knew that Johnny didn't kill Mary Ellen. But if he didn't, who did and why? These were the questions he had to answer for himself and, more so, for his constituents.

Almost as soon as he arrived, the phone rang, and he answered.

"Boss Sheriff, this is Lige Wade. You know me, I has the boat launch and rental on the river."

"Yes, Lige, I know who you are. What can I do for you? Has someone stolen a skiff?"

"Naw Sir, nobody stole no skiff."

"Then, what can I do for you?"

"Sheriff, I may know sumpum about the lady that got kilt."

"What's that Lige?"

"I ain't gone talk about it on the phone, yous need to come to my place but don't bring nobody with you."

"Lige, you can tell me on the phone. But, if you insist, I will be right out."

"Yes, Boss, I be waiting for you."

Freddie knew Lige had a drinking problem, but he also knew he was honest and had never given anyone any trouble. For years, he had owned a boat launch and a skiff and outboard rental on the Pearl.

It took thirty minutes for Freddie to arrive at Lige's boat launch and Lige was waiting for him. There were two fishermen launching their boats, so Lige asked the sheriff to walk a few yards away out of earshot.

"Lige, what do you know about the murder of Mary Ellen Mays?"

"I don't know whats I know, but I knows something."

"You want to tell me about it?"

"I don't wants to, cause I don't wants to get mixed up in it, but I guess I gots to."

"Ok Lige, what do you know?"

"That lady rented a skiff from me on the day she got kilt. She was in a hurry, because a thunderstorm was coming. I tried to talk her into waiting but she refused. She had two jars with her. I could tell there was dumplins in one and greens in the other. It turned out she had some cornbread, but I didn't see it then. I cranked the motor for her, even though she said she knew how to do it. She took off up the river."

"Is that all Lige?"

"No, Boss, there's be more. About two hours later, I look out in the river and here comes my boat drifting past. Ain't no lady in it. I paddle out there and gets my boat and bring it to the dock. In it, I sees the dumplins, the greens and the cornbread, but ain't no lady in it."

"Is that all Lige?"

"Naw Sir. There was a little bit of blood on that flat part near the bow. I suspected something, so I pulled the boat on shore and covered it with a tarp."

"Can I see it Lige?

"Yes sir, Boss, it's back here." He led the sheriff to a tarp covered boat.

The boat still contained the food and, as Lige had said, something that appeared to be blood.

"Lige, why have you waited five days to call me?"

"Boss, youz a good man. But I was the last to see that white woman and there is blood in my boat. It ain't gone be good for a black man to be the last one to see a dead white woman. It could even be bad."

"Why did you decide to call me?"

"Boss, I knowed Mr. Johnny more than I knowed you. He didn't kill that woman."

"I know that too, Lige, and you may have saved his life. Don't touch the boat or let anyone around it. Don't tell anyone about this conversation. I will have the boat picked up. You can take off the motor. When this is over, I'll return your boat."

"Yes sir, Boss."

What Lige had said was the best clue in the case. It was now clear Johnny had not transported her to the houseboat and may not have known she was coming.

Could she have come to attempt reconciliation and to surprise him with his favorite food?

Why had she not unloaded the food and why had she not secured the boat?

Most importantly, why was there blood in the flat boat?

He had an idea. He had to make another visit to the houseboat.

Public opinion continued to mount against Johnny and against Freddie for the failure to arrest him. Freddie's biggest supporters called a meeting and insisted Freddie act. Finally, he had to do something. He decided to turn the case over to the District Attorney to investigate.

He turned all the information over to the DA. The boat, the statement from Lige, and some evidence he found at his last visit to the houseboat. He had photos and a statement from the doctor who did the autopsy and accompanied him to the houseboat the last time he went.

His decision to turn the case over to the DA came because of public pressure; but more so, it came from the fact that, after his last visit to the houseboat and taking the doctor with him, he felt sure he could exonerate Johnny. The grand Jury would be the decision maker and Johnny would not spend the rest of his life under suspicion. The DA had agreed not to arrest Johnny unless the grand jury indicted him.

A grand jury was summoned. Freddie would present the evidence almost as if he were a defense attorney.

First, he established the fact that Mary Ellen used a boat she rented to reach the houseboat which was two miles upstream. Lige testified.

He then pointed out that the food was never removed from the flat boat.

He presented what was determined to be human blood on the flat boat.

He pointed out that a person planning murder would not take a very rusty knife to be the weapon.

Finally, he laid out the evidence of what he had found when he and the doctor last visited the houseboat. His findings were backed up by the doctor.

Here's what he found:

On the top edge of the partially submerged pontoon was the key to the mystery. Age had caused the pontoon to deteriorate. On the very rounded end, where you would tie your boat on arriving, he found a small bit of fabric and a small bit of skin. He could only assume the skin was human. Johnny said he had not noticed that, and assumed in docking the boat, Mary Ellen had rammed the pontoon, causing the rusty end to become jagged and more exposed.

The fabric matched the nick in Mary Ellen's shirt fabric and the rust in the wound matched the rust on the pontoon.

The conclusion was that when Mary Ellen arrived, as she attempted to board the houseboat, she did not secure the skiff. She fell while in the skiff striking the side of her head on the pontoon. It was rusty, sharp and almost the same circular shape as the wound she had.

She bled some on the skiff but managed to climb onto the porch and into the houseboat before bleeding out. The skiff drifted downstream.

It was just an accident.

In less than an hour, the grand jury decided in favor of Johnny. There would be no arrest.

In a situation as above, there will always be non-believers. There will always be conspiracy theories. This case was no exception. It was discussed and reviewed for years. It was a popular subject when Freddie ran for reelection. He only won by fifty votes.

As for Johnny, the public showed him little mercy. He would grieve for years over Mary Ellen, her infidelity, and her dying. He blamed himself for not telling her the truth about his war injury. Maybe she would have married someone else and today be a loving mother.

He blamed himself for leaving her so hastily. Maybe he could have raised someone else's child. His recovery would be long and hard and maybe never complete.

He considered trying to make a fresh start. When the shipyard closed, it was a perfect opportunity. He applied for a job in Texas with the railroad. He knew a railroad job had good benefits and the pay was excellent. He got the job.

It was similar to what he had done at the shipyard. Dismantling and refurbishing freight cars. Hard work but regular hours, and work was really all he had to do. He knew no one.

A couple of years passed. He had lived like a hermit. His home was one room in a boarding house with people that would come and go. No one asked him about his past and that was fine with him. In 1958, he bought a Magnavox high fidelity phonograph. It was on sale, as it was believed that stereo sound would be available before year's end, and it could be converted. Other than an outboard motor, it was the only semi-expensive thing he had ever purchased for himself. The first album he purchased was Elvis Presley's Golden Hits.

He spent hours in his room listening to "Loving You" and "That's Where Your Heartaches Begin." A few weeks later, he decided to go to an Elvis concert in a nearby town. For some reason, he bought new, more appropriate clothes. They were the first he had purchased, other than work clothes, since Mary Ellen died. After shaving and dressing, he looked in the mirror with new confidence. He felt alive again.

The concert was packed and there were no reserved seats. He chose a seat by an attractive woman that he assessed was of similar age, 34. She was a brunette, tall, dark eyes as best he could tell, and beautifully dressed. She had a healthy, athletic look but not unfeminine. They acknowledged each other but little else was said.

The concert continued. Elvis began his song, "That's Where Your Heartaches Begin." Shortly after the song started, he looked at her and could see tears streaming down her face. He realized he had to try hard not to cry himself. It occurred to him that they both had something in common, heartache. He wondered what hers was. Unconsciously, he placed his hand on hers. She squeezed it.

The concert ended and he exited the hall. He intentionally stayed around the entrance until she exited. Their eyes met. She walked straight toward him as if she had been summoned.

He could tell she was a truthful person and had no reluctance to bring up the hard subjects. "Looks like you have had some heartaches too. My name is Jane.

"Nice to meet you, Jane." He didn't remember to give her his name. "Can I walk you to your car?"

"Sure, it's three blocks away."

"That's ok, I need the fresh air."

The conversation as they walked was easy and gentle. As a romantic interest, he had only known Mary Ellen. She had always been there since grade school, and he hadn't developed the skills of dating.

Too soon, in his opinion, they reached the car. "Would you like to have dinner with me? I'm sorry, I am assuming that you don't have a boyfriend and are not married."

"Your assumption is correct and, yes, dinner would be fine. I need it. There is only one thing..."

"What's that?"

"You haven't told me your name."

"Oh, my Lord, my name is Johnny Mays."

"And I am Jane Dalton." She began to scribble a phone number.

On their first date, they both commented that neither had been so at ease with another of the opposite sex. It seemed like there was nothing they couldn't discuss. On that night, little was said about eithers previous spouses except he told her his wife died in an accident and she told him her husband, a policeman, was killed on duty. Both discussed it with ease, but not in depth.

On the dates that followed, there was no question a relationship was developing. Could there be something to this relationship? Johnny was beginning to question himself. He had decided that, after what happened with Mary Ellen, he would never be untruthful in another relationship, if there was to be a relationship.

For over two years, Johnny had lived in the boarding house as a recluse. He reasoned that living in a boarding house would not be a turn on to someone as perfect as Jane. He moved to an apartment. Soon, their relationship got more intimate.

One Sunday afternoon in July, she asked him to go on a picnic at a local lake. She would pick him up and have everything they needed. He could not help but think that it was the anniversary of Mary Ellen's death. The thought kept reappearing in his mind. He hoped he could pass it off and enjoy the day.

The blanket was spread, the food was unpacked, and Johnny knew it was time to be honest with Jane. He would not deceive her in any way.

He told her the story of Mary Ellen's accident, that she was pregnant, but not by him since he could not have children, and his being suspected of killing her. He emphasized that he could not have children so strongly she started laughing.

"Johnny, do you think I care? I am 35 years old; I have not gotten pregnant yet and, let me be honest with you, I have had the opportunity. I could care less if you're sterile."

It was a good day. There would be days he would think about Mary Ellen, but the guilt had lessened.

Six months after their first date, Jane and Johnny married. It was a Justice of the Peace wedding, but Freddie drove over to stand with Johnny. Freddie liked Jane and felt she was good for Johnny.

Johnny could not believe that he had found happiness again and he felt even better he was not hiding anything. Jane was the happiest she had ever been.

They bought a cabin on the same lake they had picnicked on with no nearby neighbors. Both could not wait to get home from work and be with each other. They seldom went anywhere and, except for work, always went places with each other. That is the way they liked it.

About a year after their marriage, Jane got home before Johnny. She didn't know how she was going to handle it, but she decided to lay out the old Navy duffel bag and block his boat trailer with her car.

She sat a bottle of champagne in ice with two glasses and made some pimento and cheese sandwiches, his favorite.

"What's up, Babe? Why the champagne?"

"Special occasion."

"What occasion?"

"Notice your duffel bag. It's been sewn shut. You're not going to put anything in it. Notice your boat trailer. It's not going anywhere."

"What are you talking about?"

"I'm pregnant and don't even suspect it's not yours. I have you an appointment with a urologist tomorrow to prove that you're not sterile. Now finish that champagne and let's go to the bedroom. You have to take a sample for the doctor. I borrowed a baby food jar from a friend. That's what you put it in. This is gonna be fun."

Johnny believed her. He had questions and concerns, but he believed her. It occurred to him that Mary Ellen's baby could have been his. There was that guilty feeling again. In a few minutes, it passed.

The next day he gave the sample to the nurse with embarrassment. In a few minutes, he was called to the examination room. In a few more minutes, the doctor came it.

"Mr. Mays, you have a weak sperm count but you should have no problem having children."

Nine months later, a son was born. He was named Freddie.

The houseboat has been gone for years. Its demise is unknown.

THE PINK WHEEL

It has always puzzled me that sometimes the things you want most can cause you the most trouble. My dad was an old man when he told me what happened. By that time, the psychological damage was done and mostly healed; but, for a brief period in my preteen years, the bicycle caused me both joy and grief.

I had asked for a new bicycle for Christmas. I had never owned a new bicycle and the old one I had was a hand-me-down from my brother. It was at one time, and for the time, a fine bike. It was called an English Racer. When I inherited it, it was too big for me, and it had no brakes. The hand brakes had been removed. To stop it, you had to put your foot forward and press against the front tire. Over time, this caused the front wheel to wobble.

On that Christmas morning, there it sat, beside the small pine tree that mother had erected to give our house some feeling of Christmas. It was a Western Flyer. I knew it came from the local Western Auto as my dad traded there often. I had seen that brand in the store. It was a boy's bike, but immediately I knew something was wrong. It was solid pink. I knew that was a girl's color and, in those days, gender bias was very real, at least in rural Mississippi.

To this day, I would like to know what went through the mind of the marketing department that created such a color for a boy's bike. I also wondered why my dad had bought it for me. As I have already said, only years later did I find out. At the time however, I was just thrilled to have transportation. At least it was better than a bike with a wheel that wobbled and had no brakes. Well, maybe not.

I was not prepared for the ribbing I got from my friends when we met up a couple of days after Christmas at the Crossroads, our favorite muster ground. Jimmy was the bully in our crowd. In one way, I disliked him; but in another way, he was our protector. He was bigger, a couple of years older, street smart and known to not take much off anyone regardless of size. Mother said it was because he didn't have a mother. She was gone, dead or something. We never knew.

Jimmy had a bike that was even worse than my old English Racer. It had two different sized tires. This was out of necessity, not for performance, as they design them today. There was no chain guard so the chain would rub against his pants leg or bare leg in the summer, the grease giving him an even more fearful appearance.

I was the last to arrive at the Crossroads, but I think the word had gotten around. All four of my buddies had put their bikes on the side of the gravel road, just waiting for my arrival. Jimmy also was the loudest and most dramatic of the bunch. He dropped on his back and rolled in the gravel, much like a dog we had one time that had hydrophobia. He was laughing at the top of his lungs.

"Hey, did you get pink lace panties to match?"

I was infuriated, but I knew the sympathy of my other friends was not with me and I would just have to endure the humiliation, which I did.

One day in the spring, we met at my grandmother's. It was afternoon and she was sitting on the porch. I was her favorite and she always stopped what she was doing to spend time with me.

In her yard, we all had our bikes and she came to where we were gathered. "Son, when did you get that pretty wheel?"

Not only had she said it was pretty, but she called it a wheel. I knew old folks called bicycles wheels, but my friends didn't. They thought it was hilarious.

More humiliation. "Where is your pretty wheel?" they would ask at any opportunity.

A year passed. Jimmy became more distant, and it was obvious that living with his daddy, a heavy drinker, was not going well. If anything, Jimmy became tougher, and you might say meaner. Looking back, I now know there was physical abuse; but, in those days, some parents thought they had the right to do as they wished with their children. There was little, if any, intervention from anyone.

We saw him less and less and, to some degree, his absence was welcomed. He dropped out of school in about the 9th grade. We heard he picked gladiolas at the gladiola farm during the season. He also picked up loblolly pinecones and sold them to the forestry department. He finally got a semi-permanent job at a combination store that had concessions such as candy, Cokes and hamburgers, as well as sold gas, changed oil and washed cars. He did the automotive chores.

Over the next year, the humiliation of the pink bike got so severe, I parked it in the barn and seldom, if ever, road it. It had junk piled on top of it and was more or less hidden from sight.

Jimmy, in the meantime, had gained the trust and confidence of the owners at the store where he worked. He was now in charge of closing, counting the money and dropping it in a locked iron box.

It was the hottest August in memory with no rain since mid-June. The gravel road in front of my grandmother's house was now a ribbon of dust that drifted into a dense haze with just the passing of a breeze.

I walked to her house to water her ferns, as arthritis prevented her from lifting the watering can to reach the hanging plants. I think that was the way it was, at least that is what she said.

"Son, where were you going in such a hurry on your wheel yesterday?"

"It wasn't me MaMa. I haven't ridden that bike in months."

"You are the only one I know that has a pink wheel, unless you are a girl." Even MaMa had to rub it in.

"It was dusty and I didn't see the rider, just the pink wheel."

"Wasn't me, MaMa."

In a few days, we heard that Jimmy had left town. Rumors had it that he had stolen the day's receipts from the store where he worked; about $40.

Another year passed.

Jace Adams worked hard but hardly kept his head above water. He was a great father and husband, but making or managing money was not his forte. His only child was 10-year-old Reba, whom he worshiped.

I heard him say she wanted a bicycle for Christmas, but he couldn't afford one. It made me think.

My cousin Bernard was a good welder and had a cutting torch. He could remove the crossbar on my pink wheel, and it could pass as a girl's bike much better than it did for me as a boy's bike. I told Mr. Adams he could have it for five dollars. He was excited.

About three weeks before Christmas, I went to the barn to deliver it to Bernard. It wasn't there. I had no idea what had happened to it. I hated it for Reba's sake and thought how much it would have meant to her and how much humiliation it had caused me.

Little thought was given to the bike or Jimmy after that. They were certainly not connected. Years passed. It was 1994 and I was visiting my father. It was one of my last visits with him as he suffered from emphysema as the result of smoking 3 packs of Camel cigarettes a day for 69 years.

There was a knock on the door. I answered and, standing behind the screen was a large guy with a weathered complexion. He was very muscular, with calloused hands and scars above each eye. Something about him looked familiar. It took a moment, but I recognized the Jimmy that I had known 36 years prior.

I looked past him and parked on the street was a late model pickup truck. In the bed was a pink bicycle. I knew some mysteries were about to be solved.

Jimmy came in, cordially addressed my father, and sat on the same couch he had sat on a few times, years before.

"Where have you been?" I asked.

"I've been in Louisiana and Texas."

"I see the pink bike. Now, there was only one of those, and I had it. So how does the bike fit into your story?"

Jimmy began to unravel a story that was almost unbelievable. If I had not known how tough and resourceful he was, I wouldn't have believed him.

"You see, my dad was a mean drunk. I got tired of it. I heard my mother was living in Natchitoches, Louisiana so I decided to run away and live with her.

"I stockpiled some food I stole from the store I worked at. Things like Vienna sausage, Spam, cookies, and the like. I then stole $35 before slipping into your barn that night and stealing the bike. I think the store owners wanted me to get away, as they made things awfully convenient. I knew you didn't care anything about that bike.

"I left the next day about mid-afternoon. I rode the bike about 10 miles and hid in the woods for three days to make sure no one was looking for me. I knew my father didn't care what happened to me, but I was concerned the law had been notified due to the missing money.

"I rode that bike all the way to Natchitoches, Louisiana. It took me five days. I lived with my mom, got a job as a deck hand on an oil rig, and I have worked in the oil patch ever since.

"I decided to pay back what I owe. This is the first time I have been back. I didn't even know my father was dead until ten years after it happened. Didn't much matter anyway.

"I found out a couple of hours ago that the store owners have long been dead, so I gave that money to a beggar on the side of the road. Then I came here to return the bicycle."

"I hated that bike. You could have just kept it," I replied

It did not occur to me that my dad's feeling would be hurt by that statement, but I could tell he looked perturbed at what I said.

Jimmy visited for another few minutes before saying his goodbyes. After he had left, my father's demeanor was even more distant. I realized that I needed to explain. I sat with my dad and told him about all the teasing I had gotten when I was younger. I asked him why he had bought such a bike in the first place.

He explained, "Back in those days, times were bad. Not many working people had checking accounts, so we got paid in cash. I got paid at noon on Christmas Eve. I always went from creditor to creditor and paid what I could pay on my bills.

"It was late Christmas Eve and I realized that I had a few dollars left and I knew you wanted a bike. I didn't like the color either, but it was the only one left. I guess it is safe to say no one else wanted it either. Western Auto marked it down five dollars to get rid of it, so I bought it. Even after all these years, I just assumed you still had it. I never knew it was missing."

The bike was in perfect condition, as it was never ridden after its trip to Louisiana. I didn't want it, and I had two boys. I was not about to expose them to the same humiliation I had. We decided to put the bike on the side of the street where people left their junk. Three days later, it was still there.

Thinking back now, I know I was foolish to have felt ashamed at having a pink bike. I realize how much my dad had sacrificed to buy it.

I also think about how Jimmy had teased me about the very thing that turned out to be his escape. His salvation had been my humiliation. Funny how things turn out, isn't it?

SNAKE IN THE GRASS

It is remarkable that the old sign is still legible. Nature preserved it by accident because it partially fell from one of the posts holding it years ago. That turned the face side down, away from the sun and rain. After some study and mentally inserting some faded letters, the writing was decipherable.

With so much television and drama at the click of a remote, there is no longer the deep intrigue to dwell on local unsolved mysteries of the past. There was a time when the stories of those happenings were passed from generation to generation, with each taking from, or adding to, the original tale.

For some reason, many of these fascinating mysteries did not make the newspapers and these oral tellings and recitings are the only hint we have of the strange or mysterious event.

Such was the story of the disappearance of Charles Powers. Not one mention of his disappearance and the aftermath can be found in the obituaries of the time, but there is a grave marker in a local cemetery that denotes a Charles Powers. The headstone reads, *Born in 1945, Died in 1961.* That's probably him; and, if it is, it gives credibility to the rest of what was told. The Willow Ridge Bluff sign is also a positive clue.

Charles and his family lived about five miles east of town. Their home was one of a half-dozen or so on a ridge that rose from the lowlands, or from what locals called, the marsh. These homes were not elaborate but homes of sufficient size and quality to make a desirable neighborhood. More rural than urban, the only undesirable aspect of living in the country were the mosquitoes. It was as if they were starved for human blood.

In the mile and a half between the ridge and the marsh was a wide variety of flora and fauna. At the highest point of the ridge were tall pines mixed with water oaks; but, as the terrain traveled toward the marsh, the pines subsided and Live oaks became more prevalent. The view of these oaks covered with moss formed a picture-perfect Louisiana postcard. Past the oaks and moss, the land transformed to support palmettos, willows, and marsh grass.

For hundreds of years, this ecosystem provided a well-stocked habitat for all its inhabitants. The oak trees provided acorns to support an abundance of squirrels. A small stream wound its way around the ridge, forming a habitat for beaver, mink, and wild hogs. There were rumors of black bear and, yes, the always mythical black panther. No one could offer proof of either's existence in the form of a cadaver, so the nearest proof was an occasional sighting and killing of a bobcat.

Early Native Americans feasted on this bounty and, later, trappers supported their families on the food and hides the area produced. The trappers and the Native Americans were gone by then. There was more money to be made at the brickyard. The animals had been left to multiply for years. They were abundant. This environment was pristine and, if life needed a rebirth, this would be its Eden.

Charles' mother worked at a general store in town and his dad worked at the shipyard. They drove to work together before 7 a.m. and Charles caught the school bus at 7:30. He would return a little after 4 p.m., but his parents would not get home for at least another hour.

The locale described provided a perfect cornucopia for a kid with an avid fantasy for the outdoors. Charles was a dependable, independent kid and, in the summer, spent his spare time fishing where the river touched the terminus of the ridge. In the fall and winter, he spent his after-school hours and Saturdays hunting.

More of this story can be confirmed by remnants of another sign that still can be found near the highway, not too far from the ridge. Back then, there was a roadside zoo hidden behind a wall made of plywood signs. The signs had pictures of lions, monkeys, apes, alligators, and snakes. It was not a place that the locals were particularly proud of, but tourists on their way to and from New Orleans were lured in. There was a general admission charge and a few animals, but no lions or snakes with six-inch fangs as advertised on the signs.

Even though there were none with six-inch fangs, the most numerous members of this menagerie were the snakes. There were many local species of snakes: cottonmouths, copperheads, corals, and rattlesnakes. There were two boa constrictors that were said to be from South America, but only the gullible believed them to be anacondas. For an extra twenty-five cents, you could see the "deadly cobra" kept in a separate room. Finally, for fifty cents, you were able to go to the crocodile show. They were alligators, not crocodiles; but the show culminated with the handler putting his hand in the open mouth of the largest of the reptiles. Each visitor most likely left fleeced of a dollar, a more substantial ransom at that time than today.

On the ridge about a mile north, Doctor Sumrall lived with his wife and grandson, Scott. Twenty years before, he and his wife had built a large home on 150 acres of some of the most beautiful land in the parish. It was at the point where the ridge abutted the river, forming a bluff. It was a favorite place for Charles to hunt and fish, as in those days, "No Trespassing" signs did not exist.

Doctor Sumrall was now retired but had recently volunteered to fill the unexpired term of the coroner who had suddenly passed away. Being a part-time coroner was an easy job, but a large, twenty-year-old home and 150 acres of land required upkeep. The upkeep was something the doctor did not enjoy now as he had when he was younger. The area was booming with new industry to the north and south. Subdivisions were being developed in the most remote places. He reasoned that he could subdivide the land into lots and develop them as needed, a few at a time. He had some preliminary survey work done and the sign made, but he had not pursued the idea any further.

Doctor Sumrall's grandson, Scott, was twelve years old. He was living with them temporarily while his parents worked in Central America for United Fruit. Scott, like Charles, enjoyed the freedom of country living; but, being younger and less experienced than Charles, did not have the in-depth knowledge of the outdoors.

Scott affectionately called his grandmother "Moms" and grandfather "Pops."

"Moms, I saw a big snake back where those survey men had cut the grass."

"What did it look like son?"

"It was long and black and kind of skinny."

"Probably just a black runner. They're good snakes. They eat mice and rats. Never kill a black runner or a king snake."

It was only a few minutes until Doctor Sumrall arrived.

"Pops, I saw a big black snake where the surveyors were working. Moms says it may be a black runner, but I think it was a cobra."

"There are no cobras around here, and no long black snake from this area is venomous. What makes you think it was a cobra?"

"Because it lifted its head and looked straight at me. Like you see on T.V."

"You probably saw a coachwhip. Did I ever tell you about a coachwhip?" and a deep smile appeared on the doctor's face.

"No sir."

"They say a coachwhip is the fastest snake there is. One reason they are so fast is they can put their tail in their mouth and form a hoop. Then they chase you by rolling like a tire or a hula hoop. If it ever happens to you, you must jump behind a tree or over a fence to escape. If they catch you, they will whip you to death with their tail and then stick their tail in your nose to see if you are breathing."

"That's not true Pops."

"Maybe not, but that's what I heard when I was a kid. Some people call them hoop snakes."

"I still believe it was a cobra."

On that late September afternoon, it was almost dark when Mr. and Mrs. Powers came home from work. Charles was not there. His rifle was missing and an empty box that had contained .22 caliber long rifle hollow point ammunition was on his dresser. There was no cause for concern as this was not unusual.

By 8 p.m., his mother began to worry; but his father, if worried, did not show it. At 10 p.m., they called the sheriff.

Two deputies arrived and, after consulting with the family, reasoned that Charles had gotten lost and would be home when it got daylight. It would be a warm night, so probably there was no reason to worry. Unfortunately, he did not return home the next morning.

At noon, a full-scale search was underway. The high school dismissed classes so that the boys could help in the search. They found nothing.

On the fourth day, Doctor Sumrall saw buzzards circling on the most remote part of his property. He was aware of the missing boy but wanted to believe the buzzards were circling for a dead animal. He reluctantly went to the trouble to investigate.

What he found, he tried to believe was not true. In a slumped position under a tree, he found the body of young Charles Powers. Charles was wearing shorts, a t-shirt and U.S. Keds tennis shoes. Due to the unusually warm temperature, the body had reached a significant degree of decomposition; but, as a coroner and more as a father, he knew the hardest part would be telling the family what else he was seeing. Charles' exposed skin, legs, arms and torso under the t-shirt, had been chewed and partially eaten by animals.

The body was removed to the morgue which was a small room in the funeral home. Doctor Sumrall, accompanied by the sheriff, stopped to inform the family. He encouraged them not to view the body but would let them know the cause of death as soon as he had finished his examination.

It was late in the afternoon when Doctor Sumrall paused for the day. He had found no reasonable cause of death. The body had no signs of an accidental gunshot or foul play. It had been too warm for the boy to have suffered from exposure. He was baffled. He informed the family of the preliminary findings, or the lack thereof. He also asked them if Charles had any known health problems. If he did, the family was not aware.

During the night, Doctor Sumrall woke several times. He knew it was an improbable possibility, but his mind kept remembering the snake that his grandson had seen not far from where the body was found. At daylight, he returned to the funeral home and rolled the body from its cooler.

Starting at the thigh and going to the feet, he meticulously examined the body. In some places, there were just loose pieces of flesh due to the animal activity. Then he saw it. Could it be? There was one puncture wound just above where Charles' sock would have been. It could be a snakebite. In his practice he had treated many. Where the other fang mark should have been, the flesh had been chewed away. Snakebite was a possibility he now had to consider.

Dr. Sumrall drove to the small roadside zoo, paid the admission charge, and went immediately to where the snakes were kept. He then attempted to pay the additional twenty-five cents to see the cobra. The owner appeared from a back room. They had previously met when the doctor had treated one of his employees who had been bitten by a copperhead. He had an undeserved dislike for the owner. The owner had not paid for the treatment of his employee, but that was not unusual. Many patients could not or would not pay.

"That room is closed."

"Why?" Doctor Sumrall asked.

"The cobra died last week, and I have not been able to get a replacement."

Somehow Doctor Sumrall didn't believe him, but he reasoned that maybe he had formed a prejudiced opinion. He returned to the funeral home, trying to keep an open mind.

After making some phone calls to snake bite experts, he was directed to a cobra expert in Florida, Mr. Bill Haast. Mr. Haast had been bitten by cobras so many times his blood could be transfused and used as anti-venom. Just a few years before, eighteen-year-old Irene Raub had been bitten by a cobra at a nearby snake farm in LaPlace. Mr. Haast was flown by Navy jet to New Orleans for the transfusion, but she died while they were en route. No one knew more about snake bites than Bill Haast. Mr. Haast told him that, after that length of time, combined with the elements and animal exposure, it most likely could not be proven to be a snakebite.

Doctor Sumrall remembered all the frank and to-the-point conversations he had been involved with over the years with his patients and their families. He knew there was no easy way to present what he knew about Charles' death to the family. He knew that, as a father, he would want to know the truth. On the other hand, he had told families the truth before and wished he hadn't.

Would it be easier on the family to think he died of natural causes or as the result of an escaped deadly snake? Can a sixteen-year-old die of natural causes?

He knew that if the public heard there was an escaped cobra in the area, there would be mass pandemonium. He knew that his piece of land would always be the spot that people would morbidly point to and say, "That is where the cobra lives." He would never be able to sell the first lot. Selling lots was no longer important. At that moment, he made up his mind to never develop the property. He would not let any conflict of interest influence his opinion.

He had duties to his profession that he had to uphold. He had a duty to Charles' family and a duty to protect the safety of the community. Any decision he made may conflict with one or more of these duties.

After much thought, he made his decision, and his conscience was clean. Sometimes a lie, especially if you are not certain of the truth, is appropriate. On the death certificate, he wrote Undetermined Causes.

Dr. Sumrall has long been dead; but, to this day, the land has not been developed. The only evidence of the event are the two dilapidated signs and Charles' grave.

If it was a cobra, it was never seen again.

BLANCHE

If you have an image in your mind of a young women living in 1908, I expect it is quite different from the reality of Blanche. The truth is, there was no reality in this Blanche.

A Puritan or Victorian model of femininity she was not. Beautiful and elegant she was, but she was not your sweet, stay-at-home Southern belle. One reason for this is she was not Southern. Blanche lived in New Orleans, but she was not from New Orleans. New Orleans had its own shady side, but Blanche was from Chicago.

The street smarts that she brought with her from Chicago may have been part of her allure. Men, even respectable men, could not resist her. Young men whose parents had raised them to be in church every time the door opened would forget all they had learned about the wages of sin just to be with her one night. Forgiveness could be asked after the fact; but for the time being, they would gladly indulge in the sins of the flesh with Blanche.

Andrew was perfect prey for Blanche. The son of one of the wealthiest families in the South, Andrew had been educated at some of the best schools in the country and abroad. He was trained in religion on the pews of the most popular fundamentalist churches in the South. Until he met Blanche, that training had been influential in his life, especially the part about maintaining a chaste and pure life.

Andrew had a high position in the family business. It was not given to him, he earned it. He was educated and trained for the position and was a dedicated officer of the company. At twenty-four years of age, he was a high wage earner with an additional wealth of assets inherited from a deceased family member.

Six foot two inches with perfect posture, his wealth, good looks, and blonde hair made him a most eligible bachelor. He had rented an apartment at the poshest hotel in the city, The Grunwald. He was known to spend his evenings in the lobby, studying the sales and financial reports of his company and sipping a Sazerac, his favorite cocktail. Never was he seen in the company of a lady.

There was another key player in this story. His name was Duke Conti. He appeared in town and rented a room at the Monteleone Hotel. He advertised himself as a magician, a seer, a psychic, and a healer of hearts. Extremely thin, he looked and dressed like a Middle Easterner. He became a popular attraction, performing in the hotels and entertainment establishments of the city.

Andrew and Duke met by coincidence (or was it?) in the lobby of Andrew's hotel. Andrew was examining company documents and drinking his Sazerac. Duke was performing in another area of the hotel for some conventioneers. As he exited the performance, Duke made a point to pass near Andrew and ask if he had enjoyed the performance. Andrew informed him that he had not seen the performance and had not been aware it was taking place.

To Andrew's annoyance, Duke pulled a chair and sat directly across the table on which the Sazerac was sitting. He then reached in his pocket and offered Andrew a free pass to the next evening's show. As he handed the pass to Andrew, he accidentally tipped the drink glass, spilling its contents onto the table.

"I am so sorry. Signal your waiter, if you don't mind," Duke said. "I will order you another."

Andrew stood and looked around the lobby for the waiter. When his eyes went back to the table, the table was perfectly dry, and the Sazerac glass was full.

"How did you do that?" Andrew asked.

"Truth is just an illusion, my new friend, just an illusion."

Andrew stuffed the performance pass in his suit pocket and politely wished his new acquaintance a good day. Andrew knew then that he would be present at the next night's performance to see what this magician had to offer.

◇◇◇◇◇◇◇◇◇◇

Andrew got to the performance thirty minutes prior to showtime to get a good seat. He did not know that all seats had been reserved, and he had been granted a seat directly in front of the stage. That is when she appeared.

She wore a floor-length green gown. Her reddish hair fell long to teasingly cover her cleavage. In the center of the low-cut dress, she wore a cameo, ivory most likely, but it carried traces of color that seemed to be coordinated with her hair, a rouge tint you might say.

She was assigned the seat next to him. In the gentlemanly fashion he had inherited, he assisted her with her chair and then introduced himself to her. She extended her hand, and that is when he became totally infatuated.

Years later, he would try to explain what it was that swept him off his feet and, for a short time, ruined his life and finances. He could not be sure. She was beautiful. She dressed a little sinfully, but not cheaply. Her complexion was nearly flawless, with just a touch of rouge that made her cheeks resemble those of a new China doll. Her fragrance, it was rose water of a quality he had not even scented in Europe. Looking back, he thinks it was her touch, though he still cannot explain it fully to this day. He felt an electric tingling as her hand touched his; not an unpleasant tingling, but one he believed that day was a signal that she was the one. His short hunt for the proper lady was over.

Another couple joined them at the table, but they were insignificant to him. The show was also insignificant. He was only interested in her. As the lights went up and the show ended, he asked her to join him for dinner the next night. He said he would send his chauffeur to pick her up. She gave him the address of the Desoto Hotel, one of the top three hostelries in the city.

They dined at Antoine's. He was a little surprised that a lady of such elegance could not read the menu, even though it was in French. The trade-off was she seemed to adore the accent with which he explained each course, and he loved the attention. They drank heavily, more than he was used to.

By the end of the meal, he was certain he had met his soulmate, the one he had only dreamed about, dreams fueled by such classics as *Romeo and Juliet*. He knew she felt the same way too. They were in love. That was the sum of it. Why wait?

They did not. That night, she did not return to the Desoto. She went with him. His experience in the matter of love was limited, and she pretended hers was too. It didn't matter. They... that is, he, was in love.

Andrew's father was no fool. Something about this Blanche did not seem right. Even though he admired his son's business acumen, he did not trust his romantic experience, or lack thereof. He hired an investigator to check out Ms. Blanche from Chicago.

His first discovery was that she was not registered at the Desoto Hotel. She was tracked to a small place of near squalor on Rampart Street. He also learned that Blanche was very talented, but not in a way that would benefit his son. There were other things Andrew's father learned, but he felt it best to tell Andrew as little as possible.

His father was not given the opportunity. A telegram was received informing him that Mr. and Mrs. Andrew Coflan were en route to Europe aboard the RMS Adriatic. They would take an extended honeymoon, visiting both England and France. They would return in six weeks.

The newlyweds returned to New Orleans in late March and immediately ferried across the river to Andrew's family home. Andrew was eager to share his beautiful Blanche with his parents.

Surprisingly, his parents were seated on the veranda when he and Blanche arrived. They showed none of the graciousness or hospitality he had wished for or expected. Nothing was said to give him an indication that anything was wrong, other than the cold reception. When he attempted to show Blanche the home, his mother stepped in front of him.

"The house is not clean. You did not tell us you were coming. It is not presentable for guests. You can't go in," she said.

She pulled her son around the corner of the veranda, out of hearing distance from Blanche. "That strumpet's not coming into my house."

Little did Andrew know that his days of fanciful marital bliss were over. That night, Blanche told Andrew that she thought the marriage was a mistake, and they had rushed things too much. She told him she would be moving back to the Desoto the following day. Of course, she would expect him to pay the rent, since they were married. Stunned, Andrew agreed.

Andrew was heartbroken. His evenings were no longer spent in the lobby of the Grunwald drinking Sazeracs. He had stepped up to Absinthe. The essence of the wormwood was strangling out the memories of her, but only intermittently.

Much as Duke had appeared three months prior, he appeared again. He questioned Andrew's well-being, as he was unkempt and out of order in appearance. Andrew freely told him the truth.

"My friend, love, like truth, is just an illusion," Duke beamed. "Did not I tell you that I was the healer of hearts? Did I not tell you that I have the gift; the gift to return your lover to your life. You have nothing to lose. What is her name and where can she be found?"

"Her name is Blanche, and she lives at the Desoto."

"I will call on her tonight. Expect a return of her favors by noon tomorrow."

At exactly noon, she appeared at his office.

"Can we talk?" she asked.

She came in and he closed the door. She cried, apologized, then locked the door. He was happy.

The next afternoon, Duke came by Andrew's office.

"I must admit, I had my doubts," Duke related to Andrew. "She had the hardest heart I have ever healed; and, I must be honest, it probably will not last without more intervention. But, let us see, my friend. It has been my pleasure to be at your service."

Either by mystic powers or just plain coincidence, Duke was correct. After a week, Blanche moved back to the Desoto.

This time, Andrew made the trip to the Monteleone, another of New Orleans' famous hotels, to see Duke. Andrew agreed to hire Duke for the sum of $10,000. It worked. She came back again, then left, just as before. Duke's services were acquired several more times, until Andrew had spent almost $40,000.

Without telling Andrew, his father hired the Pinkerton Detectives to check out this mystic, heart-healer named Duke. When their work was completed, he went to his son's office and closed the door.

The investigation revealed:

Duke had served time in Mexico City; New York City; Austin, Texas; Greenwood, Mississippi; San Francisco; and Seattle – all for fraud and scams.

Implicated with Duke was Blanche, AKA "Boom Boom" Blanche, queen of burlesque, AKA Bigamy Blanche, having three husbands simultaneously.

Duke was arrested and scheduled for trial. The trial would reveal an intimate relationship between Blanche and Duke that continued even during the short time she was living with and married to Andrew. The family did not need that publicity, so the charges were dropped.

Andrew filed for divorce, and she counter filed. He wrote her one last check for $3,900 and the divorce was granted.

Little is known about what happened to Blanche. It appears she and Duke were arrested for a similar scam in Minnesota. After that, there is no known record of her.

Duke, on the other hand, turned to an honest living. He became one of Vaudeville's biggest stars. When he died in the 1950s, he had amassed an estate of $3,000,000.

Andrew found honest and true love and lived a very successful life.

RING ON A CHAIN

Proverbs 22:6 KJV

Richard Davenport slurred the opening lines of his sermon just as he had many times before. No, it wasn't alcohol induced; but, nevertheless, a demon he could not control. On most Sundays, his sermon delivery was perfect; but when it happened, the congregation knew, but they didn't know the reason.

He knew why it happened and knew why he became distracted and confused, but he also knew there was nothing he could do about it, no matter how hard he tried. Well, there was something he could have done about it, but it would have come at a heavy cost. It would have ruined lives; his, and especially, hers.

Regardless of what she did, he could not, or would not, do that to her. He was older and wiser now and, as a minister, had counseled so many people he knew that when we do not achieve our goals, we often place blame on others. She had selfishly hindered his career. He both blamed and resented her, but he still loved her.

He was seminary educated and had a good pulpit presence. He knew just when to inject the right inflections that made his sermons always interesting and spell binding. At 60, he knew being the lead pastor in a large church of his denomination would never happen. Churches somehow don't believe a man who has not married and raised a family could have the necessary life experiences to lead a major congregation.

Looking back, his career had been a long journey. He was raised in a conservative, fundamentalist religious denomination. They were often judged by the way they dressed. As a child, he was deeply immersed in the faith and believed in everything that his fiery, short minister would say. He believed in the strange sounds he heard coming from the throats of the believers. He believed that a true believer could drink poison or handle snakes and God and/or the Holy Spirit would protect them. He had never seen snakes or poison in his church but believed it could happen. That was called faith and it was instilled in him at an early age.

It was a doctrine that truly relieved one of his anxieties. If you believed, you could give your troubles to God and he would provide. He learned that other denominations preached this, but his truly believed it. As a young boy, it worked for him and was comforting. He had never been hungry, and all his family members were healthy. Of any monetary blessings his family received, an adequate share was given to the Lord. It seemed fair to him. They paid rent for a place to live, why not reward God for health and happiness?

The hormonal change of adolescence began to create a storm within him. At first, he prayed and often quoted the scripture, "Get thee behind me Satan." He couldn't believe that all the things his minister said about sin and temptation were now happening to him.

He became embarrassed when his mother would come to school for any function. She would be wearing her dark dress that extended to her ankles, with her hair braided tightly to her head. The other mothers wore shorter dresses with bright colors and their hair was cut more like Jackie Kennedy's. He wished his mother dressed like that.

He had been forbidden to go to school dances. Dancing was a sin. He could not go to the city swimming pool because young ladies would be there and would not be properly dressed. His church called it "mixed bathing."

He could play sports, as the Lord loves a healthy body, and even his pastor encouraged him to do so. If the pastor had any desire to keep Richard within his flock, this may have been bad advice. Richard excelled in sports.

His athletic ability and his natural good looks made him a class favorite.

He realized there were other things in the world besides his church and what they believed. He never doubted that God loved him, and that God would provide, but he questioned why God had to be so confining.

School activities occasionally would interfere with his church obligations. He would become very conflicted. His pastor insisted he must serve God first, and his coaches emphasized teamwork. He was at a crossroad in his life. A crossing which would be years in the navigation.

In those days, church was a big part of most lives. Not only was it a big part spiritually, but a big part socially. Sunday school parties and picnics were an integral part of Christian fellowship. The First Methodist Church even rented the city pool and had a swimming party and picnic. Surely the Methodist girls didn't swim in long dresses.

With each passing year, despite his prayers, the clash between his religious teachings and his leanings toward being "worldly," as the minister used the term, grew more intense. The summer before his senior year he would remember as the apex of the conflict.

He turned eighteen that summer and made a decision that would forever change his life. He would no longer go to church. As much as his parents and his minister insisted, he refused. He would hear them pray for him, as if he were committing a crime. He realized that, in their opinion, he was committing a sin; a sin that could cast him into eternal Hell, and that was worse than being a criminal.

He went swimming at the pool. Yes, the girls did wear bathing suits. He smoked a few cigarettes now and then, and even drank an occasional beer. He went to after-football game dances too. He loved the new freedom he had. That is when he became infatuated with Cindy.

Who could blame him? Cindy was the prettiest girl in town. Her long, dark hair was teased and pulled to the top of her head. It was the era of big hair. She wore some makeup just because it was the thing to do, but she really didn't need it. Her clothes were purchased each year when she and her mother went to Atlanta. She was easily the best dressed girl in the school.

He still prayed and was mindful that what he was feeling was just as the preacher had said it would be. He was being tempted by the Devil. It didn't matter. He would follow the Devil's path, at least for a while, and ask for forgiveness later. He remembered the Prodigal Son.

Every class has one, the girl that has and is everything. She would be elected most beautiful, most stylish, most likely to succeed and president of her senior class. Cindy was also the head majorette and, even with the relative modesty of the uniforms of that day, he was attracted to her like no force that had ever guided him. He remembered her beauty and still remembers that she had the prettiest legs he had ever seen.

No one knows how romantic chemistry works; but, regardless, she had the same attraction to him. Soon they were inseparable. When he got his senior class ring, he never put it on his finger. It went on a chain, and he proudly placed it around her neck. She was his, and she liked that too.

Her father was very prominent, successful, and had ambitions for his daughter. He and her mother had mapped out her life. She would go to college at least. Maybe become a doctor or, at least, marry one. She would be happy, and they would provide whatever support she needed to become who they wanted her to be. Richard did not fit into the equation.

They first forbade her to wear the ring. She complied. Then, as the romance deepened, they forbade her to see him.

Cindy did not want conflict with her parents. She would appease them on the surface, but she would not give up Richard. Her parents were pleased when she announced she had a date to go to the movies with someone who they strongly approved of. Danny lived just down the street from Cindy. What her parents didn't know was that he was Richard's best friend. Danny would deliver her to Richard just out of sight of her parents' home and bring her home at 10 p.m., which was her curfew.

Just prior to graduation, a picture was taken at a class party that appeared in the local newspaper. Richard had his arm around Cindy. Her parents saw it and made the decision. She would spend the summer in Europe with a group of graduating seniors from around the state.

Richard blames them. If they had not planned to send her away, maybe things would have been different. From time to time, he looks at the old photo taken by Danny that special morning. The picture is in black and white, but his mind replaces the lack of color with vivid hues. The dress, he remembers, was beautiful. Pink with white polka dots, she accented it with short, white heels and his ring proudly displayed around her neck. His usual dress was blue jeans, a white T-shirt, white socks and loafers. That day, he wore dress pants, a white shirt, and wingtip lace-up shoes.

It was a Friday. He remembers that also. The picture was taken in front of the goldfish pond at the high school. They got there early under the pretense of a special study hall and class pictures. In her purse, she carried her birth certificate and a makeup kit.

By 9:30 a.m., they had crossed the Alabama line. Just as they were told, there it was, a big sign: Justice of the Peace, Marriages my Specialty. By 10 a.m., they were Mr. and Mrs. Richard Davenport. The Justice of the Peace told them of a nearby motel his brother owned and soon they were together.

Oh, the stupidity of youth. Only then did it occur to them that they were going to have to tell her parents, and his, too. They started home at 2 p.m.

Cindy's father had been suspicious that she may still be seeing Richard and was determined to keep an eye on her. He was well-connected in the community and good friends with the high school principal. The principal agreed to keep him informed of anything unusual. The principal had seen Richard and Cindy that morning, but when roll was called and turned into the office, they were not present. He called Cindy's father.

Danny was called to the office. After threats of being expelled and not being able to graduate, he revealed that they had eloped to Alabama. Cindy's father called the state police.

While returning, within five miles after crossing back over the state line, a red light appeared behind them. Richard pulled to the shoulder of the road. The officer went straight to Cindy's side of the car.

"Are you Cindy Miller?" he asked.

She answered, "Yes sir."

"You are to come with me."

Richard still remembers her using her maiden name. He was hurt. She was his now. Then the officer asked her if she and Richard had gotten married.

"No sir. We were going to, but we decided against it. We were going back home to tell my parents that we decided not to."

This took Richard off guard.

Richard drove home following her and the officer. At the edge of town, she convinced the officer to let her talk to Richard and the officer pulled the car to the side of the road.

She ran to Richard's open car window. "Until we can work this out, I am going to tell them we didn't get married. We changed our minds."

She didn't wait for his answer. As she and the officer turned toward her house, he turned toward his.

Final exams started Monday morning. She was an excellent student and was exempt from having to take exams. She would not be at school. For two weeks, he had no contact with her. She was restricted from using the phone and confined to the house. The next time he saw her was graduation night.

She avoided him. After the ceremony, he pushed his way through the crowd, hoping to talk to her. "Richard, I leave for Europe in the morning. We will work all this out when I get back. Do not tell Danny we got married. He believes we changed our minds. He told me you told him that and I appreciate it. I must have some time."

It was the longest summer of his life. Each day, he awoke and went to the mailbox. There was no letter from her. How long does it take for a letter to come from France? How was she? Didn't she remember she was his wife? June turned to July and July to August. Not one word from her.

Danny found out that she would get home on August 15th, but there was bad news. She would be going to the University on August 17th. Her belongings had already been moved to her dormitory room.

He had put his plans for college on hold. It had never been a strong priority anyway. Suddenly, he realized that, at least for a while, he had a void to fill in his life. He remembered the coaches at the junior college had shown an interest in giving him a football scholarship; but, at the time, he was not interested. Maybe now he would consider that.

August 15th came and went. He knew she was home because he could see the light in her room when he passed. Why didn't she attempt to contact him, he wondered.

On the morning of August 17th, Richard's mother placed a letter on his dresser. It was from her, and he sat on the edge of the bed to read it.

Dear Richard,

We messed up. That does not mean I don't love you. It means that we just must postpone making it public. My parents want me to go to college. I want to go to college. If they had any idea that we are married, they wouldn't pay for it. I will hurry through. I will go to summer school and graduate in three years. Even then, I think we should have a regular wedding and not tell anyone about Alabama. Please keep this a secret, as I know you will.

I love you,
Cindy

260

Richard took the football scholarship offer and excelled academically and athletically. He was there for two years. Offers from major colleges were coming in. He could complete his education, but what about Cindy? He had not heard one word from her in two years. True to her word, she went to summer school; but certainly, she came home from time to time, but made no attempt to see him.

He had decided to accept a scholarship to one of the major universities that had offered and was making plans to report for early August practice. He was in the driveway loading his car. She drove up. As she approached, he could tell she was crying.

"Richard, I have a problem. I am engaged to be married during the Thanksgiving holidays. You will see the announcement in the paper soon. I thought I should tell you."

"Cindy, we're married. You can't get married to someone else."

"No one knows about Alabama. I can't tell him. He is very jealous and thinks he is the first boy I ever kissed. He would die if he knew I was married. We can never tell. Promise?"

As if a dream, he was speechless as she faded out of sight. It would be a long time before he would see her again. A couple of years later, he saw her father, who made a point of saying what a fine young man she had married. Richard thought to himself, *she sure did*, but he knew her father wouldn't understand.

The next two years were a blur. He played in a few games but was no star and graduated with just passing grades. What was he to do with the rest of his life?

It was the most desperate time of his life. He drove to the church where he was raised. He looked to the hillside where the cemetery was, and had more than a casual thought of ending things and being buried there. Then something told him to pray. Not even as a believing child had he prayed that hard.

So much of what he had been taught spiritually returned to him that day. He thought of the passage from Proverbs that reads: *Train up a child in the way he should go: and when he is old, he will not depart from it.* He would not depart. He would be a minister.

He prayed each day for guidance and felt that he should pursue the ministry in a mainstream doctrine. He would go to seminary and become a Methodist minister. She had been Methodist.

It was a long journey. First, through seminary, then assignments to small rural churches. Then, associate minister at a larger church and, finally, a series of medium-sized churches where he was the sole pastor. He realized not being a family man and not having a wife had hindered him in his career. He also knew he had never forgotten her. He knew he would never make her a criminal by revealing she was a bigamist. He knew that, if he married, he would be a bigamist himself. That was the way it was, and that is the way it would be.

As the years passed, her image was frozen in his mind. To him, in his mind, she didn't age or lose any of her beauty. He had tried his best to not let losing her ruin his life and had made some headway. Then it would happen. Some young lady in her late teens or early 20s would attend a service. Not just any young lady, but one that looked like he remembered her.

That is when he felt the lump in his throat. That is when he stumbled over the lines of his sermon. That is when the hurt was fresh again.

That Sunday, when it happened, it was different. He noticed a lady, an older lady and not a member of his congregation, enter and sit on the very last row. He paid little attention. As his sermon continued, he noticed something strange about the lady sitting in the rear of the church. From where he stood, he could not be sure, but she appeared to have a ring on a chain around her neck. That would be unusual for a 60-year-old woman. Strange and predictably, it brought back that familiar feeling he wished would never reappear.

Unable to concentrate, he repeated the last few lines and a scripture he had previously spoken. Just as the service ended, she left the building and he never got to welcome her or satisfy his curiosity as to who she was or why he was attracted to her.

Three weeks later, she came back. She arrived late and, rather than sit in the rear like most late-comers, she walked almost to the front and sat in a seat by the aisle in his plain view. She wore the ring and she had on a pink dress with white polka dots.

He stopped his sermon and leaned on the pulpit. He was silent for what appeared to the congregation to be minutes. A doctor in the audience started toward him, assuming he was ill. He regained his composure.

"No, I am fine, really, I'm fine, just trying to avoid getting hiccups." The doctor retreated but took a seat near the pulpit just in case.

As customary, when service dismissed, he walked to the entry to wish the congregants a happy week and thank them for coming. She lingered in the front of the church until almost everyone had gone. He hoped she had not left by a side door.

Then she approached. She had a smile on her face and extended her hand. Softly, she said, "Yes, Richard, it's me."

She then placed an envelope in his hand and left without saying another word. He hurried to his car, turned on the engine and air conditioner and hurriedly opened the letter. He remembered the last and only letter he had received from her. He still had it and had read it a thousand times. He recognized the handwriting.

Dear Richard,

This letter takes all I have in me to write. First, you kept your end of the bargain. You never told. I did not intend for you not to find happiness and marry, and I know you did it partly to remain legal, but mostly for me.

I made two mistakes in my younger days. One was marrying you and the other was marrying Tom. The mistake with you was that we were just too young, and you did not fit the mold my parents had in mind for me, but I loved you. Marrying Tom was a mistake for almost the opposite reason. I married who my parents wanted me to, not who I loved.

Our marriage was not a great one. He cared more about his patients than he did me. I saw him very little, and when I did, he was dead tired. He never abused me; he was just not there for me. He was not at the bedside when our only son died of cystic fibrosis at five years old. He was in the Cath lab treating some ninety-year-old man, whose heart had already beaten for a full lifetime.

He provided well and made good money. Money was something he loved, next to his patients and ahead of me. I never wanted for anything material. He died of a heart attack himself, treating a patient in the emergency room. It was four o'clock in the morning. The only real memories I have that I cared to salvage from that marriage were those of our son.

I will never have to turn my hands at anything. I am still finding large sums of money he had invested with my name on them, that I did not know he had. So, you can say, I guess he loved me in his own way.

I have come to realize that young people can be in real love. I think we were. Were we?

We must talk, I will be staying at the hotel. Here is my cell number. We must talk, and soon.

Love,
Cindy

They met and they talked.

The next Sunday, he based his sermon on three stories from the Bible. He put a little twist on each. They were the Prodigal Son, the Story of Ruth and the Prophet Hosea.

When he closed his sermon, he removed his vestments and laid them on the pulpit. He paused for at least a minute and then said:

"Ladies and gentlemen of this congregation, it has been my pleasure to serve as your pastor these past six years. We Methodists don't usually last that long at one church, but somehow you good people kept requesting me and no one else made any offers. I want to thank you for that opportunity.

"Just because I am a minister does not keep me from having unsatisfied dreams and desires. As of today, I am not going to be your minister anymore. I have something I have to pursue."

He walked from the podium, up the aisle. As he passed the last pew, she stood and took his arm. As they walked away together, he reflected on his sermon from Hosea and whispered to her, "Come, Cindy. Let's go home."

Four Years Later...

The crowd was excited. It was the largest attendance the church had had in years. With open arms, they welcomed their new senior pastor and his wife, Brother and Mrs. Richard Davenport, to the First Pentecostal Church of Pine County. It was the largest church in the area. Cindy wore a long dress but departed from the stereotype of a Pentecostal preacher's wife. After all, it was 2005.

The skirt she wore was white with pink polka dots. She also wore a pink blouse. A long-sleeve jacket of pink had been tailored for a perfect fit. She still had a beautiful complexion; so, in keeping with her position as the wife of the minister, she wore no makeup. Well, she did wear just a little lip gloss. Her hair was still long and pinned to her head much as it was in high school, but not teased. Breaking the tradition of not wearing jewelry, she did have a wardrobe secret. Hidden under her blouse, on a chain, was his class ring. She never looked more beautiful. His sermon was flawless.

Train up a child in the way he should go: and when he is old, he will not depart from it.

The scripture had come full circle.

IT HAPPENED ONE CHRISTMAS

Be not forgetful to entertain strangers: for thereby some have entertained angels unawares. Hebrews 13:2

My dad worked construction and occasionally he would take a short-term job out of town. It was not practical for the family to accompany him, so my mother and I would stay at home alone. Dad would come home each weekend or every other weekend. In 1958, he was working in Houma, Louisiana.

Dad was a very generous person and wouldn't turn his back on anyone in need. He may not be able to solve their needs financially, but he would give whatever aid he could and most likely provide them with a meal. Usually that food would be served at our house and prepared by my mother.

The world was safer then, or at least I think it was, but not as safe as to allow some of the liberties Dad took. He would never pass up a hitchhiker that he would see on the roadside. Not only would he give them a ride, but he would also invite them into our house to spend the night and get a couple of meals. That is how we met David.

I can't remember David's last name, but I know it was Louisiana French, and I think it was Savoie. Dad picked him up just out of Houma. He said he was going to Memphis. He was not an unclean beggar type, even though his clothes were well-worn. He carried nothing with him, as if he had left without planning. David just appeared to be someone who needed a ride and he had found the perfect benefactor.

Dad brought him to our house on December 23rd, two days before Christmas. Mother found blue jeans belonging to my brother, a shirt, socks, and underwear and had Dad insist he showered and changed. She washed his clothes and the next day patched the knees of his pants with iron on patches.

The next day, Christmas Eve, he asked Dad to drive him to the intersection, as he would have a better chance of catching a ride. Dad said he would but invited him to spend Christmas with us. He didn't hesitate and gladly accepted. Little did I know that this would be the start of a connection that would influence all our lives.

Mother never cooked turkey for Thanksgiving or Christmas. She always baked chickens. We raised chickens and David readily volunteered to kill and dress the two we would need for the holiday dinner. Mother was impressed. Dad would have never volunteered to do that, and I was probably too young. David had a way of attracting the attention of each family member.

Mother dug around in my brother's closet, who was in college and not home that Christmas, and found enough outdated clothes to assemble a reasonable wardrobe for David. He was not giving any indications he was ready to leave and, surprisingly, it seemed Mother and Dad were enjoying his presence.

In our family, the period between Christmas and New Year's Day traditionally was a time for hunting. Sometimes I would hunt alone and sometimes with other friends or family members. I asked David if he wanted to go with me and he readily accepted.

We did not have an arsenal of weapons like some hunters do today. As I recall, there was a 16-gauge single shot shotgun, a Remington .22 caliber semi-automatic rifle and a .22 caliber single shot rifle. The single shot .22 rifle was the gun he chose, and I always used the shotgun.

We entered the woods that adjoined our property and he said he needed to sight in the rifle. I had used the rifle but never thought of adjusting the sites. I suppose the previous user had a shooting form similar to mine.

He took a match and fastened it to a pine tree by sliding it behind the bark. He then walked backward thirty carefully measured paces. Steadily he aimed the rifle and fired. He then examined the spot where the bullet hit the tree and made some sight adjustments.

He repeated the process, but this time he struck the match. He struck a match for the next seven shots. I had never seen shooting like that; and, as an eleven-year-old, he was my new hero. He told me he was raised hunting in Louisiana and then was an expert marksman in the U.S. Army in Korea. He made that day a successful hunt.

It was New Year's Day and he said he must be going. We asked him why he was going to Memphis and he surprised us by saying he wanted to be in the movies. He then told us he had been an extra in a movie called *Band of Angels*, filmed near his home in Louisiana. They paid him fifty dollars and he had heard they were going to film some Elvis Presley movies in Memphis. It was easy money.

We wished him well and made the usual assumption about Dad's hitchhikers that we would never see him again. Dad drove him to the intersection.

With all the activity of the holidays, it was a couple of days before mother got around to cleaning the room where he stayed. He had carefully made up his bed in Army fashion, tucked hospital corners; but, of course, Mother was going to change the sheets. When she removed them, she found three envelopes. One addressed to her, one to Dad, and one to me. In each was a one-hundred-dollar bill. That was big money back then. Dad probably wasn't making three hundred dollars a month.

It was a good thing David had left the money, because in about a week Dad became ill with pneumonia. He was hospitalized and missed three week's work. The money was a Godsend. Mother quoted a scripture something to the effect of entertaining angels unaware. David was her angel.

Eventually Dad went back to work but the money, including what was left for me, was long gone. The last thing Mom needed was for the local sheriff and a Louisiana law enforcement officer to knock on the door. They explained to her that David had robbed a store in Louisiana and stolen four hundred dollars. He had been apprehended and now we were in possession of stolen property and would have to return it.

There was no way to do that. My parents didn't have three hundred dollars laying around. They knew the money was not rightfully theirs, but nevertheless, they couldn't pay it back. After negotiations, they arranged to pay it back at thirty dollars per week.

Four years passed. One summer Sunday, an old auto came up the drive. It was David. Mom and Dad treated him with a warm welcome and mother made a place at the table for our Sunday dinner. He filled us in on the last four years of his life. He spent a year in jail and then got assigned to a work release program. He learned carpentry and, for the last year, had worked for a contractor, but that job was completed, and he was looking for work.

He was in luck. Dad was now a foreman on a pipeline being built by Brown and Root. He needed a carpenter and sent David through the proper channels to be hired. It turned out he was an excellent carpenter and excelled in his work.

In a few months, that job was finished but both he and Dad were asked by the company to move to a new site in Texas. Dad declined, but David accepted the offer. It must have been ten years before they saw him again. I was grown and no longer lived at home.

Again, it was a Sunday, and I suppose he remembered my mothers Sunday dinner when he knocked on the door. In the driveway was a new Ford Ranchero. He was dressed in navy blue pants with a starched khaki colored shirt. Again, mother set the table. He was still with Brown and Root and was now a supervisor.

Sometime in the 1980's he came for the last time. It was Sunday. Mother set a plate for him again. He explained that he had retired from Brown and Root and bought a few acres of land in Northeast Texas. Dad had long been retired and he and my mother lived on a minimal fixed income.

Before he left that day, he explained that if it had not been for that Christmas ride to our house, his life would have turned out differently. He told them that he owed all his success to what our family did for him during Christmas in the late 1950s. He handed mother an envelope and told her not to open it until he was gone.

As soon as he left, she opened the envelope and there was thirty one- hundred dollar bills. That is the last time they saw him. Mother said the Lord always returns gifts tenfold.

THE JOURNAL

He hadn't always done so but, for the last twenty years, he had religiously kept a journal and made detailed daily entries. That was when he first started reflecting on his past rather than on his future. It's an age thing. There were so many things he enjoyed recalling, as if the past was brighter than the future or even the present. He was reminded of the Biblical passage "and your old men shall dream dreams".

By some standards, he was an old man as it was two days before his 76th birthday. He would spend it alone, as his wife of fifty-three years had passed three years prior. His only son lived 300 miles away and would not be with him. He didn't mind too much as this gave him the opportunity to reminisce. In his mind, he could make the past like he wanted it to be. He packed a few items of clothing, his blood pressure medicine, a toothbrush and comb in a gym bag. It had been years since the bag was used for its intended purpose. By mid-morning he was in his truck on his way "home."

Southerners do that. He was going "home." Home meant where he was reared, not where he had lived for 50 years; not where he had worked and raised his son. He thought about his son. He blamed himself for being the first to break tradition and there was some guilt.

When he was growing up, it was customary for you to stay in the general geographical location as your parents. When they got old, you brought them into your house, or maybe you still lived in theirs. There were no retirement centers or nursing homes in those days, at least not in rural communities. Many people had their funeral in the same house they and their grandparents were born in. That was then. Things were different now. Moving halfway across the world was commonplace now. He remembered his father's disappointment when he decided to move to Louisiana.

It is not that he had not been back home. When his parents were alive, he made the three-hour drive often. After their death, not so much. Occasionally, the nostalgia created by the absence grew strong and he would go back. It had been three years. The homing instinct was intense.

He parked his truck in front of an upscale hotel, checked in, and then sat in the lobby looking through large plate glass windows that gave a view of the town's main street. He studied each face that passed. Did he know them? Would he recognize them? He knew he looked a little different now, so he had to assume the same of them. Finally, this activity did not satisfy his reason for coming. In fact, he was not sure why he came or why he ever came at all after his parents were gone. To remind him, he opened his journal.

As he scanned the pages where his thoughts had been transferred to paper, he noticed a redundant theme. Surprisingly, it was not of family, not of past romances. It was about a place; a place that had become more special in age than it had been in youth. A place he had known simply as the pasture. A place he had not revisited physically in fifty years but returned mentally often, more often now than in the past. Now he would go physically.

It was a forty-acre tract of land that was located across the road from his childhood home. It was not his family's land, not now anyway, but it had once been. That was before the war, the Civil War that is. Basically, it covered a long, sloping hillside. The highest part was to the north west and it sloped eastward and southward toward the road. There was a stream, well a ditch, that ran through it that would be dry most of the time, but summer rainstorms would swell it with water, turning it into a torrential wet ribbon.

In twenty minutes, his truck neared the site. He pulled into a long-abandoned driveway, parked, and put a CD in the player. He wanted music that was slow and haunting, something to not overpower his mind. He chose a Carly Simon album.

The drive where he parked once was a dirt trail leading to a now fallen sharecropper's cabin. Luther and Carline Johnson had lived there. They had two children as he recalled. The children must have been about ten years younger than him.

Mr. Putnam owned the land back then, but he had moved to town, so Luther was the caretaker. Luther most likely got a few dollars a week to keep up the farm and a plot of land to raise food for his family. He had a milk cow and a hog as he reflected in his journal.

He remembered and wrote in his journal about that day, the last time he had seen the Johnson family. He noted it was cool, almost a cold winter day. He watched as a mule drawn slide loaded with the few items the Johnson's owned moved slowly down the driveway and turned onto the shoulder of the road. Carline walked behind, carefully watching the children that were stacked among the few articles they owned. Luther led the mule.

The cow was tied to the rear and walked along side Carline. He remembers there was no hog. Maybe they had sold it for traveling money. After all, it was hog-killing weather.

He tended to ask questions in his journal, as if the paper they were written on would magically leach a written answer. Where were they going? Why were they going? He would never see Luther or Carline again and no one else ever lived in the cabin.

"So many unanswered questions," he entered. Such as Mr. Putnam never farmed that land again. Was it not profitable? He did, however, have the field bush-hogged once a year. This provided a playground for himself as he reflects on those occasions so many times in his journal.

A journal entry caught is attention. At the top of the page was written "Hay." It read:

I remember that year Mr. Putman leased the property to Mr. Walker. Mr. Walker planted hay on it. In late summer, it was harvested and baled. I remember the smell; the earthy, almost yeast-like smell of the bits of hay left behind. As fall came, I would lie on the hill and watch the birds soar, wishing I had their freedom. I envied their freedom to move effortlessly and from their lofty position see all that happened below. What an advantage they had over us, especially me. I envied the birds. I vowed someday I would fly.

Another adjacent entry, "The Kite." It read:

I could not control the flight of the bird, but I could control the kite. The pasture was a perfect place to launch the dozens, maybe hundreds I made. The secret was the weight of the string. I used #8 sewing thread. One went past Pistol Sasser's store, almost to Norfield. That was over two miles. I sent messages to the kite by writing the message on a piece of paper, cutting a slot in the paper and putting it on the string. The wind would blow it up the string. I wish I could recall the messages.

"The Dove Hunt" read:

Mr. Putnam let me plant an acre of corn. It was a legal way to attract dove. I loved to dove hunt then. I thought they had a chance. I was not a good shot and my only gun was a single shot shotgun with a sawed-off barrel. I read one day that doves mate for life. That bothered me. One day, I wounded a dove and did not kill it. I killed it by bashing its head on my gun barrel. I never hunted dove after that.

I grew to detest hunters who kill for the joy of hunting only. I have tolerance for those who eat what they kill, but no tolerance for those who claim they eat the game but lie about it, as if to justify their plundering of nature. I do remember a few who hunted to keep their families from starving. Even though it was illegal, the community looked away when they hunted out of season.

There is a lot I don't know. I never saw a deer or wild turkey then, but I hear they are plentiful now. Maybe there is something to game management.

He cut the CD player off and exited the truck. He first walked to the site of the old Johnson Cabin. Some stones from the piers it was sitting on remained. The well and the rack that housed the windlass were still standing. Surprisingly, the corn crib that had looked as if it would fall in was still there and looked almost the same.

In the eaves of the roof on the crib were wasp nests. He remembered how often he would rob the nests, using the wasp larvae as fish bait.

He was curious. Was the hole still there? The hole where it was rumored

Mr. Putnam had dug up the wooden keg of silver and gold. Rumor had it the recovered treasure gave Mr. Putnam the where withal to move to town and soon quit farming. Most people did not believe it. He had written in his journal that he believed it.

The land and the entire section, over 600 acres, had belonged to his great-grandfather before the Civil War. He did well with the land. Cattle, hogs, horses, corn, cotton, chickens, and 16 slaves made him one of the most envied landowners in those parts. That was before Grierson came.

He knew the story well. It was a family secret but, like all secrets, it leaked out. It started when Colonel Grierson of the Union Army made a Calvary raid through the heart of Mississippi. The purpose was to detract attention from what Grant had planned for Vicksburg; but, to add to the scheme, they plundered farms and destroyed railroads.

On the evening of April 29, 1863, Grierson arrived with 1700 horse soldiers on his great-grandfather's small plantation. His grandfather willingly complied with Grierson's wishes for food for his men and horses. He had heard that 12 miles north, the landowner had refused, and his home, barn and crops were burned. They also took his livestock. Also, with 1700 rifles aimed at him, what else could he do? If he had resisted, they would have taken everything and burned his place, possibly killing him also.

The next morning, Grierson thanked his great-grandfather but, before he left, his men unload a wooden keg. Then the Colonel called the farmer in and explained to him what he had to do.

He told him, "You have been cordial to my men. I wish you no harm, but you must do one favor. During the raid, we have confiscated a significant amount of silver flatware and some gold.

"We will be going into Louisiana and crossing the Mississippi River. I want you to bury this keg with the gold and silver in it. You are the only one to know where it is buried. After the war, and we will win, I or someone on the Union's behalf will come for it. It better be where you buried it."

That morning, the Union soldiers left, burning the depot and fifteen rail cars in the next village before making their way to Louisiana.

Great-grandfather carried out the wishes, mainly because he was a man of his word, even if the promise was to the enemy and because he was thankful for them not burning his property. Only he knew where the keg was buried.

After that day, the locals blamed him for siding with the Union and shunned him as well as vandalized his property. They set fire to a corn crib and, while fighting the fire, he collapsed and died. No one knew where the keg was buried, or so the story goes.

It is not known how Mr. Putman found the location, or even if he did, but it is plausible. He walked to the fence line and the depression in the ground could still be seen.

He then referred to his journal again. It prompted him to reflect on the ditch. As a young boy, he played in the ditch often. On the corner of the property by the highway was a Clabber Girl Baking Powder advertising sign. It was old and a new one was erected. He and a friend had asked if they could have the old sign and the sign company not only gave it to them, they gave them a dollar to dispose of it.

The two boys placed the sign across the dry ditch and it became their fort for the next couple of years. They played in it for hours.

When it would rain and the ditch would swell with water, they would fashion a small boat out of a 2x4 and race it until it disappeared under a culvert at the highway. They imagined their boat eventually would make its way to the Bogue Chitto River and then to the Pearl River and then to New Orleans.

It was now late afternoon and he made his way back to the truck. He returned to his room at the Inn and to his perch in front of the glass window. It had been a long time since he had done something that he did not consider logical. It was time. He could afford it, and he would.

The next morning at the courthouse, he located the name and address of the present owner. He was a Putman, possibly the grandson of the one he had known. He then went to a real estate office to inquire about the value of land such as the pasture. He was told about $1,500 per acre. That would be $60,000.

With this information, he called the landowner and arranged a meeting. He explained that he wanted the property for nostalgic reasons only. He made an offer of $65,000.

He had been told by the real estate agent that $1,500 was based on a willing seller and a willing buyer. Unfortunately, in this case, the seller was not willing. He immediately increased the offer to $100,000. The owner explained he really did not need the money. That made him want the property even more. It was like trying to buy back your past from someone that will not return it.

"$180,000 and that is my final offer, but I want the mineral rights."

Mr. Putman responded, "I only have half, but you can have half of my half."

It was agreed. They would take care of the paperwork the following day. He asked the manager of the hotel to recommend a person who could transfer the title. She recommended the attorneys down the street and looked up the phone number. He called and gave the receptionist his name, the name of the seller, and the location and an appointment was made for the transfer of the property the next day at 3 p.m. He notified Mr. Putnam.

At 3 p.m. the next day, he entered the attorney's office without knowing the firm's name or the attorney that would close the transfer. He and Mr. Putman were escorted to a nicely furnished room. Three walls were filled with books and the other wall with the degrees of the attorneys.

In a few moments, a distinguished black gentleman walked into the room. "Sir, I am Luther Johnson and I will preside over this transfer. You see, I used to live on that property."

He was taken back by this news and immediately asked about his parents.

"Well, sir, after Mr. Putnam quit farming, he told Dad he could use as much of the land as he wanted to farm. The problem was Dad had no money to buy seed and fertilizer and, not owning the land, none of the merchants would give him an advance. He had to go.

"He struggled and eventually got work at the sawmill. After that, he did ok, as we say, for poor folk.

"I joined the Army at seventeen, spent ten years there going to school when I could. I came out with a college degree. I took my GI Bill and went to law school. Here I am. You know, I think about that old place every time I pass it. Dad loved it. Sharecropped there over 20 years. I took him back about 15 years ago and let him walk the property. It was kind of sad. That was just before he died. Mom's gone too now. My sister is still living, however."

The property was professionally transferred. Mr. Putnam took his check and left. He and Luther talked as if they had been childhood friends for some time and then it was time to go. They shook hands and he started for the door. He then turned.

"Do you do wills?"

"In this town, we have to do everything."

"Prepare my will please."

"What do you want to bequeath?"

"Take these notes and put them in that legal language. I'll come sign it tomorrow."

"I, being of sound mind, do upon my death bequeath property I have acquired from Putman on this date to Luther Johnson Jr. and his sister."

"Why would you do that sir?"

"It's my birthday."

He never stepped foot on the property again.

❧ ◆ ☙

THE SINNER'S BENCH

It was a small frame church located on an out-of-the-way gravel road in what was already the most remote part of the county. The congregation had never been large; but, if needed, the building could seat about ninety people. That was ample, as on a good Sunday, the attendance was about forty. If more than fifty attended, that would have been considered a special occasion and the collection plate would have been passed twice.

The building consisted of one room. As you sat, facing the front of the church, there was what some might call an altar. It was where the pulpit was placed, and it more resembled a small stage. Immediately in front of the stage was a table used for communion services. The table had some writing engraved on its face, but that was turned away from the crowd since the writing was in Latin and no one knew what it said or if it was scripturally appropriate for that denomination.

In front of the table, facing the church entry, was an aisle; and, on each side of the aisle, there were several rows of benches. These benches were made of wood slats that would creak or moan as some of the crowd swayed while singing their favorite gospel hymn in the a cappella environment.

On each side of the stage, placed perpendicular to the rest of the benches, was a very short bench that would only seat three people. The benches' original purposes were not known. Maybe they were just made to fit the confined space. Each was known as the "Sinner's Bench."

It became a custom, a very loosely defined custom, that a congregant who wanted to confess his or her sins would sit on this bench and, at the appropriate time, would stand and confess those sins to their fellow "Brothers and Sisters in Christ," as their fellow worshipers were called.

It should be known that the women wanting to confess would sit on one side of the church and the men would use the other side for this undefined ritual. Men tended to confess their sins more often than women. Only twice can it be recalled that a woman came forth; and, of those, the only confession from a woman that people remember clearly was delivered by Missy Bullock.

Missy was eighteen years old, a recent high school graduate, and maybe the prettiest girl in the county. Through her junior and senior year, she only had one boyfriend and they were inseparable. There were rumors that they had been seen parked one night on some lover's lane. It also had been rumored they were caught skinny dipping at Bluff Springs.

It was thought she had broken up with her boyfriend, as he had not been seen lately. Word got out that she wanted to make a public confession of her sins on the following Sunday. What she would reveal promised to be good; so, that Sunday, the crowd approached maximum capacity. It was assumed she would tell of her transgressions on the lover's lane and at Bluff Springs.

Her confession appeared sincere at first. She related that she had been rude and disrespectful to her mother and asked forgiveness. She quoted the scripture about honoring your mother and father.

After this, she paused. It was as if she had looked everyone in the audience in the eye individually. The silence must have lasted a minute. Everyone anticipated a steamy confession and sat spellbound.

She began, "The real reason I am here this morning is to advise this congregation that every bench in here should be named the Sinner's Bench. You see, you are all gossips, busy bodies, and spreaders of falsehoods. No one has ever seen me skinny dipping, because I have never skinny dipped. I will not deny that I once parked on Fire Tower Road. I have kissed my boyfriend, and I know who saw me. The reason I was there is that was the night my boyfriend – who was also my fiancé, I might add – told me he had been drafted and would be joining the Marines, so our wedding would have to be postponed.

"Now, the person who saw me is here today. He was there that night, and not with the wife that is sitting beside him now."

With that, every eye in the building moved to see if body language would reveal who the sinner might be. Every man in the group felt he was a suspect.

Missy closed her confession with, "God forgive us, as we have all sinned."

She then walked straight up the aisle and out the door. She never returned. On that day, the church lost the first pretty lady in the congregation. They would lose another.

Most of the confessions, if not all, were from the heart of the repentant, hard working people. People who worked even harder to please the Lord. As Christians today, some were more open about their relationship with Jesus than others. Some were irritated, or made to feel uncomfortable, with the confessions. Others were deeply touched by them, to the point of tears.

As most of the confessions were from the heart, most of the confessions were harmless sins, or that is the way some categorized them. For example, Brother Ernest asked forgiveness for cursing when his prize bull got out of the pasture and was hit by a car. Brother Sanders said he was guilty of envy; he had wanted to buy a new Buick, but his credit would only allow him to buy a Ford. Brother Rick had a Buick, and Brother Sanders wanted one too.

Some would just ask the congregation to pray for them as they had sinned. Not stating a specific sin often made the fellow members even more curious.

If the news got around that, on a certain Sunday, someone was going to confess, you could count on a good crowd in attendance. That is what happened when Brother Hollis told some of the members he had a confession to make and planned on doing it the following Sunday.

When Sunday came, Brother Hollis left Sinner's Bench and stood up in front of the communion table. He was a plumber by trade and tried to explain the nature of a job he had been hired to do. The long and short of it was that he could not find the quality materials that were specified for the job, so he had substituted a lesser quality product without adjusting his price accordingly.

The audience, as usual, left disappointed. About a year later, Brother Hollis again was seated on the Sinner's Bench as the crowd began to arrive.

Everyone was sure he was going to relate another typical, small-time sin that no one really cared about. However, this time it was different.

He stood in front of the communion table, just as he had the year before; but it was obvious he was disturbed and began to sweat and stumble over his words as he tried to relate the events that had landed him in this extremely uncomfortable situation. The more he squirmed, the more certain the crowd became that this promised to be good, so all ears listened carefully.

In the audience was an attractive wife and mother who was half his age. Her name was Sister Louise. She sat not ten feet from where he was standing.

He then began to relate that he had been hired to do some exterior plumbing work for Louise and her husband. A root had grown through the drainage line blocking the flow. He then said that he had arrived early, about 6:30 a.m., as it was summer and he liked to work in the cool of the morning. He had previously traced the drainage pipe from the master bathroom, so that is where his work began.

He then stopped and hesitated. All eyes were on Sister Louise, and you could tell she was very uncomfortable with what his future words might reveal. She had no idea that this confession had anything to do with the plumbing work at her house. Sister Louise had been married before, which, in itself, was a sign of loose morals as far as some of the congregation were concerned.

He then revealed that the curtain was open on her bedroom window. She was home alone, as her husband was an engineer on the railroad and did not get home until about 10 in the morning. Brother Hollis said it was an accident, but he just happened to pass by her window as she was coming out of the bathroom, dripping wet from her bath. At first, he hurried by, ashamed that he had accidentally been in the wrong place at the wrong time. That is when he said the Devil took a hold on him.

He said he could feel the Devil pull on his arm and lead him back to the window.

"Well, I couldn't have helped myself if I wanted to. You know, the Devil, he is a big strong fellow. He assured me she would not see me. So, with the Devil pressing me hard, I watched her. It took her about fifteen minutes of fixin' her hair and putting her make-up on before she even put on her underwear.

"But I got to tell you truth, I want to confess all. I came back three more days and watched. I could have repaired that pipe in two hours, but instead I replaced it all the way out to the road. The Devil told me to. He told me it was ok, but not to charge them for the pipe, and I didn't. I am proud of that."

Sister Louise had already left the building before Brother Hollis related the part about coming back three more days. I am sure someone conveyed all the details to her. She was never seen in that building again.

There was another confessor, one that used the bench many times. His name was Toby. At that time, Toby was in his 40s, but he had the mind of a twelve-year-old. About once a month, Toby would be seated on Sinner's Bench. The young folks liked Toby, they could relate to him, but the adults had become intolerant of him. They dreaded when he would decide to repent, which happened often.

Toby did not divulge the nature of his sins. He just asked for forgiveness by Jesus and the Church, as he had been a sinner.

A lady was heard to say, "Why don't they tell him that, as stupid as he is, he will get to heaven on a baby ticket. He doesn't need to confess."

One Sunday, some of the teenagers asked Toby why he confessed so much. His answer was simple and profound.

"I confess because I have sinned. We all sin and fall short of the glory of God. One sin is just as bad as another in the sight of God. You see, I am not smart. In fact, I have heard them say I am dumb. I will never be great or amount to anything. Therefore, I must make sure God loves me."

Many years later, I attended that church. The Sinner's Bench was still there. A few of the old-timers, the ones my age, remember when sins were confessed, but they say it has not been done in years.

Last year, I attended that church again. I sat on the bench. Toby had been dead for years, but I remembered his words.

"We all sin."

Toby's simple summation may have been the greatest expression of repentance to flow from any bench in that tiny church. As I sat there, I realized that bench needed me to fulfill its purpose.

Guess what? I needed it too.

Photo Credits

Pg 23: RIOS269611, CC BY-SA 4.0 <https://creativecommons.org/licenses/by-sa/4.0>, via Wikimedia Commons

Pg 57: Joe Haupt from USA, CC BY-SA 2.0 <https://creativecommons.org/licenses/by-sa/2.0>, via Wikimedia Commons

Pg 69: Konstantin Makovsky, Public domain, via Wikimedia Commons

Pg 103: TheMightyGrog, CC BY-SA 4.0 <https://creativecommons.org/licenses/by-sa/4.0>, via Wikimedia Commons

Pg 139: Greg Gjerdingen from Willmar, USA, CC BY 2.0 <https://creativecommons.org/licenses/by/2.0>, via Wikimedia Commons

Pg 199: Small gravel pit in Birchfield Wood by Steven Brown, CC BY-SA 2.0 <https://creativecommons.org/licenses/by-sa/2.0>, via Wikimedia Commons

Pg 205: Kingkong954, Public domain, via Wikimedia Commons

Pg 211: Pine woodland South of High Moor Farm by Gary Rogers, CC BY-SA 2.0 httpscreativecommons.orglicensesby-sa2.0, via Wikimedia Commons

Pg 217: Daniela Kloth, GFDL 1.2 <http://www.gnu.org/licenses/old-licenses/fdl-1.2.html>, via Wikimedia Commons

Pg 235: Macieklew, CC BY-SA 4.0 <https://creativecommons.org/licenses/by-sa/4.0>, via Wikimedia Commons

Pg 241: Rajendra Dhar, CC BY 3.0 <https://creativecommons.org/licenses/by/3.0>, via Wikimedia Commons

Pg 267: Bert Kaufmann from Roermond, Netherlands, CC BY 2.0 <https://creativecommons.org/licenses/by/2.0>, via Wikimedia Commons

Pg 279: Basher Eyre / All Saints, Old Burghclere: pews

www.ingramcontent.com/pod-product-compliance
Lightning Source LLC
Chambersburg PA
CBHW040519170726
48295CB00012B/261